TWINKLE, TWINKLE LITTLE STAR

BEN BARZMAN

Twinkle, Twinkle
Little Star

G. P. PUTNAM'S SONS

New York

PZ
4
. B297
. TW

TO NORMA

"*Our earth is but a small star in the great universe. Yet of it we can make, if we choose, a planet unvexed by war, untroubled by hunger or fear, undivided by senseless distinctions of race, color or theory.*"

TWINKLE, TWINKLE LITTLE STAR

1.

THIS IS being written hastily.

It shouldn't be written hastily. I don't suppose anything should, especially this.

But we've all agreed that time's running out. Either it's written now or it might just as well not be written at all. For my part I would have liked time to sit myself down and try to figure out some of the deeper implications of what went on.

They say no. Write it down fast, they say. Get down as many of the implications as you can on the run and the hell with the rest.

Maybe they're right. Just the same, despite all the haste, I can't help taking time off to notice the monumental irony of having to write in a hurry about one of the most important events of the century.

Century?

One of the most important events of civilized time, if you ask me.

When I think about it a little more, I realize that perhaps it's not just my private monumental irony. It's probably an irony which belongs to all of us who happen to be living in this little flicker of time which is the present. Almost every day brings an event which, by rights, we should have a century or so to think over and work out. But things keep happening so fast that there doesn't seem to be any odd hundred years lying around loose for either you or me.

So I'm writing this hastily.

Even so, I'm going to be as careful as is humanly possible about the way I present it to you. We have practically no proof that what happened really did happen.

All we have, really, is one dozen red roses. Of course they happen to be just about the most fantastic red roses you ever saw. But you can't walk up to the world holding a dozen red roses and say, "We've just been eyewitness to, and lived through, one of the most important and remarkable events of all time, in proof of which we ask you to take a good look at these roses."

Eventually we may do that too.

We also thought of calling a press conference and breaking the story that way, but the more we thought about that, the more apparent it became that *that* wouldn't work either.

For example, supposing I were to spring the following story on you:

PARIS, Dec. 12—At slightly after ten o'clock last night your reporter encountered a three-headed woman of about twenty-two years of age in the corridor of his apartment house, Number 8, Quai d'Astorg. The three-headed woman, all three of whose heads were beautiful, and who was very smartly dressed, inquired after a Monsieur Turoffsky. Your reporter replied that Monsieur Turoffsky, a Jewish sculptor, was presumed to have been killed by the Nazis during their occupation of Paris and that his apartment was now occupied by your reporter. Your reporter then invited the three-headed woman in, but she, visibly distressed, thanked him kindly and left . . .

Although I know that the very casualness of the style in which it's presented might make you wonder momentarily, actually, after you read the story a second time, you would not only be bewildered and incredulous, but you would also wonder what the point was. Something as momentous as a three-headed woman can't be slid under your noses just like that. You'd want to know about a lot of other things.

After a while you'd begin to say to yourself, "What's all this about a three-headed woman? Who are you anyway? What is this—a joke? Who else saw this three-headed woman?"

I didn't see any three-headed woman. I was just using her as an example to get you in the right mood. What we saw was infinitely more fantastic and, at the risk of seeming repetitious, let me reiterate, infinitely more important than a three-headed woman; and I imagine the implications, both scientific and every other way, of the existence of a person with three heads must be enormous.

As you've probably gathered by now, I'm not a scientist. I can't tell you much about the scientific background of what took place.

All I can do is to try to tell you about myself, about some of the people involved and about some of the events which I now feel led up to that most incredible adventure.

When I spoke of the three-headed woman, just about everything I said, except that there was such a three-headed creature, is true.

I am a reporter, actually a sort of foreign correspondent for a group of Canadian-French language newspapers owned and published by a man named Debret, who is my maternal uncle.

I live at Number 8, Quai d'Astorg, in the top-floor apartment which once belonged to a Jewish sculptor named Turoffsky, who hid in a false ceiling which you get to from the roof. Despite that, he was found by the Nazis and certainly killed.

I have been living in Paris for some years.

The way I got here is because my Uncle Debret, who is quite an important character in Eastern Canada, wanted me out of Canada.

As I look back it seems to me my Uncle Debret was always wanting me out of Canada.

You might even say that Debret considered Canada not big enough for the two of us even before I was born. At least that's a fair conclusion which could be drawn from Debret's attitude toward my father.

According to my sister Ella, who is older than I and should conceivably know, Father was neither French nor Catholic and that was why Debret had never approved of him. My opinion is that Debret saw in Father a man whose life was not guided by considerations of immediate self-interest. To Debret this was, of course, the telltale mark of the mortal foe.

When in 1930 Father finally coughed himself to death as a result of being gassed in World War I, Debret told Mother that he had always known that Father would end like that. In Debret's book it was always guys like Father who got themselves gassed and then went off and died, leaving a widow with two orphaned children, and, my Uncle Debret implied, on his hands.

Although I was only seven at the time, I remember the way my Uncle Debret looked at me. He didn't have to tell me. I had a feeling. Some day Debret would want me out of Canada.

Most disconcerting was the fact that I was what nearly everyone would have called a particularly inoffensive child. I never talked back and above all I never argued.

I was not like my best friend, Wilfred MacIntosh, who had that wonderful unself-conscious way of taking for granted that life was to be lived and that he had a right to live it the way he wanted to. He owed nothing to anybody. *He* talked back. *He* always argued.

Mother, Ella and I lived in Vancouver, British Columbia, which is as far from Montreal, where Debret was, as you can get. Mother taught school and Debret bothered us only occasionally.

When I was fifteen he came to Vancouver on one of his periodic fishing trips. Naturally he stayed with us, even though the house was small and he could have afforded the most expensive hotel.

He and I went out fishing for salmon (I didn't really want to go with him but he insisted) and we had a big argument about the bait.

Not that it matters. When the salmon are running up there, you can use part of an old shoe for bait.

I caught three of the biggest fish he had ever seen and he caught nothing.

That night, just to top it all off, Wilfred MacIntosh came over and started getting me into my first real trouble. As I've indicated earlier, Wilfred was my closest friend. He and I used to get up at five o'clock and run all the way from Mt. Pleasant to English Bay where we would take a swim.

Well—Wilfred got into a big theological discussion with Uncle Debret. It was at a period when Wilfred was interested in such topics as life and death and space, and what's behind the stars. Wilfred had just read a couple of books on the subject, which is more than Uncle Debret ever had, and it was a joy to behold the way fifteen-and-a-half-year-old Wilfred made a horse's ass out of Uncle Debret—to such an extent that the moment Wilfred triumphantly left the house, Uncle Debret said he was nothing but a bloody atheist and demanded that I give up being friends with him.

Debret raised such a stink about this that the word got around that Wilfred was an atheist, and although he was not particularly interested in the question, it became a point of pride for Wilfred to be known as one. He even went so far as to write an article, "Atheism for the Teen-Ager," for some particular sect's magazine.

The summer of 1939 I was sixteen. Wilfred and I graduated from high school and were at loose ends when the famous incident which sent me out of Canada for the first time took place.

It was a lovely afternoon in June. Wilfred and I were both idly watching the big ocean-going liners being loaded when Wilfred casually remarked that he thought a big war was coming. I suppose the fact that one of the liners was the *Empress of Japan,* and that they were loading scrap iron on another Japanese ship called the Something-or-Other *Maru,* must have had a little to do with his chain of thought.

Wilfred then went on to say he thought we both ought to picket the ship. Otherwise, he said, the chances were that the scrap would be shot back at us.

I think I've already pointed out that I'm not the picketing type. Picketing gets some people angry. I don't like to get people angry—at least I didn't then.

So I sat by and watched Wilfred make a sign out of a piece of cardboard, nail it to a board, and go into a one-man picketing job. A crowd gathered. Several Japanese officers came down from the Something-or-Other *Maru* and started to argue with Wilfred, who just kept on picketing. I'm still not sure how it happened, but somebody bumped Wilfred and he almost fell into the Inlet, at which point Wilfred swung at one of the Japanese officers.

I couldn't stand by and watch my best friend get hit, especially when a couple of other Japanese sailors joined in.

You may remember, if you can go back as far as 1939, the international incident *that* created.

Also, of course, old Uncle Debret came flying out as fast as he could and all hell broke loose. He went screaming to Mother about how I was the dupe of an international conspiracy and didn't we realize what all this did to a man in his position.

Wilfred took it all very calmly; in fact his eyes lighted up when I told him that Uncle Debret had said it would be a great idea, just great, if I got out of Canada before people found out I was his nephew. Because Wilfred thought it was just great too. It would give him and me a chance to look around the world and see the big cities while they were still around to be seen.

2.

Uncle Debret was so enthusiastic about our going that he not only made arrangements with somebody who owned a fleet of ships to get us on one of the ships as stewards, but he also personally spoke to Big Jim about having me do some travel pieces for the *Vancouver Sun* to pay my way.

I didn't particularly want to go. I wasn't quite sixteen at the time. The idea of shipping out for a round-the-world trip, especially with Wilfred, was pretty frightening. I always wondered why we continued to be best friends. On almost everything that counted I was always on the opposite side.

Wilfred would argue heatedly with me and when he'd get angry, as he invariably did, I'd dummy up. He would take that to mean he'd convinced me, until the next time we'd get on the same subject, I would take the same position, and he'd get furious and ask me why in the hell I hadn't continued to argue with him. I'd tell him and he'd say Jesus H. Christ—and for some reason or other we'd stay friends.

I was absolutely certain Mother wouldn't let me go. You couldn't let a sixteen-year-old (barely sixteen) just pick up and toot off around the world—especially with somebody like Wilfred.

Well—

You could.

Not that Mother really wanted me to go, but the fact that she didn't want me to go—especially with Wilfred—only convinced her that it was a sacrifice that she had to make.

The second big kick in the teeth was Big Jim.

I was sure *he* wouldn't want me to go. I was nuts about Big Jim. He had come up from San Francisco where he had once been a leading newspaperman and drunk. He had come to Vancouver the way you would go to Pago Pago to drink the rest of your life away. But then he met Mother. She had made him throw the bottle away and by God he never touched a drop since and he worked his way back to be City Editor of the *Sun*.

Well, when Big Jim said that a sixteen-year-old writing travel pieces was a terrific idea, it was impossible to get out of it.

Third big kick in the teeth was that almost nobody seemed to feel that the world was *not* going to be blown to pieces. Also I got the general impression that almost nobody felt that anything could be done about it.

Except a few people like Wilfred who wanted to picket.

We did go, Wilfred and I. We shipped out first on a passenger ship going to the Orient, mostly Japan. Yes sir. Indeed sir. We didn't do bad for kids not quite sixteen.

We saw Nagasaki and Hiroshima while *they* still stood.

Wilfred and I went to the medium-class geisha houses, visited the sex shop at Kobe, stole the official album from one of the biggest brothels at Nagasaki (it had pictures of all the girls in it, with a few words of comment about each one in wonderful Japanese-style English—all you had to do was look at the album and make up your mind). I kept sending Big Jim long and dull articles about the officially approved tourist spots, and private letters about the geisha houses and bordellos. What Big Jim did without telling me was to rewrite the letters a little bit and print *them,* and throw all the articles in the wastepaper basket.

The letters, incidentally, were very successful.

But the big European cities had top priority on Wilfred's list as the most probable candidates to have the stuffings kicked out of them, so after knocking around in the Orient for a few weeks, we got ourselves transferred to a Europe-bound freighter.

We landed at Le Havre in the late summer of 1939. From there we thumbed a ride to Saint-Malo. It was a very hot day so I took a swim while Wilfred went looking at the medieval wonders of the town.

I saw Marie-Ange on the beach at Saint-Malo and that was as much of Europe as we got to see.

Marie-Ange was wearing one of those bathing suits which later were to be called bikinis. It was the first time I had seen a girl practically naked that way in public, and I couldn't take my eyes off her. (Neither could anyone else on the beach.)

The next day Wilfred wanted to push on but I insisted on staying. I had to meet the bikini. Later, when Wilfred joined me for a swim, I pointed her out to him and told him I had been trying to meet her.

He went right over and started to talk to her. I followed a few minutes later and he introduced me to her.

They were deep in a big discussion when I got there. They were always in a deep discussion after that.

I would sit by their side on the beach listening to Marie-Ange and Wilfred talk about the serious things Wilfred was talking about at that point—art, beauty, life, sex, God, love. Most of all they both seemed interested in what it was that made a thing beautiful.

Wilfred even argued with *her*. They both got very angry with each other. He kept saying that anything that made life better or richer was beautiful.

She said then why should we not consider a milk bottle more beautiful than a Grecian urn?

Wilfred said that when people discovered the best design for a milk bottle, she would see for herself that it would then be the most beautiful thing in the world.

I didn't argue with her. I just sat by and watched them, especially Marie-Ange and the movements of her body. Every now and then I would take time out and play with her three-year-old sister Tou-tou who followed me everywhere and giggled no matter what I did.

A cartwheel was the funniest thing that had ever been invented. A somersault would fracture her. A wrinkling of the nose would set her off into peals of hysterical laughter.

Every now and then Tou-tou would have a sudden change of mood. No matter what I did she wouldn't laugh. She'd stare at me with her big round brown eyes and say, *"Tu es fou,"* which is French for "You're nuts."

Marie-Ange would think up new arguments for the next day. She said that right now, here and now, the milk bottle *was* very useful and not as beautiful as a Grecian urn.

It stumped Wilfred and he began to shout even louder. That night I took Marie-Ange for a walk on the high wall which enclosed the town. She started to tell me about how during the Middle Ages Saint-Malo and its great wall was considered practically invulnerable and what an *imbécile* my friend Wilfred was.

Those few days I hadn't been able to do anything but think of Marie-Ange and the feel of her body when I'd accidentally touched her.

When we got to a dark part of the wall I suddenly took her in my arms. I guess whatever had been working on me had been working on her too because she wasn't even startled. I kissed her with all the clumsy fury of a lonely, scared, eager adolescent and she kissed me back the same way.

To tell you the truth, for a second there I was a little frightened by the intensity with which she threw herself into the embrace. When I had been dreaming about it I hadn't visualized her that way.

I think I said something about this being wrong. Maybe I just tell myself now I did. That she seemed so young. . . .

I must have said something like that because I remember her getting very angry and saying she was as old as I was and everybody knew girls were twice as old as boys of the same age. Besides, once I had started something like that, did I think I could just stop?

We found a dark warm corner in the sand and as I felt her body close to mine, part of me was saying, "Wilfred is crazy about her. You're betraying Wilfred." While another part of me was saying, "It serves him bloody well right for always arguing."

And then I forgot to think about Wilfred or about how old Marie-Ange was or about the coming war and let myself merge with her in a blinding ecstasy that left us both awed, exhilarated, disturbed and delirious with a crazy kind of happiness.

She whispered that I was not to say anything to anyone. She mentioned I was especially not to say anything to that big *imbécile* Wilfred, and the next day on the beach she continued the argument with him about the milk bottle and the Grecian urn.

The only difference was that now she listened more and seemed a little less heated about her arguments. Every now and then we would look at each other and Wilfred didn't seem to notice a thing and neither did anyone else. (It was then I learned that surprisingly enough, it doesn't show on you.)

From then on I could hardly wait for the night to come and for her to slip away and meet me in our corner near the medieval wall, then go down to the warm sand where we'd make frantic love.

After that, although I didn't realize it consciously, Marie-Ange became part of every woman I touched; her lips were there, her arms, her body and the fierce ardor of her passion—from then on.

I'd been getting urgent letters from Mother saying it was time to come home. War could break out at any second. Then Big Jim wrote saying he too now thought it was time. After a few days it became obviously stupid for us to stay on no matter how much we wanted to.

The last night we were alone together, Marie-Ange gave me a picture of herself and Tou-tou in bathing suits. I put it in my wallet and it's been there ever since.

Yet a very strange thing happened when Wilfred and I came to say good-by to them. Marie-Ange threw her arms around Wilfred and held him that way for a very long time. He kissed her and said he would come back to her after the war was over and would bring her a milk bottle and a Grecian urn, and when they broke out of the embrace Marie-Ange was crying. She kissed me on both cheeks the way you do for a good friend.

It was Tou-tou who cried for *me*.

We got out on the last ship, which was the *Champlain*. Wilfred stuck around in New York figuring he ought to see *it* while it still stood, but I beat my way back to Canada.

Then the war happened.

I went back to school and to life in Vancouver. I lost track of Wilfred but found out later he hung around the States seeing all *their* big cities. As soon as I was eighteen I enlisted in the Royal Canadian Air Force. I didn't want to particularly, but it was what I thought I ought to do.

There was a big party for me the night before I left for the training camp in Eastern Canada. Mother and Ella and Big Jim rushed around all night pouring punch and serving cakes and they were all very noble about it—no tears—and the next morning I left.

The first guy I met in camp was Wilfred. He'd enlisted too. He looked at me sourly and said, "I told you we should have picketed."

He kept saying that all through the war. Every time we went out on a bombing mission he would say, "Next time you picket."

3.

WILFRED AND I and Old Wonderful Walter Carr, a young Yank medic Wilfred had met during a blackout, were having a drink in a Kensington pub. It was nice and snug there, with its heavy blackout curtains and its windows taped to make them concussion-proof. Old Wonderful Walter was trying to tell the bartender a joke. To my knowledge the bartender had heard that joke at least three times. It was one of the most popular jokes of the war.

Wilfred gulped his drink down hurriedly, said he'd see us later and left. He didn't want to waste an evening on jokes. But Old Wonderful Walter couldn't be stopped like that. He kept right on with the story.

It seems there were two goddam American G.I.s riding in a goddam London cab which, it being wartime, had no tires, no springs and practically no seats. After about ten minutes of being bounced around in the goddam contraption, one of the goddam G.I.s leaned forward, tapped the cabby on the shoulder and said, "Hey, Mac—You know what we do with goddam cabs like this back in the States?"

After thinking it over seriously for a moment or so, the goddam cabby leaned back and said, "As I understand it, mate—you'd either drink it or make love to it."

Having come to the point of the story, Old Wonderful Walter waited hopefully for the laugh. Instead, there was the loudest and most terrifying explosion I've ever heard or felt in my whole life, and we were all knocked off our feet.

After the glass stopped breaking and the room got down to earth again, we picked ourselves up.

"Goddam point killer," Walter said automatically.

He was white as a sheet. I could hear him distantly through the compressed ringing in my ears.

We both watched a couple of the customers who were still down. I think they thought they were dead. Sometimes it affects you that way. It takes you a couple of seconds to realize you're not dead.

The two customers reluctantly got to their feet.

"Jesus," Walter said. "Jesus H. Christ, but that was close."

He shook his head to clear the ringing away, then we both began to hear it at the same time.

Somewhere, and not too far from us, a little girl was screaming. Little by little that scream pushed everything else in the room out of the way and took over completely.

The big impulse was to rush out there and claw around at the debris, but we could already hear the shouts of the salvage crew. There was no point in interfering with their work.

Meanwhile the screaming kept right on.

The bartender went around kicking broken pieces of glass out of his way.

"Let's go take a look," Walter said uneasily.

"You go take a look," I said to Walter. "You're a doctor. You studied for years for just this moment. You go, Walter."

He looked at me peculiarly and left.

The screaming kept up. It was all I could do to keep from screaming myself.

I'll tell you why, lady.

A week before I had been on a bombing mission to Saint-Malo.

All week I hadn't said anything to myself. All week I hadn't admitted it was sneaking up on me.

Target for tonight, gentlemen. Saint-Malo.

Saint-Malo, sir?

Yes, Lieutenant, Saint-Malo. Why?

Nothing, sir.

I don't know.

I suppose I could have said, "Sir, if you don't mind, sir, I'd rather not go on this mission, sir. You see, sir, Marie-Ange and Tou-tou live in Saint-Malo. Marie-Ange is the girl whose photograph I carry in my wallet. The girl in the bathing suit. As a matter of fact, sir, you once admired her to the extent of permitting yourself to whistle when you saw the photograph. If you don't mind, sir, I'd rather not drop any bombs on them."

You can't tell. It's conceivable. I might not even have been court-martialed.

Only I kept my mouth shut. Tight.

And so did Wilfred. Tight as a drum.

Over target, sir.

Now he's sirring me. He means me.

Bombs away.

Please God. Please Marie-Ange. Please anybody. Hide yourself, Marie-Ange. Find some hole for yourself and Tou-tou. Hide Tou-tou's head in your lap.

I poured myself another insane drink. To tell you the truth, at that period of my life I didn't really enjoy whisky. My idea of something to drink was a nice, big, frosted creamy root beer; or even ginger beer. But I kept wasting this perfectly good Scotch whisky.

Marie-Ange was covered with blood and was holding a broken milk bottle in her hand and was screaming for me to come look.

Not that I really believed it. I believed it only in the way you believe somebody has broken into your bedroom when you hear a sound at night. You know darn well it's not so, but you have to go and see.

I left the bottle with the bartender because I knew by now I wasn't too sure on my feet. I was right because the minute I hit the darkness outdoors I fell flat on my face over some rubble.

Some character with a helmet and an earnest civilian face helped me to my feet and explained to me about the screaming.

Twelve-year-old girl, she was. He'd known the family. Mother, father and three children. All girls. Father was a sort of bookkeeper-accountant, you might say.

It was a German bomber, just happened to be passing by and thought it would drop in on that sweet little English family. After it had dropped in only the twelve-year-old was left. The others had been killed.

She was the screaming.

I told him I wanted to get over there. I wanted to help her.

He repeated that everything that could be done for her was being done. His tone implied that this was no place for a nice young Canadian flyer.

What the earnest civilian face didn't understand was that I just wanted to make sure that this twelve-year-old English girl wouldn't cut herself with a broken milk bottle.

He followed me doubtfully as I stumbled over the rubble. A moment later I saw Walter's silhouette hunched over something. Alongside of him stood another grim-jawed character with a helmet. He was holding a shielded flashlight on the girl.

"Shock," Walter was saying stupidly. "Nothing wrong physically. Shock."

It was getting so I had to restrain an impulse to clamp a hand over her mouth. Finally even the grim jaw in the helmet couldn't stand it.

When he sensed that Walter had given up, he said to the little girl irritably:

"Here, here! We've had enough of that!"

At that point I got so mad I could have poked the bastard, even though, at the same time, I knew exactly what he meant. Instead I pushed him aside roughly so that he staggered a little and the silhouette of his tin hat changed angles, and I swept the little girl off her feet and held her tightly in my arms.

I rocked her the way you would rock a baby, with my face pressed hard against hers. I kept mumbling over and over:

"It's all right. It's all right. The bottle didn't break. It isn't broken at all. You see? It's all right. It's all right. The bottle didn't break. . . ."

I kept right on saying those words over and over and over again until they lost their meaning in the sense that we ordinarily understand meaning, only they took on a meaning I had never known before. It was a meaning that communicates itself more through touch, smell and a sense of the proximity of another living being. I felt a great cocoon weave itself about the two of us, shutting out the rubble, the falling bombs, the shattered bodies and the grim figures.

She stopped screaming. I kept on saying "It's all right the bottle didn't break" over and over again until somebody stabbed me in the eyes with a blade of light. It took me several seconds to become aware of the darkness, the rubble, the sounds and the people about us.

"The ambulance's come," Walter said softly and the flashlight went off.

I looked down at the little white blob which must have been her face and I had the impression that her eyes were wide open and she was staring at me.

"I'll put you in the ambulance," I said to her.

She groped for my hand and found it, then held on to it frantically. Still carrying her, I followed Walter. We worked our way over the rubble and toward the street.

Somebody opened the door of the ambulance and I tried to put her in, but she wouldn't let go of my hand.

Walter and the ambulance driver and a couple of others waited silently as I tried to pull my hand loose, but she wouldn't let go. Finally the ambulance driver asked hopefully, "Would you like to come along, sir?"

Of course I didn't want to go, especially when Walter whispered, "Somebody ought to be with her when she comes out of her shell—when they break the news to her."

I'd had it. Besides, I'd just remembered that it was tonight the Yank nurse at the Yank air base had said she'd be free.

So I went with Walter and the kid.

I sat alongside of her in the ambulance holding her hand.

I sat alongside of her as they gave her a shot and put her to bed. She kept hanging on to my hand and staring at me.

Then she dropped off to sleep.

"What was that you kept saying to her?" Walter asked as we walked out.

"Nothing," I said.

"It sounded like something about a broken bottle," Walter insisted.

"You were hearing things," I said. I left him but by the time I got to a telephone the Yank nurse had gone off with someone else.

4.

A COUPLE OF days later Walter reached me by telephone and said that the kid was just as sweet and nice as she could be and he thought I ought to drop over and see her because apparently no one else had. They hadn't been able to find any relatives.

The day after his call I got a little note from her. It seems her name was Jane Bridon-Jack and that she had asked Dr. Carr who I was and he had told her. Dr. Carr had said he didn't think I'd mind her writing to me. She was in a little convalescent home not far from London. If ever I got leave she would be ever so pleased if I would come and have tea with her and she remained Your Most Obedient Servant, Jane Bridon-Jack.

I guess I've told you enough about myself so that it will come as no surprise to you when I tell you I did go to see her and took the box of chocolates which Mother and Big Jim had managed somehow to get to me.

She was up and dressed and was a very skinny little thing with the most solemn face I've ever met. She didn't smile once during the time I was with her, but she thanked me soberly for the chocolates, and we had tea together and she said there was some talk about her being evacuated to Texas where Dr. Carr had a cousin.

Just as I was leaving, she said she had something for me and handed me a piece of foolscap.

I opened it later. It was a long poem which she had written. It was called "I'm Trying Hard to Understand," and if any one of you wishes to see it, if he or she will remain after class, I will be pleased to show it. In the meantime be good enough to take my word for it that it was a very sweet, thoughtful poem by a twelve-year-old kid who was trying hard to understand. There were moments when everything seemed horrible and confusing, but then she'd hung on desperately because of people like Walter and me who had made her feel that some day she would really understand.

I showed the poem to Wilfred and he read it very carefully.

I saw the kid three or four times after that, mostly each time something came from home. I didn't say much to her and the visits were usually very brief.

Finally I got a phone call from Walter Carr.

He had managed to arrange for the little girl to be evacuated to some distant cousins in Texas. A Dr. and Mrs. Whitman. Goddam wonderful guy, Pops. Leading American biophysicist. He and Bunny (that was Mrs. Whitman) had a big house near the University campus and no kids. The girl was leaving soon. It had all happened fast, the way those things do once they happen. Did I have time to go out to see the kid the next couple of days?

I said I wasn't sure—I would try.

The kid thought a lot about me, he said. He hoped I would keep in touch with her. They had investigated. It was true. She had no relatives. She was very much alone. He said good-by and a couple of days later his outfit shoved off to stick a knife in the soft underbelly of Europe.

I've often wondered what would have happened if Jane had not been evacuated to the home of a biophysicist. What if it had been the home of a butcher—or a shoemaker?

I know now from what did take place that it wouldn't have mattered. She still would have become what she became. And what happened would have happened anyway—

I *know* that now. I know it in a way that few human beings have been privileged to get the answer to a question which begins with

What if?

The next day I got a note from Jane saying she was leaving in frantic haste and how everybody thought that was the best thing, and she felt beastly that she hadn't been able to see me again (she made it sound as if it was her fault) but hoped that I would keep in touch with her. It meant so much to her.

Wilfred asked me what I was going to write to her.

I said I thought it was enough for me to be going out on these bombing missions. I felt I was doing my share just by doing that.

He said he thought it was important that I write to her.

We had a little argument right there at the air base.

Finally he said, Okay, *he* would write to her. Would it be all right if he signed my name to the letter? Coming from him it wouldn't have meant anything to her.

I said, Sure. Fine. Great. Write to her. Put my name on it.

He did.

His first letter was a reply to her poem. About how it was important for people like her to understand the real causes of what had taken place. He didn't go into the real causes, but he promised some day he'd tell her.

Her response came back as fast as the wartime postal system could work. The letter gushed all over itself. What a Wonderful Letter, she wrote. It Made Her Feel She was no Longer Alone. She would Write to me Constantly. And Some day We would Talk Together. . . .

I showed her letter to Wilfred. I was sore. I said however you looked at it he had saddled me with the responsibility of this kid. I didn't want it. Wilfred should have signed his own name to the bloody letter. In the last century guys like Wilfred would have been missionaries.

Wilfred said, Okay, okay. He'd take on the responsibility. He'd answer her letter. A human being was worth it.

I said, "You just bet you'll answer it," and before I knew it, something which had been smoldering since I had betrayed him with Marie-Ange burst into flame and we had the worst argument of our lives. And because *I* had betrayed *him,* I started the fight.

I said all he thought about was changing people.

He replied, Why not? Did I think people were perfect?

And I flung at him, No—but did he think he was perfect enough to take on the right to change people his way?

Well—

It went on like that.

It was never really the same between us after that. We were much more careful with each other. We avoided talking about subjects we might not agree on.

He did answer every letter she sent. He'd show me his answer. I'd read it and say sure—okay—why not? And his answer would go off.

Her first letter was called Thoughts on First Flying in an Airplane. She had been evacuated by plane. It was all about how wonderful Man's Mind Was and how Incredible it was to Soar and Sit above the clouds and See the world you've known become Geometric Bits and Pieces.

Of course this came at a time when each time we got into a plane it was a nightmare. I was sure each time we'd never come back. And we had plenty of chances to watch the world below become Bits and Pieces.

From then on I'd just glance at her letters and pass them on to Wilfred. There were Thoughts on First Seeing Texas. Thoughts on Becoming a Woman and how Frightening and Beautiful it was to think that now she could Reproduce Another Human Being; then there were less agreeable thoughts, no longer in upper case.

Thoughts on how the Negro was treated in Texas. There had been an incident in a bus. Apparently Dr. Whitman and Bunny hadn't been able to explain it to her satisfactorily. I remember thinking that the letter had a quality of panic and feeling angry and baffled that Wilfred had sucked me into this thing.

He and I came close to another hot argument.

Wilfred said he thought it was time I learned that by being a human being I had acquired a responsibility; I ought to try to think, to take a position. Besides, he said, this was obviously an extraordinary little girl.

He read out loud one part of her letter in which, for the first time, she mentioned her personal tragedy. She said that there was something similar about a bomb coming out just out of nowhere and dropping, by terrible chance, on their flat and killing her mother and father and two sisters Phnee and Mundy who had never done anything to hurt anyone in their whole lives, and hating a man because of his color. It was exactly like what she had just seen on the bus when a Negro had been beaten and almost hanged by a group of whites for no reason at all, simply because he was a Negro.

Wilfred read it out loud, he said, because we, he and I, were now dropping bombs on people. We had even dropped bombs on people we loved. . . . (I suddenly realized what the Saint-Malo mission must have meant to him.) That unless we tried to understand we were worse than carnivores, who killed for food.

Then he said that he would take his leave in the States and visit the little girl in Texas.

I said that was great. I could hardly wait for him to get leave.

Wilfred wrote her a long letter and because he and I were sore at each other, he didn't even bother showing me a copy before he signed my name to it.

But I saw a copy of it later when I went through his effects.

I am glad [he wrote] that this incident with the Negro happened to you at this point in your life. It will show you much more clearly what the real world is like. You mustn't let that reality frighten you. You must constantly remind yourself that there is beauty, responsibility, rich potentials—especially in your life. I can now see you do have special capacities for experience and special gifts for understanding those experiences. But you mustn't remain aloof—I think you'll find that your gifts will not come to flower unless you mingle with people, try to know them and their problems and try to help them as best you can.

That was the letter.

It made a big impression on her. In fact I have a hunch she memorized it.

Wilfred didn't ever get to Texas. On our thirty-fourth mission out together we were hit. Whatever it was that hit us was so big that at first I thought that somehow we had lost altitude and crashed, but at the same time I felt a searing, blinding, completely incredible pain. I must have screamed as I turned toward Wilfred, and I remember dimly his making a vague, oddly broken gesture toward me, lifting his arm as if he had started to say something.

It was his last gesture in life.

I'm glad he and I took that trip. I'm glad he saw Hiroshima and Nagasaki and a few other places.

There were times when I hated him. But he was my closest friend.

He was gallant, honest and real. I know that if he had lived, he would have spent a lot of his time picketing.

5.

EVERYBODY BEHAVED as though my wound was the greatest wound that had ever been inflicted on anyone. It was something like the baby bear's porridge. Not too hot, not too cold, and not too sweet—but just right.

I would walk again, but whether or not I would ever run again depended on a lot of things. But then who needs to run? The only time civilized man needs to run is either in war or when he plays tennis. Who really needs to play tennis?

Me, Doctor. I need to play tennis. I may say I was a very good tennis player before I got hit. One of the dream images I kept having all the time I was in the service was of hitting a tennis ball as hard as I could with a beautiful, clean, sweeping shoulder drive and watching the white ball zoom over the net and land deep in the back court.

But I guess you can't have everything. There was no question of the fact that it was, in many ways, a pretty high-grade-type wound. The war was over for me, but it was not enough of a wound to put me in the mutilated class and make it difficult for people to be with me. It was enough of a wound to get me back to Vancouver, to Mother and Big Jim and my sister Ella. It was also enough of a wound to have the government pay me a sum of money on which I could live comfortably.

I wrote a short note to Jane in Texas telling her I had been hit, that I was convalescing, and that if I didn't write very often she would understand. The truth was that as a result of Wilfred's death she had become even more remote to me. Despite that, she continued writing me at least twice a week and the letters were just as intimate and revealing as they had been at the beginning.

About once a month or so I would answer her briefly; just saying that I was getting better and what the weather was like.

I fished and took walks, lay around in the sun on English Bay, took a trip to Victoria, talked to Big Jim and to Mr. Godfrey, who taught English composition at Britannia High, about the milk bottle and the urn. It was obviously out of Big Jim's line, but he knew that there was something else I was looking for behind it, and tried to help me find it.

Mr. Godfrey took it seriously and gave me a lot of books on æsthetics and the *Nature of Beauty*.

Yes, sir. Yes, ma'am. It was a great little wound. Men worked a whole lifetime and got less than what I got for that wound. Why, I had it all, everything those ads promised you at the age of sixty, if you had lived a good thrifty upright life.

Fish. Smoke a pipe. Read books. Take up a hobby.

Liked by everybody. Do anything you please. Go anywhere.

See what I mean? I was Secure. I had Nothing to Worry About. I had what I had fought to guarantee. I had what I had been trying to promote for myself all my life before that.

In a dull and unostentatious way I had never been unhappier in my whole life, or lonelier.

Then one day the cannon in Stanley Park, which usually booms out the curfew at nine o'clock, kept booming.

People poured into the streets.

The war was over. People kissed each other, loved each other, and it was all great.

From that moment on I became obsessed with the idea that if I could find out what had happened to Marie-Ange and her sister Toutou, the feeling of oppression would leave me.

I sent one letter after another to her at Saint-Malo. I would imagine a letter coming back from her, telling me that she was fine, and Toutou was fine, and how they were rebuilding Saint-Malo—or even how she was either married, or about to be married.

But no answer came. Instead, I got a note, a long time after I sent the first letter, saying that that address no longer existed.

I tried writing to the Mairie of Saint-Malo and various other official agencies. I once got a reply that somebody would look into the matter for me and inform me as soon as they had definite word.

Of course they didn't inform me. It was easy to understand why. They had the job of putting their whole country back on its feet.

Jane kept writing regularly. She was in college now, studying physics, I suppose because of Pops Whitman being a biophysicist, but also, she said, because they had discovered that she had some extraordinary aptitudes, especially with numbers. Once or twice she invited me to come down to Texas. The Whitmans would love to have me, and she was sure the sun was good for me.

I wrote back and told her that contrary to popular belief Vancouver had a rather mild and benevolent climate, and that I was getting along fine.

Big Jim had given me a job on the *Sun*. Nothing important.

Human interest stories. About people and their dogs.

Interviewing condemned prisoners.

I did pretty well at it. Big Jim thought I had the makings of a fine newspaperman.

Somewhere in the background of those years the Chinese Communists won in China, and the Cold War broke out. The Americans had inaugurated their Marshall Plan and the Russians were quarreling bitterly with them in the United Nations, but I went quietly on my way writing stories about fortunetellers, murders and divorces, the sort of thing most people read first when they open the newspaper.

Which brings me to 1950 and the incident which was the beginning of my Uncle Debret wanting me out of Canada again. Ironically enough it also had to do with Wilfred.

For some reason I never understood, after all those years a couple of guys from the atheist sect for which Wilfred had written his article on Teen-Age Atheism turned up suddenly one day and asked me if during his last moments Wilfred had made any mention of God.

I thought about my answer carefully. Even though I didn't want to get into any arguments, I couldn't betray Wilfred.

I told them Wilfred had been knocked off so suddenly that strictly speaking he had no last moments the way we know last moments.

They then went on to ask if, at any time we were in combat, Wilfred had seemed particularly to have turned to God.

I said I thought that Wilfred was usually pretty busy when we were out over enemy territory.

That was all I said.

6.

THEY WERE what you might call aggressive atheists. They weren't just content to let it lie there. They had to make something out of it. They wrote an article called "One Atheist Who Remained an Atheist Even in the Fox Hole" and quoted me as an authority.

Several newspapers picked that up and before you knew it, there was quite a controversy brewing.

Debret called from Montreal and ordered me to deny everything. I couldn't do that. I hadn't given any opinion of my own. I was only telling what I had seen.

He then asked me to put Mother on and he burned her ear off about didn't I realize what it did to him and his position to have his sister's son talk that way and be publicly identified with ideas of that kind?

Well, neither Mother nor Big Jim brought any pressure to bear on me, and Debret finally let it go at that.

But a short time later on the occasion of the anniversary of Wilfred's death, his high school club belatedly dedicated a plaque to his memory. I was asked to say a few words and I did. I hadn't realized beforehand that there would be considerable interest in this little ceremony, largely on account of the atheist business. Several reporters were there and they went to town on the fact that there was no religious ceremony of any kind; although it seemed to me that it would have been most unusual if there had been.

On this one Debret flew all the way in from Montreal, had a long talk with me, the gist of which was he wanted me out of Canada.

This time he would like me to stay away more or less permanently. He offered me a job.

Paris correspondent for his news syndicate. My French was good enough.

There was only one condition. I would have to give him my word I would never write any atheist propaganda. Or anything else subversive.

I began to feel that no matter what I did, if I stayed, I'd have

Debret on me—and there was no reason for me not to go. Big Jim and Mother were comfortably married. My sister Ella was engaged to a tall thin character named Tommy Gerard who had sheep interests near Kamloops.

And the condition Debret had imposed didn't seem so difficult.

Besides, I could get to Saint-Malo.

Much as I hate flying and the sight of a plane and despite the fact that I could have gotten cut-rate passage on a boat, I was suddenly in a hurry. Once I made up my mind I couldn't bear to stay.

I don't know what the family thought, but they seemed to understand. Ella made some half-baked attempt to get me to stay for the wedding, and when I said I wouldn't, gave up.

A couple of days later I landed at Le Bourget, took a room in a cheap hotel in Paris, checked my bags there and took the first train to Saint-Malo.

The center of the town was a hollow mockery. Most of the places Marie-Ange had pointed out to me were gone. The wall around the town was the only substantial thing that had been left standing.

Yes, sir. We sure had done a job on that town.

Even at that date they were just beginning to rebuild, but because it was early winter very little was going on. The area in which Marie-Ange's house had stood was about the worst hit of all.

There was a little *épicerie* doing business in a battered old rickety makeshift shop. I asked if they knew anything about Marie-Ange.

The old lady looked at me with angry suspicious eyes, wiped her hands on her apron, disappeared in the back and came out with a young man, I guess her son. He came over to me and asked what I wanted.

I told him I was looking for Marie-Ange Rouleau. He didn't seem to understand. I asked him how long they had been in Saint-Malo and it seems that they had been there several generations. I described Marie-Ange to him. Also Tou-tou.

Both the old lady and the young man kept staring at me. Neither one said anything. I told them how I had met Marie-Ange.

It wasn't that he didn't know who she was. He knew only too well. He and the old lady shut the *épicerie* and took me with them.

They took me to a little cemetery right outside the town. Marie-Ange and Tou-tou were buried side by side.

They had been killed in an air raid in June 1944. June 7th.

Where were you on the night of June 7, 1944?

Now don't get excited. It wasn't me.

On the night of June 7, 1944, I was in a hospital, flat on my back. It wasn't me. I didn't do it.

On the matter of the broken milk bottle. It's true the bottle was broken. But I didn't do it.

You didn't?

No. I didn't. I found out today. The aforementioned milk bottle was broken on the night of June 7, in the year of our Lord nineteen hundred and forty-four. And for your information, I was not there. Understand? I cite as evidence exhibit A—two tiny gravestones in a cemetery outside of Saint-Malo. *Marie-Ange Rouleau. 1924–1944. Décédée, 7 Juin 1944. Aurore Rouleau. 1936–1944. Décédée, 7 Juin 1944.* . . . On that night, gentlemen, I happened to be in a military hospital. . . . Official affidavits supplied on demand indicating dates and places.

I stood there in the gray cold staring at the two little tombstones, remembering the feel of Marie-Ange's body and the way Tou-tou had laughed and the way she had said I was nuts.

I felt sick.

Marie-Ange had lied to me about her age.

She had been barely fifteen. . . .

I couldn't stand the old lady and her son looking at me. I got away as quickly as I could.

I took the *rapide* back to Paris.

7.

FROM THE first moment I hit Paris, things fell into place for me. While I was getting myself accredited as a foreign correspondent, I ran into a guy named Izzy Gomez whom Wilfred had met in London. Wilfred had often spoken of him with admiration. Before the war Izzy had distinguished himself as a reporter showing how certain editorials in

American newspapers were duplicating Nazi propaganda word for word.

Izzy is half-deaf, having had an eardrum punctured in Spain, where he had been a correspondent. He talks in a very high-pitched voice and is very excitable.

For some reason or other he took a liking to me. Maybe it was because of Wilfred—or because he felt flattered that a Canadian remembered his name. In any case, Izzy had been very friendly with the Jewish sculptor named Turoffsky who had been killed by the Nazis, and it was through Izzy that I fell into that beautiful apartment the moment I hit Paris. The rent on it was the prewar rent, which is about seven dollars a month.

Izzy introduced me to the woman he was living with—Giselle. She was about twenty-seven, the widow of a veteran of the Spanish Civil War. Her husband had been captured by the Gestapo and tortured to death.

Izzy had a little office which he offered to share with me.

Within a few days after I landed in Paris I had an apartment, two good friends, an office, and I was in business.

Every now and then I would remember Marie-Ange.

Jane?

I couldn't even remember what she looked like. I had written to her saying only that I was leaving Vancouver but not saying where I was going. She had then written asking Mother to let her know where I was. Mother sent the note on to me.

I didn't answer it.

Then Mother sent me another note from Jane.

She was still an undergraduate at the University of Texas but was doing research with Pops Whitman. It was exciting working with him, but she missed badly the letters I had sent to her before. There was no one there to whom she could talk the way we had talked in our letters. I had always been so clear; I had always sensed the problems with which she would be confronted before they happened. She was very troubled. It would mean so much to her if I would write again. Was it because I had been wounded that I felt I no longer wanted to talk about such matters?

I remember thinking idly that she was probably close to nineteen then. I wondered what she looked like.

Naturally I didn't answer. She wasn't really expecting an answer from me. The guy she was expecting it from was dead.

And somewhere in the background of these years the war in Korea broke out; the French were fighting in Indochina and I kept hearing from Izzy about how Vishinsky and Dulles had crossed swords at the Security Council meeting.

If I'm hard put I can remember also that Stalin died, the war in Korea ended, the King of England died, there were various women in my life, and that my good friend Izzy Gomez had given up, a long time ago, trying to talk to me about the stories he was filing.

I recall also that there was McCarthyism in America and a lot of outcry in France about the execution of the Rosenbergs. Every now and then I would wake up in the middle of the night and think of Wilfred and Marie-Ange and say to myself that my God, I was over thirty. . . .

Then one night I went to a UNESCO reception. I went for the usual two reasons: one, to find a story my Uncle Debret would not consider too controversial (that's no mean feat); and two, to see if there were any leftover dream girls lying around who could give my life substance.

The reception was being held at the apartment of Vicomte de Something or Other who was a big shot at UNESCO. It was a big, lovely, crystal-chandelier-lighted, brocaded, Louis the Fourteenth kind of an apartment, and it seemed to me a promising background for anybody's dream girl.

It turned out to be a very serious evening. They even served some sort of a mildly spiked fruit punch, not to get people in a mood so they could be sold something, but actually to keep people from getting thirsty so that they could concentrate on the business of the evening. The business turned out to be the rehabilitation of a couple of hundred thousand disturbed children who were still left over when the account books of the last war were being gone over.

Just about the time when I was wondering how I could beat a graceful exit I heard a voice behind me say:

"Well, I'll be goddamned."

I turned and there was Wonderful Walter Carr, big, curly-haired and as boyish as ever. He was a little high. He greeted me by throwing his arms around me and kissing me on both cheeks the way French generals do when they decorate a soldier.

"What are you limping for, hey?" he asked.

"I got shot in the rear," I told him. "Cut a nerve."

"Cut a goddam nerve, hey?" Walter repeated enthusiastically.

It seemed he was working out of Geneva where the Foundation kept an office. Switzerland was full of wonderful goddam vitamins, some of which I needed, Walter said, to make the nerve grow back.

The idea of sending me vitamins seemed to fill him with joy and it was all I could do to prevent him from sending me a heat lamp which he said I also needed to treat the wound.

"How you making out, boy?" Walter kept firing at me. "Lucky bum to be in Paris. Just happens to be about the best damn city in the world. What you doing?"

I told him about the deal my Uncle Debret had worked out, and how by driving myself nuts I had managed only to spend about a thousand bucks a year of my own money. I was now down to five thousand bucks, and I had sworn not to go below that point.

Walter was watching me very carefully with that warm, attentively eager and engaging medical look of his.

He asked about my sex life. I told him it wasn't particularly fascinating.

It was then a matter of ordinary courtesy for me to ask how his sex life was.

His face lighted up, but he still kept looking at me keenly while he talked. To say, incidentally, that Walter's face lighted up is to say a lighted Christmas tree lighted up. Walter's face is always lit.

His sex life was wonderful. He was married to an incredibly beautiful and lovely Italian girl whom he had met when he and his outfit were piercing the soft underbelly of Europe. She was a countess, but you'd never know it (whatever he meant by that). She had been educated in England, Switzerland and France and she had brought a stability and tranquillity into his life he had never known before.

He stopped.

"Okay," he said at last. "Tell me about it."

"About what?" I asked.

"About what's eating you," he replied.

I dutifully tried to think of something that would satisfy him.

"Nothing's eating me," I said at last. "Nothing that's not eating most people."

"Yeah," Walter said reflectively, still staring at me. "Yeah, sure." Then suddenly something happened to his face which was as though all the bells in all the village churches had suddenly started to ring out. "Jesus," Walter said. "Jesus H. Christ."

"What's the matter?" I asked.

"Nothing," Walter said after a moment. "Nothing at all." He poured a soup-bowlful of cognac. "Just drink that down, boy, and relax."

I eyed him suspiciously. I didn't like the bells ringing, and I didn't like the way he obviously kept getting more and more excited about whatever it was he had thought of.

Despite the fact that we drank a huge amount of the Vicomte de Something or Other's cognac, Walter kept his guarded secret closely guarded. When I dropped him off at his hotel that night I could see that the minute he got to his room he would put the operation into motion, but what with all the drinking, I completely forgot to tell Walter that I was leaving to cover the Cannes Film Festival the next morning and that I would be gone two weeks.

8.

THE NEXT morning I called Walter a couple of times at his hotel, and even once at the Foundation's Paris office, but he wasn't in, so I left word for him at the hotel that I was leaving for fourteen days or so, and that I hoped to see him sometime on my return.

It was a wonderful two weeks, at least for me. I always enjoy the film festivals at Cannes. The sun is lovely.

By the time I got back to Paris I had a nice tan, and with it that glowing phony feeling of health which a tan always gives me.

In the stack of mail waiting for me was a series of indignant notes from Walter.

The first few notes from him were Call me, Walter. Call me as soon as you get in, Walter et cetera.

After a while it degenerated into Okay, you son-of-a-bitch, don't call me. I just want you to know that Jane's probably coming to Paris, Walter.

That one rocked me.

I sat down before I read his last note. It was a lulu.

For a long time now Jane Bridon-Jack has been writing me, asking me if I knew where you were. She's been trying to get away from Texas and over to Europe, but Pops and Bunny wouldn't let her go just like that. She hasn't been too happy there. Naturally you being here makes the picture different.

A lurking foot shot out of the darkness and kicked me so hard that my teeth jammed.

Why, for God's sake, does my being here make the whole picture different?

So I just wrote and told Jane that you were here. To tell you the truth I was a little surprised myself at the rapidity and, I might say, intensity of the response. To cut through all the formalities, my boy, by the time you read this letter, that is, if you're really going to stay away two whole weeks, Jane will in all probability be in Paris, and calling you. Incidentally, I have a couple of other reasons for having done this, but in the meantime, before you blow your cork, I just want you to know that I've seen some pictures of her lately—and listen—it's nothing you would want to chase off with a baseball bat. Also, it so happens she's a genius—at least that's what Pops says, and I would be inclined to trust him on that score. She apparently can do calculus and things like that in her head. So when you boil it down to its essentials, a beautiful genius with a three-dimensional figure who is predisposed toward you is about to be where, if you tried, you could get to see a lot of her. My medical opinion is that it would be to the advantage of both of you. I trust that your natural tendency to be a stinker will be kept somewhat under control and you will remember that she's a terrific, sensitive girl who's had a terrible shock in her background and treat her accordingly. Believe me, I remain your faithful servant in this and other matters, Old Wonderful Walter Carr.

I let the letter drop out of my hand the way you would drop a two-hundred-pound weight that somebody had casually handed you. I looked through the other letters. There was one from Texas from Dr. Chester Putney Whitman. It said in part:

It has not been easy for me to come to the decision that I had the right to presume to write to you; nor, once having made that decision, to compose this letter. Overcoming the scientist's natural hesitation to make any excursion into the area of feeling, I should still like you to know that Jane has become, to Mrs. Whitman and myself, everything that the family which we were denied might have meant to us. We know she has been anxious to return to Europe because she has felt that somehow in Europe she could resolve certain conflicts. Whether or not this is true, I cannot estimate. But I do know that whatever Jane is to be for the rest of her life may well be determined in the very near future. Further, I feel most deeply that she is destined to make great and valuable contributions to the science to which she has chosen to devote herself, and I need not tell you as to what paramount point of importance that science now finds itself elevated.

It may be very old-fashioned of me but knowing the esteem and the very special regard which Jane holds for you, I felt that by communicating what I have to you, you who like us have been chosen to bear the responsibility of this important young life, would see fit to take that responsibility with the seriousness with which it deserves. These days, what happens to the extraordinarily gifted people like Jane has become a matter of national responsibility. I should only note that neither Mrs. Whitman nor I would wish you to interpret this as meaning that we should like to protect Jane from having the normal experiences, even painful though they be, concomitant with her age. Forgive this intrusion. I trust that you will accept it in the spirit in which it has been offered. Sincerely yours, Chester Putney Whitman.

Then when I looked over Walter's letter again and mixed it with Chester Putney Whitman's, I got what my friend Jake Mendelberg used to call a first-class mishmash. I wished deeply and fervently at that moment that both Wonderful Walter and his distant cousin the biophysicist and this great delicate flower of a girl would all go somewhere and unostentatiously drop dead.

But my little surprises were not quite over.

There was another note on the subject. This one was from the party of the first part—Jane Bridon-Jack herself. It was a *pneumatique*.

A *pneumatique* is a letter that you can send to anywhere in Paris and have it reach its destination within a couple of hours, providing, of course, you send it from Paris.

Here's what it said:

I'm staying at a little hotel called Hotel Parnasse and its telephone number is Danton 39-77. I've just gotten in and I must confess I had a pretty rough time of it in the plane although everyone says it was a very smooth flight. I didn't get much sleep so I'm very tired. I think I'll sleep all night and all day (I sometimes do that when I'm overly tired) until tomorrow night when Walter's note said you would be coming back, at which time I'll call you. But if you feel like telephoning, please do. I won't mind in the least being wakened whenever you would like. As ever, Jane.

The *pneumatique* had been sent late the day before.

What I wanted most at that moment was my hot shower but I knew that the moment I got in it the bloody telephone would ring. I have an obsession about that anyway. The moment I get relaxed and ready to enjoy the shower I'm sure I hear the phone ringing, or somebody knocking on the door.

I forced myself over to the telephone and a big routine went on with some character at the other end. It turned out to be the concierge of her hotel.

"Mademoiselle Bridon-Jack," I said wearily into the phone.

"*Qui?*" the character asked.

"Bridon-Jack," I said. "*Breedon-Jacques.*"

Finally he said, "*Breedon-Jacques!*" as if he had made the discovery of the century.

"*La petite Américaine,*" he said.

"*Anglaise,*" I said savagely. "If you will but regard her police registration form which is still before you, you will see she is on a British passport."

"You are correct," he said coldly at last.

I knew then I had made an enemy for life.

"She sleeps," he said.

"Awaken her," I ordered. "She is expecting me."

There was a long cool pause.

"Very well," he said at last coldly. "It is as you wish." I heard the gurgling sound as he rang her room.

A high, thin, rather childish feminine voice said hesitantly, "Hello—"

I said, "Hello—Jane?"

She said, "Yes—"

I said, "How are you?"

"Wonderful," Jane's voice came back. The childish, sweet tones were throbbing with excitement.

I waited for her to go on, but she was apparently waiting for me to go on.

I always lose at that game. I'm always the guy who talks first, I told myself bitterly. Wilfred was the only guy, outside of my opponents, who ever won. I decided this time I was going to win. I would wait her out.

I waited so long that the telephone operator cut in asking, *"Terminé?"*

"Pas du tout," I said savagely.

"How are *you?*" Jane finally asked.

"Okay," I said.

"You must be tired," Jane said. "I looked up Cannes on the map. It's all the way across France. Did you drive?"

"Yes," I said. "I drove."

"Are you too tired to have dinner with me tonight?" Jane asked. "I want very much to see you."

"I'm not too tired," I said ungraciously.

"It's now a little after six," she said. "I imagine you got in only a little while ago."

"Yes," I said, "about half an hour ago."

"I should think you'd like to rest for an hour or so," she said. Her accent was a curious mixture of Oxonian and Texas drawl, but what was stranger was the mixture of maternal assurance with those childish tones. "Then you'll probably want to take your time bathing and dressing. I could come by your place—say at eight-thirty—or is that too late for dinner in France?"

I stared at the telephone incredulously.

"It's not too late," I said. "But there's no reason for your coming around to my place. I—"

"I wouldn't mind," she said. "Unless you'd rather I didn't."

"Well, that's not it," I said. "I have a car, and I know Paris."

"It would save a little time," she said.

I blinked at the phone again.

"Okay," I said finally. "You know how to get here?"

"Yes," she replied. "The man at the desk drew me a map last night. I'll see you at eight-thirty."

"Fine," I said.

We hung up.

Well, fellows—

Although on the surface she sounded like she might turn out to be not as big a pain as one might have anticipated, you never know—

Lie down and rest awhile, little man, she had said. You must be tired.

You never can tell. There's an outside chance she could turn out to be something interesting.

I didn't get very far convincing myself of that. Since I've been in Paris I've been continuously surprised at how many people from Vancouver, B. C., visit France. And most of them turn out to be cousins of one of my buddies in the R.C.A.F. or friends of friends of Ella's.

Among the last had been a girl, rather pretty in a sour sort of way, who had come to study art and then hated Paris. It had become a personal issue between us. The reason she hated Paris boiled down mostly to the fact that a person couldn't find either decent toilet paper or the same remedy for diarrhea that she used in Vancouver. (Incidentally, one might be forced to admit that Western Hemisphere toilet paper is slightly superior, but the local medicine for the runs is second to none.)

There'd been too many of that kind for me to be too hopeful about Jane. Besides, the idea of her being here bothered me. It evoked Wilfred and a host of disagreeable thoughts.

I decided I would make an effort with this one. I would take her to Versailles. We would do the Louvre. I would (out of deference to Chester Putney Whitman) take her to the more dignified night clubs, nothing too risqué. I figured hopefully that maybe two weeks would do it.

While I shaved, I forced myself to imagine that skinny solemn little twelve-year-old turning into something, but all I got was a small, horsy-type lady with dry blond hair and eyes red from looking into too many books.

I decided to change shirts as well. The white shirt with the soft collar would set off my Cannes tan very well indeed.

I had never looked better in my whole life. I was thinking what a shame to waste it on Chester Putney Whitman's genius when there was a knock on my door.

I looked at my watch. It was eight-thirty all right, and I could hardly believe there had really been a knock on the door. Everybody else I've ever known to visit me took the elevator. I'm on the seventh floor, which is the top, and French staircases are steep. I always hear the elevator stop at my floor and I know it is somebody for me, because there's nobody else on my floor.

I was a little irritated to be surprised that way.

I opened the door.

Well—leaning against the doorpost and breathing hard was a small, golden little thing with golden hair and golden eyes. She still had her Texan tan and she also must have known that white sets off a tan well, because she had on something cool and simple and very white.

She was neither skinny nor gawky.

As Walter had said, she was definitely three-dimensional.

Don't ask me if she's beautiful. I can't tell. I don't know if most people would think she's beautiful.

Me—I think she's beautiful. I think she's the most beautiful thing that was ever made. I thought so the first moment I saw her there in my doorway.

9.

HER FACE was tilted up with such intense expectation that it was almost funny. Also what was almost funny was the way she smiled and lowered her head in such obvious relief.

You see she had been staring at me as hard as I had been staring at her, and the way she had smiled and lowered her head in relief conveyed so obviously that she had been worrying about what *I* would now look like, and liked very much what I looked like.

If that sounds immodest, I'm sorry, but that's the way it was. Most people would have taken pains to hide the fact that they had been anxious about what you would look like; even more especially a girl would certainly have hidden the fact that she was glad you looked the way you did. Also, I'm sure no other girl I know, or had known, would have knocked at the door while she was still out of breath. I'm sure she would have waited until she was all composed, had looked at herself in the mirror, done her lips, and straightened her dress.

But not her. She had knocked the moment she felt like it.

She slipped around the doorpost and inside the apartment and I shut the door behind her.

"Why didn't you take the elevator?" I asked.

"I felt like climbing stairs," she said with a half laugh.

So did I.

"I walked from the hotel," Jane said. "We don't live far from each other. I guess Walter arranged it that way."

"I guess he did," I said.

Old Wonderful Walter Carr, the world's greatest doctor. From now on I would recommend him far and wide.

And as for you, Chester Putney Whitman. I think I understand.

Jane leaned back in a chair letting her head hang forward, her arms droop heavily at her sides, her shoulders slump and her legs slide straight out from under her.

"Bunny always makes me relax like this when I get very excited," she explained. "It's a vulgar form of Yoga. Does the posture bother you?"

"No," I said, "the posture doesn't bother me." There must have been something about the way I said that, because I remembered she craned her neck and looked up at me. I was a little bit embarrassed because actually the way I had said it made it sound exactly the way I had meant it to sound—that, at the moment, I couldn't think of anything that she could do that would bother me. So, to make it sound a little better, or to cover up, I hastily said something about the fact that Wilfred used to stand on his head for twenty minutes every morning. . . . Good for his sinuses, he used to say. Also kept your hair from falling out.

"I remember him," Jane said. "You mentioned him several times in your letters. What happened to him?"

My wound began to throb.

"Wilfred was killed, the same time I got hit," I said.

She straightened up.

"I'm sorry," she said.

"That's okay," I said. "Would you like a drink?"

"No thank you," she said, "I don't need one."

She was looking at me all the time. I was trying to figure that look out.

It's true, isn't it? her eyes were asking. It's true and you're going to make it come true for me, aren't you?

I kept trying to make my eyes say Sure it's true.

I think I succeeded—temporarily that is.

She was saying, "I like your apartment very much."

It *is* a nice apartment. It has a huge two-storied living room with an enormous window through which you can look and see the Seine and about a thousand years of Paris. There's a balcony bedchamber which you reach via a beautiful old winding staircase which spirals gently up. Bits of exquisitely fashioned fragments of sculpture which Turoffsky did are scattered about the room pretty much the way Izzy and Giselle found them.

She picked up a hand that the sculptor had done, caressed it gently, then put it down.

I said, "How long are you going to stay in Paris?"

You could see the physical signs of her tensing up.

"That depends on so many things," she said. "I've . . . I've really come to continue some work which was begun in Pops's laboratory . . ."

I must have looked surprised.

"At least I hope to be able to continue it," she said with an uneasy laugh. "You haven't by any chance ever heard of a man named Ion Morescu?"

I said I hadn't.

"He's a biophysicist, too," Jane said. "He's living very close to Paris, in one of the suburbs I believe—" She pulled out a little notebook she carried with her and read, "Villa des Cinq Fusillés, Fontenay-aux-Lilas—do you know it?"

"I know Fontenay-aux-Lilas," I said. "It's not far. About fifteen minutes by car."

She got very tense again.

"Good," she said. "Dr. Morescu had come over to America in the early part of the war as a refugee. He worked in Dr. Whitman's lab. Then in nineteen forty-two he disappeared leaving all his notes behind. There wasn't very much, but I think I see a possibility . . . of something immensely important. No one else thinks so . . ." She took another breath. "Now if I can only talk Dr. Morescu into continuing the work with me . . ."

It was hard to realize she was a scientist. You had to revise all physical images you'd had up until then of what you thought a scientist looked like, or acted like.

"Why shouldn't he want to work with you?" I asked.

"I don't know," she said, "but I wrote to him, and he wasn't interested. Of course I couldn't put very much in a letter. If Morescu won't work with me, I don't have much of an excuse for staying. And I want very much to stay."

"When will you know?" I asked.

She exhaled.

"I'm not sure I'd want to know too soon if he were to say no," she said. "I thought I'd wait a week or so. Then I figured I might as well get it over with. I'll see him tomorrow."

"I'll take you," I said. "Sure you wouldn't like a drink?"

"I'm sure," she said.

She was silent for a long time. I started to put my jacket on. When I turned, she was looking at me again the way she had before. Not trying to hide it at all.

It had gotten quite dark by now. Behind us, lights had popped up all over the river. The excursion boat *Bateau Mouche* came floating down the river like a big golden bubble. We watched the river in silence for a few moments.

I asked her if she was hungry, and she said she was famished, and I said Okay let's go. We decided to walk to Patrick's on Montparnasse, about a fifteen-minute walk.

It was a fair to middling good spring night, not one of the best, a little on the coldish side, but apparently the Parisian lovers didn't think so. They were out in full force. You could hardly pass a tree or a shadow of any substance without finding a pair of lovers looking at each other as if there were some important message in code on the other's face, touching each other, kissing and sighing. Also I remember having the impression that there was a lot of laughter abroad.

Patrick's was loaded with people I knew. It couldn't have been better or more exciting or more what a little golden-haired thing with golden eyes might have dreamed Paris was.

Asa Cubit, the painter who claimed only a Ukrainian such as he could paint a Paris landscape, was there. So was Latze Gaza, the news photographer. He told Jane that before any modern war was planned, both sides inquired if he would be available to photograph it.

Then there was George Henneman, the foreign correspondent for a big Yank network. And of course, best of all, Izzy Gomez and Giselle came walking in. Izzy's jaw fell when he saw Jane and realized she was with me. He switched on his hearing aid (a top compliment from Izzy) when he leaned over to talk to Jane in his high-pitched voice, and kept wondering what I had ever done to deserve sitting next to a girl like that. Giselle took an instant liking to Jane and Jane to her, and considering they were two of my best friends, it made it just great all around. It couldn't have been greater if it tried. Every male at the table kept trying to explain things to Jane.

Then Jason Foster came over. He's a big, very handsome fellow. His excuse for coming over was that he had once been one of Izzy's great friends, but since he had taken to working for some overseas Yank agency he and Izzy had not hit it off so well.

There was so much talk and about so many things, I actually can't remember how Cubit got off on his mobiles. Henneman and Jason were working over the possibilities of a war with Russia when Cubit started talking about his friend Chaiman, a modernistic sculptor.

"So I said, 'Now listen to me, Chaiman,' " Cubit was saying. " 'Let's face reality. The future of sculpture is in the past; even with sculpture that moves like your mobiles. Nobody really wants it. Sculpture was for the stately homes of yesteryear.' " By this time Cubit had almost everybody's attention, except Jason's, Henneman's and Jane's. These three were talking to each other *sotto voce*. "So I gave Chaiman a great idea," Cubit said a little irritated that he didn't have everybody hanging on each word. "The idea of the century."

Jason and Henneman were really interested when they discovered Jane might be doing some research.

Then Cubit said very belligerently:

"Aren't you people interested in my idea of the century?"

Jason and Henneman were forced to let go of Jane and even Izzy switched on his hearing aid and we all waited for Cubit to go on.

"Mobiles for cemeteries," Cubit went on dramatically. "Instead of lifeless headstones—imagine—headstones that move. Mobiles . . ." He made a dreamy gesture with his hand to describe the movement. "But that's only half of it. The other half is . . . to make the mobiles radio-active-proof. Don't you see it?" he asked softly. "There's going to be a big atomic war. Ask Jason. Ask Henneman. They both live on that assumption. Now. What's left after the war? Or who's left? . . . No-body. Nothing. Except billions and billions of radioactive-proof grave markers—mobile crosses, crescents, stars—moving languidly each time a radioactive wind blows." Here he shut his eyes dreamily and made a lyrical gesture with his graceful hands. "The world of the future—"

I looked over toward Jane. It was not exactly the kind of talk I would have prescribed for that special evening and for a girl who had lost her family in a bombardment. But that's the way it is with these picturesque Montparnasse encounters.

You never know.

Jane was very pale, and for a panicky moment I thought she was going to be sick. Instead she looked searchingly from one face to another, her eyes resting on each face a long hopeful moment and then going on.

I think they were all vaguely conscious of some kind of a challenge coming from her. The way she looked at us, you had the feeling that she was saying, "Surely someone will have something to say about this picture of the world of the future?"

When people tell you that there is a danger the world will return to chaos it's impossible to grasp it. What Cubit had done was to give us a tangible hint of chaos. The terrible image with the languid movements of the grave markers in a deadly radioactive atmosphere was understandable.

10.

FOR THE rest of the time Jane and I stayed, Cubit's specter sat with all of us at that table, and it was impossible to disregard it. A lot of professional egos who were accustomed to having supper with various kinds of specters, the Gazas, and the Jason Fosters and the Hennemans —to whom a specter like a national calamity is something to be turned into a well-made photograph—or a well-thought-out report—or a well-turned phrase—all had a try at this one.

They turned phrases and made jokes—all except Izzy, Giselle, Jane and me.

Izzy had never accepted the idea of living in a world of specters and neither had Giselle or Jane. So they kept quiet.

As for me, I'd gone up in a plane thirty-four times and risked my life each time. I'd been shot up. I'd dropped bombs, and each time I'd dropped part of my life with them.

So specters were out of my line. I don't know then what to say about them.

The moment came when people just sat around trying not to look at each other, trying not to say that a radioactive-proof cemetery with billions of dead was not something you could brush off with a light word.

Finally Jason, in that easy, well-trained way of his, made some diplomat's joke which I don't remember, and when nobody laughed, said, "Well, I guess that breaks the evening's back, doesn't it?" . . . And left.

A short time later Gaza and Cubit got up and the party was over.

On the way back to her hotel Jane was quiet for a long time, holding herself so close to me I could feel the movements of her body as we walked and could sense her fear.

Behind us the sidewalk cafés were beginning to pile their chairs one on another.

As though she knew I had been working it over in my mind all this time she said, "You haven't told me what you think of what Cubit said."

"I haven't given it a great deal of thought," I said. "I suppose it's because I really can't imagine an atomic war happening."

She looked at me in puzzlement.

"I can," she said. "Very easily."

"Then let me put it this way," I said. "I know there won't be an atomic war in the same way I know that people in those apartment houses won't suddenly start throwing themselves and their children out of their windows."

She looked over at me and then up at the squares of light which glowed in the slumbering façades.

"If you're not sure," I said, "we can stop here a minute and see if any of them do jump."

"If you don't mind," she said, "I'd like two or three minutes to think over your last point."

I thought it was a gag at first but then I realized she was serious. She's done it many times since then. It's always on the level as she was that day. She takes two or three minutes off and thinks.

Just as she did that night.

I waited in silence, staring up at the darkened windows.

"Your point is very well taken," she said at last. "What you're saying is that we mustn't underestimate the fundamental urge to live. No matter what other complicated drives are superimposed on people, that simple instinct will always emerge as paramount. People want to live."

She turned to me with one of her smiles and my heart jumped like a fish leaping high out of water and I said to myself, No matter what the discussion is, this is one girl you can talk to logically. And she'll listen. She's wonderful, I thought.

I folded my arm around hers and held it pressed tightly next to me.

We swung off at a brisk pace and I could feel her fear dissipate itself as she clung to me affectionately.

I've fallen in love with her, I said to myself. I'm going to marry her. She's the woman I'm going to have at my side all my life.

The dark doorways were dotted with lovers but the early languid lyricism was gone. For them it was now the hour of the hot furtive gesture before they went back to the lonely reality of their lives.

Never again would I be lonely. Never again would I wait for the evening with dread. Never again would I have the feeling that life was passing me by.

The lights were out in the foyer of her hotel. The bilious concierge was reading yesterday's paper by one naked light he allowed himself.

"Welcome to Paris," I said.

"Thank you," she said.

"I'm glad you came," I said.

"So am I," she said.

I leaned over and kissed her—on both cheeks, the way you do in France when you say good night to a friend of the opposite sex.

Despite Cubit and his mobile grave markers and Jason and Henneman and their atomic war, it was a pretty good world.

Just about the best.

At 8:30 the next morning I telephoned Morescu. He answered the phone himself, a soft, rubbing voice that was almost unintelligible. I apologized for calling at this early hour, but since I was calling on behalf of Mlle. Bridon-Jack . . .

Morescu cut in. "She is here?" he asked in perfect English. His voice was almost completely without inflection, only the tiniest sort of flip at the end of the last word to indicate his astonishment.

I said she was here and very anxious to see him. Would it be possible for him to see her that morning, since I could then drive her out, which would make things much easier, as she had little French and knew nothing at all of Paris? He hesitated a moment, then said Yes, he would be pleased to see us at ten-thirty if that was convenient. I replied that it was and hung up.

Jane was waiting for me in the lobby of her hotel.

She looks great in the morning, I said to myself as she came rushing out to meet me. She was obviously so glad to see me as to elicit the rather open envy of a bearded American art student who lived in her hotel and who had been opening one of his canvases off to one side in the lobby in the hope of attracting her attention.

As we left she smiled at the Beard. I asked her if she knew him and she said no, but he obviously had wanted to talk to her only had been too shy.

We had breakfast at the Coupole, which is near her hotel and which has a waiter who should be used as a model for all breakfast waiters in the world. When he brings you your *croissant* and *café au lait,* his manner is that of one who knows breakfast is a solemn and difficult moment when conversation is not particularly indicated.

From behind Jane's back he nodded to me, indicating this was the best of those he had seen me having breakfast with and that he approved of her highly.

Jane had toast and orange juice. She didn't want anything hot, she said. She was very nervous.

I told her that Morescu had been very nice on the telephone. I told her that another good sign was that Pops and Bunny had let her go. Pops had known Morescu, or at least I assumed he had, since Morescu had worked in Pops's laboratory. If Pops had let her go, he must have had some feeling Morescu could be talked into it.

She had a characteristic way of looking at you—a half-smile, slightly wistful, slightly loving, slightly promising, and regretful that what you say is not so.

"That's not one of the reasons Pops let me go," she said. "He hoped I . . . I'd get Paris—and other things—out of my system . . . lots of other things."

She downed the rest of her orange juice and looked at her watch. "Shall we go?"

11.

IT WAS easy finding Fontenay-aux-Lilas and Morescu's broken-down villa. As we drove up, the high decrepit gates were pushed open. We were invited in by a tall, lean man of about fifty, with a very friendly manner and a pleasant face. He disappeared, cutting across the immense grounds and over into the equally decrepit villa. About two minutes later he reappeared at the doorway and waved his arms in a signal for us to come in.

We drove around to what must have once been the grand entrance for the carriage trade.

René, the man who had met us at the gate, gestured us past the heavy apparatus of old wood, iron and stained glass which was the front door, and into the house.

It took us a couple of seconds to adjust our eyes to the almost funereal light and our lungs to the sudden unventilated musty coolness of the hallway. You had a feeling that several generations ago some air had been captured and imprisoned and was now slightly stir crazy.

René pointed to another door and pushed it open, then leaned in and asked to be excused as he had to go back to work. A voice came back thanking René and we entered into what I suppose you'd call a library. Wooden shutters sealed out most of the light except that which came from a little gooseneck student lamp, which stood on a desk littered with thousands of papers, innumerable ash trays, books, and God knows what else.

A man rose from a chair behind the desk and started to come toward us. That was Morescu.

There was something about him that baffled me at first, but after a few minutes I realized what it was.

Morescu looks like a photograph of a man—his coloring, the look in his eyes, even the way he talks.

Like a slightly old-fashioned, slightly faded photograph full of grays and muted blacks.

Once upon a time, when he was fully alive, he must have been swarthy, but now he's sort of cigarette-ash gray. His eyes have the look of tin foil in a photographer's old-fashioned flash bulb after it's been burned, as though some momentary flash of incandescence had used the eyes up.

He was wearing a double-breasted ash-flecked jacket, a woolen muffler, and a cigarette was burning at a peculiar angle, almost even with his forehead, out of a battered gold cigarette holder.

"Forgive me for not coming out to meet you," he said in perfect English and in that very soft rubbing voice, "but there is so much sun today, and I am a heliophobe." He turned to me with an apologetic gesture for explaining the word: "I dislike the sun." His mouth twisted a little into what the facial muscles seemed wistfully to recall as a smile and he said, "Is it possible that you are Miss Bridon-Jack?"

"I think so," Jane said with a wisp of a smile, "although what with the excitement of seeing Paris for the first time and . . ." She looked at me and then at him, and added, "All the rest—I'm not quite sure."

Morescu was staring at her. You had the feeling he was looking at an old album; she was out of his own life.

"I'd forgotten anyone could be so young," he said very softly. He turned to me. "If you will be good enough to dust off those two chairs you will be able to sit . . ."

"Dusting off" the two heavy armchairs he indicated included removing from one of the chairs a heavy marble bust (I think it was of Lavoisier), inducing an elderly dog named Rip to find a warm spot elsewhere, trying to disentangle a broken umbrella from behind the seat, and pushing the torn leather back in place so that the rather menacing interior of the seat was partially covered.

Morescu watched Jane and me go through all this with the polite disinterest with which he did a great many things; a little like the way a ragged but elegant tramp would watch a window in a fashionable haberdasher's being dressed. He was interested but in a very distant and objective way.

Once we were seated he looked at us neither expectantly nor any other way. I had the feeling we could all have sat there for hours without Morescu feeling in the slightest uncomfortable.

Mr. Eternity.

After a while Jane began to feel ill at ease.

"You got my letter, I believe?" Jane asked. It was exactly as though she had said, *"Somebody's* got to start this conversation."

"Indeed," Morescu replied pleasantly. "And you got mine?"

"Yes," Jane said. She waited hopefully a moment, but he gave no indication whatsoever that he would budge.

Suddenly Jane sat up with a prim kind of determination and blurted out, the way a schoolgirl blurts out a recitation she has learned by heart, "Mr. Morescu, I think your estimate of the possibilities inherent in your conceptions is unduly pessimistic."

Morescu inclined his head in a slight graceful movement of acknowledgment.

"So you indicated in your letter," he said. The smoke ribboned lazily up over his eyes.

"I think," Jane went on, "that your hypothesis may be one of primary importance."

She had obviously said *that* in her letter too. Only this time Morescu didn't even feel obliged to point it out. He continued to sit, distant, impassive.

"I would like you to look at what I've done with your work," Jane said. An edge was beginning to appear in her tones.

"Why?" Morescu asked.

"Because," Jane said, "I think you and I can work this out together. I can't do it alone—" Her voice throbbed with eagerness. "I believe this is enormously important."

She was so ardent, so young, so alive, that it must have touched him dimly. He smiled at her.

"If only you'll work with me," Jane finished wistfully.

The smile on his face died. The cigarette holder dropped. He frowned.

"I cannot do any more research," he said. "I cannot."

He said it the way you would say a thing was physically impossible. I believed him. I think Jane did too, but it didn't stop her.

"Why can't you do any more research, Dr. Morescu?" Jane asked.

There was a big silence and Dr. Morescu turned white and his hands trembled.

"When the two of you came into this room," Morescu said, "it was as though someone had brought me a bouquet of flowers. Although I dislike the sun, I love flowers. It was as though someone had brought me in some daffodils." He pulled out the tiny glowing stub of his cigarette and let it burn out in a huge iron ash tray. "I will tell you why I cannot do any more research," he said.

"I was more or less happy working in Dr. Whitman's laboratory as a refugee scientist. I had all I needed and no one bothered me." Morescu asked quietly, "Do you know why I left so suddenly?"

"No," Jane said nervously.

"I was lured by the Nazis," Morescu said. "The bait was my wife and daughter." He hesitated. "My wife was Jewish—and of course my daughter was thus half Jewish. They had disappeared in nineteen forty. I searched all over Europe for them." He frowned, continued with difficulty. "One night a compatriot of mine appeared suddenly. We talked in that huge room which is on the south side of the house." He stopped.

"Yes, I remember that room," Jane said.

Morescu nodded.

"We talked till midnight," Morescu said. "My compatriot told me that he had seen my wife and my daughter alive in Paris. That was all he told me. He said he hadn't even had a chance to speak to them. If he had said more I would have been suspicious. If he had said less—"

The unusual effort seemed to tire him. He seemed sorry he had begun.

"I got to Paris through Portugal and Spain," Morescu went on wearily. "Every move of mine must have been watched. The moment I got to Paris the Gestapo paid me a visit." He stared at us blankly. "It was true. My wife and child were alive."

He pushed himself to his feet. He was all cigarette-ash gray now.

"A German colleague of mine had known of this research." Morescu made a slight gesture toward Jane, as if somehow it was her research now. "I was offered a deal. The lives of my wife and daughter if I continued to work with this same colleague . . ." He seemed to have lost the thread of his thoughts. Suddenly he wheeled about as though he had heard a piercing cry. Then he came back to us and said, "They're both dead."

He sat down.

He didn't say any more. It was as though he considered what he had told us an adequate explanation for not wanting to go on with the research.

For a long time we avoided each other's eyes. The story affected me strangely. My wound began to throb. I began to find the silence heavy.

I got up and said, "I'd like to open a window."

I walked over and fought for some minutes with a window which obviously had not been opened for at least two generations.

Jane was standing very close to me.

"Are you all right?" she asked quietly.

I looked at her in surprise. "Of course I am," I said.

"You . . . you were limping so badly," she said.

"It's my wound," I said. "Funny how I can go for months—then wham—something hits me . . ."

"May I get you something?" Morescu asked. "Coffee perhaps?"

I wished they would all stop looking at me, although I realized it was because they didn't want to look at each other.

I sat down.

They sat down.

I could feel Jane thinking hard.

Finally she sat up again, this time even more primly.

"You promised you'd let me talk to you," Jane said to him. "I came all the way here to talk to you . . ."

Morescu was very agitated. "Surely you must understand why I cannot . . ."

"It will take me two weeks or so," Jane said relentlessly. "At least that—for me to have a fair chance to tell you what I see in this work . . ."

"Two weeks?" Morescu asked uneasily.

"Yes," said Jane.

He pointed to the litter on his desk. "I have some friends at the Sorbonne," he said, "who occasionally give me work as a translator. It is the way I live."

"We could talk at night," Jane said.

"There is no transportation at night," Morescu said. "You would be unable to get back to Paris . . ."

"I have a car," I said. "I could pick her up."

He looked at us. I'm sure we were both hanging on each word as if our lives depended on it.

He smiled. Almost-smiled, that is. When he almost-smiled, you realized he must have once been a most attractive man.

"It is a kind of conspiracy, I see," he said with gentle weariness. "But I agree. Come speak to me for two weeks."

"Thank you," Jane said. "Thank you very much."

He was eying us quizzically, her mostly, as he walked us to the big front door.

"You do not mind that I am convinced that this work has no possibility?" he asked of her.

"Oh, I mind," Jane said seriously. "I mind very much. Only I think I can unconvince you."

We shook hands. He bowed. We left. He disappeared back into the cigarette smoke.

In front of the car we looked at each other.

"We did it!" Jane said in intense whispers. "We did it!"

We drove off quickly. When we were about a kilometer away from the house she let out a "Yippee" that I'm sure was heard clear on the other side of the river. At least an elderly fisherman on the other bank almost fell into the water.

"He's given me two weeks!" Jane shouted. "Two whole weeks! Yippee!"

The third one was on me.

Qu'est-ce-que c'est que ça—Yippee? *Qu'est-ce-que ça veut dire?*

A far-Western exclamation, *mon ami*. It is used on very rare occasions. When one is delirious with joy one says, with great exuberance, Yippee!

An approximate translation of Yippee, *mon ami,* could be I am young, she is wonderful, I am in love and life is sweet and exhilarating to the touch.

Two weeks—

12.

Two weeks later, on Saturday evening, just as I was picking Jane up at her hotel, and as a matter of fact just about the time we were stepping out of the hotel's tiny lobby, the churlish concierge called

Jane over and said there was a communication *téléphonique* for her. She ran like hell over to the phone which is alongside of the desk.

It was Morescu all right. He had finished studying her notes. He had given the matter very careful thought. If she would come out on Sunday he would tell her what his decision was.

Well.

We spent most of the evening going over each nuance of each word of that telephone conversation but there was no way we could figure out what Morescu might really have decided. The very fact that he didn't tell her on the telephone seemed like a bad sign. If it had been yes he probably would have said yes on the phone.

Or would he? And if it had been no, mightn't he have preferred to say no simply on the telephone and avoid painful scenes?

Morescu was obviously the sort of man whose main drive in life right now was to avoid painful scenes, in fact any scenes whatsoever. So a man would think, Jane reasoned, that it would have been infinitely simpler for him to have said, "Look here, I've thought it all over and I've decided please go somewhere with your notes and your problems and quietly fade away."

But then, of course, Morescu was somewhat beholden to Pops. After all, Pops had taken him in as a refugee and treated him to the fat of the land. You couldn't just say to Pops's adopted daughter, Go get lost.

On the other hand because of what was involved, that is the potentialities military and otherwise, it might very easily be the sort of thing a man like Morescu would not care to discuss on the telephone. Especially after what he had been through with the Nazis. But then he could simply have said yes, and if Jane had threatened to let her excitement get out of hand, he could have most paternally suggested that they discuss all that on the morrow, *tête-à-tête*.

By the time I brought her to the hotel she was pretty jumpy and I was worse.

"Do you mind not coming out with me tomorrow?" she asked suddenly. "I'd rather go alone." I was startled by the idea. "I—I want to get used to the long Métro ride—if—if he should say yes. I'd like to make sure I can get by on my own French—"

I was very hurt. It seemed to me she was pushing me out. I was scared by how badly I was hurt.

I guess she realized it, because she turned to me with a warm smile.

"I might as well tell you the truth. I want to be alone if he says no. I want to be able to go to pieces—or anything else I might want to do—comfortably. I couldn't if you were there."

I was relieved.

"I understand that," I said.

I felt myself come back to life.

A little before noon the next day, which was a Sunday, I met her at the Sortie of the Port Royal Métro. Long before she saw me, I saw her come walking up the enormous flight of steps.

From the distance it was impossible to get any idea of what the answer had been. But as she came close I realized she was pale and frightened.

My heart lurched. I thought, Old Morescu turned her down. Now she'll go back. I'll lose her.

I was panicky.

When she reached the head of the stairs she paused to catch her breath, then said:

"I'd like to walk."

I watched each move she made anxiously. There seemed to me no doubt that the answer had been no.

I would ask her to marry me right then and there and we could go back to Vancouver, only what the hell would she do in Vancouver? Teach?

Why not?

Or for that matter we could get married and live in Paris. A while anyway. She could continue research here.

Montparnasse was practically deserted. I guess everybody was getting ready for Sunday lunch. In France Sunday lunch is more or less the reason you keep living a gray life in some lousy job the rest of the week. Everybody gets dressed up, and everybody eats out with his girl friend or his family.

All at once there was a peculiar throbbing sound which I did not recognize. People poked their heads out of windows and stared off down the empty boulevard. After a moment the throbbing grew distinct enough to be identified as the disturbing sound of muffled drums. Then people began pouring out of apartments, children came running over, and from right under our noses a gendarme materialized and began redirecting traffic.

Moving slowly down the boulevard was a somber cortege, a silver and black horse-drawn coach covered with flowers. Right behind was a military escort of honor and a muffled drum corps.

The gendarme explained to us that it was the official reinterment of the body of Louis Braille; that he was now being reburied in the Panthéon in a place of national honor.

While I was translating all this to Jane the cortege came abreast of us. Hundreds of blind children followed the coach, holding each other's hands as they walked slowly forward. Behind the children came many hundreds of blind adults, tapping their way along with their white canes, making a rhythm almost like that of the drums.

"These children," the gendarme explained to us in hushed tones, "are mostly war-blind. They are being cared for in governmental institutions."

"But there are so many of them!" Jane exclaimed with a kind of incredulous horror.

"Even a very few blind children," the gendarme said, after I had translated, "seem like very many. But you are right. There are surprisingly many children who lost their sight as a result of the war."

After the parade passed, Jane and I sat down at a sidewalk café and ordered coffee which she didn't touch.

For a long time she was silent. At first I thought it was because of the blind children. Then I began to realize she was in some terrible inner conflict. She was trying to work something out in her head and she couldn't.

Without realizing it, she was rocking slightly as if in pain.

"Jane—" I said, the way you wake up someone you love who's been in a deep sleep.

She looked up at me and away.

"Strange how it worked out," she said with a kind of gentle bitterness. "Right after my family was killed, it was hard for me to do anything—even to read. Innocent words like 'cat' would make me think of our cat. It had had one blue eye and one yellow eye. I saw its body in the debris. And 'boy' would make me think of the boy who used to play with my sister Mundy. So I retreated into mathematics. The world of numbers seemed safe. Now look at me and my numbers."

"I don't understand," I said. "What happened?"

She still didn't answer.

"Morescu refused?" I prompted.

She looked straight at me.

"No," she said. "He didn't refuse."

I looked at her in consternation.

"He's willing to work with me," she continued, "if I still want to go ahead."

"If *you* want to go ahead?" I demanded. "What does that mean?"

"Dr. Morescu pointed something out to me which I should have realized myself," she said painfully. "In my girlish excitement about my work I overlooked it. But I've got to face it now. This research of ours could provide the basis for the most terrible instrument of war yet conceived."

For about ten seconds that had me on my heels. All I could think was that she might leave Paris, leave me, go out of my life. I'd lose her.

"If you take that attitude," I said numbly, "you've got to stop being a scientist. Any really important discovery these days can be used in war."

"Then maybe I should give up my work," she said.

I was appalled. I saw that she had faced up to that possibility too.

"Isn't there anything else your work could be used for?" I asked desperately.

"Yes," she said after a moment. "It could make an important contribution to our understanding of basic life processes—and in other fields too. Providing it wasn't used to wipe out whole continents."

She was serious. Whether she was right or wrong, she really believed that.

And it was an ordinary Sunday morning in a very usual little Parisian café. Ordinary men and women in their Sunday best were seated about us.

"You yourself said we mustn't underestimate people's will to live," I said. "No continents are going to be wiped out."

"It wouldn't be planned that way," she said. "It would begin with other weapons." Some horrible image passed through her mind. "There wouldn't be war-blind children this time. Not even radioactive cemeteries. There'd be nothing," she said simply.

"Even if you decided not to go on with it"—I was hanging on desperately—"someone else would discover it."

"Oh, no," Jane said grimly, "not this one. This was a fantastic stroke of luck. In the normal course of scientific inquiry it might be years—if ever—before it was again discovered."

"And if it died," I said coldly, "with it would die all the benefits that it might bring. Face that too."

I suddenly realized my tones had become harsh and belligerent.

"Don't attack me," Jane implored. "Help me. I'm trying to think it out. I don't know what to do. You *are* right—it *is* a frightful responsibility either way. It would be a terrible thing just to let it fade away. It's a great discovery—" She was trembling. "This is a pretty rough thing to ask a girl to decide on her own."

I felt like the world's biggest rat.

"Couldn't you go ahead with this and see what it develops into?" I said gently. "If it did become something monstrous—couldn't you destroy it then?"

"I don't know," Jane said uneasily. "I'm not sure we could control it at that point."

"Why couldn't you?" I persisted. "You can do what you like here in France. No one will ever bother you. Private research is not supervised."

Jane frowned, then said she'd like two or three minutes to think that one over.

She took the full three minutes this time. I kept watching the café clock.

"The choice is what you say it is," she said finally. "Either I give up my work . . . everything I've prepared myself for . . . everything I can do so well . . . or I go ahead with this project." She brought her coffee cup near her lips, held it there for a fraction of a second, then put it down without having tasted the coffee. "I'm going ahead with it."

This time I had to keep myself from shouting "Yippee . . ."

After that I took her for a drive along the Seine, past Notre-Dame and all the bridges. They had never been more beautiful.

We had lunch in a restaurant I know in the Wine City. It had never been more charming or more colorful, what with hanging salamis, wine bottles and slightly obscene posters. Old M. Georges, who has been running this restaurant for forty years, came up and brought his enormous menu, on top of which is a drawing of a naked woman smiling brightly as she's being boiled in a pot. I guess the idea is that in that particular restaurant no sacrifice is too great for a good meal.

Or maybe, Jane thought, it was meant to indicate that this is a restaurant of tasty dishes like the lady being boiled.

M. Georges went out of his way for us. Jane does that to people. He made us sample some of his latest wine purchases, and then brought out Mme. Georges and introduced her to Jane, explaining briefly that she was none other than the model for the naked lady who was smiling sweetly as she was being boiled. Mme. Georges laughed loudly, said that things had changed a little since the time she had posed, joined us in a glass of wine. By the time the steak came, Jane was laughing and the fear which had been circling behind her golden eyes flapped its huge black wings and took off and a flock of dazzling-colored birds sang, twittered, whistled and wheeled about in what was suddenly a beautiful soft blue sky.

We had both convinced ourselves it really was all wonderful.

13.

JANE WROTE to the Whitmans telling them of her decision. She worded the letter very carefully because she didn't want to say too much, even to them, about her work. She simply said that neither she nor Dr. Morescu was certain as to where the work would lead (which could mean anything) but that Dr. Morescu, who was a sweet and gentle person, had been disposed to join her in investigating the possibilities.

The Whitmans replied that they were pleased that she would work with Dr. Morescu. There was much she'd learn. She was not to worry about money ever. They had opened a dollar account for her in Switzerland and had arranged for traveler's cheques to be regularly available for her in Paris. There followed a long list of admonitions from Mrs. Whitman about warm clothes, simple diet and the benefits of her Yoga relaxation exercises.

The next couple of weeks after that Jane spent in getting herself adjusted. Weekdays she'd get up every morning at 6:30 and take a Métro out to Fontenay-aux-Lilas.

Every evening I'd meet her at the Port Royal Métro station. We'd kiss on both cheeks and hurry out to dinner.

She'd turn in early.

Saturday noons I'd drive out to the villa and pick her up and we'd lunch together in Paris. In the afternoon we'd wander around the old *quartiers* of Paris and Sunday we'd go to the Louvre.

She was bubbling over with excitement of Paris, her work, and what a fascinating human being Dr. Morescu was. He was slowly coming back to life.

It was all so new, there were so many impressions to exchange, so much to see and do, that a month went by before we got around to ourselves.

Late one Saturday afternoon Jane asked me to drop her off at the hotel. She wanted to change for dinner.

There was a message waiting for her. Wonderful Walter Carr was in town with his beautiful countess.

We telephoned them and before you knew it, or at least before I knew it, there he was and his countess *was* beautiful and great fun and Old Walter was looking earnestly at Jane and me and saying "Goddam" every time he looked at us. Before I knew it again, as it happens often in Paris, a full-fledged dinner party was going on in my apartment.

Izzy and Giselle came over, also a guy named Rufus Boehm and his wife, friends of Walter's and Izzy's. He and his wife were both very attractive people and he was doing some kind of research at the Cancer Institute.

Gaza came over with a Eurasian model who was the rage of Paris and an American motion picture director who kept telling everybody that he secretly disagreed with American foreign policy as it was then practiced. He kept making passes, more for form's sake than anything else it seemed to me, at Walter's wonderful countess, the Eurasian model, Jane and Mrs. Boehm. The only woman excluded was Giselle, I suppose because of the way Izzy frowned at him every time he came near.

Since everybody had brought champagne there was a sort of spiraling gaiety. Each time a new bottle would appear, we would pop it and drink it. When the next caller appeared at the doorway incredibly with a bottle of champagne, this in itself caused renewed outbursts of gaiety and called for more champagne.

Everybody liked and enjoyed each other. The American director turned the full force of his charm on Mme. Fénelon the concierge, who looks a little like a spring onion. She had come up to complain about all the noise, but before you knew it, she was telling the American director the story of her life. This held us all spellbound because aside from the fact that he was a little drunk, he spoke no French whatsoever and understood less.

Izzy even turned on his hearing aid. Walter stood by fascinated, mouth open, and when Mme. Fénelon came to the part of her life in which her husband, who had been a *garde-champêtre,* a sort of game warden, left her for the widow of a rich peasant, the American director made a wide gesture of sympathy and understanding as if to say, "What can one do? Life is like that," held Mme. Fénelon's head close to his manly breast, gave her another glass of champagne and gesturing for her to be very quiet on account of the other inhabitants of the apartment house, ushered her out.

He insisted that Mrs. Boehm tell him what Mme. Fénelon had said and listened to her with the same kind of sympathetic intensity, went downstairs and came back with four magnums of champagne all iced, which last caused Walter's countess to get out on the little terrace and sing, in a lovely warm voice, a series of what, we discovered later, were slightly dirty Neapolitan love songs.

Finally about two in the morning they started to leave. Everybody by this time was kissing everyone else. Walter kissed me on the forehead, then kissed Jane on the mouth, I kissed his countess and Giselle and Izzy kissed everybody on both cheeks, and Jane and I were alone staring at each other.

I said I didn't think there was any good reason why she should go back to the hotel, and she looked at me with those lovely golden eyes of hers that seemed to me at that moment the purest color I had ever seen anywhere. She was silent a long time—too long, I realized later —and said finally yes, she didn't see any reason either why she should leave.

After that was said, there was the awkward moment which seems to me to be usual at times like that.

Jane got up and emptied a few ash trays.

Madame Thérèse who comes in to clean my place three times a week doesn't come on Sundays.

"I hate the smell of stale cigarettes in the morning," she said.

Jane went to the bathroom. I straightened up a little, piling the champagne glasses and dirty dishes in the kitchen sink. I opened all the windows and stacked the empty champagne bottles over on one side.

When Jane reappeared she looked a little strange. I realized after a moment it was because she had wiped all the lipstick off her face and had let her hair down.

I found her exciting that way.

She walked over to the center of the room and leaned over, letting her head and arms hang loosely in her pose of Yoga relaxation.

Looking at me upside down like that she said:

"You know you've never really told me much about yourself."

I had to twist my head to talk to her.

"That's funny," I said. "I'm a favorite topic of mine—what do you want to know, for example?"

"For example," she said, "what do you write about?"

You don't usually expect to have a serious conversation with some-one whose head is hanging down that way.

"Nothing," I said.

She blew the hair out of her eyes so she could look at me. I won-dered how much you could catch of the expression of a man's face from an upside-down point of view.

"I'd really like to know," she said.

"I'm telling you," I said. "Don't underestimate it. It's not easy to take nothing and make it seem important and interesting."

I was just marking time. I wasn't really interested in what was being said. It was simply a way of getting to the moment when she'd be in my arms and I could tell her how much I loved her.

"You're joking," she said pointedly. "You write serious things."

I was beginning to get impatient and uneasy.

"No," I said, "I wasn't joking."

She straightened very slowly. When she was up, she stared at me.

I thought she was giving herself a chance to get adjusted to right side up.

"Why do you write about nothing?" she asked.

"It's the only kind of story my uncle will print," I said. "I've got to make a living."

I started to move toward her. She made an almost imperceptible movement away from me.

"You won't write about the parade of the war-blind children?" she asked.

"I don't know who would print a story like that," I said.

She looked at me in consternation.

"You don't understand," I said quickly. It was getting out of hand. "I once sent my uncle a story about the man who had first introduced the eating of horse meat in Paris—and how the grateful horse meat dealers had erected a bust in his memory in the Horse Market. He wouldn't print it."

"But why not?" Jane asked.

"He said it was skillfully disguised Communist propaganda," I said. "Picturing the French as a nation driven to the eating of horse meat."

She looked around a little as if she weren't sure where she was, then shook her head.

"Don't you try to write for anyone else?" she asked.

"No," I said, "it's a full-time job trying to make enough to live on out of him."

For no reason I could think of I suddenly had an image of Wilfred and his letters and I felt a surge of anger. Then I remembered he was dead and the anger faded and I hated myself.

There was another empty champagne bottle under the buffet. She must have seen it when she was upside down.

She walked over to it, picked it up and carried it to the kitchen.

I waited for her near the kitchen door.

She came in and stopped right at the door.

"I expected someone different," Jane said.

Okay.

You can't argue with that.

I turned and started to walk away.

The way I walked out of the plane in that muddy field in Wales, with something sticky oozing down my leg—past the streaming figures that were running toward what was left of Wilfred.

Until she called:

"Wait!"

I turned.

She was still standing by the door.

"Don't go," she said.

I went over to her and took her hand and kissed it, saying, "I love you."

"I came to Paris because of you," she said, as though thinking it out loud. "I can't think of any really valid reason why you and I shouldn't live together. The fact is—"

I didn't let her finish the sentence; instead I took her in my arms hungrily and held her to me, kissing her. Maybe it's because there was too much at stake—my whole life, for example—maybe that's why I felt a sudden uncertainty, almost a fear. Maybe it was because for the first time in many years, as I held Jane in my arms, I had a sudden image of Marie-Ange. I think perhaps something of all this communicated itself to Jane—for I had a fleeting impression of cool lips pressed against mine eagerly, when suddenly she was pushing at me blindly, fighting her way out of my arms. She looked ill.

I stared at her in horror.

She was saying, "Sorry, terribly sorry," and then the moment she seemed to have the slightest hold over herself, she pulled me back toward her desperately. But at the touch of her body against mine she became frighteningly rigid and I could feel her force herself toward me with a terrifying intensity. I held her off at arm's length and said, "Jane! What is it? What's wrong?"

She moved away from me. She looked like someone who had stepped out of a car accident.

"I don't know," she said in whispers, "I don't know."

"Perhaps it was the champagne," I finally managed to say.

I knew it wasn't that. I also knew with some sure instinct that if we didn't get over this moment we might never get over it. I came toward her again. She pulled me to her frantically and this time she half screamed as she struggled out of my arms and broke away and stood a few feet away from me.

"Oh, darling," she said, brokenly. "Oh, darling."

"Tell me," I said.

She made a conscious effort to control herself.

"I can't help it," she managed to say. "I don't mean it to happen."

"Tell me," I insisted.

She leaned over in the Yoga position for a second.

"Each time you kiss me," she said, "I can hear screaming. And I see coffins and a graveyard." I thought she was going to be sick.

"Has it happened before?" I asked.

"No," she said.

"Just with me," I said.

"I don't understand," she whispered. She was frightened. "I'm very much attracted to you physically. More than I've been to any other man. I . . . I'd like to think about this."

I let her sit in a chair and think about it.

Then she got up and repeated, "I'm afraid I don't understand." She was dead white.

That wonderful little head that could take three minutes off and understand anything, couldn't understand this.

I thought fleetingly of Marie-Ange and Tou-tou and said to myself that some day I would put flowers on their graves.

"No idea at all why?" I asked.

"None at all," she said. "I don't seem to be able to think." She was speaking clearly now. "It does not appear to be related to any conscious attitude I may have toward you," she said.

"I *understand* that," I said.

"I'm so very sorry," she said painfully. "I wouldn't want to hurt you for anything."

"It's all right," I said.

She came quite close to me and took my hand and said, "I hope you're able to be patient with me." She was looking at me imploringly. "Because I need you very much."

The way she said it made me go numb with fright.

"There's lots of time," I said. "I'll wait. We'll take it easy. We'll work this out. Because I love you."

Well, sir.

I was patient for a long time, at least it was long for me. I understand that the late Dr. Kinsey mentioned some man who went for thirty years without any of what the late Dr. Kinsey called sexual outlet whatsoever.

14.

I DON'T KNOW exactly what we became to each other. I guess we were like married people who don't sleep with each other but who see each other all the time. I became like the dentist husband, let's say, of a famous actress. No matter how hard they both try, he can never enter the magic circle of her work.

On Saturdays when I'd drive out to the villa to pick her up, I'd shake hands very warmly with Morescu and ask him how he was.

He would say in French he was very well indeed, and ask me how I was. After I'd said I was fine, the ice would begin to form. Then Jane would try very hard, like making some bright observation about how interesting it was that Morescu and I always spoke French when it was only chitchat and English for the serious talk.

Morescu would smile and shrug and I would hazard the opinion that perhaps it was because English was somehow a more serious language, but I would add hastily that French was a serious language too. Just about then I would beat a most precipitate retreat and once or twice I thought I heard the two of them sigh with relief.

At night when I'd come for her at the Métro station, she'd start to tell me about her work with great enthusiasm, and begin to explain what it was about. But then as she got into it more and more, no matter how hard we tried, we'd both begin to realize that I would never really understand what they were doing, and we would let it go at that. Actually I got a rather hazy idea that Morescu had done some kind of an experiment in which he had duplicated, as closely as was theoretically possible, the conditions which might have existed when the world was created, and as a consequence had observed certain phenomena or rather a phenomenon for which Jane had worked out the mathematical verification. Apparently it was this phenomenon which was causing all the excitement.

Every now and then I would help them install some piece of equipment into the large upstairs room in Morescu's villa which, without my realizing it, began to look like a real laboratory.

TWINKLE, TWINKLE LITTLE STAR   73

We'd have dinner together almost every night. She'd tell me about her day.

I'd tell her about my day. I'd bellyache about my Uncle Debret. I'd tell her about Mother and Big Jim and Vancouver, British Columbia, and Kamloops where my sister Ella is now with her husband.

We'd see Izzy and Giselle a couple of times a week. Once or twice a month we'd eat sukiyaki in a Japanese joint. Weekends I'd spend out at the villa where Morescu had set aside a room for me—and sometimes Jane would spend the night at my place.

Don't get excited. In separate beds always.

And there was an enormous amount of talking done. Jane was interested in everything. The only other person I'd known who loved to talk that way was Wilfred.

Jane would discuss things with almost anybody and argue with almost anybody. But you always had the feeling she was doing it because she wanted to find out.

I would listen mostly, because I enjoyed watching Jane and listening to her especially when she was in a very hot discussion. Someone would present an argument which was new to her. She would stop and startle everybody the way she had startled me that first time by saying, "I'd like two or three minutes to think that over."

She would take the three minutes, after which she would sometimes say, "No. I believe you're wrong." Or just as often, "Yes, I believe you're right."

And the discussion would go on.

About six months after I first met Jane it all began to creep up on me. I remembered a very attractive Icelandic art student I had interviewed who had seemed willing to listen to reason.

We had an affair which was a first-class nightmare. Forgetting the fact that she was rather odd (she painted in total darkness on the grounds that that excluded all outside and distracting influences and she never slept nights), she must have sensed that every time I touched her, I was thinking of someone else. She took to calling me in the middle of the night. When I would get to the telephone she would hang up. Don't ask me how I knew it was she. I knew.

One night she insisted on staying at my place until morning. What I think happened is that Mme. Fénelon or Mme. Thérèse, the charwoman, told Jane.

Anyway when I came home that night, Jane was waiting for me. She was in a flimsy nightgown and had used a little too much of some perfume with a sexy name and was looking like a virgin ready for the sacrificial knife. She had set the table with a red-checkered table-cloth, two candles, some red wine, a roast chicken and a couple of thousand hors d'oeuvres.

Also, since it was winter, there was a discreet fire in the fireplace and the electric heater was on.

Although the apartment is fairly well heated for a seventh-floor apartment, it was still a little too cold for what she was wearing.

I shut the door and said as gently as I could that I thought she ought to put something warmer on. She said that she was quite warm where she was, to which I replied that the gown was so thin, what with the flames behind her, a man could see right through her, to which she replied seriously that that was part of the general idea, and would I mind coming over to her.

We were both scared to death.

She reached out with her two hands and our finger tips touched, and even from that slight contact I knew, and I think she knew, but she controlled herself.

"Damn," she said defiantly, "don't stand there like a fool! I'm getting cold."

I pulled her toward me roughly and swept her in my arms, holding her to me as tightly as I could, and this time there was absolutely no response from her. No matter how hard she tried. Nothing.

I got her my heavy bathrobe and wrapped it around her and she sat down near the fire and began to cry in that soundless way she has of crying, while I sat next to her just caressing her lovely troubled little head gently and lied about how it didn't really matter.

From then on, from time to time, she'd tried throwing herself at me in the same way.

In my past there had been many an occasion when I knew the lady I was with was being effortfully co-operative rather than responding with all-out enthusiasm and I was able to take it in my sexual stride.

But not with Jane. I didn't want her that way.

I tried several times to think about marrying other women. It just wouldn't work, even though I wanted very much to have a family, to bring my wife back to Vancouver and to have her meet Big Jim and

Mother and Ella and Jake Mendelberg and the others. But I wasn't able to. Even though I thought I was getting to the age where it would begin to be too late to start a family.

I saw Jane two or three times a week. We spent all the important holidays together. In between times she worked—and I took up, as Debret would say, with other women.

And somewhere in the background of *those* years, Gaza was killed stupidly in the war in Indochina by stepping on a mine; the thawing out began and Izzy became more hopeful with the Geneva Conference (he and Giselle got married); the Soviets exploded *their* H-bomb; the warm spell ended and the Cold War got colder than ever. The French and the English and the Israelis made the lightning thrust on Suez as the Russian tanks moved in on Budapest. There were riots in Little Rock.

I saw Jason Foster from time to time. He'd always inquire about Jane and her health and her work. And latterly I had noticed he'd been looking harried.

Henneman became very important and we almost never saw each other.

I heard Rufus Boehm and his wife were separated.

We saw Walter and his countess very often. They were trying to have a child. They hadn't had any luck but Walter was very cheerful about it. He said he guessed there was nothing for it but to keep right on plugging away.

And Jane changed.

She dressed the way Parisian women do and it became her enormously. She made friends everywhere she went. Even when we'd stop in some odd café for a casual cup of coffee, the café people would always remember her from then on.

René and Marie, the people who live in the caretaker's cottage on Morescu's property and who take care of the villa as best Morescu will let them, were crazy about Jane. I noticed that everywhere she went people would brighten when she came in. Even though she'd talk and argue with almost anybody.

She turned twenty-six and became more desirable than ever—and each time I'd see her I'd want her more and more.

15.

WHICH BRINGS me to the fall of the year 1957. I don't know whether you remember the week the Russians sent up their first Sputnik. That was quite a week.

We were all excited about the Russian baby moon as most people were. Jane was very preoccupied and for the first time since I had known her seemed to be completely lost, caught in some crazy kind of excitement in which I could not participate. When I picked her up at the villa, she and Morescu stopped talking when I came in. They said good-by to each other hurriedly.

I took her to a little bistro on the Île St. Louis which she loved. But that night she barely noticed she was there. I had to ask her twice what she'd like to eat. When she finished ordering I asked her if anything was the matter.

She said, "Yes. Something's happened. We're entering a climactic phase of our work."

I asked her if it had anything to do with the Russian-launched satellite and she frowned a moment and said there couldn't possibly be the remotest connection.

(She was wrong. There was a remote connection, as we discovered later.)

Then she said that for the next few weeks she was going to stay at the villa and would I mind not calling or seeing her. Just for a few weeks.

There was a big silence.

I don't know why I did it. Suddenly and to my surprise I heard myself say, "Jane, I can't go on like this. I can't keep seeing you the way things are between us."

She said tightly, "It won't be for much longer. In a little while we'll know—whether we've created a monster."

"What's that got to do with us?" I asked.

"After that," she said distractedly, "I'll be able to think of us." She reached out for my hand. "Hang on a little while longer. I need you very much now."

I hesitated.

"I know what you've been through," she said, "and that's another reason that now that we've had some tangible proof of our work, I want to work day and night to finish it as quickly as possible."

"Okay," I said, "I'll hang on."

For over two weeks after that I didn't see or hear from her.

I wrote an article about the French press reaction to the Sputnik even though I knew Debret wouldn't print it. (I was right. He didn't print it. The French press wasn't unfavorable enough to the Russians.)

Knowing it would end soon made that period unbearable. I tried many things like taking out Gaza's Eurasian model, but after about ten minutes she realized what was going on. She said she would pat my head, or hold my hand, or get drunk with me while I told her my troubles, but one thing she wouldn't do was to have dinner with someone who kept forgetting she was there. All that came out of that was a big hangover for me the next morning and a suggestion from her that if I ever got over it, to call her.

So I busied myself writing stories that wouldn't upset my Uncle Debret, wandered around feeling like a piece of modern sculpture, the kind that has a big gaping hole where the heart and guts normally are.

Giselle began to look at me worriedly; Izzy kept frowning and saying "For Christ sake" every time we were in the office together; occasionally he would even whirl around toward me, turn on his hearing aid and say, "What did you say?"

I would shake my head, and he would say irritably, "For Christ sake," and go on typing away some scurrilous story about Yank policy, peck and hunt on his battered typewriter.

One day I came in late in the afternoon and I could tell from the look on Giselle's and Izzy's faces that something was up.

I was right. Jane had called. She was at her hotel and I was to call her.

They both pretended to go back to their work, but I noticed that Izzy's typewriter wasn't going as I walked over to the phone. Naturally I went through the same broken-down routine with Jane's concierge at the hotel. First of all he kept saying To whom did I wish to speak? and I would repeat Mademoiselle Bridon-Jack, and he would say there was no one in the hotel by that name, then I said it was I calling, and she had asked me to call, then he replied that Mademoiselle Bridon-Jack had come in only a few minutes before after having been hard at work, and looking very tired, and he was sure it would be much more prudent to permit her to sleep, and why didn't I call her tomorrow? So I told him that as a matter of fact she had asked me to call her back, and then he tried something about being certain she was about to bathe. Finally he rang her and then suddenly there was her voice, warm, vibrant, so very alive even after being worked over by the Parisian telephone system, and with that quality of immediate gladness as she heard my voice.

She said that she was fine and that they needed my help, and could I pick her up in the morning at her hotel, and would I like to come out with her to the villa?

I said I would be glad to pick her up and go out with her. She asked me how I was. I said I had missed her very much, and she said she had missed me very much too, and we made a date for nine o'clock the following morning and I hung up.

Izzy was able to continue with his work. Giselle looked somehow relieved and for a few moments I felt wonderful as if something had been solved, only that night I slept practically not at all.

I kept tossing and turning and my wound kept howling like a hungry dog as I tried to think it out.

Why did they need me? What could have happened which made my help important? Maybe they wanted my advice. Maybe . . .

Finally I fell into a very troubled sleep.

The churlish concierge at Jane's hotel the next morning said for me to go up, she was waiting for me. He made it sound like an insult, but I had other things on my mind.

Jane was about half dressed, that is she was in a *robe de chambre* and had obviously been arranging a lot of papers when I came in and boy she flew right over into my arms and I held her for a long time with her head buried in my jacket. When she looked up at me she was saying:

"Are you all right, darling?"

I said I was lousy, that it had been awful.

"I know, darling," she said quickly. "What can we do? I'll do anything."

I said the only thing I could think of was for her to go to a head doctor, and she said, Okay. She would go, if I thought it would help. Now—after what had happened—she thought that soon she would have time to go to England. She felt that even though her French was now pretty good, trying to tell your troubles in French to a French psychiatrist might not be so good, especially as she didn't know the words for some things. So she would go to England. Only . . . it was strange, wasn't it, that it was just with me that it happened?

I had a sudden flaring, burning thought about the American motion picture director and whether she had just gone off sort of experimentally with him, all in the spirit of good honest scientific inquiry to make sure it was just me, but I stamped that one out quickly and said, Hell I was ready to go to a head doctor too if it would help.

Only this idea somehow didn't do much for either of us. I don't know whether it was that both of us, deep inside, knew what the matter was, and that it was not really something a head man could help us on, or just the general nervousness of the moment.

Jane said that they now had concrete evidence that Morescu's theory and her mathematics were not just flights into the upper strata of modern science. While she was talking she was gathering papers which she explained she wanted to take out to the villa and burn just in case, later on in the day, they felt they might want to.

Since she didn't seem to want to explain much more than she had, I didn't press the point. She was working very quickly and nervously and said that she was anxious to get the stuff out of the hotel room as quickly as was humanly possible.

I piled her papers and notebooks in a couple of paper cartons while she disappeared into the bathroom and slipped into a dress.

I remember noticing the dress. It was blue, a soft sky blue, and I remember telling her how well it became her. She said that Bunny had sent it; that she had gotten a package and a long letter from Pops; the most important point of the letter, she said quickly, was that they were fine and missed her and were planning a visit.

I also remember that for some reason or other when she mentioned that Pops and Bunny were coming, I had a distinct feeling that we were approaching a climax. One way or another our lives would change.

16.

IT WAS a lovely, uncommonly warm morning in early autumn. The trees along the roadside looked as if they'd had a very good summer and were wearing the latest fall colors with elegance and chic. French peasants, stooping over the forlorn tail end of their harvest, would straighten up and holding his or her hand over his or her forehead and immobile for a second, would look out as we drove past. Here and there a child, sitting in its *tablier* on the banks of an irrigation ditch, a hand clasped lazily over a raised white knee, would laugh and wave to us. They all seemed to understand, to imply that they knew that the vehicle which had just passed contained two lovers, and the children's laughter and the peasants' pause seemed like some kind of benediction.

Jane was leaning back in that Yoga relaxed position of hers (I think mostly in an effort to stave off car sickness), head high and back, body slack, when she said:

"Didn't you once tell me you knew Morse code?"

"Yes," I said. "Wilfred and I studied it when we were cadets in high school. We each got five bucks for passing the code examination."

She was so preoccupied with other things that it wouldn't have mattered to her if I had learned Morse code from a Buddhist monk.

"It may be useful today," she said tensely.

"You getting messages in code?" I asked.

"We don't know," she said. "You see we had expected some sort of impulse—" Then she caught herself. "It'll be much simpler to explain when you get to the villa and see for yourself."

"Okay," I said.

"We're burning everything except one set of notes," Jane said. "We're arranging the apparatus so that it can be moved . . . or destroyed in a hurry." She rolled over a little and snuggled against me. "We've discovered something," she said in a voice so matter of fact that it sent shivers down my spine. "And I think we'll know for certain this afternoon."

"Okay," I said.

I didn't realize how fast the car was going, until she touched me with an imploring hand. No matter what, at more than sixty kilometers an hour she gets sick.

I slowed down. She took a deep breath.

After a while she said, "Do you know why they call it the Villa of the Five Who Were Shot?"

"Five guys got knocked off near the villa," I said. "René told me about it."

"Did he tell you who they were?" she asked.

"Resistants," I said.

"They were kids," Jane said. "The oldest was seventeen. They had helped Morescu escape."

It seemed to me the day changed a little on that one.

It seemed to be colder.

Morescu must have been watching for us from the ground floor of the villa because almost the split second we drove past the tall broken-down gate posts and swerved onto the grounds, the heavy front door creaked open and Morescu came toward us.

Even on this unusually gentle and autumnal day he wore a heavy double-breasted ash-flecked jacket and an ample wool muffler and of course the perennial cigarette was burning jauntily out of his battered cigarette holder.

He was very excited, which anyone who knew him could surmise from the facts: (a) that he had come out into the sun which he hated, to greet us; (b) he was half running.

The most you could ever hope from him even in an emergency was a sort of brisk walk. But now he was almost running.

The moment the car stopped, he had opened the door on Jane's side and they both looked at each other. I realized with surprise how deeply attached they had become to one another.

They kissed each other on the cheek and then he turned to me and nodded and we shook hands warmly. Then as usual we had nothing much to say and stood looking at each other awkwardly.

"I hear something's finally happened," I said, noting with surprise how callow my words sounded.

"Yes, well," Morescu said in tense but still elegant tones. "If you will come in out of the sun, perhaps we will discuss it at length."

He was in a high good mood, for he folded Jane's arm in the crook of his in a remembered gesture of paternal gallantry, and we walked down the path to the great staircase.

"It has always amazed me," Morescu was saying as we moved toward the house, "the manner in which you of the Anglo-Saxon world worship the sun, exposing yourself to it endlessly like primordial lizards. I find that when I am in the sun there is nothing else I can do but be aware of the sun. I cannot think, talk, work, or even play in it. It is blatant, crude, oppressive, and only a lower order of life with an extremely depressed metabolic rate should ever expose any part of itself to it for any length of time . . ." We were at the door, that heavy, poorly functioning apparatus of wood, old iron and cracked glass which he tried to open with a flourish, but succeeded only in causing to stutter slowly away from the frame until finally there was an opening large enough for us to enter. He then managed to shove the door back and you could feel Morescu returning to his element.

As for me, the almost funereal light from the high stained-glass windows, and the sudden unventilated musty coolness gave me, as always, the feeling that if I didn't consciously breathe, something would happen and I would gradually stop breathing altogether.

But Morescu stopped nervously before a highboy which stood in the hallway. On the marble top of the highboy stood an old battered coffeepot full of a jet-black liquid. It rested on a badly dented silver stand under which a spirit lamp was coldly burning, keeping the horrible liquid hot.

"I am happy that Jane has brought you," Morescu said as he set about pouring us three coffees, and although his hands were trembling, still, from the way he poured, by God if you didn't imagine the pot was some lovely silver urn and the thick little cups most delicate and graceful porcelain. "I am sure you will be able to help us."

I said I hoped I could be of some use.

"When Jane first came," Morescu went on, and somehow you had a feeling that he had a feeling that he was making a statement, or that his words were being recorded, "full of enthusiasm for the work which I had abandoned, I think she had much more of a sense than I of the potentialities implicit in that work. I felt at the time that it was only because she was very young that it was possible for her to envisage such extravagant promise." He sipped the coffee as though the acrid substance were aromatic and delicious. He reluctantly put the cup down, then looked out at us both with his burnt-out face. "I am inclined now to feel," he said, picking his words carefully, "that Jane's vision was somewhat conservative. There are indications that we may have found something which could open a whole new chapter in the fabulous story of modern bio- and astrophysics."

Jane was standing a little awe-struck before that last statement of Morescu's. It reminded me of the way she had stood the first time I had shown her Rodin's statue of Balzac in Montparnasse.

Knowing her as I did, I waited for the scientific disclaimer—the cautious qualification, the guarded reservation. You know the way scientists are. Everything is carefully hedged.

But neither one of them made any further qualification. A whole army of cold bugs began to crawl up my back, eating the skin off as they worked their way up.

"Although we do not fully understand the nature of the phenomena with which we have been confronted," Morescu went on, "we do understand that we are in the presence of phenomena never before, to our knowledge, submitted to scientific scrutiny."

His hands were trembling violently as he lifted his cup once more to his lips and realizing it was empty, put it away with infinite regret. "Only . . . we are not certain yet as to its . . . real significance."

He stared at the empty cup, lifted the coffeepot, swished it about to make sure it too was empty, which it was, then moved away and up the staircase.

I sighed as we followed him.

Once upon a time the belle of the château must have come sweeping down that staircase in crinoline and hoop-skirted glory to make her dramatic entrance. Now, with the somber-colored light coming from the glass which reached from top to bottom of the château, it looked like a big-scale fish ladder, up which human fish would fight their way.

And there I was marching on to witness one of the great scientific discoveries of our time.

Or so they said.

A moment later we got into the huge main upstairs room, which they had converted into a laboratory.

The mood changed completely.

The room itself was lighted by numerous curtainless windows, spotlessly clean. Their purpose was to let in the light, which they did admirably.

The room was full of many things, but it was a completely un-fussy room. Each object looked as if it knew exactly what it was sup-posed to do and did it. Everything else had been sent packing.

There was a group of compact-looking, regularly spaced, motor-like machines which were fed by a series of what I call brain wires.

Each machine stood over a stone basin of the kind which is some-times used for laundering.

Although I had been in this room hundreds of times before, the moment I entered I had a sudden feeling that I was in the presence of something momentous. It wasn't only because of what Morescu had said but because of a physical sensation I felt in the room. My attention was slowly pulled, and then held with a sudden grip, on a central machine, to which all the other brain wires, machines, motors, seemed to be directed, and which sat enthroned on a long marble-topped table.

Under this central machine was what at first looked like an enor-mous jewel: a crystal-clear container enclosing a colorless liquid that now seemed possessed of some magnificent luminosity, the quintes-sence of the pure light one gets from clear sweet water, and although there was at that point no sound, no movement, I seemed to feel something pouring into that liquid.

The three of us went directly to that container, neither Jane nor Morescu having to tell me that this was the big attraction. Jane's and Morescu's excitement intensified the closer we got to it. Morescu sent an additional thrill of anticipation down to my toes by doing some-thing I have never seen him do before. At a distance of about ten feet from the container, he solemnly snuffed out and threw away a whole cigarette which he had absently lighted a few seconds before, even flailing his arms about to clear the air of the tiny wisps of smoke which spiraled up from the crushed cigarette.

The two of them stood alongside of this liquid silently, looking at each other, then looking at me, both watching it in fascination.

"Some time ago," Morescu said very, very quickly, "we installed the crystal glass container which you see. In the container was her-metically sealed a quantity of sterile water. Both the water and the interior of the container had been made as sterile as possible, that is to say as devoid of contact with living organism of any kind as it was scientifically possible for Jane and myself to make it . . ."

He stopped, as he frequently did lately, and frowned a little, as though he had suddenly lost his chain of thought. After a moment when it became apparent that he would not quickly find it, Jane went on, taking over suddenly; what was always fascinating to me was the natural easy way she spoke—as much at ease as when, some weeks before, she had discussed Garibaldi with the local Italian delicatessen owner.

"We used the sterile water simply as a type of filter. I think I told you that Dr. Morescu, on the basis of astrophysical data in his possession, surmised the existence of a ray as yet unknown," Jane said. "I think you know too that I was able to supply mathematical verification for the existence of that ray. After he and I had satisfied ourselves that the mathematical aspects seemed sound, we developed the apparatus you now see . . . for channeling the ray . . ."

Morescu, having had the thought picked up by Jane, was relieved. Now again the incredible excitement was surging through the room.

"We had absolutely no tangible proof of the existence of this ray," Jane went on, "until some days ago, when we noticed a periodic agitation on the surface of the water. At first we attributed it to the vibrations of passing traffic, or the trains. We have even considered the possibility that it could be some kind of emanation from the Soviet-launched artificial moon which is still circling our planet. But it is obvious to us now that it cannot be. This is a manifestation from stellar space being channeled through our conductors . . ."

She pointed and we all three looked up to where she pointed. Morescu moved closer to Jane in excitement.

There, near the ceiling, poised over the machine which sat over the crystal container, was what seemed to be the bag of an old-fashioned vacuum cleaner.

As I watched it my hand suddenly got cold.

17.

THE BAG was shuddering, and when I say shuddering I'm not being literary. It was a movement almost human in its quality; if not human, at least alive. The shuddering was rhythmic as if it were doing some peculiar kind of breathing.

Someone was touching me on the shoulder. I jumped, but it was only Jane pointing, indicating that I should look down at the liquid.

Whatever was causing the vacuum-cleaner bag to breathe, or shudder or however you want to describe it, was passing through and into the viscous colorless liquid, making a series of very strange ripples, or dimples. I say strange because there would be a few large ripples, then there would be a small dimple. I don't mean to say they always came in that order, but that there were two kinds of ripples, one large and the other small.

When you throw pebbles into a liquid, the circles ripple out varying in dimension; but these two ripples never varied in size. The large one would always be exactly the same size as though its area had been carefully measured, and the same thing was true for the small one.

Over on one side behind the container, I caught another movement, something busily moving up and down. By the time I got a good look at it, Morescu was explaining it.

"That," he was saying, "is a simple graph operated by electro-cellular impulses. As you see, the head, which is something like a pen point, records the size and frequency of the disturbance and the time of its occurrence."

With that, Morescu reached over and picked up a roll of paper and unrolling it, revealed a paper band about three inches wide on which the graph had recorded the disturbances of the last few days.

On one side of the little squares which covered the band were written the hours of the day, and alongside, the day of the week and the month. Each time a large dimple had occurred, the graph had made a deep dipping line and for the smaller dimple a smaller dipping line.

They were both handling the band the way a very fancy jeweler would handle an enormously valuable gem.

I stared at the band for a long time. Something on my face must have told Jane about a strange thought that had come to me as I stared at the band.

"It means something to you?" Jane asked in a half whisper.

I said, "This ray of yours is obviously a middle-aged and prosperous English banker."

They both stared at me with a slightly irritable interest, as though I had said something childish at a moment of utmost gravity.

"Well," I said quickly, "it doesn't start work until ten-thirty in the morning . . ." I pointed to the readings on the graph. "Then it quits exactly at twelve at which time it indulges in a two-hour lunchtime. Now it deigns to work again from two to four, at which time it knocks off for tea or a brandy, then at six on the nose it locks up for the day." They were now following the graph as I was saying my piece. I added lamely, "At six it probably goes to its club for a whisky and soda."

There was a long silence.

Jane tried a little laugh, but it was not too friendly.

"Well," she said, "*that* was a rhythm we did not particularly remark . . ."

"Or to be more precise," Morescu went on, trying to keep this false ball in the air, "we did remark that the phenomenon occurred only during daylight hours, but," and then he bestowed a rather sour, almost paternal glance like a pat given by a father to a little boy who insists on making bright but inappropriate remarks, "I should never have thought to refer to a rhythm in the occurrence of astro-biophysical phenomena as English banking hours."

Jane was watching me intently now as I studied the graph.

"Is there anything else you see?" she asked. "In code, for example?"

"There's a lot of jumbled letters," I said.

She got very excited.

"But there *are* letters," she insisted.

"Let's put it this way," I said. "There's a big dimple and a little dimple. If you consider the little dimple a short and the big dimple a long—that is the dit and the daw of the Morse code—you get, as for example here"—I pointed to the graph—"the following sequence of letters—pbqrsktehg—"

I wrote the letters out for them. P-B-Q-R-S-K-T-E-H-G.

I dare you to try to make something out of that, but you've got to hand it to the scientific mind. They studied that jumble of letters for a good ten minutes, backwards, forwards, upwards and downwards. Finally they both shook their heads in defeat.

It didn't mean anything to them.

"But mostly," I said, "I find the following sequence—dit-dit-dit-daw. Three shorts and a long. It keeps repeating over and over again."

"Yes," Morescu said thoughtfully. "I have assumed it was in response to the message I'd sent." As I looked at him with interest, he went on. "We believe that not only have these impulses been coming to us, but there is some sort of an impulse which we apparently are able to transmit in return . . ."

He reached up to the base of the vacuum-cleaner bag where there was a shutter which moved horizontally between the bag and the liquid. The shutter had to be worked by hand. If you were strong enough, you could do it rather quickly but at a considerable strain on your arm.

Now Morescu grasped the shutter and worked it back and forth, each time shutting off anything that passed between the bag and the liquid—working it four times that way—three shorts and a long, then leaving the shutter open, waited.

A short time later the liquid dimpled with three small dimples and one large one. Morescu repeated the manipulation and the result was the same a second time.

Something was running around in my head as I watched—some mouse of an idea that I couldn't quite get my hands on.

Morescu stepped away from the machine. I made an inquiring gesture asking whether I could try the machine.

Morescu made a sweeping gesture of invitation. I went over and clicked three short clicks and one long.

As I watched the response I caught the little mouse of an idea.

"I know what it is," I said suddenly, "that was the V signal of the B.B.C. during the war. The opening of the Beethoven Fifth Symphony—" I hummed it for them. "Ta-ta-ta-tum . . ."

There was a stunned silence.

"The V signal of B.B.C." Morescu blinked in amazement. "That's very odd—isn't it? I mean—I wasn't consciously aware I was using it. You see I started sending it. It was only after I sent it that the response came with the identical signal."

I turned to them.

"You absolutely sure this is coming from space?" I asked.

"Very sure," Morescu said.

They were both hanging on each word and gesture of mine, a very pleasant novelty for a guy to whom they had never even tried to explain what they were doing.

"Because," I said, "what might be happening is that the impulses *you* are sending might be coming back to you."

Neither one replied for a moment.

"It's not possible," Morescu said quietly after a moment.

Jane looked from his face to mine.

"We would like you," she said, also speaking in very soft tones now (they both seemed to be afraid somebody would overhear them), "to send a message in Morse code. Can you do that?"

I said I could do that.

If I sent a message and if that message really went through space and if an answer came—*that*, to say the least, would be very interesting.

I turned back to the shutter. I could feel the other two holding their breath.

"Hello—hello—" I beat out, working the shutter as rapidly as I could.

Morescu said we would have to wait a long enough time for the impulse to travel there and back. I didn't ask him what he meant by "there" . . . .

Then after a long time the answer came back.

"*Hello—hello—*" exactly as I had sent it.

That could have meant anything. But . . .

Suddenly—

Something was coming. In Morse code. And in English.

I started to transcribe but it was coming too fast for me. All I got was:

"*Why—have—you—*"

Then I couldn't get any more.

Jane and Morescu had moved closer to me to see the message as I had written it. There was a little gasp from them as they saw those three words.

The liquid was dimpling all over the place but I was no longer even trying to get it. It had been years since I used the Morse code.

"Hello—hello—" I worked the shutter in a frenzy. "Regret cannot decipher you are sending much too fast for me stop."

We waited tense minutes again. Then the answer came.

I'm giving it to you exactly as it came. I still have the paper and the messages I wrote at that moment.

You can't tell. A museum may want them some day.

"*Sorry,*" the reply came. Now it was coming much slower so that I could decipher easily. "*Why have you been sending three shorts and one long over and over again are you in distress standing by stop.*"

The three of us studied that message a long time.

"You still think this is coming from outer space?" I asked in whispers.

Now I was whispering.

Nobody was listening.

That is, I don't think anybody was listening.

They were both very upset.

"It seems to me," I said, "that somebody is transmitting to you, on what I would say is an ordinary wireless transmitter—probably not too far from here—the same way the Russian satellite is transmitting."

Morescu's hands were trembling.

"The phenomena we are now observing," he said quickly with very, very quiet emphasis, "are astrophysical in nature. These emanations are coming from space much beyond our planet. I would hesitate to tell you even how far beyond . . ."

"Okay," I said. I was talking fast too. "Maybe it is coming from far away. But it's coming in Morse code and in English."

I showed them the band but neither one of them even seemed to want to look at the band. They were too busy looking at each other in complete perplexity.

"I think," I went on, "that your apparatus apparently generates something like the impulse which is sent out by an ordinary wireless set and is apparently sensitive to the reception of the same impulses."

I began to feel like the invisible man who could move among and see real people but who couldn't make himself heard.

"Maybe that's important," I said. "Maybe your discovery will replace the old-fashioned wireless transmitter . . ."

"Let's go on with this," Jane said in a very still voice, as though she hadn't even heard me.

"Sure," I said.

She took a deep breath. "Please send the following message: 'Who are you—'" she dictated slowly, "'and where are you transmitting from?'"

Well, I sent that message. It certainly was the simplest way of clearing up that little mystery.

Then we waited again. Hours it seemed to me.

The liquid began to dimple in slow, regular dimples; slow enough for me to decode easily.

"*This*—" came the response, "—*is LXI London.*"

Whatever small and die-hard doubt had been hanging on inside of me came out waving a white flag and its hands held high.

18.

MORESCU NOW looked sick.

They both stared at the words I had written on the paper as though they were things that crawled.

"It's just not possible," Jane said in dismay.

"I couldn't have been mistaken," I said. "I took down the dits and the daws as they came."

Morescu was thinking hard.

"Have you ever heard of an LXI London?" he asked.

"No," I said, "but that doesn't mean anything."

"Please ask them which London they are," he said quietly.

I craned my head and peered to get a better look at him.

He looked sane.

"This shutter is pretty heavy," I said. "I don't mind working it for you, but listen. That's London, England. If it were any other London, like London, Canada, or London, Illinois or Iowa—I'm sure the Yanks have a London somewhere—the other London would always say so. Only London, England, would say simply This is London."

"Please ask them anyway," Morescu insisted nervously.

"Which—London?" I beat out.

They answered.

"We are London England why do you ask and who are you stop."

The last part of the message had come faster.

I sighed.

It was all over for me anyway. Somewhere along the line Jane and Morescu had gotten their figures wrong. Maybe a flyspeck had looked like a decimal. Maybe—

Behind me Morescu was groping for a chair. I brought two chairs.

"Is it possible we could have been so wrong?" he asked.

She didn't answer. She was the only other person in the room qualified to answer.

"But still," he went on after a bit, "I find it strange indeed that they should ask why we asked who they were . . ."

"It's for the reason I mentioned before," I said. "Everybody assumes London is London, England. They're surprised anyone would ask."

Oh, I was so sure of myself, I tell you. I would have taken heavy bets and given heavy odds.

Luckily, there were no sporting people around just then.

The liquid had begun to dimple again.

"*Who—are—you—please—respond—standing by—*" the message came.

I read it out loud to Morescu and Jane. Jane sighed. She turned to Morescu inquiringly.

"Shall we tell them that we are an experimental station right outside of Paris?" she asked.

"Yes," Morescu said, the weariness making his words seem almost cut off for lack of breath. "Yes. Tell them that."

I didn't move. She turned to me and looked at me questioningly.

"Would you send that message?" she asked.

"I will if you insist," I said. "You're the boss. You must know what you're doing. For example, you must know that a person can get himself and herself into a big and unpleasant crock of trouble for unauthorized transmission by wireless. The French authorities . . ."

"Oh, hell," she said, cutting me off quickly. "We told you—we are not transmitting on anything like wireless."

"Okay," I said.

I sent the message.

The long wait—

The reply was a question.

"*Paris—France—Question—Stop.*"

"Now why would they ask that?" Jane demanded.

"Maybe LXI London is also expecting something from outer space," I said. "Maybe they were hoping we would say Paris Mars—or Paris Moon—or Paris Saturn."

Listen.

I was just trying to introduce a light note.

They were both taking it very badly. As well they might when you thought about it. Two years' work at the very least and how many years Morescu might have put in on his own before that. And to have let his wife and child go off rather than continue with something that was to wind up this way.

"It's less surprising they should ask," I put in, "after all messages coming from Paris, France, in English seem a little odd."

Morescu accepted that explanation.

"Please tell them that we are Paris, France," he said heavily.

I told them that we were Paris, France.

The answer from LXI was another question.

"Why have you been disregarding international agreements and transmitting during times set aside for distress signals?"

There was a good twenty seconds' study of *that* message and then Jane turned to me.

She was dictating straight to me now, the way you would to a professional telegrapher. No apologies. No "Would you mind sending this, please?"

Just:

" 'We,' " Jane dictated and I transmitted, " 'have disregarded international communications regulations because we have not been transmitting on conventional wireless transmitter.' "

After the usual long wait the answer came so rapidly I never would have got it if I hadn't recognized what they were saying.

"Please stand by," the answer came.

There was a long silence. For some reason or other, Jane and Morescu were still hanging on to something.

I was trying as hard to figure out what the hell they were hoping for. I gave up.

"Let's face it," I said finally. They both turned to me, pale, tense. "I think London has been p-ohed because you guys have been disregarding international regulations on distress signals. Communications people would take that seriously. Now they are trying to get a fix on us so they can report our exact location to the French authorities and have us picked up."

"We have been sending out signals for several days now," Morescu said gently. He was talking with the gentleness which people who have suffered a great loss talk. "If they had wished to trace us, they could have any time in the last few days."

"But it's harder, maybe, with this ray of yours," I said. "You say it's not at all like conventional wireless . . . ."

"You can't have it both ways," Jane said. "Either London, England, has been receiving our messages, for some reason Morescu and I will never understand, as conventionally transmitted wireless messages, in which case they could trace us. Or they have not received our messages as conventionally transmitted wireless messages."

"Okay," I said. "What do *you* think this is?"

"I don't know," Jane said, frowning down at the penciled message. "I just don't understand it."

Well. I'm the type of fellow who is always willing to face all possibilities. If not exactly face them, at least give them a passing glance.

"If you're sure these messages are coming from outer space," I said, "there are two possibilities. One"—they were both watching me with hopeful interest—"that the people who are sending the messages are lying—which somehow I don't believe. Or two—that there is another London, England, floating around in outer space somewhere."

I was gracious enough not to add "which somehow I don't believe" after the last part of the sentence.

Morescu straightened himself wearily.

"I am not prepared to make any conclusion whatsoever," he said heavily. "At the moment I cannot explain the fact that these messages have come nor the fact that they purport to have come from London, England."

It was apparently a painful admission for him to make. There was a slight and rankling little implication that perhaps he was rationalizing and refusing to admit defeat.

But just at that moment the liquid began to dimple again. Jane pulled on my sleeve urgently to attract my attention so that I would not miss any of the message.

Now this one was a humdinger.

"*Are — you — Paris — France — Eastern — Hemisphere — Planet — Earth — Stop,*" the message came.

Now why the hell would anybody want to ask that? Not unless anybody who was asking that had some reason to expect that the answer might have been something other than Eastern Hemisphere Planet Earth.

"'We—are—Paris—France—'" Jane dictated in slow and hushed tones, like soldiers marching at a royal funeral. "'Eastern—Hemisphere—Planet—Earth—who—are—you—stop.'"

Now you see it's conceivable that they had asked us if we were of the planet Earth because they were not. Don't ask me to tell you what we thought they might have been. At that point something happens to my mind.

It mercifully stops thinking.

Anyway the answer came:

"We — are — London — England — Eastern — Hemisphere — Planet —Earth."

There was no mistaking that.

London, England, Eastern Hemisphere, Planet Earth.

One hour's flying time by plane.

You could call by telephone and there would be only a one or two minutes' delay.

Then the liquid began to dimple again.

"LXI London—calling—Paris—France—please—stand—by—stop."

We stood by. Breathlessly now. The message came again:

"Now been definitely verified contact with you one of major developments of our time utmost importance you stand by urge you stand by please reply stop."

The excitement was jumping like forked lightning on a night of a summer electrical storm.

"Standing—by," I replied at once.

There was a moment when nothing happened.

"They don't sound like people who are trying to trace unauthorized transmissions," Jane said.

"No," I said, "they don't."

We stopped talking. The liquid was dimpling again.

"LXI — London — calling — Paris — France — can — you — give — us — solemn — assurance — your signal — will — be — kept — open — at — all times — until — further — communication — from us — stop."

I looked at the other two. They both nodded quickly.

"Paris—France—calling LXI London," I sent back. "You—have—our — solemn — assurance — signal — will — be — kept — open — at — all — times — until — further — word — from — you — stop."

Their reply was as follows:

"Thank you are relying on you human life may depend on your assurance what time are you what day of week what month stop."

I looked at my watch. I realized with a shock that we had been there for hours.

"We are fourteen hundred zero six o'clock," I replied. "Saturday month October stop."

"*You are four minutes slow please synchronize your time with ours at fourth dit your time will be fourteen hundred ten minutes zero seconds.*" There were four dits. We all set our watches. "*What are weather conditions over Paris stop.*"

"Perfect autumn day," I replied. "Clear slight wind south southeast visibility excellent what do you have in mind stop."

There was a slight pause before the reply came.

"*Following is message we are authorized to transmit to you—urge you suspend all further communication permitting clear channel keeping your signal open under all circumstances urge you further stand by at all times please reply if you agree stop.*"

We studied that message quickly.

"Let's ask them what this is all about," I said. "They obviously don't want to tell us. But maybe if we ask them . . ."

"Yes, certainly," Morescu agreed quickly.

I transmitted:

"Do not understand why you consider this contact major development please explain standing by stop."

The answer came quickly:

"*Regret cannot add to authorized message please confirm assurance open signal at all times stop.*"

I looked at Morescu and Jane.

"What shall I say?" I asked.

"Confirm it," Jane said.

I sent back:

"Paris France to LXI London confirming assurance signal will be kept open at all times standing by stop."

"*Thank you for confidence stand by good luck all around.*"

The liquid stopped dimpling.

I reached up and pulled the shutter out so that it was permanently open.

The tension was unbearable.

"What do you think will happen?" I asked.

They were either too jumpy to answer or didn't know.

"Somebody should be on the roof making observations," Morescu said uneasily.

Knowing how Morescu hated the sun, I said I would go, only unfortunately I was the only one who could send and read Morse code. Finally Morescu decided he would go alone, and that Jane would stay with me.

It was important that she be in the laboratory.

He hurried off.

Jane was pacing nervously, absently.

I said I still didn't believe the messages were coming from outer space.

She stopped pacing.

"I don't know what to believe," she said in distress. "If this were emanating from any distance at all, there could not possibly have been this coincidence of time. We were told to synchronize our watches. LXI either had reason to think the transmission would be effected with sufficient speed so that our times could be made to coincide—or—" She hesitated a long time. "Or they computed the time difference. They did not say, 'It is now such and such a time here.' They were telling us our time. Maybe they knew. Or . . . perhaps the Soviets have sent up a manned satellite . . . and these broadcasts emanate from them."

"If they have," I said, "why should the Soviets go through all that about LXI London?" I stared at her for a moment. "Could it be that they would do that as a disguise—a blind?"

"They don't work that way," Jane said. "At least I don't think they do. And besides—I timed the intervals in between messages. It's about twice the time it takes light to reach us from the sun . . ."

"What does that mean?" I asked.

Jane shrugged and walked over to a nearby desk where she busied herself with pages of calculations. For a long time there was no movement other than her hand as she wrote and no sound other than the slight soft rubbing sound of her ball-point pen on the paper.

19.

AT EXACTLY four thirty-five—sixteen hundred three five—Morescu came staggering into the room.

Both Jane and I went hurrying over to him.

He sat down in a chair weakly. Jane gave him a glass of water. After a moment he revived sufficiently to manage a weak smile.

"The sun . . ." he said. "I am not accustomed to it. As you know. I'm afraid it's made my head turn a bit." He took a deep breath and sat up. "I would have come in much sooner only I have been observing something which is rather interesting." He waited another moment before he could go on. "The birds have been behaving strangely . . .

"They seem to be attracted to a particular area about the roof," he went on. "Also they seem to be there in unusual numbers. Unfortunately the sun is so bright I could not accurately observe." He made a restraining gesture as Jane and I started toward the door. "René has a pair of binoculars. Borrow them from him. Do not go up on the roof. I do not think we should make ourselves—remarkable. Also René and Marie have prepared lunch for you," Morescu went on. "If you don't mind we will change places. I will stay here in the laboratory where I belong. If there is a message, it will be recorded anyway. Besides, I shall call you the moment anything happens."

Outside it was incredibly warm. I heard later that it was one of the warmest October days on record. The sun was still shining and the atmosphere was alive with a sense of things to come.

René came hurrying over to Jane and me with a pair of binoculars. I passed them to Jane.

She studied the roof top for a long time. Whatever it was she saw only increased her uneasiness and anxiety.

Finally she handed me the binoculars. They were the old French army kind from World War I. They magnified about eight times.

I could see clearly some distance above the roof. Birds of all kinds, sparrows, pigeons, and even swallows, were wheeling and swooping about the upper right-hand part of the roof—the part covering roughly the area in which the machine stood over the crystal container from which the glowing light was emanating. Some of the birds seemed to plunge directly into the area which led in a diagonal line from the laboratory window off into space; once getting into that area, they seemed to be drawn, and not by their own means, down the diagonal line until it appeared almost certain they would hit the roof; then they would again swoop free. It became apparent too, as I watched, that the birds were returning time and again to that area, repeating the procedure exactly each time, until after a while they would veer off and away.

At first I was not sure whether I was seeing that or imagining it; then suddenly a flock of pigeons which had been roosting on a nearby tree, with one of those inexplicably sudden movements that flocks of birds seem to have, wheeled en masse into the diagonal line, and this time there was no doubt. I could watch their plump bodies fall in a diagonal line until I was sure they would be dashed to death against the roof, only at the very last fraction of a second they seemed to be sucked under and away to soaring freedom.

"Do you think anyone else is noticing that?" Jane asked anxiously.

"I do not think so," René replied. "The sycamore trees hide the villa sufficiently from the roadside on this side, and on the other"— he pointed across the river—"luckily the Seine is sufficiently wide here so that one could not detect the movement of birds with the naked eye."

We all looked across the river.

It was true. At that distance you couldn't make out the movement of birds.

The only way the crazy behavior of the birds over our roof could have been noticed would have been if some watcher, equipped with binoculars, happened to have focused directly on that particular spot.

Jane and I took turns with the binoculars, keeping that area under surveillance for a very long time. It must have been much longer than I thought, because after I handed the glasses back to Jane I realized that Marie and René and little Jean-Pie had had time to set their lovely old Restoration farm table outdoors right behind us, at a point from which we could eat and continue to watch the birds.

Jane protested. She said she was much too excited to eat. As a matter of fact, I felt exactly as she did. My insides felt like an old rope on which a sailor had tied some fancy marine knots.

Marie paid no attention whatsoever to either of us. She simply remarked, dryly, that neither one of us had eaten since breakfast and here it was deep in the afternoon. Whatever it was we wanted to observe could not possibly be observed better by two people made lightheaded by hunger.

I remember thinking vaguely how white and beautifully worked the tablecloth seemed. There were crystal wineglasses and old silver. Marie had arranged the table so that it all looked like a dazzling jeweler's display with ruby-red wine and golden French bread and golden Normandy butter.

The table and the meal were like things and events which happen in a dream. You don't seem to concentrate on what you're looking at —or at least the emotional effect of seeing that which is before you is completely different from that which it normally is.

The birds kept wheeling in and out of the area about the roof. Maybe it was the *apéritif* which I downed and the wine I drank in unconscionable quantities, but it seemed to me that there gradually began to be a change in the birds; they appeared to be taken over by a constantly increasing excitement until they were throwing themselves about with reckless abandon and shrill exhilaration. Without realizing it, I kept on drinking more and more wine. Also I remember thinking I was eating like a horse without having the slightest idea of what it was I was eating.

Marie and René and Jean-Pie kept moving in and out of focus bringing food, moving in a kind of hushed silence, stopping every now and then to look in awe at the birds.

That René and Marie had gone to such lengths with the setting of the table and all only added to the tension. Their actions implied that something momentous was in the making. To top it all off, René brought out a very old bottle of cognac. For the first time during the course of the meal, Jane looked away from the roof as she watched René pour the hundred-year-old brandy, and her face was very solemn. The fact that she didn't try to stop René scared me even more because Jane would never have let René pour that brandy unless the moment *was* most extraordinary.

We drank the brandy slowly.

Then René and Marie and Jean-Pie took the table away and I felt myself suddenly overwhelmed with fatigue. My mind began to function as an independent apparatus having no relation to me. I began to think of Wilfred and how, one soft summer day, we'd been watching a log boom. We'd been asking ourselves useless questions, and as we idly watched the boom float down the Fraser River we'd asked ourselves how a waterlogged log felt.

Jane and I got up (Jean-Pie had brought some blankets and some pillows). I remember saying to myself with a pang that if Wilfred had been there with us I would have been able to tell him how a waterlogged log feels and I remember feeling slightly bitter and thinking that it wasn't fair that Wilfred was not there with us.

Marie came back and suggested that it would be a good idea for us to take turns resting after all that food and excitement. She went on to say that even if both of us shut our eyes at the same time, she would be constantly where she could keep an eye on things, and if Monsieur Morescu should want us, René and Jean-Pie intended to do a little work virtually below the window of Monsieur Morescu, who could call to them with the greatest of ease.

After Jane had kissed Marie for her thoughtfulness, and she and René and Jean-Pie had gone off, Jane said that if I liked I could just lean back a bit and rest, she'd do the watching.

Down below us, peaceful, somnolent, like an old tramp stretched out on a park bench, the Seine drowsed past us. The grounds sloped gently so that you could lie on your back, as I did, and with your arms folded back under your head, idly watch the barges float by, feel the lazy river wind play about your hair, and look over at the lovely face, so tense and serious, and see the same wind toy with her golden hair, the way a lover touches the hair of the woman he's just made love to.

Suddenly Jane began to beat down at the ground with her knotted fists.

"I can't stand it," she whispered fiercely. "I can't. It's been so long. Weeks. I've been waiting too long—I—"

I sat up in alarm.

"What if nothing at all happens?" she said.

"Something will happen," I said.

I was scared.

"All clear now," she said after a moment and with a wan smile. "Only I've got to get my mind off it. Help me."

We were silent, but it was a silence in which you were counting the particles of time one by one.

"Lean back," she said. "It's all right now." I leaned back. "It doesn't feel like October, does it?" she said with obvious effort.

"It feels more like my favorite month, May," I said.

I realized afterwards that she hadn't responded as quickly as she should have.

"Why is May your favorite month?" she asked.

"Because of Victoria Day," I said. "Victoria Day falls in May. We'd picnic—it seems to me it was always beautiful on Victoria Day. Wilfred and I used to go to Grouse Mountain and catch baby trout in a handkerchief that had four strings tied to it, one at each corner. We would put a little rock in the center to weight the handkerchief down and when a baby trout—they're called fingerlings—would come hovering over the white handkerchief we'd pull it up and catch the little fingerling alive."

For a moment she seemed to have lost herself. Her head was far back and her lips were parted and her eyes were looking straight up, as if she were seeing my Grouse Mountain.

"What would you do with the baby trout?" she asked quietly.

"We'd keep them in a tub of running water," I said.

I was on the brink of turning to her and taking her in my arms. I was thinking to myself that never had she felt closer to me.

"My family was killed in the month of May," she said suddenly in flat tones. "Some day I hope to be able to think of the month of May and think of your little fingerlings—and of you." She thought another moment. "Maybe after LXI tells us what this is all about."

It seemed to me the sweetest idea that had ever been dreamed of in anybody's heart. Her finger was idly winding a curl in a cowlick which I can never get to lie down as a good little cowlick should.

Neither one of us said anything for a long time. We just lay there, listening to the river and the creaking river sounds, and me dimly aware of her finger in my hair.

"Fishy fishy in ze brook," I said. I was beginning to get sleepy. "Pappa catch zem wiz a hook." The wind was drowsy and warm. "Mamma fry zem in ze pan. Baby eat zem wiz eez hand."

We used to recite that, with a fake French accent, when we were kids. I remember thinking vaguely about the birds which were wheeling about the roof of the broken-down villa, and a broken-down middle-

European scientist who was fooling around with vacuum-cleaner bags which shuddered, and strange messages in Morse code, and a Russian moon circling above us, and a golden-haired girl I loved lying at my side, not knowing, of course, that I was about to witness one of the most important incidents of modern times, and ever alert, as a good reporter should be, I fell fast asleep.

20.

I AWAKENED THE way an athlete takes a high jump—slowly at first, then *voom* I was sitting up, scared down to the core of my shinbones.

It had got almost dark.

Jane was no longer at my side. I was still lying on the grass, but the whole world was one growling, roaring sound—anger and fear translated into raw sound—and I realized there was an enormous airplane diving down at me, swooping so low that it seemed to shake the trees, the house, the very ground around me. I fell flat on the ground and just as I was sure the monster was going to crash on me the plane roared up again and off, leaving me feeling as though I were in the midst of a mass of shattered glass.

I guess I lay there flat on the ground for about twenty or thirty seconds. I had some fleeting wild idea that war had been declared, that the plane that had roared overhead had dropped a bomb, that everybody was dead, until gradually the deafening reverberations dwindled off, leaving only a menacing silence. Vaguely and strangely it seemed to me I heard a feminine voice from somewhere nearby call for help and also call my name.

I speculated on how much someone would have to offer me to get me up and on my feet. (In moments like that the goddamnedest things occur to you—you don't seem to have any real control of what you're going to think.) To save whatever remnants of self-respect I had left I tried to tell myself that I had hallucinated the whole thing —the roar, the plane, the cry for help, my name . . .

Then there were sounds of footsteps rushing toward me, and no amount of talk could hallucinate them away, and I finally got myself up and turned.

René and Jean-Pie were running like mad toward me, streaking across the grounds.

"I saw it! I saw it!" Jean-Pie was shrieking. "Enormous. So low." He was flapping his arms almost hysterically, imitating a plane diving. "Almost on the house . . ."

"*Mon dieu!*" René said breathlessly. "This plane . . . flying toward us with an incredible rapidity . . . then there was this thing in front of it. This thing which swooped down and seemed to fall somewhere nearby . . ."

It was all tumultuous, like trying to talk under a roaring waterfall.

"What thing?" I shouted at him.

"A type of bird," René answered, still breathless. "I wasn't able to get a good look. But I thought—like a huge bird . . ."

"No, no, no!" Jean-Pie shrieked, passionate with excitement. "*I* saw it! It was a type of flying bonbon, the kind that comes in gold paper —all wrapped . . ."

I turned to stare at Jean-Pie. Normally he was a sound kid. Even a bit on the serious side. What was especially disconcerting was that even René didn't think what Jean-Pie had said was outside the pale of sober consideration.

But another sound came from behind us. We all turned quickly. Morescu was stumbling toward us pushing himself as fast as he could.

"Jane—" Morescu panted. "On the roof." His breathing was painful, wheezing. "She was watching on the roof. The plane. It was caught the way the birds were. But I heard the plane coming . . . and I . . . I cut off the signal. Only Jane's not there. She's not on the roof."

I think in the next fraction of a second of silence René, Jean-Pie and I had the same horrible image of Jane and the diving plane, for before I could even get myself launched, René was running toward the villa's back staircase. I started off after him with a great lurch.

I guess it had been a long time since I'd done any running. Or maybe it was the lurch. Anyway I got about six feet when I felt a stunning pain hammer at my wound and I could feel my thigh muscles double up under me and I pitched head over heels. Even while I was falling, I made a frenzied gesture for the others to keep on going, and as I worked frantically rubbing at my thigh muscles, out of the corner of my eye I could see the three of them make it to the house and disappear.

I was working furiously on my thigh and calf, trying to massage the agony out, when I heard a strange rustling nearby.

It was the sound of a body moving in the brush. I made it to my feet. The sounds from the brush became more violent, as though something alive were thrashing about.

Dragging my leg behind me, hopping on the other leg, I staggered over to the brush.

For a moment I didn't see anything.

Then I saw something which was caught in the branches of a nearby tree, about ten feet off the ground.

Something which had a golden glistening glow about it.

It was a nude woman, and she was trying desperately to untangle herself. She twisted and saw me and I saw her.

I'm going to try to tell it to you as accurately as I can. It's a little hard for me now not to cover it with wonder and amazement, but here's how it really happened.

I stumbled closer and suddenly realized it was Jane.

I'm not sure, but I think I rushed crazily toward her. As I came nearer I realized she was calling my name. Then she must have gotten herself free because she fell, crashing down on me as I lunged for her. That succeeded in breaking her fall and we rolled helter-skelter into a wild rose bush, until panting, scratched, bruised (at least *I* was bruised), we came to rest, she on top of me and both of us on top of my wound.

Well, when things got back more or less in focus, my back and arms and face were burning raw from the scratches and I was afraid to move because of the thorns. It was the craziest combination of sensations. There I was, holding her in my arms, and she had nothing on at all (or so it seemed to me). But at the same time, I was wishing she would get off me.

I felt her diaphragm working in that curious alarming way and I knew just from the movement that, in the midst of everything, she was going to be sick.

Which was okay with me as long as she got off me.

Despite her nausea she got up carefully so as not to make any movement that would hurt me, then held her hand out and helped me up and we stood there the two of us looking at each other.

We were both breathing hard and in the midst of all that turmoil I was saying to myself:

Here you are and there she is, the woman you love, and for the first time you're seeing her completely naked. Her breasts are smaller than you thought but very beautiful just the same. Her waist is incredibly tiny; on the other hand her hips and thighs are much more rounded than you would have imagined.

At the same time (if that's possible) I was realizing that she was not naked at all, if you wanted to get technical about it; her whole body was covered with that wonderful transparent stuff which I had seen in the crystal container in the laboratory. Of course in terms of hiding anything it was about as efficacious as a layer of cellophane might have been. Then she began pulling the stuff away from her face, not frantically, as one might have expected, but the way a woman would wipe off a beauty cream, and I realized numbly that her mouth and nose had been covered too, which last jumbled the impression in my head even more. How had she breathed with that stuff around her? What had happened? What was she doing in that tree naked, and what was that stuff she had smeared all over? And in about two seconds, if she continued to stand that way before me, I would sweep her off the ground and into my arms.

The stuff made a slight sucking sound as she pried it loose, and once having got it loose, she took a deep exploratory breath, trying it out for size. Just as I *was* about to sweep her into my arms, she gave me the kind of downcast look people who are about to be sick sometimes make and turned, staggering away toward the river.

I started after her almost instinctively, but behind her back, without turning, she made an imperious waving gesture telling me to stay where I was.

So I stood there. It had all happened so fast I was still breathing hard and my psychological churn was still churning at top speed.

From back of me came the sound of frantic footsteps. I stumbled out of the brush to see Jean-Pie come running toward me in a way that kids seem to run, as if they are being blown up by explosions and you expect arms and legs to go flying off in different directions. By the time he got to me he couldn't speak for lack of breath, and could only point toward the roof and make violent gestures indicating that they had not found Jane on the roof.

Finally I was able to say, in between deep breaths, "She's all right. Go back. Tell them she's all right."

He blabbered something again. I guess it was hard for the sound of the human voice to penetrate past the sound of his own deep breathing. When he did understand he started off again as explosively as he had come, then as suddenly, stopped and turned. It was remarkable, if you were in a position to appreciate it, how quickly he was able to make the complete transition from utter action to utter immobility.

"You're covered with blood," he panted. "The whole back of your shirt."

"Never mind that," I gasped. "You'd better get back and tell them—"

But by now he must have suspected that there was something interesting afoot.

"Shall I get you some iodine?" he asked with a great show of concern.

There were unmistakable sounds of Jane moving in the bushes near the river.

"You must always take care of scratches," Jean-Pie went on sententiously.

"Get back there now, will you?" I said. "I'll take care of the scratches myself. And tell them everything's all right."

My tone must have made him realize I really didn't want him to hang around so he nodded and reluctantly ambled away, stopping every now and then to look back, but seeing I was watching him, finally took off.

The moment he was out of sight I hurried back to the brush in the direction she had taken.

It had got a little darker, but not *that* darker. When I found her, she was leaning and half sitting in a pose of utter relaxation on some wild berry vines the thorns of which made rose thorns look like dull fellows. I could see the thorns clearly and I could see her clearly and I realized that between the time she had gone off and Jean-Pie had come, there had been some small doubt in my mind as to whether I had actually seen her; perhaps it had all been because I was drunk. But there was no doubt in my mind now. She was real. Her bare body was real, and so were the thorns which she was leaning on.

I thought, She's probably delirious. In delirium there's a kind of anesthesia.

But she didn't look at all like a girl who was in a state of anesthesia. As a matter of fact she looked a little crestfallen and apologetic, as if I had caught her doing something she oughtn't to have been doing. Which all made it even wilder and more nightmarish because only people who are fully dressed can really afford, psychologically, to manage such nuanced expressions as crestfallen and apologetic. To pull that off, standing naked as the day you were born, is quite a feat.

I remember her mumbling something, which only added to my confusion, about anti-flight-sickness pills not being very efficacious against failures.

That's what she said. I couldn't begin to figure out what anti-flight-sickness pills she was talking about, nor what failures. I didn't even try.

"Don't move," I said dazedly. "I'll lift you straight up." And I started to move gingerly toward her.

"What *is* the matter with you?" she asked.

I remember thinking to myself how much more English her accent had become. Probably covering her nudity a tiny bit that way. Nothing like an English accent for that.

Of course I thought she seemed strange. But then everything seemed strange.

The light was now a pearly gray, and it was getting hard to detect slight changes in expression.

"You're sitting on wild blackberry thorns," I said.

She seemed to frown as she stared at me.

"But I've got this stuff on," she said, almost sharply, as though that were an explanation. Then as though to give the point more emphasis she straightened and walked barefooted across the thorns and to within a few inches of me.

By simply moving the position of my body I could touch her, we were that close to each other.

"What's going on?" I said, my head whirling. "What happened here?"

"Nothing," she said with a sigh. "Not a damn thing."

I stared at her for a long time. If she continued to stand there that way, I began to realize that a gigantic centrifugal force which was developing inside of me would whip me over to her in a matter of seconds.

"You'd better get out of that stuff," I said.

"Yes," she said slowly, "perhaps I'd better."

She hesitated a second then began pulling the stuff off, keeping her eyes fixed on me all the time, inserting her fingers between the substance and her skin, beginning right alongside of her mouth.

I turned and started to walk off. After all, this was fairly intimate activity and I needed a second or two to keep from falling off the tightrope I suddenly found myself on.

"I'm afraid you'll have to help me," she said softly, stopping me. "I shan't be able to get it off by myself, you know."

Her voice sounded different. It was not only the accent now.

I came to her and put my fingers on her shoulders on the part she had not yet cleared and although I knew it was not her skin I was touching, I had a strange, bewildering and wonderful tactile thrill from the touch of the stuff which covered her.

For a few seconds I worked it off her. Somewhere in the deep distant subconscious, hundreds of questions were clamoring to be asked, but I think you'll understand why, under the circumstances, I did not ask them.

Not only did that substance feel alive, but it looked and felt like the softest thing in the world. Yet when I tried to pick it up by scraping at it with my fingernails, I made no more impression on it than I would have on the hardest steel alloy.

"You'll have to slide your fingers between it and my skin," Jane whispered. "You know that's the only way—"

She seemed excited and yet there was a tiny suggestion of irritation in her excitement, as I did as she said. I slid my fingers between her skin and the stuff and I was able to pull some of it away from her. I was about to say, I realize, I was able to "persuade" the stuff away from her, for I remember a definite feeling that the stuff was reluctant to leave her body, for which, under ordinary circumstances, I might not have blamed it. Only now it kept twisting and slipping away from my fingers so that I was constantly pulling at it and coming in contact with Jane's bare skin and by the time I had managed to get the top half off down to her waistline, I was almost frantic with wanting her.

I stopped abruptly.

"Do hurry!" Jane said softly. "I'm freezing!"

I hurried. I stopped only one other time and that was when I had gotten the stuff off to a part of her which I felt our complicated relationship did not give me the right to continue. But this time all she had to do was shiver a bit with cold. I needed no other prodding. I went on savagely, pulling the stuff clean away from her body, almost to her knees.

I could see that now she herself could, even with a little difficulty, get rid of the rest, which she did, bending gracefully and pulling it off the way you would stockings, so there she was in that half gloom completely nude before me, and at our feet the lovely substance which had covered her made a radiant little pool.

For the first time in a long time I looked directly at her and this time, even in the half darkness, there was nothing nuanced about the way she looked at me.

I suddenly forgot all about roaring sounds and messages and what she was doing naked in a tree and I pulled her toward me savagely, crushing her close to me. I don't know whether there was even a faintest movement of hesitation but I sought her lips frantically, suddenly bracing myself for the terrifying moment when she would go rigid.

Only it didn't happen.

Far from it. Instead her lips and her body and her whole being came out to me, flew toward me, to my lips and to my body and to my whole being, with a great free wonderful wanting and needing, exactly as I and every other man who has ever breathed had dreamed endless times before. I kissed her over and over again dozens of times until we were both breathless and half delirious, each time savoring the incredible sense of release from the awful specter which had haunted our love before.

I remember wondering vaguely why the miracle was taking place, until I stopped wondering about anything and was conscious only of the exquisite body of the woman I loved.

21.

IT WAS very dark. She was lying at my side and I kept touching her to reassure myself that it was all real and because I enjoyed touching her. She was curled up against me and I could feel her breath on my face and we had told each other for about the ten thousandth time how much we loved each other; rather, the way it went was she would whisper, "You do love me, don't you?" I would whisper back that I loved her very much. Then we would lie there silent, with our happiness a palpable thing you could feel, for about two or three seconds, when she would again ask me did I love her? and I would reply I did.

We were curled up in the blankets Marie had brought.

The sky was full of stars and you could hear the river sounds come with that soft muted quality that sounds in the night seem to have.

I asked her if she felt like talking. She asked me again if I loved her and when I repeated that I did, she sighed and said Yes, she was ready to talk.

I said, "Tell me how you got in that tree."

"I don't know," she said. "It was all a blur. Lights whirling and a feeling of falling and a huge strange object and there I was . . ."

"Lights whirling?" I asked in bewilderment.

"When I first went out," she said.

"Wait a minute," I said grimly. "Maybe you'd better begin at the beginning. You covered yourself with the stuff. Why?"

"You know why," she said gently.

"I don't," I said.

She hesitated.

"I was attempting an interspatial journey," she said at last.

I stopped looking at the stars and turned over to look at her, but all I could make out was a blur of white.

"An interspatial journey?" I asked stupidly.

It was stupid because I knew goddam well that's what she had said.

"I don't understand," I said, when she didn't answer. "How were you to take that interspatial journey?"

"You know how I was going to take that journey," she said almost drowsily. I realized that she thought I was kidding.

"But I haven't the slightest idea how you were planning to make an interspatial journey," I said.

There was a subtle change in the whole mood then. For one thing I was beginning to get a little worried. It was all sounding off-key again, the way it had when I had first found her in the brush.

"Obviously I was going to travel on the beam," she said. "Surely you weren't that unaware?"

"Well I *was* that unaware," I said, and added, "Jesus."

"Jesus what?" she asked sharply.

"You mean you got from the roof to the trees?" I asked.

"That would seem to be about what happened," she replied with a sigh.

I thought *that* over for a long second.

"You might have been killed," I said. I pulled her toward me and held her tightly to me.

"The theoretical odds were considerably in our favor," she whispered, her breath tickling my lips. "At least we thought so . . ."

I kissed her.

"You thought so, you thought so, you thought so," I whispered to her with a kind of savage mockery. "Don't you know you must never risk your life ever again?"

"Yes darling," she said softly. "I know."

"Why didn't Morescu go instead of you?" I demanded.

"But I'm younger and healthier," she said.

I kissed her again.

When we broke out of the kiss we were both gasping.

I waited a second.

"Why did anyone have to go?" I was whispering too now.

"It was the only way to substantiate our assumptions," she said.

"Who cares about your assumptions?" I said almost inaudibly. "What if you had been able to reach the moon . . ."

She pushed herself away from me. Just a bit.

"Why should we have wanted to go to the moon?" she asked, puzzled.

"Wherever in the hell you were trying to go," I said.

"We were trying to reach the earth," she said.

Be careful with that feather, son. Don't keep waving it around that way. You might just sweep me away. Now I pushed her a tiny distance away from me and tried to look at her. But of course by then it was pitch-black.

"The earth," she repeated. "The other one. Morescu and I have developed a hypothesis that there is another earth, the exact twin of ours."

I don't know what I had been thinking, but that last reply of hers reassured me.

"So that's what this was all about?" I asked with a kind of gentle condescension.

"Yes," she said with a sigh. "That's what this was all about. And there's considerable astrophysical evidence to support our hypothesis. Not to mention those signals."

"You mean you thought those signals were coming from a twin earth?" I asked.

"Yes," she said.

"But they were coming from just a few miles away," I said tenderly. I held her very close to me again. I felt suddenly very superior and protective.

"But they weren't coming from just a few miles away," she whispered insistently. Of course I didn't really care any more. I didn't care about anything except the feel of her close to me.

"Where do you think those signals were coming from?" I asked indulgently.

"They could have been coming from the twin earth," she whispered, with a slight touch of defiance.

"It would have to be one hell of an identical twin," I said wryly. "Where they spoke English, had the Morse code . . ."

"Of course," she replied calmly. "Why not?"

"And another London," I went on.

"And another Paris," she continued.

I could tell from her body that none of this fazed her in the least bit. Apparently she and Morescu had thought about all these possibilities, and had learned to live with them.

"I might as well try to explain to you how we came to this theory," Jane said softly, "so you won't think us utter idiots—or are you interested?"

I kissed her again—passionately.

"Fascinated," I said. I blew gently on her ear, tickling her. She shuddered a little. It gave her goose flesh. She waited for me to stop.

"Well then," she began in a quite formal lecturer's tone—no mean feat when you get a picture of the circumstances. "In working out the conditions which might have prevailed when the earth was formed we encountered an interesting phenomenon . . ."

"You told me that part," I said. I began to blow across her lips. She found the sensation almost unendurable. She wriggled her head away from me.

"Do you want to hear this?" she demanded.

"Yes," I said. "Only tell it quickly."

"I shall tell it my way," she whispered primly. Then she went on. "We had, to the best of our knowledge, duplicated on a miniature scale the physical conditions under which our planet must have developed. Each time we achieved those conditions we noted that not one mass, but two masses formed. At first we thought that there was something wrong with our calculations, but after a while we decided to observe the further development of the two identical masses." She stopped. For emphasis. "They developed exactly alike. In precisely the way identical twins develop. From that we were led to the hypothesis of an identical planet, the twin of ours, somewhere within a calculable area within our universe's space—with a development in all probability identical with ours."

I didn't particularly want to rub it in but it seems to me we always take a peculiar kind of pleasure (if we are completely honest with ourselves) in the failure of others, even when they're very close to us. Maybe it's one way of enduring the defeat. And besides—it really didn't matter now.

I let my hand wander over her face.

"And of course," I said softly, carrying it to what I thought was its logical absurdity, "if the other planet developed exactly like ours, there must be another Canada, another England . . ."

"Yes," she replied firmly, "that would follow."

"And another you and another me," I went on. I was beginning to enjoy it now. "And if they've really developed the way we have, there would've been another Morescu working on exactly the same experiment with you."

"Naturally," she said. She stopped and thought. "Only there could be some deviations. In the last few years we've learned a bit about the laws governing social development; in that sense then we've learned how to exercise a certain control over our environment. We could expect, accordingly, some variations . . ."

I laughed quietly. It all seemed so wonderful to me—even these flights of fancy.

"A good thing too," I said. "Otherwise, if you'd been right and had actually made it—I mean the flight—you might have landed exactly in the other Morescu's back yard and there might have been another me waiting for you, asleep by the river." I stopped. "I'm sorry you didn't make it," I spoke so softly that she had to strain to hear me, even though she was in my arms, "because then there would have been another you and another me in each other's arms like this and I think that would have been wonderful."

Then she said, "Don't you think we ought to get into the house?"

"Yes," I said.

"And would you," she asked, "as is belatedly fit and proper, carry me over the threshold?"

I said I would. Gently I broke out of her embrace, got to my feet and groped around in the darkness for my clothes, when suddenly I stepped on something soft.

I felt a thrill of horror, for I was sure I had stepped hard on her hand. In my anxiety to move away, I stumbled backwards and went over with a crash, falling to one side with all my weight.

The full force of the fall carried me against what, I discovered later, was a thick branch which caught me in the dead center of my wound.

In spite of myself I made a piercing sound of pain—a sound that must have been made even worse by my trying, with a physical effort, to stifle it.

Almost immediately she was over at my side. She remained that way close to me, silent, and then after a moment I realized she was stroking my forehead gently and the blackness began to recede slightly. I held her hands and kissed her finger tips . . . and stood up straight.

"I'm sorry," I said, surprised at how torn my voice sounded.

"*I'm* sorry, darling," she said. "Whatever happened to you?"

I realized she was standing nude in the cold and she was shivering. I fumbled for and found the blanket and covered her with it.

"I started to fall," I said, "and landed on a branch—which got me in my wound."

There was a slight silence and then she asked quietly:

"What wound?"

When I didn't understand, she repeated with an urgent insistency.
"What wound?"

"The wound I got when we were hit," I said quietly.

"Hit?" she asked. There was a kind of hysteria about her now.

"The . . . the same time . . . Wilfred got killed," I said.

She gasped. "Wilfred killed?"

"Now listen," I said uneasily. "You knew Wilfred got killed— What
is it?"

"When?" she repeated almost frantically. "Tell me! When?"

"In the war," I said gently. "I wrote you and told you about it."

"War?" she whispered. "What war?"

"The last war," I said, still very gently.

She's hysterical, I thought, my heart sinking. It happened, not the
way we'd thought it would. But delayed. Terrible.

There was another sharp sound from her. Then there was a long
silence and I could feel her standing rigid there in the darkness.

I found my lighter and lighted it, holding it high so I could see
her face.

She was very white. Her face was glistening with two tears.

"What is it?" I asked. The light fluttered about like a dying moth
on her face, her body seemed to be turned toward me strangely.

"Sorry," she said and her voice sounded contrived and unreal. "It's
nothing . . ."

I started toward her. She recoiled a little. No mistaking it now.
"There *is* something," I said.

"No, no," she said shivering. "The excitement. I . . ."

She made a vague gesture. I swept her off the cold ground, blanket
and all, and held her to me. For a second I had an impression of the
old Jane—of something remote, inaccessible. But that flared briefly
then died in the darkness and I felt her curl up close to me and felt
her warm breath and then her lips gently on my cheeks.

"I'm sorry for your wound," she whispered. "I'm sorry about
Wilfred."

I waited for her to explain more, but she didn't. I knew then that
the day, and the days and days of tension before it, had been too
much for her. But she'd be all right, I told myself over and over. She'd
get over it. We'd broken down the wall which had kept us apart and
we'd come together at last.

There might be a momentary relapse now and again but the miracle had happened. We'd won. We were together.

Holding her in my arms that way I carried her across the dark grounds, up the steps, and, as she had asked, "belatedly over the threshold," and up the grand staircase where the starlight caused the stained-glass windows to cast eerie shadows.

I had the feeling that her eyes were wide open and that she was watching me strangely, but I was afraid that if I looked down at her I'd fall.

I carried her into my room and sat her down on the bed. I turned the light on and realized with surprise, as I looked at the clock on the commode, that it was only eight.

When I turned to her she had not moved. She sat there, just as I had put her, staring at me.

I sat down on the bed alongside of her when suddenly she reached over and took my hand and I realized that there was much more in the way she was looking at me—something very complicated. Wistful, disturbed and very excited. I was about to ask her why she was looking that way when there was a knock on the door.

She pulled the blanket over her clear up to her chin. I hesitated.

But the knock was repeated, urgent and frightened. I went to the door.

Morescu was standing in the hallway. I opened the door and stepped out, shutting the door behind me. Without consciously meaning to, Morescu half leaned as though to see around the door. He seemed to wonder why I had so carefully shut it behind me.

In the dim hallway light I could see that Morescu was frightened. It seemed to me he had aged considerably since this afternoon; his face was haggard and his hands were trembling violently.

When he spoke it was in intense whispers.

"The police are here," he said.

Maybe it was because I knew his story. Or maybe it was because of the way he said it. I felt myself go cold.

"I'll be right down," I said shakily.

He reached over and touched my arm for support. It was the first time since I had known him that he had made any gesture whatsoever toward me. I suddenly realized he was in a far worse way than I thought. His touching my arm was the way someone close to you leans on you for support in a moment of great stress.

I went back into the room.

"Why did the police come?" she asked.

"They must have noticed something," I said. "Jane—what really happened?"

"Happened—when?" she asked strangely.

"René and Jean-Pie claimed they saw something flying through the air at treetop level," I said. "And how *did* you get in that tree?"

"I told you I don't know," she said quietly. "I don't remember that part."

"Do you remember about a plane?" I asked.

"No," she said very slowly. "I don't remember about a plane."

Her face was curiously expressionless.

"What was all that about flying on a beam?" I asked.

She thought for a long time.

"I think you'd better see the police," she said.

"It might help if I knew what really happened, before I spoke to the cops," I said.

"Do you have to tell them anything?" she asked, in that strange calm way.

"I'll tell them only what we want them to know," I said.

"Then," she said, "don't say anything to anyone—not yet. I'd like to have a chance to think. It's been a bit too much. I'm not sure I understand it all myself. I need some time to think."

"All right," I said finally. It seemed fair enough.

I got up and washed my face hurriedly, then put on a tie and a jacket and combed my hair. At least one of us should look like a solid respectable citizen.

When I turned to her for a moment she didn't even see me. She was lost somewhere.

I bent down and kissed her lightly. I was halfway straightened when she threw her arms about my neck and pulled me down to her and clung to me with a crazy intensity.

"Oh, darling, darling, darling," she kept whispering the word over and over. It was strange too because when I wanted to kiss her she avoided my lips. She just wanted someone to cling to.

I sat down on the bed.

Morescu could wait a few seconds more, and so could the cops.

Because I had waited a long time for this to happen. All my life, when you really thought about it. And I was scared. For I knew something was wrong. Very wrong.

I held her close. She was sobbing but it was out of joy, wonderment and fright—the way you would be if the most incredibly beautiful thing in the whole world had happened to you.

It *had* happened to her, but it wasn't what I thought.

"I'll get rid of the cops as quickly as I can," I whispered, "and then I'll come right back. Wait for me here."

"Yes," she said quietly.

I leaned down again to kiss her and again she avoided my lips before she realized what she was doing. Then as she became aware, she pulled me toward her, with a conscious effort, and kissed me hard and long.

22.

IN THE GRAND cobweb-decorated salon (Morescu would never let Marie and René do any real cleaning here, since, he kept insisting, no one was ever to do any real living here) which even more than the hallway looks like a big fancy fish bowl because of the strange glass all around it, Morescu and two French policemen were waiting. All three were holding a cup of Morescu's terrible coffee; all three seemed to be enjoying it. If I had needed any further assurance that the two men were French, this would have been it.

One of the two men, a man of middle age with a rather cold face which suddenly surprised you with an unexpectedly pleasant smile, was wearing a sheepskin coat with a fleece-lined collar. The other, a younger heavy-set, red-faced man, had an easy air of authority about him, wore a dark shirt, a dark tie and a well-cut brown corduroy jacket.

The sheepskin opened the proceedings.

"I am very sorry to disturb your Saturday evening," he said, "but there have been some incidents of a rather unusual nature in this area.

We are anxious to know if you could be of any assistance in helping us find an explanation for these incidents."

His manner, his tones, made me realize that anxious as I was to get rid of him and his colleague, this would have to be played carefully.

Morescu seemed to have regained his composure somewhat. But that was only a surface estimation. His hand trembled so as he brought the coffee cup to his lips that he actually spilled a little coffee and had to step away to avoid being stained by it. I realized the two cops had noticed it without seeming to notice it the way some cops do.

I said that, being a law-abiding citizen, I would as always cooperate to the fullest in any matter in which the police were interested. What sort of interesting incidents, I asked, had taken place?

Neither of them, it was obvious, even vaguely considered the possibility of answering that question.

Instead, the corduroy kid, with that wonderful quality that experienced cops seem to have for behaving exactly as though statements they don't want to hear weren't even said, asked me very, very politely where I had been at approximately nineteen hundred hours that day?

Despite all my other preoccupations, and despite the two-thirds of me having stayed behind with Jane upstairs, nonetheless I was beginning to notice this man in the well-cut corduroy jacket and I was beginning to have a sense of his authority, and with it a chilling sense of the importance of what had happened.

I was trying desperately to think where my answering that question would lead. At nineteen hundred hours, as accurately as I could determine, Jane and I had been in the garden together. Aside from wanting to protect Jane as much as possible, I realized that she and I would have to keep our stories straight. We hadn't had time to agree to a cover story.

While this was all whirling around, there was a sound at the door and we all turned.

Jane came in.

I remember wondering how she could have got dressed so quickly and realizing, in a hazy way, that the moment the cops' eyes lighted on her, their whole manner changed, and I even remember vaguely remarking to myself, "How very French it is of the cops to react this way. From now on they will be in this investigation with everything they have."

But all that was really only of subsidiary interest, I was only mechanically aware of it. Because I suddenly felt myself go sick.

She hadn't more than glanced at me. Nothing of the great thrilling experience we had gone through together communicated itself from her to me. The woman standing there was poised, weary, serious and under great strain.

This was not a woman who had just given herself to me, nor to anyone. This was not a woman on whom there lingered the faintest afterglow of ecstasy experienced a short time before.

I didn't give a good goddam about the rest. About the plane, or the beam, or the mystery. All I wanted to do was to rush to her and shake her and remind her and reawaken her.

But of course I was able to control myself. I listened the way you listen to echoes as Morescu presented her to the cops. They both apologized again, the sheepskin jacket smiling, and the corduroy kid making wonderful use of his quiet elegant authority.

But Jane was reassuring them quietly and begging them to go on.

The corduroy kid repeated his question to me. Now that Jane was here I could answer it without the fear of having her contradict me later.

I said slowly and distinctly, "At nineteen hundred hours I was outside, asleep in the garden."

Watching Jane as I said it.

The reference to the garden had absolutely no effect on her. She continued to look tense and anxious and I thought that she was either the world's greatest actress—which was a terrible thought. Or— Well, there was no alternative possibility that I could persuade myself to think about.

The sheepskin jacket was asking if we had seen, or been aware of, anything unusual at that hour?

And while the three of us, Morescu, Jane and I, were ostensibly trying to remember, a very strange thing happened.

First of all, the outside lights jumped on illuminating the grounds. It could only have been René who had turned the lights on and under the circumstances it was almost impossible to understand why. He knew as surely as we did that the darkness was our ally. He knew too that we were anxious to avoid attention.

All of us in that salon of course immediately turned our attention outdoors and through the beer-bottle-brown glass of the huge dormer window we saw René and Marie and Jean-Pie come running out of the shadows and stop suddenly and peer off, all three looking in the same direction.

I looked in that direction and had time to catch a fleeting glimpse of a figure which was disappearing into the darkness of the road ahead.

The figure was very vague and far but nonetheless I had the very disturbing sensation that it was familiar. Then seconds after I had seen it, I had a strange message communicated to me, as though a whole series of inner messages had been finally synthesized.

The figure that had been swallowed up in the darkness ahead had been Jane.

Immediately I turned to look to my right. Jane was there, standing alongside of me. She hadn't moved.

Morescu was pale and looking at Jane incredulously.

Both the cops had by now hurried to the window and were peering out.

There was a sound at the door and René and Marie came bursting in. Their eyes immediately sought and rested on Jane.

The two cops were watching René and Marie now.

"Is there anything wrong?" the corduroy kid asked quietly of René.

"No," René said after a moment, and with great calm. "There is nothing wrong."

"Someone just left," the sheepskin kid said. "Who was that?"

"I was expecting a visit," Marie said evenly. "My friend must have come and not finding us in our cottage at the gate, and the house dark, left. That is why we turned the lights on. We hoped it would make her realize we were here. But apparently she could not stay anyway."

The corduroy kid studied Marie intently. Both Marie and René had been in the Resistance. They had done very dangerous work. They were prepared for the kind of scrutiny to which they were now being subjected.

Finally, after an unendurable ten or twenty seconds, the corduroy kid nodded and Marie and René withdrew. I'm sure the moment they were in the hallway with the door shut behind them they went rushing off.

I had to tell myself that Marie and René would do everything possible to find out who it was that had gone off down that black road.

"You say you were asleep in the garden at nineteen hundred hours?" the sheepskin jacket was asking me with polite surprise.

"Yes," I said. "I'd had to work last night and had almost no sleep. It was a very warm afternoon."

They digested that. Morescu and Jane were hanging on each word nervously.

"Nothing disturbed you?" the corduroy kid asked.

"Not that I remember," I said. "Was there something that should have disturbed me?"

"Yes," the corduroy kid said after a long reflection. "There was a noise which should have disturbed you." He turned to take in the three of us. "No one here heard a loud noise?"

Jane, Morescu and I promptly shook our heads. Almost in unison.

"That is very odd," said the corduroy kid, "because your neighbors some two hundred meters away reported hearing the noise in question."

Morescu poured himself another cup of coffee, or tried to. His hands were shaking even worse than before. Jane had to pour it for him.

Her hands were steady.

"Two hundred meters," I said, "is quite a distance for certain types of noises. What kind of a noise did you have in mind that you think it odd we didn't hear?"

The corduroy kid looked at me very carefully. I realized he had come to some kind of a decision. "The noise," he said with a sort of bland dryness, "that a large airplane would make in coming down very low—so low that it almost crashed."

I had a hunch now what kind of a decision the corduroy kid had come to. He had decided that we were stalling. He had decided he would have to take some other line of attack.

It would mean he would get the hell out. It would mean I could run down the road and look for that silhouette that had disappeared. Or maybe René had already found her.

"Now that you mention it," Jane said, "I remember vaguely a large growling sound but it happened so far over there"—she gestured behind her—"that it didn't impress me particularly."

"Airplanes fly often over this area," Morescu offered. "And frequently much lower than they should. Once or twice it has occurred to me to complain."

"Why haven't you?" the sheepskin jacket asked.

Morescu looked at him in perplexity.

"It is a question of temperament," I said rather sharply. "Monsieur Morescu is not the kind who makes complaints."

They thought that over very gravely. Then the corduroy kid nodded as though he accepted that.

"Would you permit us to look around?" he asked very apologetically. "Not that we suspect anything. It is simply to ascertain if perhaps something of which you yourselves are not aware has taken place."

"It is hardly likely," Morescu said with quiet dignity, "that anything having to do with the noise of a plane, to take the example you have chosen, could have passed unnoticed by all of us."

The two policemen made no real effort to press that point. It was very obvious that they had both decided on some other plan and after elaborate apologies, and a very gallant good-by to Jane, they left.

23.

"THEY'LL BE back as soon as they've acquired the proper documents permitting them to search the house," Morescu said. He could barely speak. "We must start dismantling at once."

In fact he started off toward the door.

I stopped him.

"That figure we saw out there in the darkness," I said. "Who was that?"

"I don't know," Morescu said. He pulled himself together. "We haven't had a chance to talk together. You . . . you were not . . . Jane and I couldn't talk to you . . ."

"What do you mean Jane and you couldn't talk to me?" I demanded. "Jane was with me."

"He means after the plane came at us," Jane explained quickly. "We—"

"But you *were* with me," I said. "Jane! In the garden!"

"But I was in the laboratory," Jane said. "I left you asleep in the garden. There was never any further word from LXI. Then that noise and—"

I cut her off. I pointed wildly in the direction of the road.

"You know who that was walking toward the road?" I demanded. "That was you . . ."

She moved away from me as though she thought I'd suddenly gone nuts.

"But I was here," Jane said, her voice strained and tense. "I couldn't have been out there. What are you talking about?"

I looked at them both the way you would when you think you're losing your mind, or somebody's playing a bad joke on you. Morescu was shaking his head in agitation.

"After the plane roared down almost crashing," Morescu said, "we found Jane in the laboratory. Then Jean-Pie came back and said you'd fallen in the rose bushes and your shirt was full of blood. We thought you were drunk."

"I wasn't drunk," I said. "Jane was with me in the garden. This was something no man could hallucinate. It was real . . ." I went to her and took her hands. "It's got to be true. You and I . . ."

I could tell from the feel of her hands that it wasn't true. She hadn't been with me.

"We knew there was someone with you," Jane said tensely.

"*You* were with me."

"No," Jane said quietly. "*I* was not."

I felt myself go empty and cold.

"What was it?" I asked in a whisper. "What's happened?"

"I haven't any idea," Jane said frightened. "Unless, because of the state you were in . . ."

"No," I said. "No. Don't try to do that to me. It *was* you and me."

Morescu was leaning against the window for support.

"It is evident," Morescu said quietly, "that something of extraordinary importance has taken place. We must have time enough, free from the police, to find out what."

Before we could continue there was a sound in the hallway and the door burst open and René entered.

He'd been running and was out of breath.

"There's another policeman," he said. "A strange one."

I grabbed hold of René by his lapel.

"You saw someone go off down the road," I said. "That's why you turned the lights on even though the flics were here. Who was that?"

René pushed my hand away from his lapel gently.

"I don't know," he said. "It was very dark."

"You thought it was someone," I persisted.

"I was wrong," he said. He took a deep breath. "I cannot keep the policeman standing out there much longer."

"I've got to go out there after her," I said.

"Wait," René said. "The place is surrounded. You mustn't do anything precipitate. Marie and Jean-Pie are out looking for this girl we saw disappear. It would be much better if you behaved very normally."

"I've got to find her," I said. "They can handle the flics themselves."

René stopped me by force.

"I assure you," he said quietly, "that if you go out there you'll have every flic in this area following you. Whoever that girl is . . . do you want the police on her?"

That stopped me.

Whoever that girl was, as René had said, either she had a good reason to leave, in which case the worst thing I could have done would have been to lead the cops to her—or she wanted to avoid us. If she wanted to avoid us, I would never be able to find her on my own at night.

"Bring in this strange policeman," I said to René. "I'll stay."

"Yes," said René, halfway out by then. "It's much better."

Jane was staring at me strangely.

"You thought you were with me?" she asked in a whisper. "With *me?*"

"I *was* with you," I said. "I saw you. I . . ."

"You couldn't have seen me," Jane said with the kind of tone you would use on somebody you're afraid might become violent in a moment. "Let's get that straight. I was not out there. I was in the laboratory. Everyone saw me here. Jean-Pie. Everybody . . ."

I looked at both of them quickly.

"What's going on here?" I demanded. "Why are you so anxious to convince me I wasn't with you? Why didn't you come down and talk to me or take a look at me between the time the plane came down and now?"

"Because Morescu and I were trying frantically to figure out what happened," Jane said. "Jean-Pie said you told him you were all right, and that you chased him away . . ."

I pointed my finger at them both.

"I was with you," I said to Jane.

Even while I was saying it I was thinking, If a man were to want a thing bad enough, maybe a man would hallucinate it. Maybe a man would conjure it up with such force as to make it sound, taste, feel like reality . . .

"You were under very great tension," Morescu was saying distractedly. "As we all were."

Sounds from outside put a quick end to that part of it.

"Please," Morescu went on in great agitation, speaking very rapidly now. There was a knock on the door. "There are certain things you must know." He spoke so rapidly it was almost impossible to understand him. "Everything is now arranged so that our notes and our equipment can be got out in a hurry . . . if we can get past the police. René has worked out a plan. The moment we have got rid of this policeman we will put everything in the back of your car. René will make a diversion while you make your escape."

The knock came again.

"You haven't any idea of what it was that happened?" I asked. "Who that girl was—what—"

Morescu shook his head. "I have not the slightest idea," he said quietly. The knocking became more insistent now.

"*Entrez*," Morescu called out.

Then we waited—motionless—and René and the policeman entered.

He was a strange policeman all right.

I think of him as Snookums. I suppose because it's hard to imagine anything more inappropriate than that name. Snookums was tall, dark, and was obviously not French. His hair was cut in what the French call *brosse*, and what the Americans call crew cut. He wore the sort of clothes many Americans wear, loose and informal. I judged his age as about the same as the French cops, but his face seemed younger, less disturbed by life.

When he first walked in behind René, he studied Jane, Morescu and me with a frank professional stare. His way of looking at you had an offhand intensity which gave the impression you'd seen him before a dozen times or so in Yank movies.

"If I'm disturbing something important," Snookums opened the proceedings, "I could come back another time."

"No," Morescu said curtly. "Now is just as good as any other time. But first, please—who are you?"

"Police," Snookums said.

"French police?" Morescu asked.

"No," Snookums said, "I'm not, I'm just police. I'd like to ask you some questions which you won't have to answer unless you want to."

He implied also that he would not answer any further questions about himself.

His French was perfect. From the look of him I had expected him to have an accent, but he had none. The only thing that was noticeable about his French was that he spoke it the way people who have learned a language very well speak it—a little too formally.

Morescu did not even ask him to sit down. We all remained standing. It was one way of saying we were in a hurry.

"It will all depend on the nature of your questions," Morescu replied quietly.

"I'm afraid you'll have to tell us which police you represent," Jane said.

"In matters of this kind," he replied, "one is never precise. If you check on me you will find I'm police all right. Why are you worried?"

"Go ahead with your questions," Jane said coldly.

Snookums made none of the preliminary polite coffeehouse palaver. He came right out with it.

"I understand you're doing some research here," he said.

"That's correct," Morescu said.

"What kind of research are you doing?" Snookums asked.

There was something almost admirable about the beautiful, almost stupid, simplicity of his approach.

"We are doing research," Morescu said, "on a highly abstract problem which cannot possibly be of interest to you."

"I see," Snookums said. "But what field is it in? Physics? Chemistry?"

"To explain it to you adequately," Morescu said, "would require you to understand higher mathematics. It is that abstract."

Snookums looked deliberately from one of us to the other.

"Who's sponsoring this research?" he asked suddenly.

Morescu was thrown off momentarily. I could see he was trying to think through the implications of that obviously unexpected question.

"Nobody's sponsoring this research," I said in English, with irritation. "They're doing it on their own."

Snookums turned to me the way a dog which has already killed one rabbit would turn to a second rabbit.

"American?" he asked, still continuing to speak French.

"No," I said, still in English. I wanted to find out if his mother tongue was English. "I'm Canadian."

"What do you do?" Snookums asked, continuing in French. I must have scowled because he added very quickly and with that same flat, frank evenness in his tone, "That goes for you too—you don't have to answer any of these questions either."

I looked over at Morescu and Jane.

"I'm a journalist," I said still in English. "For several French language newspapers."

Snookums took a pause. You could almost see a moving finger in his head riffle through an index file which he kept in his head . . . Newspapermen—American, Australian, Armenian—British, Cambodian, Canadian— Ah yes . . .

There—under the B's— Once involved in international incident picketing Japanese ship. Wilfred MacIntosh. Pilot with R.C.A.F. Shot down . . .

I don't think he had me listed. I had the impression he pulled out an imaginary little black book and gold pencil and in a crabbed mental hand made a mental memorandum to himself to look me up.

"Why should they be doing research on an abstract problem?" Snookums asked me in French.

"Why not?" I replied. It was getting harder and harder for me to control myself. "Some people do abstract art. Some people do research in abstract science. It's to gratify man's thirst for knowledge— an aspiration toward the finer things—or wouldn't you understand that?"

Snookums had a fine capacity for not letting himself get provoked. He looked me over coolly, then turned back to the other two.

"You were here in France during the war, weren't you?" he asked Morescu suddenly.

"Yes," said Morescu after a moment.

"Weren't you doing research work for the Germans?" Snookums asked.

"No," Morescu said. He cut a cigarette in half and with trembling fingers stuck one half in his battered holder.

"What happened to your wife and child?" Snookums asked calmly.

"They were killed," Morescu said tonelessly.

"How do you know that?" Snookums asked.

Morescu now looked up at him. Terrified.

"I assumed so. They were taken away from the Vélodrome d'Hiver," Morescu said. "I saw them there."

Snookums frowned.

"You were given permission to visit them at the Vélodrome d'Hiver?" he asked.

"No," Morescu said almost inaudibly. "The Nazis did not give me permission to go there. Only doctors were allowed to see those people. A friend of mine, a Jewish doctor, told me they were there. I waited three days and three nights in front of the building. Under the elevated tracks."

Morescu stopped talking for a moment.

I remembered what René had said about that terrible incident. Thousands of Parisian Jews, old, young, babies, men, women, adolescents, rich, poor, middle-class, healthy, sick, had suddenly been rounded up by the Nazis and thrown into the huge sports arena, each one by then having foreknowledge of the terrible, wanton, meaningless end that loomed ahead. Their screams could be heard for all the days they were kept there; a continual blending of some fifty thousand agonies into one horrible cry, so unendurable that the people who lived for blocks around in that area fled from it in terror. Only the Nazis moved about it methodically, making note of possessions, age, weight, sex.

The sound of that one unendurable voice became an image and that image was reflected even now as he stood before us in Morescu's burnt-out eyes; the elegant little Continental scientist who had stood in front of that huge, barnlike building for three days and three nights listening to that voice, knowing that his wife's and child's cries were part of the texture of it.

"I saw them for a moment," Morescu went on, his voice dry as dust, "as they were brought out on the morning of the fourth day. They were loaded into vans, both of them." He slumped a little, and then waited a moment before he could go on. "There was not one known survivor from that journey."

TWINKLE, TWINKLE LITTLE STAR 131

"Why do you think the Germans permitted your wife and child to be killed?" Snookums asked.

"I don't know," Morescu said woodenly. "Perhaps they felt that the project was not that valuable after all. Perhaps they felt I was not really doing my work . . ."

"That doesn't sound much like the Germans," said Snookums. "I would have thought they would have kept your wife and child alive. Even if your project might not have seemed worth while, they needed scientists of your caliber. I don't understand why they would have permitted your wife and child—"

Suddenly something burst inside of Morescu.

"I do not wish to answer any more questions!" Morescu said stridently. "Now get out of this house! And you will never return unless you have completely legal documents which authorize you to return! Understand?"

Snookums thought about it exactly as he would have if it had been the mildest sort of question.

"I'm sorry," he said and there wasn't the slightest suggestion of regret in his tones. He turned to Jane. "Perhaps you would not mind answering a few questions?"

"I would mind," Jane said in English. "You are no longer welcome here."

Snookums nodded and then said, *"Au revoir."*

Which as you unquestionably know means, "I'll be seeing you soon," and Morescu, correct to the last, ushered him to the door and out.

There was a few seconds' silence as we listened for Snookums's footsteps to disappear down the pathway.

"I'm so sorry," Jane said softly to Morescu, "I didn't know it happened that way . . . I . . ."

Morescu looked up at her.

"It's all right," he said shakily. "For a moment there he led me to think . . . that perhaps . . . the Germans had not killed them . . . that perhaps they are still alive—" and as Jane started to say something he added quickly—and ruefully, "No. They're dead. I know that. Only we are alive and there is something of vast importance about to happen to all of us—and that is the essential—is it not?"

"Yes," Jane said almost inaudibly.

Morescu turned to me.

"I can think clearly now," he said. "We must waste no more time trying to puzzle out what could have taken place. Whatever it is, we must find out first before our discoveries become public. You agree to that?"

I'd promised that to Jane a long time ago. I told Morescu I agreed. The sound of running footsteps stopped Morescu.

René, Marie and Jean-Pie came bursting in.

"More police," René said. "On the road outside . . ."

He motioned excitedly toward the highway.

I whirled on Marie and Jean-Pie.

"What about the girl?" I demanded.

"Disappeared," Marie said when she caught her breath.

"We'll look for her," René said. "We know this area better than you do." He turned to Marie. "You must not let the police in. Even if they now have a document. For at least ten minutes. Understand?"

Marie nodded. She took Jean-Pie by the hand and the two of them rushed away to stave off the police for ten minutes. From then on it was all like a well-planned nightmare.

We rushed upstairs. The laboratory had already been dismantled. There were three small briefcases full of papers. René snatched them up and several other small cases, took the keys of my car and hurried down the stairs with his burden.

I remember vaguely Jane telling me that there were three cases which she had marked with crosses. In the event of danger I was to destroy them. Burn them was the simplest. Then she quickly showed me the contents of all the other boxes. It was all there, the apparatus to which I had become so accustomed that it was with a pang that I saw it all had been packed away—the hair curler wires, the vacuum-cleaner bag, the wonderful radiant stuff, the electrodes, the crystal containers—friendly objects I had come to love.

Jane was speaking with great calmness now. She gave me a list on which there were instructions on where to hide the various objects about my apartment. She had thought it out carefully and with an incredible memory for details.

The crystal containers I was to put in the bottom of the buffet where an old chandelier was stored. People would think they were parts of a modern lamp. The wires I was to put in the broom closet where I kept lengths of old wire. The vacuum-cleaner bag I was to fill with the radiant stuff and put it too in the broom closet.

The instructions could not have been more precise and Jane kept repeating them in simple language until she was sure I had understood it all.

Immediately thereafter began the parade down the stairs. What had taken Jane and Morescu, and probably hundreds of other scientists behind them, years to put together was dismantled and hidden away in the back of my car in a very few minutes.

Suddenly from ahead we heard the tatters of Marie's voice as she spoke to the police. Her voice was unusually loud, as though she wanted it to carry to us, and a moment later she came over.

"They had no documents," Marie said simply. "But they are keeping the house under surveillance. They are parked in the little road at one side there."

She pointed.

"We will take our Citroën," René said quietly to me, "Jean-Pie and I, and we will turn out in front of the little lane and stand there thus blocking the police car long enough for you to get away. You start your motor only after mine is under way. The noise of my motor will cover you. And of course you will not turn your lights on until you are well down the highway."

René and I shook hands. Jean-Pie emerged from the shadows and shook hands too. Then the boy and his father hurried off toward their car.

Jane would stay behind with Morescu, at least overnight. It was either that or taking Morescu with us and we had finally concluded that more than one of us leaving at once was not a good idea. In the morning Jane would meet me at the Coupole. In the meantime, if anything came up, we were to telephone each other immediately, even though the phone would very likely be tapped.

Up ahead we could hear a grinding sound as René began the process of starting his twenty-year-old Citroën. We held our breaths. At long last the motor coughed, caught and roared.

It *was* a noisy motor. Seconds later the old car lumbered off.

I shook hands hastily with Morescu, and he turned away as if giving us a fraction of a moment alone together.

Jane and I faced each other.

I swept her to me frantically.

"Something fantastic's happened," I whispered. "You know that, don't you?"

"Yes," she said in a barely audible whisper. She was deeply agitated and her body was heavy and almost inanimate.

I held her off at arm's length, then she kissed me deliberately and I let her go, feeling raw and hurt.

I got in the car. Over the roar of the Citroën I started my car and moved off behind René.

I had a last glimpse of her standing in the darkness looking at me and I thought to myself that she was crying.

Then there were too many other things to think about.

24.

RENÉ STOPPED his car in the center of the road, completely blocking the little lane. Behind him I could see the vague outline of another car. René stalled his motor as I shot out.

As I sped by, the car behind René flashed its lights angrily and a man shouted something.

I had a vague image of René leaning out of his car politely as if to hear better and I disappeared down the main highway at full speed.

About five hundred meters below I cut off the main highway and onto a minor road.

Despite my promises to Jane and Morescu, I decided I would make one desperate try at finding the girl we had all seen walk out into the night.

For some minutes I kept shooting in and out of a network of country roads, every few seconds flashing my lights on and sweeping them over the dark brush.

Then I realized that I ran a real risk of getting lost and perhaps winding up somewhere near Morescu's. If I were to get caught and if on some pretext the notes and the equipment would be confiscated, I would never be able to face Jane again.

I tore back onto the main road. I would get the stuff all hidden away as I had promised Jane and then I would come back and continue the search.

The highway was loaded with Saturday night traffic and I drove along as fast as I dared. Very gradually, as I darted in and out of traffic, I began to have the feeling something was wrong. At first it was a vague generalized feeling, then slowly I became convinced that there was something wrong with the car, or with something *in* the car. Something was burning perhaps. The feeling took on proportions almost of panic.

By that time I had reached the Porte d'Orléans.

There was so much life and traffic there that I felt reasonably certain that it was safe to pull up to one side at the first parking place I saw.

I sniffed the air. There was nothing burning. My attention was pulled to the seat alongside of me where René had put the vacuum bag with the radiant stuff. The bag was emitting palpitations and it felt to me as though the stuff were pulling at my trouser cuffs imploringly, the way a small child would, to be let out. I undid the bag as quickly as I could. I could almost swear that I heard a sigh of relief as the stuff gratefully slipped out of the bag and oozed over the seat toward me, curling up along my right thigh.

Without realizing what I was doing, I reached over and caressed the stuff as though it were something alive, for example the way I used to caress my faithful Airedale, Buster, who in her elderly years would seem to know when I was in trouble and would lay her muzzle gently on my knees and would look up at me with her deep brown mournful eyes. And this time the touch of the stuff brought with it the same sense of contentment and assurance that Buster had always brought me.

A few blocks away from my place I stopped the car and forced the reluctant stuff to return to the vacuum bag, which I then tied off tightly. The bag immediately began to palpitate, but I hardened my heart to its pleadings. I had too much else to worry about.

I had great luck with Mme. Fénelon. I think she was entertaining that night. To get past her window, which is like a huge spying eye, without being seen is extraordinary, but to pass unnoticed three times as I did, and with armloads of equipment, is a minor miracle.

Maybe it was because it was getting close to ten o'clock, which is an odd hour of a Saturday night in Paris. Most people are either in bed or set in whatever they've planned for the night.

Once I had everything safe in my apartment the first thing I did, of course, was to release the stuff on the living-room floor. It immediately moved toward me. I was hurrying so I got tangled in a couple of the brain wires. It took me seconds to disentangle them and for a moment I thought I'd never get them straight. I was so nervous I swore out loud.

The stuff, at the sound of my swearing, had recoiled. At first I didn't believe my eyes. I tried swearing again, and again the stuff recoiled.

Then I said something gentle, soft. This time the stuff came oozing affectionately toward me.

I tried it without the cuss words.

Just the harsh sounds.

It worked just as well.

It wasn't that the stuff disapproved of swearing. It just didn't like ugly or menacing sounds.

After that I carried up some of the pieces to the terrace and crawled into the false roof, putting the pieces away carefully. Even though I'd been working like a madman, and Jane's instructions were of remarkable help, I had not put everything away when I heard the grinding of the elevator and it became quickly apparent that it was coming all the way up to my floor.

I was having visitors.

At ten-thirty on a Saturday night.

It could have been a female visitor but most of the girls I know always called first as good girls should.

I jumped down out of the false roof and I swung myself back quickly into my apartment. As I got there, there was a pounding on my door.

There were still the hair curler wires to get rid of—and the stuff to put away. Tenderly I put the stuff back in the bag and hung it on a peg in the broom closet as per instructions.

The pounding on my door continued. I looked around desperately. I'd forgotten what Jane had said to do with the brain wires.

Finally I slung the brain wires over a piece of modern sculpture. They added to it wonderfully.

Then Henneman's voice came.

"Hey! Open up!"

I walked into the can and flushed the toilet so that he would hear the sound of it, and shouted, "Coming!" then took a last look around.

Some of the smaller pieces had been hidden away among the sculpting tools. Only another sculptor might have guessed they were not part of a sculptor's tools, and even then you might have argued him out of it.

The written data I had carefully distributed all according to instructions, among the pages of the autobiographical novel (which I had lately decided with great relief I would not continue). Anyone actually trying to find the scientific notes would have to plow through all the pages of my novel. As I walked toward the door, that thought gave me a kind of grim satisfaction.

It was Henneman at the door.

I let him in and he looked around suspiciously for a minute or so as if trying to find something. As always his cheeks were flushed as if he had just been freshly shaved by a barber.

"It took you a long time to answer your door," Henneman said.

It was not a gracious way for an uninvited guest to begin the evening.

"I'm a very busy guy, believe it or not," I said shortly. "What brings you here?"

He looked around carefully, then he pointed to the hair curler wires.

"What are those things?" he asked.

"That's modern art," I said.

"Oh?" he asked belligerently. He went over and looked at them, finally decided that's what they were, and turned to me.

We circled each other like two punch-drunk prize fighters.

"I'm sitting on a story," he said tentatively. "I think it's liable to be the story of the year."

"You're a lucky guy," I said.

"We both are," said Henneman. "I'm going to let you in on it." He lit a cigarette. He had a strange way of smoking. He had taken to smoking that way shortly after there was all that talk about tobacco and cancer. He wouldn't inhale. He would take a mouthful of smoke, puff out his cheeks until they became like great fat balloons, hold them that way for a long time, then quickly spit out a puff of smoke. That way there was no contact with his lungs. It was fascinating to watch. "The reason I'm letting you in on it," he went on, "is because I think you can help me."

"What's the story?" I asked.

"Manned satellites," Henneman said. He said it the way a Scotland Yard man would say Crown Jewels to a professional thief. He puffed out his cheeks again. "Manned satellites. An artificial moon with a human being in it. Something that can penetrate the stratosphere and discharge its passenger."

I held my breath. For a second I wasn't quite sure what he was talking about.

Then suddenly it hit me.

Say, Mister Bones, who was that manned satellite I seen you with last night?

Why, which manned satellite, Mister Interlocutor?

Why, the one I seen you with last night.

Why, that was no manned satellite, Mister Interlocutor. That was, I think, the woman I love. Or a reasonable facsimile.

"What about the manned satellite?" I asked.

He was watching me, watching me with an eye that grabbed hold and clung like a bloody leech.

"I've got my hooks on a pilot who's seen one—up close," he said. "Saw it clearly at nineteen hundred hours tonight right before he was coming in at Orly . . ."

That sent me reeling. If what he was saying was true, not only had I seen Jane but she had gone flying around in the atmosphere high enough to be seen by a pilot.

It took all I had for me not to show him he had me reeling.

"Nineteen hundred hours is late in the day to see a manned satellite," I said woodenly, "and besides, as an ex-pilot myself I can tell you that sometimes—in the gloaming, a man begins to see all sorts of things . . ."

"I know this pilot," Henneman said shortly. "He saw it. Besides, the object was picked up by radar."

"Fine," I said tensely. "You've got yourself an honest pilot and a manned satellite. Where do I come in?"

"Aren't you curious as to what it looked like?" Henneman asked.

"You're on the level about this?" I asked.

"Christ," Henneman said. "You don't think I'd be spoiling a perfectly good Saturday night with idle chitchat?"

"Okay," I said like a good boy, "what did it look like?"

I too needed time. Time to even out. Which way was the horizon? And Henneman would have to be handled. He could be dangerous.

"It . . . it looked like an angel," Henneman said.

I stared at him incredulously.

He stamped his cigarette out irritably.

"That's right," he said. "I'm quoting the guy. He says it looked to him, and he got a pretty square look at it, the way he imagined an angel would look. Flesh-colored. With a heavenly glow."

"Who," I asked archly, "is this pilot anyway?"

"This pilot is with the Israeli airline El Al," Henneman replied heavily, as though rubbing his lacerated body with rock salt. "He's studying for the Rabbinate—"

"Anybody else see it except this pilot who's studying to be a Rabbi?" I asked.

"No," Henneman said. "I got to the airfield just as the pilot was being cleared by the air police. Imagine my feelings when he kept insisting it looked like a goddam angel."

"Religious hysteric, they'll say," I said sympathetically.

"I don't care what they'll say," Henneman said grumpily. "Not only is its course plotted on the radar chart but also on the plane's graph. It was flying in a straight, sharply diagonal line"—he described the diagonal flight by slashing his finger through the air—"so that it could only have been a beam."

I managed, I think, to look properly startled.

"A beam?" I demanded.

"A beam," he repeated heavily. "The pilot and I have worked it all out on a graph and we were able to plot the approximate spot where the beam led to." He was looking at me with special interest. "It led to a house called the Villa des Cinq Fusillés."

"I was at the Villa des Cinq Fusillés myself at nineteen hundred hours," I said quietly.

He waited a second.

"What did you see?" he asked, watching me.

"Not a goddam thing," I said.

"You sure?" he asked.

"Of course I'm sure," I replied, trying to sound irritated.

He was put out for a few seconds.

"Didn't you once introduce me to your girl friend?" he asked finally. "A little blonde, cute as hell."

"Not cute," I said. "Beautiful."

"Okay," he grunted in ill-humor. "Beautiful. Well, I think that your beautiful girl friend and that Rumanian refugee Morescu she works with are involved in this," Henneman pronounced.

"That's impossible," I said, trying to get my eyes away from his. "I know what they're working on. It's something or other having to do with the study of the most basic forms of life—very abstract."

Then he said something which really caught my interest.

"Do you know what Morescu did during the war?" he asked. He didn't wait for my answer. "He worked on guided missiles for the Nazis."

"I don't believe you," I said slowly.

He didn't even bother trying to persuade me. "Now I'm going to let you in on another secret—top secret." He came close to me and lowered his tone.

For some reason or other I suddenly thought of my Uncle Debret and a firing squad at dawn.

"The beam in which that manned satellite was flying was strong enough to stop a four-motor airliner dead in its tracks." Henneman let that sink in, then continued, "Something held it in such a way that it could go either up or down in the path of the beam but never get out of its hold."

"Nothing like that exists," I said.

"Doesn't exist my necktie," Henneman replied irritably. "That plane goddam near crashed. The passengers and crew panicked. That's why there was this air police investigation. Do you realize the military importance of a development of that kind?"

Henneman was beginning to get himself a little excited.

"Imagine the possibilities! Imagine what you could do with a beam in which you could catch and hold the enemy planes—or enemy anything!"

Funny thing, whenever anybody talks about enemy planes, by some perverse quirk of imagination I always imagine *myself* as the enemy up in one of them. Maybe Uncle Debret is right. Maybe there *is* something fundamentally subversive about me. I shuddered a little as I suddenly saw myself in the pilot's seat, piloting one of these enemy planes, and caught in a beam and knowing that at any time, if people down below wanted to, they could send a chunk of flak right through me.

"A thing of this kind is not going to be kept secret," he went on. "Especially not by a couple of amateurs like your friends. Because one way or another somebody is going to get hold of their little secret.

And I would say it would be far smarter for it to be done through somebody like me."

He let that sink in a while too.

"I'd be able to see to it," he confided, "that they got real recognition and compensation for their discovery, and also that it went to the right place.

"And as far as you and I are concerned," Henneman continued, "I'd know how to see to it that something was worked out for us too. Okay?"

"I think you're full of crap," I said gently. "I told you—Morescu and Jane are working on a problem which relates to the nature of living matter . . ."

"I don't like to be told I'm full of crap," Henneman said. "Never say that to me." He was white.

"I'll remember that for the future," I said.

"I could have done this any one of twenty different ways," Henneman said, "and they would've all been unpleasant for your girl friend —and maybe for you. Because I *know* she and the Rumanian are in on this and so will a lot of other people. Maybe you're in on it too—I don't know. But don't fool around. This is serious and there's not too much time."

He pulled a card from a neat section of his wallet and wrote some numbers on it.

"These are all my phone numbers," he said. "You can get me any time of the day or night. If you're smart you'll convince them to get smart and work with me."

I took the card.

"A last piece of advice," he said. "If your girl friend and her Rumanian colleague have really succeeded in inventing what I think they have, then you can expect that you will be followed, your telephone tapped and even *your* place probably wired for sound."

He looked quickly around the room, as though trying to figure out where the microphones would be placed. Then he turned quickly back to me.

"Anyway," he concluded, "it would be a good idea for you to act as if that were the case."

"We're in France," I said. "The French don't work that way."

"Who's talking about the French?" Henneman said and stalked out of the room.

25.

THIS NEEDED thinking out. Nothing panicky. Calm reflection.

I tried to reflect calmly, but my brain plays tricks on me in moments like that. All I could think of was the time my friend Jake Mendelberg, who had been alongside of me in the hospital in London, had read the news that the Yanks had dropped an atomic bomb, and Jake had looked over at me gravely and said:

"Mark my words—that atomic bomb is dynamite!"

Well, at least part of the mystery was solved. We knew now why the police had come. We knew also what they were after.

They were after a beam which could immobilize a four-motored plane. And if Henneman knew about it, you could be sure every Intelligence setup in Paris must have known about it.

In a very short time we could expect to be the center of considerable activity.

But I thought about all that vaguely, distantly.

I had just about decided that I'd better get right back to the villa when the telephone rang.

I let it ring for a long time. Now, even very ordinary moves had to be carefully considered.

But as you know by now, I'm not a man who can disregard a ringing telephone.

I finally took the receiver off the hook.

"Hello?" I said in a voice so uneven that I was not sure it had carried.

"Are you there?" It was Jane, sounding very English, very precise, very controlled. Not at all like the Jane I had just left.

"Jane?" I asked.

"Yes," came the reply. "Thank God I've found you."

She sounded as though she were about to burst with excitement—exactly the way you would sound if you had been trying unsuccessfully to reach your wife for the last hour to tell her you had won the sweepstakes.

"Now don't move! I'll be over in five minutes," she went on.

"Where are you?" I asked in low tones, as though somehow low tones wouldn't be recorded.

"I don't know," she said, the words bubbling out of the receiver, "but Pierre knows exactly how to get to your place . . ."

"Who's Pierre?" I asked.

"He's one of the men I'm with," she said. "Now do stay put. I've had such a frightful time locating you . . ."

"Why did you have a frightful time locating me?" I asked.

"I'll explain later," she said.

"You knew I was coming here," I said.

"In the excitement," she said, "I may have forgotten. Just don't move—not an inch. Promise?"

"I promise," I said solemnly and hung up.

I picked up the phone again and called her hotel. She wasn't there. I called Morescu's. The phone rang for a long time.

As I waited I had the feeling I was living in that world which one imagines when one puts a sea shell to one's ear—a world of agitated sibilant turmoil, faintly unreal, wind-swept by a prevailing wind that comes from nowhere.

Jane's voice came on the telephone. It was much less English-sounding than the voice I had just heard.

"Jane?" I asked cautiously.

"Yes," she replied quickly. "You all right? Everything all right?"

"Fine," I said. "Everything's fine. Didn't you just call me?"

A little buzzing silence. Like eternity.

"No," Jane said.

There was no question of it.

She hadn't called. Either that or she was lying.

There was no reason for her to lie. Besides, I knew she wasn't lying.

"I mean a few minutes ago, here," I said.

Another buzzing silence, then:

"Oh, then," Jane said hastily. "Yes. I did call you."

"I'll wait for you," I said. "Here."

"Fine," Jane said. "Morescu and I will be over."

We were both talking the way people who think they're being overheard talk. Each word is stiff with insincerity. It's not easy. Try it sometime.

"Everything all right at your end?" I asked, even though I knew if it were not she wouldn't tell me.

"Oh, fine," Jane said with false cheeriness. (She seemed to me then to be a lousy actress.) "Marie got a letter from her family. Their cow Grisette had a calf. A bull calf. Imagine."

"A boy," I said. "What do you think? They so wanted a boy calf. Tell them felicitations from me."

Then I said good night, she said good night and we hung up.

I sat me down in an insane chair I have that comes about thigh-high to a grasshopper.

I must have been sitting for a long time because I could hardly straighten when I finally stood up.

I wiped the coolish sweat off my brow and decided I might as well shave. There was nothing else to do. I always shave when the waiting becomes unendurable.

Only cut myself four times.

No, sir. No major wound, sir. Nothing requiring hospitalization. Just *looks* like a lot of blood.

Staunched the flow of blood. Combed my hair. Put on a nice clean shirt. Left it open at the collar. Looks better that way, I decided.

Studied myself in the mirror. Was so much not myself that did not make the usual joke at myself in mirror.

I always say as I bring my face a little closer:

Not bad-looking. Would pass in the dark.

I happen not to be too particular about the kind of jokes I make with myself.

Sat down and waited.

Like a vegetable with a heartbeat.

The way you wait when you've tried to figure out an impossible situation and find that there's absolutely no answer.

After a while I got up—I decided I ought to be below when Pierre and the other man brought her home.

I dashed out of the apartment, and because the elevator takes at least twice as long to come up as you can make it on foot going down, I ran downstairs.

Mme. Fénelon and her cat Pompier appeared at their door to watch me cross the hall. I came to a full stop, tried not to appear too out of breath, nodded gravely, and went out.

I waited in front of the apartment house.

It was a soft, black night. The air was gentle. There wasn't much traffic.

I tried to think again. This time all I could think of was the Icelandic art student who painted in the dark.

It was dark now. According to the Icelandic girl, I ought to be able to think very nicely.

Come on, kid, think. There's an explanation. Why are you afraid to face it? What's the matter? Scared?

Yes.

I hadn't been waiting long before there was a loud rumbling sound down the street. Don't get excited. It wasn't an invasion from Mars.

It was only a truck. First I saw its headlights, then the rest. It was the biggest truck I had ever seen in my life.

Its presence was disturbing. Big trucks never come to that area of Paris. It is prohibited for such heavyweights, *poids lourds,* as the French call them, to circulate in certain historic and residential areas.

The truck slowed down a slight distance up ahead. A lonely gendarme, still abroad at that late hour, attracted by the sound, came running from the quai, blowing his silver whistle furiously.

If there is anything that a Parisian gendarme will take as a personal insult, it's a *poid lourd* on a street it shouldn't be on.

The gendarme made the truck stop near a street lamp. Then he began to gesticulate excitedly. A large, fleshy man jumped down from the truck and disregarded the gendarme completely, holding his arms up as though to catch something.

A moment later I realized what it was he was going to catch.

It was Jane.

She was wearing a blue dress, and she jumped from the high seat right into the fleshy man's arms.

Even from where I stood in the half-darkness, I could see she was terribly agitated. She kept looking around, even sometimes at me, without seeing anything.

I walked toward them slowly.

The members of that little group were so engrossed with each other that no one noticed my presence.

The cop was demanding to know, in a very flowery and somewhat classical French, how it was that these savages (he indicated the large fleshy man, and another man who had just joined him, by contrast a tiny, peppery-looking little man who wore a kerchief around his neck) could desecrate one of the most beautiful streets in France, and possibly in the world, by intruding their monstrous *poids lourds,* with its poisonous fumes, into this area?

She was watching the faces intently. I could feel her frantic impatience, but there was nothing I could do yet. I had to look at her first.

She looked exactly like Jane. Even the way she moved.

But what was I thinking?

She *was* Jane.

Or was she?

The little peppery man with the kerchief barely gave the cop time to finish his peroration. It was as though he knew it all, they knew exactly what the cop was going to say, he had a right to say it, but they only hoped he would get through it fast. The moment the gendarme left them the slightest opening, the peppery little man snapped back that they were quite well aware that the law prohibited vehicles of the size of the one in which they found themselves from circulating in this area. It was only under the pressure of most extraordinary circumstances that they had dared to violate the law.

The cop was listening to them with the same exaggerated boredom with which they had listened to him. Elaborately he had out his book and pencil and was carefully smoothing the paper down in order better to write the "contravention." He too had heard all this.

The extraordinary circumstances were these, the little peppery man went on. The young lady with them was English, and had lost her way outside of Paris, near Fontenay-aux-Lilas, and not having one word of French . . .

But Jane speaks French very well. True, with an English accent, but she speaks it nonetheless.

. . . they had driven her into Paris where she finally hoped to find her fiancé.

The gendarme was looking her over now. She seemed pale and frightened.

The fleshy man made a big extravagant gesture. It could not reasonably have been expected of them that they would abandon this foreigner, who was entirely without money, having momentarily left the house in which she was staying, and then having completely lost her sense of direction and not being sure of the address, so that she had found herself alone in the night and not knowing where to go until they had come along and picked her up.

I moved over alongside of her and she turned and saw me.

"Coo," she said in awe after a moment.

"Coo" is a sound which the North English make when all other sounds are inadequate.

I put my arms around her and kissed her because I figured that gesture would explain a lot and also because I wanted to kiss her. She kissed me back ardently.

The three men heaved a collective sentimental sigh.

While I was holding her, she whispered, "Do you know?"

"I don't know whether I do or I don't," I said.

Something weighing about a billion tons had just settled itself on me. Everything now seemed odd—the three men in the darkness—the huge truck—the street—the occasional Peugeot or Quatre Chevaux that came purring by.

"It's true," she whispered.

The policeman was looking at us peculiarly.

"Forgive me for not having spoken sooner," I said. My voice seemed to boom in my ears. "What these gentlemen have said is correct. I owe them a debt of eternal gratitude for having returned my fiancée to me."

The gendarme looked momentarily out of countenance. He remarked that he would have hardly chosen the two gentlemen present to play the rescuers of an English damsel in distress. He added, with a philosophical shrug, that most of the time life was like that. Finally, looking long and fondly at Jane, he said, *"Eh bien,"* which doesn't really mean anything, saluted us all politely and left.

I thanked the two drivers and asked them if I could buy them a drink. They declined graciously. They were in a hurry.

I asked for their names. I still remember them. I wrote them down. Messrs. Ribotti and Barbéris of Nice. They had driven up from the Riviera with a load of carnations and lettuce. In a pinch I believe I could get them to swear to an affidavit as to event, time and place.

Jane shook hands with them both and thanked them in English. They both gestured that it was nothing, got into the truck and drove off.

With my tongue, which weighed only two million tons, I licked my lips which felt like the two cactus plants my Uncle Debret keeps in his parlor. I leaned against a tree.

We looked at each other.

"You said something was true," I said. "What is it?" She didn't answer at once.

"I've guessed at something I'm afraid to put into words," I added.

"Would you like me to put it into words?" she asked gravely.

"Yes, I would," I said.

She waited a moment, took a little breath.

"I've flown across space," she said. "Morescu's hypothesis is correct. There *is* another earth—the twin of this one." She waited another second. "And I'm from it," she concluded.

"I see," I said.

"I flew across space," she repeated, "on a beam which comes from *my* earth . . ."

"Yes," I said.

"Everything that's happened in our planet," she said, "has been happening here—in almost—*almost,* I say—the same way."

"I see," I said.

"Twin planets," she said. "Identical twins."

The billion tons that had been sitting on me began to tell. I was leaning at a drunken angle.

In my head a crazy New Year's celebration was going off. Bottles were popping, horns were blowing, the air was full of streamers and confetti—madly gay celebrants were rushing about, weaving their way in and out of random images. The people were wearing those silly party hats that are worn at New Year's Eve celebrations. One of the images kept scurrying about shouting:

"Invasion from another world!"

Then suddenly it turned into a headline.

STORY OF THE YEAR

Then the headline grew to the size of a building and became:

STORY OF THE CENTURY

The headline kept getting bigger, filling the skies.

STORY OF ALL TIME

And then I saw my Uncle Debret's face and I was being carried through a madly cheering throng, and my Uncle Debret was breathlessly trying to keep up with the throng, while I was slowly pouring some stale champagne on his face and head. People were shouting everywhere, pointing to Jane:

"The girl from another world . . ."

And I could hear them say:

"The young Canadian journalist who found her," and Debret kept saying, *"That's my nephew . . ."* while I kept pouring stale champagne on him and he kept smiling up at me. . . .

Only strangely enough there was no real gaiety in all the strident madness—or maybe there was too much to endure all in one moment.

I knew it was true.

I stood there in the shadow of that memorable tree looking at her and part of me thinking, This tiny little thing of blood and tissue, bone, hair, lymph and other things not to be mentioned at this moment, let itself be hurtled through space, past the stars, past light, past time— to us. What grandeur there is in the human heart and human intelligence!

Yet I must admit I am made of a stuff so gross that at that very moment when the meaning of the enormous event was seeping through, my heart sank as I asked myself what all this would mean to me.

This was another girl who had thought I was another guy. We'd made love to each other under what might be called, at the very least, false pretenses.

The one time in my life that I had been sure that nothing could spoil my happiness, at that very moment, a great inconceivable event had taken place.

The moment when my Jane and I would again (and for the last time I felt) face up to our private specter was yet to come.

26.

"WHAT HAPPENED to you at Morescu's?" I asked stiffly. "Why did you disappear? Why didn't you wait for me in my room?"

"I needed time to think," she said. "I first realized I'd succeeded when we were—together—in the garden. It was such a shock. I couldn't tell you right off. Not until I'd had a moment to look around. Do you mind?"

"No," I said. "I don't mind."

"I didn't really mean to disappear," she said. "I just wanted to see where I was and what it was like. I thought we were somewhere in Paris. I had no idea it was the outskirts of the city. And then suddenly it was black and I hadn't the faintest notion where I was, or where I had been, and the lorry came with the two very nice men and I decided to take it into Paris . . ." She made a helpless gesture, as though she really couldn't explain why she had done what she had. "We never get lost, you know, in our world. No matter where we are . . ."

"I see," I said. I thought to myself, I'll ask her to explain that to me some other time.

"Then I looked your name up in the phone book," she said, "and telephoned you and here we are."

"Even *his* name is the same as mine?" I asked.

The talk we were making was purely reflexive talk, the way a chicken's body sometimes keeps on walking around after its head's been chopped off.

There was nobody around to tell us our heads had been chopped off and that like reasonable chickens we ought to topple over.

"Everything's the same," she was saying. "Only very much different." She looked at me intently to see if I understood. I nodded as though I understood. She kept looking at me.

"What's the matter?" I asked.

"You look exactly like him," she remarked with that stilted calmness. "Exactly. I'll need a moment or two to get used to it."

"You look exactly like her," I said. "You know, I couldn't tell you apart."

We didn't move.

"And yet you're not my girl," I said.

"No," she said, "and you're not my—guy. I wish you were."

"So do I," I said. "He doesn't love you?"

She hesitated a moment. "So it would seem," she said very clearly.

"Yet *I* love her," I said. "Very much. So you see it's not exactly the same. That's *one* difference between the two worlds."

"Yes," she said, "I guess it isn't the same. We must find out why the first free moment we have."

She moved a bit—just enough to assure a casual observer she was alive.

"And now," she said urgently, "you must help me get back to the villa immediately. I must get to Elmer. I've got to get in touch with our people. They must be frantic. Mother was told at the last moment . . ."

"Who's Elmer?" I asked numbly.

"He's the transmitter on which the beam is fixed," she said.

"You won't have to go to the villa," I said. "Everything's here . . . at my place. We've moved it all."

"Oh!" she said. It was a sound of the most profound relief. Then she said again, "Oh"—and stopped cold and looked at me like a little girl in trouble.

"What's the matter?" I asked.

"I'm not sure," she said strangely. "I'm afraid I'm just beginning to realize what it means . . ." She stood rooted.

"We better go up," I said. "We'll call attention to ourselves here."

"I'm afraid I can't go on," she said.

"I don't understand," I said. I understood very well. Somebody had just told us our heads had been chopped off.

"Can't—" she said. "The people. The newspapers. The broadcasts. The conferences. I can't, you know."

"Yes you can," I said. "It's easy. You'll see."

"They'll want it televised," she said. "Two billion people watching us . . ."

"Two billion?" I asked.

"I imagine so," she said, "and simultaneous translations in every language. I should think by now our whole world's been alerted. I really can't, you know."

Her tones made it sound as though she were declining an invitation to tea. Very politely but firmly.

She joined me in leaning against the tree.

"I made it," she said. "We did it—I—"

I thought she was going to let out a Yippee the way the other Jane does occasionally, so I put my hand gently over her mouth. I think it was just in time.

About ten seconds later I felt it was safe to take my hand off her mouth.

"I didn't realize I would take the responsibility this way," she said.

She seemed to be considering the advisability of going to pieces completely. She decided against it.

Instead, she shook herself and looked at me incredulously.

"Why are we standing here this way?" she demanded as though it were my fault. "We mustn't waste any time! Imperative we—at once—"

. Although she didn't specify what it was imperative we do at once, I said, "Certainly."

I managed to shift the angle of my body enough so that it was comparatively easy to set myself in motion toward the apartment house.

Mme. Fénelon, still holding Pompier in her arms, and still wearing the mangy robe which is the standard uniform of Parisian concierges, was waiting in the hallway as we came in.

She watched us in that unabashed concierge way of hers.

I nodded gravely. I was thinking, This is a solemn occasion. The details will be recounted a thousand times for history.

I remember wondering whether, in the twin planet, there was another Mme. Fénelon—one seemed enough for anyone's universe.

Jane turned and sort of half-bowed formally the way drunks do and I'm sure Mme. Fénelon must have muttered to herself the French equivalent of "Pie-eyed again, no doubt. . . ."

Jane and I got into the tiny elevator and, staring at each other without really seeing each other or anything else, let ourselves be pulled up the seven flights.

She made no comment as we went into my place. She sat down quietly in the insane chair without realizing how small it was and folded her hands. After about two seconds she looked over at me.

"It was a lovely error while it lasted," she said. "Wasn't it?"

"Among the loveliest," I said.

"I like your place," she said.

"Thank you," I said. Then, "Tell me about your world."

"It's—" she stopped. "I'm sorry, I'd have to think carefully. I don't seem to be able to think carefully at the moment. All I can say is that it seems to everybody the most beautiful place imaginable—I'm sorry."

"That's all right," I said.

"Later," she said.

"Later," I said. "Jane's coming. Do you mind?"

"I don't mind at all," she said. "I look forward to it."

She had a curious way of speaking. At least it was curious then. She spoke as though there were great excitement behind what she said, and yet it didn't affect the physical quality of her voice in the least.

"I think I'd better go down and wait for her," I said.

"First things first," she said. "You must bring me Elmer and the explanatory notes. She can come up alone—can't she?"

"Sure," I said.

"I need you here," she said.

I got Morescu's and Jane's notes. I started to sort out the pages of my autobiographical novel. She was so excited she began to read them before she realized what it was.

As I took them out of her hand, they dropped to the floor. We bumped heads as we both bent down to pick them up. Finally it was she who got the pages.

We straightened.

"What is that?" she asked peculiarly.

"It's the story of my life," I said.

"I should like to read it sometime," she said politely, handing the pages to me.

"Sometime," I said.

I kept separating the pages of my book.

"Why were you so surprised at my wound?" I asked. "And why did you ask 'what war'?"

"The last war we had was over in nineteen nineteen," Jane said, "and you couldn't have been in that one."

"I wasn't," I said. "Our last one was over in nineteen forty-five."

"Was it big?" she asked.

"I thought it was," I said. "I think there were forty million killed."

She gasped.

"Forty million!"

"I think so," I said.

"Forty million," she repeated stunned.

"Among others," I said, "Jane's family."

She made a sound of horror and pity.

"All?" she asked softly.

"All," I said.

She waited a second.

I went on with the work at hand. When I had finally separated all the pages of my novel, I handed her the notes.

She took them quickly and began to read.

I figured that while she was reading I would get the equipment down and, I hoped, without her noticing that I had hidden it. She might wonder why we had hidden the equipment that way. I thought it best that she shouldn't wonder—not yet. But she was so anxious, she followed me over toward the terrace, reading as she went, stumbling on almost everything in the room.

I got a flashlight, took the notes away from her, put them carefully on a table and together we went out on the roof.

It was pitch-black. I don't know what she thought as I crawled into that dark aperture which was the false roof. I guess she was too dazed to express much of anything.

It was hard work because I had to hold the flashlight with one hand. (The opening was not big enough for the two of us.)

I passed the pieces out to her one by one. She put them down gently.

I probed the dark area carefully with the light and satisfied myself. It was empty now. We had taken everything.

I jumped down, pushed back the plank that covered the opening.

Very carefully we carried the pieces inside into the salon, closed the shutters and drew the heavy drapes across the windows.

Then I gathered the brain wires, the vacuum bag, the small parts and, with a little flourish—the stuff.

She looked at the heap stupefied.

"Good God!" she said in a tense whisper. "Is that what I came on? Surely something's missing."

"No," I said, "that's it."

"Show me their notes again," she said in agitation.

I brought her their notes. They made so little sense to her—either that, or she was in such a state—that once or twice she read again a number of lines of my abandoned novel before she realized it wasn't their higher mathematics she was reading.

She then studied the notes with that same incredible intensity that Jane had when working, but this time I had the feeling of a furious consuming concentration.

The minutes went by. When she had finished a few pages, she glanced hurriedly through the rest. Then she looked up at me.

She was very scared.

"You're really very much behind us, aren't you?" she asked.

"We were able to contact you with this," I said.

"No," she corrected me. "*We* contacted you. The ray comes from us."

"But they made this stuff," I said, pointing to the radiant substance.

"It's our ray that made it," she said.

She stood there studying the equipment for a long time.

"I'll never be able to do this alone without help," she said.

The way she said it, I believed her.

I walked over to the telephone and rang the villa. What seemed like hours passed before it was answered.

By Marie.

That was strange, because normally at that hour Marie and René and Jean-Pie would have been in the caretaker's cottage where they lived and not at the big house.

I asked her for either Morescu or Jane.

Marie waited a couple of seconds before she answered. When she did, she spoke so carefully I knew she was being listened to.

"M'sieur Morescu and the Mademoiselle," she said finally, "left some time ago. I thought they were going to your place."

"Well, they're not here," I said frightened. "When did they leave exactly?"

"Over an hour ago," Marie said.

It would have been physically impossible for the girl by my side to have been at the villa over an hour ago.

I heard the indistinct mumble of a man's voice (which for some reason or other I attributed to the sheepskin jacket) then Marie reply that she was speaking to no one of any significance.

Then Marie came back to me and we made polite talk to make it sound good, and hung up.

"No idea where they might have gone?" Jane asked.

By then she was very scared.

I stopped still and waited for some lightning inspiration to strike me. But nothing happened and I couldn't begin to think where Jane and Morescu might have suddenly decided to go.

For the thin edge of a fraction of a second she panicked. Then she did something which she did several times afterward. She deliberately straightened and seemed to set something inside of her working. She became very calm. It's a little difficult to explain, because it wasn't at all that she became less excited. It was more that suddenly everything was under control and it reminded me a little of the way my Jane would ask for two or three minutes to think a thing over.

"I'm not sure I can put this together," she said after about twenty seconds. "But I may be slightly pessimistic because of the unusual experiences I have just had. I'll try again."

She turned quickly back to the notes and began to sort them. "Were you talking strangely at the telephone because you were worried about police listening in?" she asked without looking at me.

I nodded, trying to make it look a very casual type of nod.

"Why should the police be interested?" she asked.

I realized she too was doing the "casual" routine.

"A plane caught in a beam," I said, very offhand, as if planes caught in beams happened on the hour. "Also the plane almost crashed. Naturally the police would look into it—"

She nodded an "it-wasn't-important" nod.

"They won't bother us here," I said, wishing I could get myself to believe it.

After a second of reflection, she poured herself back on the notes.

Ten minutes went by. I know it was ten because I watched each one crawl by. Then she turned to me and she looked the way Jake Mendelberg and I must have looked the night we got ourselves lost on Grouse Mountain.

She asked me if I had been in the laboratory much.

I said I had—many times.

She asked me if I could remember how Elmer had been put together. She said it was our only hope.

I told her I thought I could. I'd try anyway.

Then she watched me with the same extreme absorption.

It was a shattering experience for me to realize that even though I'd been in the lab hundreds of times, when it came down to it my memory of how the machine had been put together was incredibly sketchy. Sometimes the harder I tried to remember, the less sure I became of anything. She would hold one of the parts at various positions and angles. Something would seem to click and in a sweat I would say Yes, it seemed to me that was right.

This frantic process went on through the whole night.

Very slowly something began to form. Whether it was like Elmer or not I could no longer tell. I was so paralyzed with fatigue I couldn't have told my head from a hole in the wall, but Jane was fresh and wide awake. She kept right on with that frantic intensity, manipulating, feeling, adjusting the pieces without letting up one second.

As the hours drained away, she developed a special technique. With her body she would hide a particular part she was putting together—then, when it was done, she would move away and expose the assembled part to me suddenly, so I would get a fresh image of it. I was to blurt out the first impression that popped into my head. Did it look right—or wrong?

I kept prying my sticky lids open and mumbling "Right"—or "Wrong."

Faint sounds of Sunday morning came. The elevator ground away and I was sure it would be the police, but then I looked at my watch and figured it was probably my neighbors going to early Mass.

I think I made some coffee. I have a vague recollection of her drinking the coffee, and my thinking the sounds of the elevator were now people going to midday Mass.

There were four phone calls.

One had no connection whatsoever with what was happening. It was a girl friend who had happened to come in from London. That call really seemed to me to have come from another world.

Another was from Izzy. He and Giselle wondered if everything was all right.

I said Yes, everything was all right.

Izzy asked me if Jane and I would like to join them for sukiyaki that night. I said I didn't think so, and I would call them.

One very nice thing about Izzy. He always knows when you don't want him to know more than you've told him.

He said good-by and we hung up.

The third call was the operator telling me that there was a call for me from Montreal and would I be there in an hour to take it?

I said I would.

Two hours later when I called the operator back, she said the call had been canceled.

I tried to figure out what that could have been, but trying to think at that point was like moving a finger about in cotton wool.

The fourth call was from a different operator, asking for Miss Bridon-Jack. There was a call for her from Texas.

I said that Miss Bridon-Jack wasn't there, but if she came in, I would have her call.

The operator left her number, and rang off. Groggy as I was, I still was able to work out that somebody had gotten in touch with the Whitmans in Texas and my uncle in Montreal.

Jane? She kept right on going strong.

The only time she'd stop was when there'd be a particularly menacing sound from the outside. Then she'd stand motionless for about ten seconds, until there was no doubt that the sound was without special meaning for us, and she'd immediately plunge back into the work.

It was one of the most exacting experiences I've ever lived through. Just imagine watching someone trying to put together an enormously complicated jigsaw puzzle, each second becoming more and more unbearable, because just as you're certain a part of the pattern is about to fall in place, it's all swept away and the unendurably patient studying, manipulating, begin all over again. Several times I had to leave (I guess she thought I went to the can or something) and get off by myself and make low sounds. I'd come back to find her as I'd left her —the personification of utter concentration.

27.

UNTIL ONE o'clock in the afternoon.

All that happened was that she paused to push back a stray wisp of hair, and looked at me. I got to her just in time to catch her in my arms as she sagged. She had a very surprised look on her face as I carried her to a chair, sat her in it, got down on my knees and rubbed her hands.

She watched me mutely with an astonished look. She couldn't speak for a moment; that is, she was physically unable to speak.

"I suppose I pushed myself a bit too much," she said, still surprised by it all.

"I suppose you did," I said.

She leaned back a little in the chair.

"We usually don't let ourselves get into this state," she said, shutting her eyes, "but in the press of time, I neglected the usual precautions. And I'm not accustomed to such drains on my emotions." I had sat down opposite to her, very close. She must have sensed it, for she opened her eyes. "Are you thinking that people in our world are with-out emotions? It's simply that we've learned to counterbalance their effects." She shut her eyes again.

"You can't keep this up," I said. "You've got to get some sleep."

"I don't want to sleep," she said intensely. "I want to solve this . . ."

"Sometimes I go to sleep with a problem on my mind," I said, "and wake up with the solution."

She thought about it a long time.

"Yes," she said at last. "You may be right. It's probably the quickest and best way of proceeding." She sighed. "I shall put myself to sleep."

"I'll come back in an hour and wake you," I said.

"It won't be necessary," she said. She walked toward the center table and poured the radiant stuff out tenderly from the sack. She let it cover her hands. It seemed to affect her like a caress. "You haven't yet discovered the nature of sleep?" she asked.

"I guess we haven't," I said.

She lifted the stuff off the table with her two hands and carried it to the base of her throat and letting it snuggle there, she started toward the bedroom.

"We go to sleep at will," she said, on the way up, "and awaken at will."

She moved quickly up the winding staircase and hurried into my bedroom. It was as though once having decided sleep was a possible solution, she was anxious to get it over with.

I came running anxiously behind her. I'd left pajamas and socks and God knows what else lying around, but by the time I got to my room, she had already slipped off the blue dress and everything else, kicked off her shoes, lifted back the covers of the bed.

Before she got in, she turned to me abruptly.

"If you have any last-minute suggestions to make," she said in very businesslike tones, "you'd better make them now. In twenty seconds I shall be fast asleep."

I watched her in a kind of foggy astonishment, not only because of her complete casualness about her nudity (which I've remarked be-fore), but also the rather startling briskness with which she was get-ting herself to bed. Our preparations for sleep are nearly always preceded, perhaps unconsciously, by a certain languor, a process of slowing down. We yawn, we scratch, we stretch, we move slowly.

"How long do you plan to sleep?" I asked.

"I'll see as I go along," she said, as though certain I would understand what *that* meant. "I may not need too much."

For a couple of seconds she went about calmly adjusting the pillow in a very businesslike way, while I tried not to stare with too much fascination at the enticing movements of her smooth bare body.

It was a little like dreaming a wonderfully real dream in which you are constantly being reassured that the dream is real except some small stubborn part of you keeps telling you very quietly that it's not real.

She turned back the blanket so that the bed seemed to beg with widespread arms. The light in the room was hushed, and the Sunday sounds which did filter through were soft and somnolent. Few things in my whole life seemed to me to have been more enticing than that bed, especially when I was not entirely convinced that she would have pushed me out if I had yielded and slipped in.

"What about you?" she asked.

"Me?" I made what must have seemed a foolish and vague gesture, indicating that I'd find something to sleep on.

I think she understood a little of what I had been feeling, for she moved toward me impulsively and I kissed her in a very brotherly way. She nodded in satisfaction, as though somehow that was what should have been done, crawled in between the sheets and holding the stuff against her cheek, let it spill over her bare throat and breasts, watched me for about three seconds, then shut her eyes and fell fast asleep—just like that.

For a moment I thought of the possibility of going out to look for my Jane and Morescu, but at the very thought of motion every muscle in my body set up such a howl that I gave in, staggered over to an armchair and fell into it.

I remember thinking I was much too tired to sleep, and wondering where Henneman was, and the sheepskin jacket, and how by now the Intelligence arm of every embassy in Paris was probably looking for Jane and Morescu.

I don't remember what woke me. Maybe I'd slept myself out.

It was dark outside as I got up stiffly out of the chair I'd fallen asleep in and staggered over to the bed.

Jane was not in it.

I moved slowly over to the door and peered down into the half-dark salon—only one tiny wall lamp was on but it was enough for me to make out Jane, dressed in an old shirt of mine, the tails of which she'd tied around her middle, and a pair of my trousers in which she lost the lower part of herself, standing hunched over something in the center of the huge room.

When she heard me she jumped a little, then realizing it was I, slumped in relief and came rushing up the stairs to me.

"I've worked out their basic principle," she said excitedly, as we descended. "It's fabulous."

She was fresh as a morning glory and her eyes and whole face were aglow with excitement and triumph. The old electricity was again crackling in the atmosphere.

"Fabulous how?" I asked, trying to shake myself awake.

"Like making an electronic microscope with a piece of glass and a paper box." She took me by the hand, led me quickly to the center of the room and pointed.

I stared.

It took me about six seconds to realize what I was looking at.

It was Elmer.

Our old friend Elmer.

Squatting majestically on my dining table just as he had squatted on Morescu's stone-topped laboratory table.

Elmer looked eager and hopeful and surprisingly prosaic for what was expected of him. Maybe it was because I was so tired but I had the impression Elmer was like a newly opened grocery store which eyes each prospective customer with a look of eager anticipation.

Jane stepped up to Elmer and manipulated things for a couple of minutes more. Then very tenderly she took the stuff and emptied it out of the vacuum-cleaner bag, in which she had apparently put it while I'd been out, and let it slide down into the crystal container.

Elmer was open, ready for business. From now on it was up to the customers.

Jane licked her lips. She was breathless with tension. The first two fingers of each of her hands were tightly crossed.

I'm glad to see they're superstitious in her big advanced world, I said to myself while at the same time I thought with a pang how lovely it would have been to have my Jane here at my side while it was happening.

If it would happen—

She bent over and touched the machine.

"Please work, Elmer," she intoned softly. "Please."

We waited, our eyes fixed on the extraordinary luminescent substance—the stuff.

It lay motionless in the crystal container, not motionless the way an inert, lifeless object would lie, but with a kind of implied agitation, as if it somehow knew how much of our hopes rested on it—and would try hard to make good.

In the darkness the radiance fell over Jane's face like a blush.

I don't know how long we watched it. At first we stood tense, unmoving, then without taking my eyes off the stuff I inched over an armchair for her and a chair for me. We sat in those chairs, hunched forward, straining, peering, hoping.

"I read your autobiographical novel," she said in very low tones. "Do you mind?"

Before I could answer, she went on—

"I wanted to get an impression of life here," she said. "It was the only way I could think of to do it in a hurry. And since you had written it up as a novel, I assumed you wouldn't consider it private."

I tried hurriedly to remember what I had written in the goddam thing, but as always, I drew a big white blank, so I just held my breath and waited.

"Who is your friend?" she whispered. "The atheist."

"That's Wilfred," I said. "I don't know whether he was an atheist or not."

There was a silence. I think we were even breathing quietly.

"I didn't read very far," she said. She was talking with studied casualness. "Didn't you ever meet a girl named Marie-Ange?"

"Yes," I said slowly. "There was a Marie-Ange."

She was looking at me. "Where is she now?" she asked.

"She's dead," I said.

She made a soft "oh" sound of commiseration.

"What did she mean to you?" she asked, after the first shock was over. "Or would you rather not talk about it?"

Surprisingly enough I wanted to talk about it. I told her exactly what had happened between Marie-Ange, Wilfred and me. Before I knew it I was telling her about Mother and Ella and Big Jim. She seemed not surprised by Big Jim, so I assumed that the man who would have been my father in her world had died too. After all, they too had had World War I. I went on to tell her about Wonderful Walter Carr and how Jane's family had been killed. I was just going to tell her about the trouble between Jane and me when I stopped.

A dimple had appeared—a tiny little vortex that seemed to send an impulse which was more like a broad smile, spreading over the surface of the stuff.

At first I didn't realize I had seen it. We had been straining our eyes too long, but I heard her sharp intake of breath and I knew that she had seen it too.

Another dimple appeared. Then another, seeming to dance in joy.

"They've found us," she whispered.

For a second we held on to each other fiercely. Then we broke away and both stared at Elmer numbly. Finally Jane made a gesture, indicating I was to try.

I moved slowly over to Elmer.

I know she didn't realize how desperately she was clinging to my left arm.

I worked the shutter with my right hand.

"Calling LXI London," I dit-dawed. "Calling LXI London," I kept repeating.

Her fingers dug deep into my arm, but you could have stuck knives into me without my knowing it.

I kept on sending urgently. I can't tell you really how long it was before the surface of the stuff suddenly started to dance with impulses and the first message from them came.

"LXI London," came the response. *"Standing by."*

My hands were trembling.

She stood motionless, lost in incredulous wonder.

"Coo," escaped from her.

"What shall I say?" I asked.

She made no response.

"What shall I say?" I repeated. "It's your people! Don't you under-stand?"

She gulped and looked at me without saying anything. I gave her a gentle shake.

"Say," she said to me finally, speaking with difficulty, "say—'This is Jane Bridon-Jack. At 1800 hours Greenwich time this earth, Satur-day, October 19th of this year, I landed on our twin planet, Earth, thus lending substance to the M-B theory of the origin of the earth and the subsequent division into two planets.'"

She said it mechanically, the way children recite a poem they've been forced to learn by heart. I worked frantically trying to keep up with her even though she spoke slowly.

"On the basis of superficial observation," she went on in that same toneless way, "evidence seems to indicate that they are considerably behind us in various phases of scientific and technological development. From the state of the façades of public buildings, and from direct observation of the atmosphere, it is quite evident that coal burning and oil burning and other direct usage of open flames for purposes of heat and energy are still the practice. Vehicles are of internal combustion type using petrol and generally much like ours in design—"

Jane stopped suddenly, for I fell back exhausted. A good thing, too —for LXI was cutting in.

"*Hold it, please,*" LXI dit-dawed. "*Perhaps you do not realize tremendous interest of a world-wide nature generated by your flight. During the first moments your report announcement was flashed to the Prime Minister and to Buckingham Palace.*"

"Coo," she said again.

"*We are now being stormed by an avalanche of questions as to your personal safety,*" the message came. "*Please report on personal position immediately. Standing by.*"

She wet her dry lips. "I am in perfect health," she dictated slowly. "Flight uneventful up until last few seconds when beam was shut off. . . . Voyage need not be in least dangerous if beam is maintained between two points."

"*Have just flashed word of your safety on world broadcast,*" LXI replied. "*Your original report now being analyzed. May interest you that we are transmitting from your family flat in Kensington, so that your family would be among the first to be reassured . . .*"

There was a momentary break then the transmission continued.

"*This is Mother,*" came from LXI.

"Oh, Mother!" she whispered weakly.

"*Can't tell you how delighted your father and I are, and of course your sisters. Do take care of yourself. Is there any danger to you from the inhabitants?*"

She turned and looked at me.

"No," she replied without hesitation, and I transmitted, "No danger whatsoever."

I needn't tell you again that there were long pauses between messages. Each time I finished, I would fall back and try to get rested.

"This is Mundy speaking," came the next message. *"All the sirens in London are going full blast and all the factory whistles. The tugboats on the Thames are tootling, Big Ben is sounding continuously —at least that's what we are told, because one can't tell which is which because every bell in every church seems to be going hard all at once. We are all so very thrilled. Mummy and Daddy hadn't told us that you were leaving even though they knew. Phnee is almost beside herself. She wants you to know how very proud she is . . ."*

Then that message stopped.

The following message came:

"Have asked family and close friends to forgive our interruption. The message of the Prime Minister is now awaited . . ."

There was another pause. She looked at me and again made that slight blowing movement with her lips.

"Coo," she said reeling a little.

Then the message came.

"When the accounts of history are drawn" (I tried to guess whose style that was) *"England, in its exploits of personal intrepidity and exemplary courage, will have a place second to no nation on earth. We are very proud that it was a daughter of this island who first hurtled the distance between ourselves and our sister earth. We are proud that it is in the second Elizabethan Era that these new vistas are disclosed. England congratulates you. We pray that this golden moment will mark the beginning of a great new era of interplanetary peace and abundance."*

Then, without pause, the crystalline substance danced out its continuing message:

"From his residence at No. 10 Downing Street, the Prime Minister of England has just addressed felicitations to Miss Jane Bridon-Jack, the first known human being to fly through space to our sister earth. Messages of congratulations are coming in now from the heads of states. We read now a statement from the President of the United States of America: 'This great deed gives further eloquent testimony as to the correctness of the historic principles by which we have been living in a community of nations. We are proud that part of the great

forces used to achieve this interplanetary voyage was supplied by the United States of America. The people of the United States of America join me in saluting Miss Bridon-Jack and her great courage.'

"We now read the statement of the President of the Union of Socialist Soviet Republics: 'This is a great achievement which will add glory to the name of world science. We join the rest of the peoples of the world in acclaiming the skill and heroism which were necessary to consummate this great victory over the forces of nature. The peoples of the Union of Socialist Soviet Republics pledge themselves to continue all efforts necessary to bring to fruition the glorious promise which is inherent in this victory and which is the culmination of thirty-seven years of peaceful coexistence of all peoples and all societies.'"

There were messages from the heads of China, of India, of France, of Italy, of the United States of Africa (at least that's the way it came over), from various South American Republics, from Australia, New Zealand, from the Scandinavian countries, from Germany. . . .

It was night by this time.

The messages showed no signs of abating.

There was a personal message from Phnee:

"For the first time in history the London Times *has headlines. And* Reynolds News *is printing a full-page picture of you in a bathing costume."*

Jane gasped. "In a bathing costume! Do you think it's appropriate?"

"You'd look good in a bathing suit," I said. "Why not?"

"I wonder which photo it is," Jane worried. "I'd die if it's the one taken at Brighton." She looked over at me. "I wonder if Phnee knows."

"My arm's ready to drop off," I said, "but if you want me to send a message across stellar space asking about what bathing suit you're wearing—"

"Never mind," she said quickly, for another message was coming in.

"Can you give us your judgment as to whether or not others making this flight would expose themselves to any conceivable danger?"

To which Jane replied:

"Have not been able to see very much but my first few contacts with the people of our sister planet make me feel that they are very much like us. I have been treated with great kindness by several people. None of these people knew my identity. Only person to whom I have revealed the truth is a young Canadian journalist now at my side sending these messages. Cannot make any real judgment on possible danger."

The answer came in the form of the following:

"We are not asking for considered judgment. We are asking for your impression, personal feeling."

Jane replied:

"I would think that others like myself will be given unstinted welcome because of advantages we will bring but that is assumption I make on basis of logic."

LXI replied:

"Have you had any opportunity to discover nature of massive bursts of radioactive energy which we have detected emanating from area of sister planet in last few years?"

Jane looked at me questioningly.

I played dumb.

I thought it was a better idea for me to keep my big mouth shut. I had an idea H-bomb explosions would not be too highly regarded. I shrugged helplessly.

Jane replied:

"No. Regret have not been able to determine causes of such bursts."

28.

IN LOOKING over the transcriptions (which of course I kept) I realize that the following then happened.

LXI asked if she had identified the objects which were circling this planet or explained the bip-bip-bip signals which had been received. To which Jane replied that she was sorry, she hadn't.

Of course she had again looked at me hopefully but I wasn't sure what my explaining that they were artificial satellites would get me— and us for that matter—into. So I stayed dummied up.

Then a message came which was obviously in code. It seemed to upset her a great deal—not upset really—affect her personally in a particular way.

She studied the jumbled mess of letters intensely and without even bothering to try to explain to me, wrote out a jumbled sequence of letters. When she'd finished she had a peculiar pleased sort of grim expression as she reread what she'd written, handed me the message to send.

I sent it and during the wait for the reply, stole a quick look at her.

She was obviously reviewing it all in her mind, fighting down some doubts and finally getting herself to the point at which she decided what she had done was fine—sort of spitting on the palms of her hands and saying, "All right. Let's just see what happens now."

Suddenly a very long message came which cut all this play short—

"An extraordinary session of the World Council which has been meeting in anticipation of such a contingency as has now arisen, has agreed unanimously with all nations participating that it is the general sense of the Council that:

1. The character of the peoples of sister planet appears to be of a benign and sympathetic nature.

2. Various delegations of scientists, technicians, artists, are now being formed and will shortly be leaving for the voyage to our sister planet. Unless, after an appropriate interval, we have formal word from you to the contrary, the first delegation will embark. This first delegation will be composed of the following:

(a) Specialists and scientists in the general field who will be able to make a quick estimate of the needs of our sister planet. They will make rapid decisions on the basis of which we will decide if further contact with the sister planet is desirable. If that is found to be the case, the delegations will be organized and sent in order that our sister planet may, as quickly as possible, benefit from such advances in science and technology as are not in their possession.

(b) Specialists who will immediately set about organizing the program which was the primary goal of your flight. Mutually directed satellites will immediately be launched.

(c) Such persons as you have already requested be given the privilege of being among the first delegation.

We will wait here the appropriate length of time for a negative message from you to reach us. You are to send such a message only if you have concrete, positive evidence of danger to the delegations."

The message ended.

She whistled and looked at me in utter dismay.

"It's my responsibility," she said, her voice shaky. "I haven't had a chance to look around. What if something awful were to happen to them? I mean—some of the most important people of our world. What shall I do? What shall I do?"

She wasn't really asking me. She was trying to transform the awful sinking feeling into words—the way we all do.

Then she did a sort of a pivot, stopping only when she was full face with me.

"If there were a reason they shouldn't come," she said, "you'd tell me, wouldn't you?"

"If I knew such a reason," I said.

"You don't know any such reason, do you?" she asked.

"No," I said. "But then I haven't the foggiest idea what dangers are involved in the flight—"

"Forget the flight," she said. "Nobody's worried about that. It's what happens once they get here."

"Here?" I repeated stupidly, stalling.

"We could ask for more time." She suddenly included me in.

"Why no," I said quickly. "Why more time? I can't think of anything bad that could possibly happen to them here."

It was true—in a way. I really couldn't. What I didn't tell her was that I just couldn't think of anything, bad or good, that could happen to them. In fact I couldn't even imagine them here.

"I could look around myself," she said. "Do a bit of quick snooping—"

"That's not what their instructions were." I cut her off. "You were to let them know if you found any concrete evidence of danger. Have you found such evidence?"

The seconds ticked by. Once she walked over to the shutter and actually put her hand on it as though about to send a message, then stopped.

"Don't stop them coming," I said.

She looked at me for a long time.

She sighed, took a deep breath as though having come to some big decision, and once having come to it, felt immensely relieved.

"Of course nothing could happen to them!" she said almost joyously. "It's unthinkable! We'd be bringing you a whole new era—"

I could see her getting set for a yell. I clapped my hand over her mouth just in time.

She smiled sheepishly as if admitting that I'd been right, then made a little gesture, the way you do when something's been irrevocably set.

I sat down.

I was in that state where you're past exhaustion.

She eyed me nervously. "You could go to bed now," she suggested hopefully.

"I wouldn't go to bed now for all the salmon in British Columbia," I said.

I love salmon.

"It'll be quite a while," she said meaningfully.

"I'll wait," I said.

"You'd better not," she said uneasily. "I mean—you've an extraordinary day ahead of you. It'd be best if you were fresh and rested."

"I couldn't go to sleep even if I wanted to," I said.

"Oh," she said eagerly, "I'll help you find your sleep—if that's what's bothering you."

"I'd rather not," I said.

"You'd really best go to sleep," she said. "I want you looking your best."

"Looking my best for what?" I asked.

"By tomorrow the delegation will have arrived," she said. "There'll be ceremonies, there'll be all sorts of official functions, celebrations. This is an historic occasion."

"You're certainly not calming me down," I said.

"What can I do to calm you down?" she asked.

"For one thing," I said, "you could tell me a little bit about your world. You haven't, you know."

She hesitated.

"I'd rather the specialists did," she said uneasily. "I'd rather you had precise descriptions."

"I'd just as soon have imprecise ones," I said.

"I can say this," she said. "Although I really haven't had a chance to see a great deal of your earth, it seems to me we dress and think and feel pretty much alike and that our everyday life is not far removed from yours. Only . . ." and here she couldn't suppress the excitement, "the real difference is that our life is . . . just . . . oh . . . infinitely easier for everybody. Easier and richer and so wonderfully pleasant." She leaned over close to me. "If I promise to tell you all I can the first chance I get, will you go to sleep? It's almost three in the morning."

I looked at my watch. She was right. Also I suddenly realized my shoulders were heavy with exhaustion and it was all I could do not to shut my eyes.

"I'll wake you the moment anything happens," she promised solemnly. When I still hesitated, she added, with a smile, "Cut my throat and hope to die if I don't." And then when I still didn't go, she added to that: "You're worried about Jane, aren't you? Well, don't. We'll take care of her."

What could I do after all that but give in? I dragged myself upstairs, got myself undressed and into bed.

Jane sat on the edge of the bed watching me. Dutifully I shut my eyes, but bright spurts of light kept popping up like corks off champagne bottles—I'd never get to sleep.

"How does it feel to be the first man to talk to a woman from another world?" she asked, in a whisper.

I said it felt good.

"We hold so many firsts," she said, "and most of them will never be recorded. Like for example you're the first man to make love to a woman from another world. And—" She caught herself.

I sat up and looked at her in alarm.

"And what?" I asked frightened.

"Nothing," she said gently, pushing me back on the bed. "Now shut your eyes." I did. "Think of the most beautiful moment in your life," she said softly.

That wasn't hard. It had taken place a few hours before.

I tried to concentrate on what she did because I thought it might come in handy. Vaguely I remember her stroking my eyelids in a curious way and while I was still thinking of the most beautiful moment of my life I felt a profound sensation of tranquillity, of deep repose, and I fell fast asleep.

Very few times in my life have I slept a sleep so deep and so refreshing.

29.

SOMEONE WAS standing over me. It took me a few seconds to remember where I was and what had happened. I opened my eyes slowly and saw that it was Jane bending over me. She was wearing an apron and there was a smell of coffee in the air.

"You'd better get up," she was saying with a gentle kind of urgency.

I pulled myself up to a half-sitting position.

"The delegation's arrived," she said. I realized she was almost breathless with excitement. "They're here now, downstairs in your salon."

I forgot all about the fact that I sleep in my pajama tops only. I was out of that bed in one fell swoop.

"Why didn't you wake me?" I wailed. "You promised."

I started to look for something. I didn't know what it was. She was following me. I hurried toward the door. She barely got there in time to cut me off.

"No!" she said sharply. "Not the way you are." I realized how I was.

"Sorry," I said distractedly. I started to look for something again. "I'm terribly sorry."

"Oh, *I* don't mind," she said, "only there are several women present —for one thing."

"Oh," I said.

"Four women," she said, "although there are only three there now. One left already."

"You should've waked me," I said.

"They came at intervals," she said. "Long intervals, and there was nothing at all unusual about their arrival. In a short while it will become quite banal."

I walked in circles again. She followed me in circles. She was as jumpy as I was.

"Where'd they land?" I asked.

"On your roof," she said. "It's ideal. We'll probably continue to use it—if you've no objections."

I started toward the outside door again. This time she barred it with her body. "You absolutely must put something on. The proceedings are being televised for our world audience."

"What proceedings?" I finally managed to ask.

"The formal greeting," she said.

"Greeting whom?" I asked.

"Greeting you," she said. "Oh, by the way." She drew herself up, doing her best to strike a formal attitude. "I have been instructed to ask your permission that the meeting between you and members of the first group of human beings to fly between the two planets be televised."

I don't know what I said. I made a sound.

She was still following me around.

"What are you looking for?" she asked.

"How the hell do I know?" I replied.

"Probably your drawers," she said.

"That's right," I said.

"Take a shower and shave before you get dressed," she said. "I'd like you to look well and have your wits about you. A cold shower."

"I left them right here on the chair last night," I said.

"The first free moment we have," she said, "I must give you the preliminary instructions in relaxation."

"You don't seem so relaxed yourself," I said.

"I know," she said. "But I'm disorganized in a very unemotional way. It's no strain on me. When you made a sound, did that mean yes, we had your permission to televise?"

"Why me?" I asked. "Why not some other more photogenic native?"

"You *are* the first person of this planet we've come in contact with," she said.

"Why not somebody who'd know how to handle himself in front of a television audience?"

"There's an enormous interest in you," she said hesitantly.

"In *me?*" I asked.

It took her a few seconds to get up enough courage to say what she had to.

"I was on the television during the night while you were asleep," she said. "I told them a bit about you . . . and . . . well, I hope you won't mind, but I read them a few passages from your autobiographical novel."

"How many people did you say were in your TV audience?" I asked.

"About two billion," she said. "Translated simultaneously into some hundred-odd languages."

"What did you read to them?" seemed to emerge from me.

"Bits and pieces," she said. "You and Wilfred. How you were shot down in the war. About Jane. Her family."

"Marie-Ange?" I asked.

She nodded.

Two billion. U. S. A. Greenland. Africa. South America. Just to mention a few that happened to cross the turmoil which was in my mind at the moment.

And Canada.

"And about my uncle?" I asked.

"Yes," she said. "So you can see," she said, "why people are waiting breathlessly to meet you."

I sat down on the bed. My bad leg was bouncing up and down.

"What'll I do?" I asked. "What'll I say?"

"Just be perfectly relaxed," Jane said. "Say whatever comes into your head."

"What if it's something stupid?" I said.

"It won't be," she said. "You know there are no cameras. You'll hardly know you're being televised."

"What if nothing comes into my head?" I asked.

One of the few times in my life I've ever been called upon to make a public utterance was the time they put that plaque up in Wilfred's memory. I hadn't been particularly nervous. At any rate, I'd thought I hadn't. I had even prepared a little speech, something appropriate and meaningless. But when I'd got up, no words had come. I had stood there speechless. I remember the faces waiting sympathetically, encouragingly, then uneasily . . . until finally one of our old high school teachers had risen and spoken simply as if nothing had happened and everyone had breathed in relief.

What if something like that happened? I asked myself.

And if the broadcast were going to their Canada too, the other Big Jim, the other Mother, the other Ella and all the other rest would be listening.

"You'll be wonderful," Jane said worriedly. "I'm sure of it. By the way," she said pointing under the bed, "there are your drawers. You must've kicked them under the bed."

"I distinctly remember putting them on the chair," I said.

"Then I suppose he must have kicked them under the bed," she said.

"He?" I asked, stunned.

"He came. He was practically the very first." She shook her head and whistled.

"What's the matter?" I asked.

"Oh, nothing," she said. "Only you *do* look so much alike. He's here now. Not in the room. In Paris I mean. He borrowed some of your clothes." She gave me ten seconds to absorb that. "Not your drawers of course—"

"That was very thoughtful of him," I said. She handed me my drawers. I didn't take them.

"If I'm to shower I won't need them yet. I may even put on a fresh pair if the mood hits me. Goddam," I said, "why did you have to read excerpts of my life to them?"

"In between arrivals I'd been asked to read something which would give an impression of recent life here," she said. "It was the only thing I could think of. But they loved it. Doesn't that mean anything to you? Two billion people loving it? So anxiously awaiting you now that in those parts of the world where it's night they haven't yet gone to bed. They're waiting for you."

"You're taking a terrible risk with me," I mumbled. "I don't know what'll pop out of my mouth."

"I'm so glad you've agreed," Jane said, jumping to the conclusion that I had agreed—but I didn't contradict her. "It's really not at all difficult. In fact you'll love it once you get into it."

By this time I had gone into the bathroom where I started to brush my teeth. She followed me there too, poking her head around me to get a look at herself in the mirror, touching her hair lightly here and there the way women do.

"Do I look all right?" she asked.

I kept on brushing my teeth but looked up.

She looked scared.

"You look great," I said. "What about Jane?"

"Don't worry about her," she said nervously. "She's fine and Morescu's fine and—"

She sounded like a mother reassuring her child.

"How do you know she's fine?" I asked.

"Because she telephoned," she replied.

"But I wanted to speak to her," I started to protest. "I—"

"It's all right," she said gently. "She thinks she spoke to you. Because *he* spoke to her. We couldn't have taken a chance letting you speak to her on the telephone. You might have given it away and someone might have been listening. We don't want too many on this planet knowing we're here. Not yet. Although of course Jane knows."

"If you didn't tell her on the phone how does she know?" I demanded.

"He told her," she said. "In fact he's with her now. But it's all right. She still thinks it's you—"

"You think *that's* all right?" I growled. "Her out with somebody— thinking it's me—"

"It couldn't be helped," Jane said tensely. "If she realized who he is, she'd ask questions that he could answer and we don't want answered yet. It was simplest for her just to think it was you."

"All right," I agreed reluctantly at last.

"I'm sorry she wasn't here with us for that very first moment of contact between us," Jane said gently. "Although actually it was not really the first and she *was* in on the very first—on Friday—and actually —she's been in on a transmission with us this morning—he and she and Morescu—"

"So she knows?" I asked.

"Oh, yes," she said. "She knows—and don't scowl because this is such a lovely day and you're to meet her at twelve-fifteen at the Deux Magots—and now I absolutely must go back and you must hurry."

I accompanied her to the door. It's a French habit to accompany people to the door. As she started to open it wide, she realized I would be in range. While she waited for me to move out of the sight lines of anyone in the room below, she practiced faces. Having finally found a special, slightly artificial face which she probably figured would be great for television, she went forth. I guess you can't just walk into two billion people without doing a little something to your puss.

I poked my head around the briefly opened door and caught the most fleeting glimpse of several men and women in my salon, but it was only a glimpse.

I had the impression they were like everybody else and that they were walking in circles too. The beings from another world didn't have wires coming out of their heads and they didn't look like cat-people or frog-people or insect-people. They looked like people-people.

I stumbled into the bathroom and shaved as quickly as a man can shave with fingers made of melting snow. Besides, I couldn't find anything. My razor wasn't where I usually put it, my shaving cream tube was topless, and the hand towel, which was moist, had been let fall on a little end table on which I keep my toilet articles.

I found myself getting slightly irritated, especially since I realized he had dropped things and been sloppy in exactly the same way I was; but that was no reason for him to be as untidy in my place. I told myself righteously that if I had landed in *his* apartment, on his planet, I sure as hell would have put the top back on his shaving cream. Of course at the same time I was appalled with myself for being so small-souled at a moment like that. Why couldn't I be of a stature equal to this great moment? I finally answered myself by saying I might as well face it—I wasn't.

When I started to dress I realized that the gray tweed jacket which was missing was exactly the one I would have worn at that particular moment and that he had chosen the very shirt I had sort of half planned on wearing.

The son-of-a-bitch had taken my favorite tie.

We had the same tastes in ties at any rate.

What irritated me even further was the realization that if he had brought clothes of his own, he had preferred mine. The quick glimpse I had had of the others indicated that they had brought their own clothes and were wearing them very nicely.

Maybe he hadn't been certain the cut of his clothes was like ours. I wouldn't know. The only person from the other planet I had met up with had arrived naked.

I had to wait a few seconds before I could pull off a little flake of Kleenex I had put on a cut on my chin to stop the bleeding. It wouldn't do to be televised before two billion people with a piece of Kleenex on your chin. But I kept pulling it off too soon and each time my chin would start bleeding again. Finally I decided to leave it on until I got to the door and to pull it off just before I went down.

I checked myself again in the mirror. Everything tallied. In fact I was all dressed except that I had only one sock on. I took off my shoe and put the other sock on and put the shoe back on. I realized I had put the other sock on inside out but by then I knew that if I didn't get myself to the door right then, I would never get myself to the door.

I tried not to think of over two billion faces glued to their TV screens, waiting for me.

I tried not to think that willy-nilly I was representing our earth and all the people on it. I told myself it was nothing at all if you faced it squarely.

I would go out there and meet some people. It was true that they had flown millions of miles through space but that didn't necessarily mean I had to go to pieces in their presence. I would be simple and dignified and take my time. All I had to do was what one did normally when presented to people. How do you do. *Enchanté*.

As I started toward the door I thought of my Jane and yearned for her. We could have walked down the steps together so easily and in case of emergency she would have simply said, "I'd like two or three minutes please to think that over."

30.

THERE WAS the sound of footsteps on the staircase and I knew I couldn't delay it a second longer. I opened the door.

Jane was waiting for me about three steps down. She was looking toward me (I think anxiously, for she seemed relieved when she saw I had remembered to put my pants on).

"Good morning," she said, enunciating each letter with that precision with which people speak on radio and newsreel interviews.

Six people were waiting below her at the bottom of the staircase, three men and three women. They were dressed pretty much as we dress and they remained looking up toward me without moving. They were studying me with a deep and solemn curiosity.

Dr. Morescu was the first one my eyes lighted on. He looked exactly like our Morescu and to put it the only way I can, even though it may sound a little foolish, there the resemblance ended. Imagine the same man just returned from a wonderful vacation looking so much younger, rested, and freed of cares and coming back brimming with nervous life. That was the difference.

One of the women was tall, gray-haired, with an angular face and a very attractive old-fashioned hairdo. Another was tall, very dark, with jet-black hair, and looked like an Oriental queen. She wore a black sari held together by a simple golden ornament at the waistline, and in her hair was a large golden comb which heightened the queenly effect.

Dr. Whitman and his wife Bunny were there. I recognized them from photographs my Jane had shown me.

And then there was Walter Carr. Wonderful Walter Carr, with the same boundless enthusiasm, energy and gaiety of our Walter—only achieving the same effect with about a third the effort.

They were all looking at me as if I were the most fascinating object they had ever clapped eyes on.

Mrs. Whitman turned away and I lost her for a few seconds; when she returned into my angle of vision she was carrying that bouquet of roses I mentioned very much earlier in the story. Despite the confusion and turmoil inside me, still I noticed those roses. Not that I had any idea of what they really were. It was simply that I knew I'd never seen roses that beautiful before.

Jane and I went down a few steps together, and I could see a tear glistening in her eye. We stopped and Dr. Morescu's hand met mine and held it motionless for a second, as though to fix that image for posterity.

"What a great honor it is to greet you," Dr. Morescu said in French with that soft, rubbing voice of his, "and what a great pleasure."

If only I could have gotten rid of the feeling that my lower jaw was a two-thirds submerged iceberg, I would have been okay. Mother says I invariably get a hangdog look the moment a camera is pointed at me. I made a big effort to brighten up.

"On behalf of the people of our world," Dr. Morescu was saying solemnly, "we salute you. May this mark the moment when a great new era unfolds for our two worlds—an era rich with unlimited promise for the kind of life few men have even dared to dream."

He stopped and obviously waited for me to reply on behalf of this planet.

A crazy voice inside of me was whispering insanely, "Unaccustomed as I am to interplanetary speaking," but I managed to stifle it and mumble something about welcoming them with all my heart and hoping their coming did mean a big change in our planet—we could use some big changes—

Then Morescu introduced me formally to the others.

The tall gray-haired woman turned out to be an astrophysicist, named Anna Soukhanova—and the dark, beautiful one in black and gold was a sociologist. Her name was Anil Sen and she was Indian.

Then Dr. Whitman said, with a touch of Texas in his warm friendly tones, how proud *he* was to be part of this delegation, Walter pumped my hand as if he'd forgotten he was holding it, and Dr. Soukhanova spoke at me for a good three minutes in what I discovered later was Russian, then startled the hell out of me by hugging me frantically.

All Madame Sen did was bow and smile. That's all she had to do. Her smile was dazzling and the bow was breath-taking.

I bowed back.

I remember thinking that their scientists were as photogenic as all get-out and wondered if that hadn't unconsciously influenced their choice for this occasion.

Then Bunny Whitman, whom Morescu had introduced as one of their leading parapsychologists (whatever that meant), came up to me and said that there was so much to be said, she felt that the best and quickest way to say what the people of their planet wanted to say to us was with flowers, and handed me the roses.

I really looked at the roses for the first time. When you see them for yourselves you'll understand what I mean. Even though they look quite like our roses they're infinitely more beautiful than any roses I'd ever seen, and I've seen many in Vancouver where we're sort of famous for our roses. These were a deep vibrant blood red and each petal was formed with a most delicate grace.

I almost went panicky. I was stuck again. You couldn't just say, "Thank you for the lovely flowers."

With two billion people watching you, you should utter only those words which could be carved in stone.

I actually did say, "Thank you for the beautiful flowers."

Jane took the roses out of my hands and put them in a vase which she had set up before in preparation. There was a subtle change in the atmosphere, almost as if putting away the flowers was a pre-arranged cue.

"You'll forgive us if we plunge immediately into the business at hand," Dr. Morescu said, his voice vibrant with excitement. "But time is short. We have come to the conclusion that our presence here can remain undiscovered, if we are very careful, for only a few hours— six or seven at most. That will take us to approximately five o'clock in the afternoon. Even after our presence is known, we could perhaps stretch it another hour, that will make it six o'clock, eighteen hundred hours . . ."

He glanced over at them.

Dr. Soukhanova set her watch. The others were listening intently; they nodded agreement.

"The time is so short and there is so much for us to do," Dr. Morescu said, "that we had hoped, perhaps you might like to help us—that is, if you feel as we do, that the importance of this day supersedes one's normal values—so that one's program might conceivably be disrupted . . ."

My program for that Monday morning had as its chief item an interview with a French-Canadian vaudeville performer who did wonderful imitations of animals and passing trains. I'd heard she was very good.

"I'm entirely at your disposal," I said quickly. "I'll be glad to do anything I can."

"Bravo!" Dr. Morescu exclaimed enthusiastically, and got right to it. "Here in Paris, two of our younger people are already out buying every pertinent magazine and newspaper they can get hold of. The contents of those papers and magazines are being teletransmitted to our people. The seven of us here"—he was now including Jane—"will go out and attempt to gather as much material as is possible in the next few hours, each in his or her special field. At four o'clock, sixteen hundred hours, we will meet again here, if you see no inconvenience in that"—I gestured that I saw no inconvenience in that—"communicate brief résumés of what we have learned to our World Council and by six o'clock, at the latest, I hope they will have been able to make a decision."

"What exactly will your World Council decide?" I asked.

No one answered for a second.

"They will decide," Dr. Whitman said quietly, when it became evident no one else would, "if it is safe and desirable to turn over all our scientific data to the people of your world and to set in motion our interplanetary project."

"What will that depend on?" I asked.

Dr. Whitman made a graceful gesture.

"It will depend simply on the question as to whether or not it would constitute a risk to the security of our world," he said. "If it turns out that you are a very fierce and warlike people"—he smiled as if the possibility were ridiculous—"then of course it would be foolhardy on our part to put in your hands an instrument with which you could easily destroy us."

31.

SEVEN HOURS, I thought. To get past seven hours.

"If the decision is favorable," Dr. Morescu cut in, "we felt perhaps you would like to be the one to announce our arrival to the people of your world. You would probably like to have an international press conference and radio, newsreel and television broadcasts."

Yes, sir.

I would like to.

Very much, to put it mildly.

I said so to them and they smiled. Indulgently, I guess, at my boyish enthusiasm.

I began staging it all in my mind. Henneman, Gomez and the boys. Every major broadcasting chain would want to participate. A continual twenty-four-hour broadcast.

People would go out of their heads for each detail.

How they looked. How they dressed. Maybe an exchange broadcast with the other world. Presenting the two Janes, and my counterpart.

"And then of course," Dr. Morescu said, "we would call for a meeting of responsible authorities from every government for putting into immediate operation the special project which is at the origin of all our activities. I can assure you that it is a project which will bring inestimable advantages not only to our planet but to yours as well."

We would present our Morescu and theirs.

I made a note to ask why it was their world had developed so far ahead of ours. Fascinating round-table discussions. Plans for the new world.

"We didn't know what to expect," Dr. Morescu was saying. "As for example, if it had been decided that we could *not* turn over our scientific secrets to you, it was conceivable we would be held by force, and," he smiled indulgently, "fantastic as it might appear to you, tortured. So, you see, we feel it is important that no one else be told that we have come until we have made sure—"

"You have my word," I said solemnly.

"Good." Dr. Morescu was very relieved. "What we should like to ask you to do for us is to permit yourself to be televised for the normal course of your day. Until four o'clock this afternoon, for example—"

"Televised?" I backed away from them. "Me?"

"We could get an idea of . . . the human side of life here in a way in which it would otherwise be impossible for us," Dr. Whitman said quickly, as though to reassure me. "You meeting people and talking to them without their being conscious that they're being televised."

Two billion people.

And the awful responsibility.

In the next few hours they would decide whether or not it was safe to bring a new era to us—a fabulous golden era. And that decision could depend on interpretations that could be made any number of ways.

The impressions they'd get from following me around for a few hours could be of crucial importance. How people lived. How they thought. What they looked like—

What if I ran into someone who shot off his mouth in a way he shouldn't? Still, if one of the delegation undertook it, it might be worse. Maybe I could steer away from anything that might give a lousy impression. I could feel my clothes sticking to my clammy body.

"I don't see how I'll be able to talk to people without their knowing," I said. "The equipment—"

"The equipment we use for such purposes," Dr. Morescu interjected quickly, "will not be at all apparent to anyone at all. It is a simple device which you will carry in your pocket and which will pinpoint you so that our beam will be able to carry images of you and your immediate environment."

They held their collective breaths and waited for my answer—not just the people in that room but two billion others too.

And being followed like that by a whole planet for every minute from now on. What if I had to go to the can? After all, from then until four in the afternoon.

"You must not worry about anything objectionable going to our people." Mrs. Whitman, the parapsychologist, must have been reading my mind. "We have our monitors in manned satellites who will see to it that anything undesirable is deleted before it reaches a general audience."

There was nothing to do after that but shake my head weakly. I'd take it on.

Apparently very pleased with my decision, they quickly formed a circle about Dr. Morescu and held hurried consultations in clipped, low tones.

All I had to do was keep going until four this afternoon. Only a few hours.

Think of six o'clock, I said to myself. Six o'clock of a Monday afternoon in Paris, France, Eastern Hemisphere, planet Earth. Word of the most fabulous event in the history of mankind would be flashed across our earth and through the echoing skies.

Jane had sidled away from the others and was quietly motioning for me to follow her—then she rushed up the stairs. I glanced around for a second to make sure no one was watching me and hurried after her.

She was not in my bedroom. As I leaned forward she beckoned to me hastily from the bathroom. I hurried in and she shut the door behind us.

"We're not being televised here," she said in low tones.

"I can't go through with this," I said. "The responsibility is too great."

"Face it," she said quickly. "You're not going to be able to hide the truth of your world anyway. You might as well let us see whatever there is to be seen." She watched a couple of seconds until I finally was able to get that down.

"All right?" she asked solicitously.

"More or less," I said weakly.

"Once you get started," she said, "you'll be fine."

"Okay," I said at last.

"Now listen to me," she went on urgently. "You must do something for me. At eleven-thirty you will go to the Café des Deux Magots . . ."

"Deux Magots?" I asked uneasily. "That's where I'm meeting Jane at twelve-fifteen."

"That's why I suggested it," she replied. "But be there at eleven-thirty, that'll give you forty-five minutes." She could talk fast when she had to. "There'll be two of our people there . . ."

She stopped. I waited.

"Who are they?" I asked. "How'll I recognize them? What'll I do with them? What—"

"You'll recognize them," Jane cut me off dryly. "And you'll know what to do."

There were sounds on the stairs. . . . She stopped.

"Jane . . . ?" Dr. Morescu's voice came floating from down below.

"How much can I tell Jane?" I demanded. "How will I know what *he's* said to her?"

"You'll see once you meet her," she said.

"Jane . . . ?" Dr. Morescu's voice was approaching, a little more insistent now.

Well—it was impossible to talk then.

"Coming!" Jane called back.

We could hear his footsteps as he entered the bedroom. Dr. Morescu saw us both leave the bathroom together. I've often wondered what he thought.

"I have something for you," he said to me, as he handed me a little golden vial about the size of a pocket watch.

I held it, fascinated. The moment it touched my hand I knew some of that wonderful stuff was inside of it. I could feel the glow of well-being in my palm. He reached over and pushed a little button and the lid flew open, and I was not wrong.

The vial did hold that radiant luminous substance.

"It's with that our television people will pinpoint you," he said. "It operates only when the lid is open—as now."

Leaving the vial open he dropped it into my pocket.

"It's fully as effective there," he explained, "and will be completely unnoticed." He made an imperative movement. "Some of our people would like to see you below."

We hurried across the bedroom and down the stairs.

A tiny crazy voice which I occasionally hear inside of me was shouting, "We're on the air!"

In the salon, Walter asked me if we had a World Health Organization. I gave him the address of the Paris Office of the W.H.O. and before I left they asked me for about a dozen or so other addresses; as follows:

A library devoted to Yoga, for Mrs. Whitman.

Centers of scientific research for Drs. Whitman, Morescu, and Soukhanova.

A leading market place for Madame Sen. (I shuddered to think what *she* might be going to investigate, but apparently they had it all planned and knew very well what they were doing.) I finally gave her directions, reluctantly, for the Flea Market, which in case you've never been to Paris, is the world-famous junk yard, antique shop, bargain counter, that stretches over several acres of very squalid Parisian landscape (which I understand the Parisian city fathers are in the process of redoing). It is hardly the sort of thing I would have chosen for two billion aunts, uncles, cousins, visiting from another planet, as their first glimpse of us.

They also asked for the names of the leading political parties of France, England, Germany, Italy, Spain and the Scandinavian countries; also the names of the newspapers associated with these political parties.

Just before I took leave of them I stopped. They all turned, the Whitmans, Carr, Madame Sen, Doctor Soukhanova and Doctor Morescu, and smiled at me, but I knew from their manner that I certainly had not underestimated the importance of what they had described as a "normal day."

At the door, Jane squeezed my arm in the same way our Group Commander had squeezed my arm the day Wilfred and I had looked up at the bulletin board and realized that he and I were the only ones left alive of our original squadron.

32.

I DECIDED to walk down the seven flights. Slowly. So for a few minutes the television audience would see only bare steps and bare walls.
But I needed time to think, to plan my "normal" day.

I couldn't let them get the idea that our world was a poor and dirty
place and that we were a harried people. As a matter of fact, it happens that I don't think our world is poor or dirty, even though I
might have to concede that, at the moment, we are more or less harried.

What would I do? Where would I go? What could I afford to show
them?

I walked down those seven flights slowly, knowing it was dead time
but figuring the hell with it. I needed an idea.

Desperately.

One thing was sure. I wasn't going to interview that French-Canadian vaudevillian. Bird calls and imitations of trains.

The thing for me to do, I decided, was to avoid the ugly sections
of Paris. Also to avoid people with extreme opinions.

The vial was open in my pocket, and I imagined I could physically
feel the beam following me.

Mme. Fénelon was waiting in ambush for me in the hallway on
the ground floor. Her cat Pompier was twitching his tail nervously,
which is always a reasonably good sign his mistress is disturbed.

I bowed very formally and walked quickly, hoping to sneak past.
She was another one it would be wise to avoid.

"I have had a very strange morning," she said, keeping in step with
me perfectly. I'll bet somewhere in her past she'd had military training.

"Strange mornings happen to everyone," I said with sententious
good cheer, increasing my pace.

"Numerous people have descended and passed my door," she went
on. "People of whom I have no recollection whatsoever of their having mounted."

She made it sound like the end of the world.

"Perhaps they came in the night," I suggested. I too was enunciating each letter clearly for the purposes of the television audience.

"I remark every individual who passes my door in the night," Mme. Fénelon said with hurt pride. (Although she exaggerated a little, it was by and large true.)

"Perhaps you are sleeping more soundly," I said, near the outside door by then. "At any rate I have noticed that you are looking very much better these days."

It only half mollified her.

"The worst of it is," she said, "that I could swear that you passed this morning at a very early hour and did not return."

"You would be half right," I couldn't resist telling her.

The innuendo was lost on her as she wound Pompier's tail around her finger. "It is not at all normal," she said, "seven or eight people going by without my noticing."

There had been only three. The other me and the two people I was to meet at the Deux Magots.

So that's how this story will be blown up later.

As I made it to the street I wondered how anyone could blow this story up beyond the size it already had.

It was a beautiful day for televising, I realized miserably as I got into my car. I'd hate to tell you how many days a year the sun doesn't shine in Paris, but of course that morning it was out full blast, pouring light on the wonderful old façades so you couldn't help seeing how black and grimy they were.

Goddamn it, I thought, why don't we wash our bloody buildings once in a while? (I stopped thinking of myself as Canadian and "them" as French. It suddenly became "our" world.)

I started the car slowly. Where to take two billion fascinated people on a selected tour of Paris by day?

Suddenly an idea hit me.

I would take my two billion guests for what my friend Art Buchwald calls "the Quick Louvre." An hour and a half spent with the accumulated treasures of centuries. Especially designed for visitors for whom you have a sort of second-cousin obligation. You have to make them think they've seen everything. Throw one masterpiece after another at them until they're groggy.

And what a wonderful place not to meet the wrong people.

Or so I thought—

Of course people might conceivably wonder if a normal day in a reporter's life would include a visit to the Louvre.

In between fighting my way through the belligerent Paris traffic, I thought up a story, so that when I got inside the building, I explained carefully to the museum guard who took my fifty francs that I was a journalist and there to do a story on the "Mona Lisa," which had been slightly injured by some lunatic who had thrown a stone at it. Funny how in my head it had seemed so right, but once I said it aloud I could have bitten my tongue off.

Fine impression to give two billion people. Lunatics throwing stones at masterpieces! I tried to gloss it over by saying that of course this was the first time in the history of the Louvre that anything like that had happened.

The guard replied sourly that he wished he had a thousand francs for every time there had been an incident like that. That's why the Louvre had to have practically one guard for every masterpiece.

Nervously I limped my way up the lovely soaring staircase. I stopped at the second landing to rest and to let the television audience appreciate fully what a breath-taking setting the endless flight of stairs makes for that lovely statue "Nike, the Victory of Samothrace."

All at once I felt somebody standing very close.

I turned.

It was Izzy Gomez.

"What the hell are you doing in the Louvre on a Monday morning?" Izzy asked in his shrill voice. "Don't tell me you've got the same stupid idea for a story as I have?"

I thought of just walking away from him. Whatever his idea was, I was sure it wasn't good for our side at that moment.

I told him I was doing an art piece. My readers had become interested in art. Mercifully, Izzy let that one go by.

"They've named one of the American rockets Nike," he insisted on explaining. "The Headless Victory. Get it?" He looked up at the statue with paternal pride. "Do you think the first person who ever named the statue would have thought that one day they would name a big bullet after her?"

I tried to steer Izzy off onto something safer, but Izzy wouldn't be steered. He was going to do a story about the ancient gods and mas-

terpieces after whom arms were being named, how people had taken
to naming rockets and missiles Thor and Jupiter.

Well—I couldn't shake him off and he accompanied me on a tour
of the great paintings. I made earnest comments about how wonderful
it was that the Louvre attracted so many hundreds of thousands of
people from all over the world. I don't know whether Izzy had his
ear piece turned off, or whether he did it deliberately. He kept com-
menting on how many of the canvases had to do with torture or death.

It *is* surprising, when you look at it that way, how much war,
crucifixion, beheading, burning and assorted tearing people to pieces
do go on in the masterpieces stored in that great museum. Izzy, of
course, made it sound as though not only had our immediate past
been one of unmitigated horror and bloodshed, but that our present
wasn't much more promising. He was jotting down names of paintings
which he would suggest to our arms progress people for what he kept
calling "bullets of the future." By the time I fled from him and the
Louvre, I was practically a nervous wreck.

The Rue de Rivoli is admittedly one of the most beautiful streets
in the world, with its mile or so of lovely old arcades, the elegant shop
windows, the surprising squares that suddenly emerge at each cross-
ing. But a man can't keep walking two billion people up and down
even that street for more than half an hour without giving rise to some
kind of suspicion.

I drifted off the Rue de Rivoli and in the direction of Les Halles,
which Zola had called "the belly of Paris." I finally decided what the
hell, I might as well go there. It's colorful and absorbing. Besides, it
was nearby.

Well—

The sidewalks around Les Halles were dotted with what at first
looked like bundles of rags but turned out to be the *clochards* or
tramps of both sexes who sleep over the subway grates where a bit of
fetid hot air from the Métro below gives them a warm spot.

I almost stumbled over a couple of them in order to avoid several
others who once upon a time must have been women. They all insisted
on coming up close (so close that I'm sure the other-world audience
got nice clear close-ups) with their streaked eyes and bleary faces,
scratching, grunting, hacking, growling at me and each other and
swigging cheap wine out of filthy bottles.

I staggered out of their way and smack into the Street of the Innocents. I didn't know that at that hour the street is lined with eager prostitutes in full regalia and fuller voice.

These particular prostitutes, for some reason or other, dress so as to look exactly like the women in the posters which used to be placed by the Ministry of Health in all the men's lavatories in Vancouver, with legends like: *Beware of Her—The Easy Woman*—with blazing hair and scarlet lips, short, seam-busting tight skirts and a décolletage that went plunging all the way down to hell and gone and back again.

The moment they saw me (I guess I was better dressed than their usual targets) they began to hawk their wares in a kind of chant, the way the street merchants sold their vegetables—and when I skittered away from them in horror, they set up such a clamor of catcalls and wolf whistles as not only to make me look like a prize fool, but to cause two roving French cops to come running and to watch me with a jaundiced eye, as though I'd done something wrong.

There couldn't have been any doubt in the minds of any audience, whether it was Lapland or Hottentot, what the girls had called out. I could only hope that Mrs. Whitman's monitors, sitting on their manned satellites somewhere in space, were quick enough on the draw to censor out a lot of that dialogue.

I was half running and didn't realize I had hit the flower market until I was in it for a few seconds.

That is breath-takingly beautiful—acres of flowers of every description arranged as only generations of working with flower arrangement could have brought about—sidewalks, stalls, trucks, ledges festooned with greens, purples, whites, scarlets—as far as you could see and smell.

I walked slowly now. A very pretty girl tried to sell me a rhododendron plant which she said had taken eight years to grow. I told her she ought to come where I lived; rhododendrons grew wild and at this time of the year covered the mountainsides. She said she would love to come some day, and would I buy the plant anyway?

I was just beginning to relax and get hopeful and to think that, thank God, at last I had found something of beauty and charm to show what I was now numbly thinking of as "my" audience. I decided to buy the plant and was about to hand the girl the money when two women and a man who had been watching from the next stall almost fell on the girl and me because she was selling flowers at an hour reserved for wholesale buyers and was therefore ruining their business.

A policeman appeared and it was all I could do to persuade him not to give a ticket to the pretty girl, who was by now in tears.

Shattered, I went back to my car.

33.

IT WAS eleven-fifteen. I drove shakily over to the Left Bank.

Always before, the Boulevard Saint-Germain had appeared to me to be very attractive as boulevards go, but this time it seemed just about the most broken-down boulevard a man could imagine; black, scraggy and with a particularly ugly Monday morning sheen.

I parked the car and hurried out, sneaking past the *pissoires* hoping they'd be unnoticed and wondering if in the other Paris they had abolished them. I've never been particularly ashamed of them before, but now they seemed disgraceful.

In the background the air felt thick with poisonous gases of automobile exhausts. It seemed to me I'd never in my whole life seen a seedier-looking bunch of people than those who had crawled out of their holes at that very moment to be displayed to our sister earthlings.

I tried telling myself that I was taking an overly pessimistic attitude. After all, this was one of the most famous boulevards in the world. Lenin had played chess in that café. Anatole France had walked these streets dreaming up his beautiful works. Picasso loved this area. Millions loved this area. Sartre came here frequently, in fact lived around the corner. Asa Cubit had his studio in the lovely Place Furstemberg right over Delacroix's atelier.

It really doesn't do much good talking to yourself. At least that's been my experience. By the time I got to the Deux Magots, I was in that state of agitation in which you tell yourself you are very calm when in reality you will settle for just not falling over a chair or bumping into a lamppost.

You may understand therefore why it was that I had almost forgotten that the other Jane had asked me to come here; I had forgotten, too, to wonder why she had made so much mystery about whom I would meet.

I scanned the faces of the *habitués* of the Deux Magots carefully, really not seeing anyone on the first time around—just blobs of faces. The second time around some of them came into focus. There was the usual assortment of artists, students, snobs and ordinary people from the *quartier* stopping in for a pre-lunch *apéritif*. Even that early in the day the café was thick with bluish cigarette smoke.

I was calm enough to recognize Asa Cubit over in one corner with his sculptor friend Chaiman. We waved to each other. Whatever else I did, I knew I had better avoid Asa and his radioactive desolation.

Even after I had covered the faces a second time, I didn't realize what I had seen.

What made me notice them was the fact that they had seen me and had half risen and were watching me. That posture was so odd that many others in the café noticed them too.

For a moment I stood rooted where I was.

Wilfred MacIntosh and Marie-Ange were standing a few feet from me.

I looked over at the others several times before I could get myself to believe what I was seeing. It was as though the faces of Asa and his friend and the rest whom I had seen before served as points of contact with reality.

Only then did I look back again.

It *was* Wilfred. And Marie-Ange was at his side. There was no mistaking it. It was they. I would have recognized them anywhere.

He had grown heavier. His eyes still had that confident yet perennially restless look and his face was flushed with excitement. I moved toward them slowly, almost painfully. In a moment they would fade away. But they didn't. They were there. They kept on being there through the frantic pounding of my heartbeat on my ear drums.

Marie-Ange was beautiful in the way many young French matrons are beautiful, with a subtly provocative sexuality.

I stopped in front of them. We touched hands—she and I—and at the touch of her fingers I tried not to think of the two little graves in Saint-Malo.

I shook hands with Wilfred and felt the vibrant pulse of his life, and the warmth of his friendship. I tried not to think that all that was left of him was a little bronze plaque on the walls of the hallway in Britannia High School in Vancouver.

Wilfred and I held our hands that way, gripping each other fiercely as if trying to communicate something much beyond words. Then the three of us sat down and looked at each other.

It was all right with me just to sit and look at them.

Just to watch them breathe and move and smile. To watch Wilfred fill his pipe exactly the way he used to, with his thumb pressing the tobacco down, crushing it into the bowl, and to realize it was a pipe exactly like the one I had bought him at Con Jones's Good Tobacco Shop in Vancouver before we'd gone to see all the big cities while they still stood.

To watch her, to feel the warm aura of her womanhood and to be reminded with each gesture and movement of the simple miraculous fact of being human beings and being alive.

After a while I realized with a shock that I'd been holding her hand all this time, even while shaking hands with Wilfred, even while we sat ourselves down. I let go and kept staring at the table top, then glanced over at them and realized that Marie-Ange had been keenly aware that I had been holding her hand, but that Wilfred was elaborately pretending not to have noticed it.

The waiter came and I ordered three coffees: black for Marie-Ange and half-milk half-coffee for Wilfred, the way they always had had it.

After the waiter left, Wilfred leaned over and said, "Do you realize how much that waiter makes a month?" Those were the first words we said to each other. Marie-Ange shot Wilfred a look, which he missed, and I had to blink to keep the tears from gathering in my eyes, because—other world or our world—it was still the same old Wilfred.

"With tips," Wilfred said excitedly, "forty thousand francs a month. At the current rate of exchange less than a hundred Canadian dollars. Now I've looked into the cost of living here a bit. Do you realize what that means?"

He slowly became aware that Marie-Ange was glaring at him.

"Sorry," he said shamefacedly, avoiding Marie-Ange's eyes.

"That's all right," I said. "Go ahead."

I wanted him to talk, I wanted to keep watching him, listening to him.

"Well no," Wilfred said, but he still couldn't help going on. "It means for himself and his wife and three children a rather . . . gray life."

"I don't think that that is why we three meet here now," Marie-Ange said softly in English and mostly to Wilfred.

"I suppose not," said Wilfred, "only I thought under the circumstances it would be fairly interesting to—" He gave up with a shrug and flashed that grin of his at me.

I thought, Wilfred is losing his hair. If you looked very closely you could notice it.

"Where are you living?" I asked Wilfred.

"In London," he replied eagerly.

"Do you get home much?" I asked.

"Once or twice a week," he replied casually.

I looked at him in astonishment. "I mean to Vancouver," I said.

"So do I," Wilfred replied. Then he realized what the trouble was. "But I've forgotten. You're a bit—behind the times in the way you travel." He leaned toward me again. "Do you realize what an incredible waste your means of transportation represent?"

He caught himself without any outside prompting from Marie-Ange that time.

"Sorry," he said. This time he looked really apologetic.

"Your Vancouver as wet as our Vancouver?" I asked.

"It's pretty wet," Wilfred said ruefully. "We haven't been able to lick that yet. But that's one of the main reasons we're here."

I guess I must have looked blanker than usual.

"Haven't they told you about the project?" Wilfred asked.

"No," I said.

"The project is climate control," Wilfred said. "Using the two planets we will be able to arrange for exactly the kind of climate on any given spot of each planet—" He looked up at me. "Imagine what London would be like with a subtropical Mediterranean climate?"

London—warm—balmy—azure-skied, or Paris—or New York—or even Vancouver—

People emerging out of the gray damp— But Wilfred didn't give me a full chance to linger.

"It would change every level of living," Wilfred went on. I remembered also how he used to irritate the pants off me by insisting on spelling everything out so literally.

"I can hardly wait for the climate control to happen to London,"

Marie-Ange said. There was an intense kind of nervous impatience about her, and when I apparently looked puzzled about her reference to London she added quickly, "I'm living in London, too, you know."

"I didn't know," I said.

She looked at me for a second and then, it seemed to me, she got even more tense than before.

"Then you didn't know Wilfred and I are married," she said.

34.

"IN FACT," Wilfred said, and despite all the other feelings I was having, I remember thinking that his tone was not exactly right—a shade too assertive, "we have two children. Girls."

There was a silence of several seconds as I absorbed *that*. I would never have imagined it working out that way. I tried quickly to reconstruct it but couldn't. Something was wrong. They were embarrassed and uneasy.

"You brought their photos?" Marie-Ange asked Wilfred.

"Well, no," he said a little defensively. "We were told to bring only that which was most essential."

"You don't consider the photos of your daughters essential?" Marie-Ange asked. Although there was ostensible humor in her tones, there was also a slight cutting edge.

"We'll have some photos sent," Wilfred said. "If things go well."

There was another heavy pause.

"What do you do?" I asked Wilfred when it got too heavy.

"I teach at the university," Wilfred said.

"He's a full professor," Marie-Ange said. It seemed to me she was making a special effort to be proud of him, a little too much of an effort. "And at his age it is unusual."

"I give a course in 'Contemporary Thought and Culture,'" Wilfred said hastily, as if aware of the slightly inappropriate nuance in her tones.

"And he's written a beautiful book," Marie-Ange said. "Both the

New Statesman and the London *Times* said it was one of the most important books of our times."

Wilfred made a gesture of embarrassment.

"I'll ask for a copy to be sent with the photos," Wilfred said, "if you like—"

I couldn't speak. I could only nod. That's what our world lost, I thought, when that piece of flak hit Wilfred and that bomb fragment tore into Marie-Ange's young body.

A beautiful woman and a beautiful man and two lovely children.

And a book which both the *New Statesman* and *The Times* had said was one of the most important books of our times.

Now Wilfred and Marie-Ange were letting the initiative go to me.

"How is Tou-tou?" I asked at last.

Marie-Ange flashed me a tender smile.

"Nobody's called her Tou-tou for years," she said. "Tou-tou is now at the Conservatoire d'Art Dramatique—in Paris. She is quite a young woman. She wishes to be an actress."

The Conservatoire is right around the corner from where Izzy and I have our office. Every day I see a flock of moonstruck aspiring adolescents make their entrance into the lofty halls of the drama school.

I would have seen Tou-tou of a morning. Every once in a while, during a break, perhaps, I would have invited her to a nearby café to have a nonalcoholic *apéritif* with me, or maybe even a glass of white wine. She would have told me about a tryout for some play, how she was trying to get into the Théâtre National or the Comédie Française. Or maybe her boy friend would be skulking in the background in lofty adolescent impatience and she would have sipped her drink hurriedly and rushed off to him.

"We heard last night what happened to *your* Marie-Ange," she said very softly. "I am so sorry."

It was at this point that I suddenly remembered all this was going on the air. I'll bet if you looked hard you couldn't find another person anywhere who could have forgotten an audience of a couple of billion people.

I pulled the vial out of my pocket hastily and made a frantic dumb show to them both, indicating that it was open and that we were on.

Neither Marie-Ange nor Wilfred seemed particularly surprised and they looked at each other as though a problem which they had been aware of before and hadn't faced up to had suddenly become un-avoidable.

They waited for a few seconds. I had the impression each was wait-ing for the other to do something. Finally Marie-Ange reached over, took the vial from my hand and transferred it to Wilfred.

He looked at her in perplexity.

"I'm not sure I understand what you mean by shutting that off," Wilfred said very carefully.

"I would never have been chosen for this first delegation," she said pointedly. "I was permitted to come only because I was asked for." She looked over at me as if I would understand. "It was a matter of personal privilege. They must have understood that personal matters would be discussed."

Wilfred took a long time to think about that.

"That does seem implicit," he said slowly, "in what has taken place." He looked over at her steadily. "You don't think I might conceivably be included in that discussion?"

"No," she said at last.

Wilfred winced and got up. Heavily, with effort.

"It all happened so long ago," Wilfred said. "I'm like most civi-lized governments. Statute of limitations. I forgive anything that hap-pened over seven years ago."

Marie-Ange shot him what was in anybody's planet a very dirty look, but immediately covered it with an artificial smile.

"It hasn't occurred to you," she said with dangerous gentleness, "that perhaps it is not because of *you* I wish to discuss this alone?"

I started to protest but she stopped me with an imperative gesture. Besides, I really didn't know what they were talking about.

This time Wilfred definitely stood up.

"That's Asa Cubit over there," Marie-Ange said quietly. "I'm sure our people would be fascinated by a conversation with him . . ."

"Wait a minute," I said. I've already indicated that of the people I didn't want on the television screens of our sister planet, Asa was high on the list. "You don't know him and—"

"*You* do," Wilfred said gently. "I'll tell him I'm a friend of yours. Besides, it *will* be fascinating to exchange a few ideas with Asa. He's one of our most admired and respected artists."

"Well, he's not very well known here, yet," I said, still trying to stop Wilfred, "and it's possible he's nowhere as interesting as your Asa—"

"Then you ought to buy as many of his paintings as you can," Wilfred said quietly. "Eventually they'll be enormously valuable."

His tones were not quite friendly but when I looked up at him I saw that he hadn't really meant to hurt me. He was frightened. Badly frightened.

"How long will you need?" Wilfred asked quietly.

"Five minutes," Marie-Ange said quickly. "Ten—at the most."

Wilfred nodded. "Ten—at the most," he said and started off.

I watched Wilfred anxiously as he crossed. If only he didn't get Asa started on his radioactive-proof mobile grave markers—

Marie-Ange's forefinger was nervously making some kind of an invisible doodle on the table top. She waited no longer than the barest decent minimum; that is, only until Wilfred had just gotten out of earshot.

"All right," she said in French, and with the directness and bluntness of a woman who has never made any bones about her real feelings, "we are no longer being televised. Now we can talk."

Maybe it was the French, or the husky, subdued tone of her voice, but whatever it was, there was a sudden crackling excitement in the air. In the midst of all that tension, with a few words, she had been able to make me feel we were alone—just she and I.

"I'm sorry," I stuttered, "but I don't really know what this is all about."

"There are things you want to say to me," she said.

"Well, yes," I said, "only I would have liked to have said them to Wilfred too. I mean I would have liked to talk to you both."

She was very upset and, I think, frightened.

"Why did you ask I be sent on this delegation?" she asked.

"But I didn't ask," I said.

She looked at me incredulously.

"It could only have been you," she said, even more upset.

"I had no idea people could be asked for," I said. "Maybe if I'd known, I would have asked for Wilfred and you."

She was stunned. She looked over at Wilfred who was by now in a deep conversation with Asa. I shuddered a little. From the look of Asa I could have sworn he was off on his radioactive-proof tombstones.

Suddenly Marie-Ange leaned over very, very close to me, so close that without realizing what I was doing I cast a worried look over at Wilfred, concerned as to how it would look to him. Wilfred had seen her move toward me, and it seemed to me that it *had* worried him.

"Now listen to me," she said impatiently. I was, of course, listening with everything I had. "How did you feel when you first heard—your Marie-Ange—had been killed?"

I was surprised how painful it still was.

"I couldn't believe it," I said, "when I looked at the tombstone. I wanted her to be alive. It seemed wrong that she wasn't . . ."

"Yes, yes," Marie-Ange was caught in some kind of excitement now. "You came back to Saint-Malo for her." Suddenly she took my hand and held it openly on the table. This time I didn't even turn to worry how it would look to Wilfred. I was caught in the excitement too. "Now tell me," she went on quickly, "if she'd been alive—that day in Saint-Malo when you'd gone up—what would have happened?"

"I don't know," I said slowly. "I really don't know."

She was getting at something. Maybe somewhere inside of me I knew what it was.

If I did, I didn't want her to say it out loud because of Wilfred.

Marie-Ange had very long lashes and I found myself remembering how when I had held her close to me, I had leaned over and blown softly on her lashes.

"He and I too first met on the beach at Saint-Malo," she said softly (it took me a second to realize that the "he" she was talking about was the other "me"), "and although we had no war . . . he too went away. Then too, it was almost six years later before he came back." She looked up at me, her eyes sad. "Now I shall tell you what would have happened if you had found Marie-Ange . . . alive." She waited a second, recalling the moment wistfully. "On the beach during one of the fabulous low tides—she would have seen you—almost a kilometer away. Not believing at first, then dropping the shellfish she'd been collecting she would have run, then as she would have seen it was really you—would have given a cry. She would have fallen in your arms and not cared who was watching, and you would have been very happy. And in the evening you would have walked on the great walls of Saint-Malo, and found the same enchanted corner—" She suddenly stopped and looked up at me. "Do you understand what I am saying to you?"

"Yes," I said.

"You would have gone up for weekends to Saint-Malo after that," she whispered with intense rapid rhythm, as though we had only a few seconds left, and it was of the utmost importance she tell me the rest, "and you would have asked her to come to Paris where you were working for your uncle, to live with you. . . . And she would have come."

It was as though I was hearing a description of a part of my life that in a way, somewhere, I had lived.

"And you would have been very happy together, until that day Jane came to Paris," her voice suddenly going flat, "and you had that violent quarrel and Marie-Ange left you, and because Wilfred was nearby (he was always nearby) . . . at that very moment she would have married Wilfred." She lifted her lashes, unveiling the full beauty of her eyes. "Only deep down in her heart throughout all these years, Marie-Ange would have known she should never have left you."

Why was she telling me this? I asked myself in panic. Was it because she had a deep need to let it out, to tell someone, and that I was better than most? Almost as good as the original—or . . . ?

She was waiting again for me to say something.

On the other side of the room Wilfred had gotten to his feet and was looking at us, as were Asa and Chaiman.

"I've got to tell you something," I heard myself say frantically. "I didn't come back to Saint-Malo just to see Marie-Ange."

"I don't understand," she said almost inaudibly. "Then why did you come back?"

I didn't want to go back over those years. I didn't want to take that awful train ride on the *rapide* between Paris and Saint-Malo, but now it was my turn.

"Marie-Ange," I said. "Marie-Ange. Listen. I'd been sent on a bombing mission . . ." I think she barely heard me. "Over Saint-Malo . . ."

She made a sound of horror.

"You?" she asked in a whisper. "You bombed Saint-Malo?" She looked around the way people in shock do. "I knew there . . . there was a war. But I thought . . . France and England . . . I . . ."

"The Germans were there," I said desperately. "We were going to invade. . . . We had to—bomb." She sat there looking at me with stricken eyes. "Marie-Ange!" I said. "Marie-Ange!"

For a long moment she didn't say anything or move.

"You might as well tell me," she said woodenly. "Was it one of your bombs?"

"No," I said. "No. The day . . . the day she was killed . . . I was in an English hospital . . . I saw the date on her tombstone . . . I . . ."

"You went back only for that," she said. "To make sure it hadn't been your bomb."

In a moment Wilfred would come.

I didn't know then what I wanted. I only knew that there was a burning anguish deep in my heart, and that somehow this lovely woman who could not bear to look at me, and who was sitting opposite me, could smooth away that pain, and that I couldn't let her go until she had.

"You must forgive me," she was saying, without any particular feeling, "but this war of yours is so difficult for me to grasp, so cruel."

"You've got to understand," I said frantically.

Her face was still blank.

Wilfred was now saying good-by hastily to Asa and Chaiman and craning his neck to look at something on the street.

"What is it you want me to understand?" Marie-Ange asked numbly.

I never did get a chance to tell her.

Wilfred had come up and stood looking at us both and I could see he was scared, and I realized we were on the air again.

"I think I saw Jane outside," he said.

"Which Jane?" I asked tensely.

"I couldn't tell," Wilfred said. "It was a quick glimpse. She was riding in one of your taxi cabs . . ."

If it was the other Jane, then something had happened. The other Jane wouldn't have come unless there was some sort of an emergency.

I started toward the door.

"She knows we are here," Marie-Ange stopped me. Her voice was calm, tired. "She may not want to be seen on the street with you. Perhaps it would be better if we were to wait here and pretend not to be expecting anyone."

I figured Marie-Ange must have had some special reason for suggesting that course of action, so I sat down and tried not to look at the street, and tried not to be aware of the awkward silence which set in.

We waited.

"I had a very interesting conversation with the noted artist Asa Cubit," Wilfred said, the way you would cover a moment of dead air —or open an educational television program. For a moment that pulled my attention away from any other preoccupations as I took time off, inside of me, to hold my breath and hope that Asa hadn't been *too* interesting.

"What did you talk about?" I asked tensely.

"We exchanged ideas on the relationship between beauty and utility," Wilfred said. "I mentioned to him the problem posed by the ordinary milk bottle when considered in relation to a Grecian urn—" He stopped suddenly. "What's the matter?" he asked with concern.

It was a second or two before I could answer.

"Nothing," I said. I know my voice was thick. "You still discussing that problem?"

"It's the most controversial issue of our time," Wilfred said. "And some of our most bitter arguments have developed over that very question. Special delegations have been sent to our UNESCO and have been hotly debating their points of view. Personally I feel that—"

"Please," Marie-Ange said in almost inaudible tones.

"Sorry," Wilfred said and stopped, the animation fading from his face. "Only look . . ." He pointed at Marie-Ange whose forefinger was moving nervously on the table top. "Watch her finger." We did. Marie-Ange completed the movement before she consciously arrested it. "She's been doodling a Grecian urn. She's been doing it for years."

Marie-Ange *had* been doodling a simplified version of what surely could have been taken for a Grecian urn. She was startled by the realization that this was what she had been doing for years. Then something must have caught her attention, for I saw her stiffen. Jane was standing in the doorway.

She was wearing the blue dress, so it could only have been their Jane.

35.

SHE SAW us, made a very discreet movement to indicate she had seen us, turned slowly, and with elaborate casualness looked behind her, then came walking toward us.

Marie-Ange nodded to her and there was a very definite nuance of unfriendliness in the greeting. Jane flashed a quick worried smile at Wilfred, who returned a smile which, like everything Wilfred did, was exactly what it was intended to be with nothing hidden—warm, friendly, glad. Then she sat down, very near me, so near that I had the feeling she was asking me to protect her from something.

"The police have gone over Morescu's villa," she said, speaking in a very conversational manner as though wanting to impress anyone who might be watching that whatever it was she was saying was only of casual importance. "They came with a search warrant and I've been followed by what I assume are police. It's important that I manage to elude them. I can't be interrogated. Whoever they are—they're outside waiting."

I glanced at the clock.

"My Jane will be coming in a few minutes," I said. "Maybe she and I could lead the police away from you."

"That's exactly what I was thinking," Jane said.

Marie-Ange was watching her with open interest.

"There was a cable for you," Jane said to me, "from Canada. The post office phoned it in. I took the call and although the pronunciation was almost impossible, I'm sure I got it right."

I braced myself. I'm still sufficiently the small-town boy to believe that a cable can only mean bad news.

Who could it be? Mother? Big Jim? My sister Ella?

"It's from your Uncle Debret," Jane said. "It reads: 'Arriving Orly fourteen hundred hours twenty Flight 614 Trans-Northern Airlines. Meet me. Regards Debret.'"

Debret!

Why was he coming at this very moment? Someone must have asked him to come. Someone very influential. And that someone had convinced him it was of sufficient importance for him to drop anything he was up to at the moment and fly over. Which in turn meant that behind the surface, ostensibly so tranquil, many unseen figures were moving, moving fast and knowing what they were doing and what they wanted.

I looked around. It all seemed the same. No one seemed to be paying any particular attention to us.

"Uncle Debret will have to come in alone," I said, shaken. To tell you the truth, I was terrified of meeting him at that moment. "I can't take time off to meet him now. Afterwards, I'll pop over to his hotel. I'll—"

"You won't be able to pop over to his hotel," she pointed out, cutting me off. "You don't know which hotel he'll be in."

"He'll call me," I said desperately.

"We'd rather he didn't call your flat," Jane said. "It would be much better if you and Jane took him to his hotel."

I didn't want Debret and Jane to meet. I couldn't let them meet. I was one person to her and another to him, and they would realize it and it would be ghastly.

"Is it that important?" I asked grimly. "It means much more to me to talk to Wilfred and Marie-Ange. We've only had a few minutes . . ."

"We could go along," Wilfred said promptly. "It would be extremely interesting for our people to see an airport" (suddenly that enormous weight which was the television and that incredible audience came back to rest on me) "and I'd be very much interested"—it seemed to me that now Wilfred's tones became a bit grim—"to see what *this* Uncle Debret is like."

All I needed now was a meeting between Wilfred and my Uncle Debret. That would do it.

I groaned a small silent groan. "How would I explain you?" I protested.

"We'll work that out," Wilfred said confidently.

"Very good," Jane decided briskly. "Before your Jane gets here I shall disappear into the ladies' room so that when the four of you go off to the airport it will seem like normal activity. The police who were following me will follow you and won't be in the least bit suspicious, because you can be sure that whoever was following me must have known about the cable from Uncle Debret, since it was phoned in and they were surely listening . . ."

Wilfred got to his feet.

"Marie-Ange and I will go out on the street and wait for Jane," he said. "Even though she doesn't know us, we know her and will be able to explain quietly . . ."

I sat there helplessly, feeling myself caught in a very fine web.

"See you later," Wilfred said, as he and Marie-Ange started out.

"Later." Marie-Ange gave the word a peculiar emphasis. Jane shot her a quick look, then Marie-Ange and Wilfred left.

I began to breathe again. That unseen televising eye makes you feel as though you are in a deep freeze.

"Well?" Jane demanded as though certain I would know what she meant by that.

"Was it you who asked that Marie-Ange be on this first delegation?" I asked. "Was that the coded message?"

"Part of it," she said.

"Why?" I asked.

"I don't know exactly," Jane said. "I hoped vaguely . . ." She never finished that. "Nothing at all happened?"

"Lots happened," I said, "but since I don't know what you were specially hoping for, I don't know what to tell you about."

"If it had happened," Jane said quickly, her tone hopeless, "you would have known without my having to tell you."

"Then tell me," I said almost irritably. "Maybe I can help. Maybe it did happen and I don't know it."

She looked at me for a moment then glanced toward the street.

Wilfred and Marie-Ange, who by that time were very near the street door, had obviously just seen something which had caused them to move a little more rapidly streetward.

"I'd better go now," Jane said quickly.

"Wait." I stopped her. "Something's happened—the delegation's come to a decision—"

"No," she said quickly. "Not yet. Only it's all far less certain than I at first imagined." My heart lurched. "I mean I thought it was all cut and dried. It isn't." She reached out quickly to reassure me. "Don't take that to mean we've decided against. It's only that we were all so sure. This"—she made a wide sweeping gesture—"was just a routine formality, we thought. It's . . . it's not a routine formality. The prob-

lem is based on much more delicate considerations than we sup-
posed . . ."

"You can't decide purely on the basis of what you see and hear
today," I said. "*One* day . . . that's nothing . . ."

"There's no other way," she said hurriedly. "We've got to make a
decision before we're discovered. And we'll be discovered today . . ."

"You could come back," I said frantically. "Even if you decide
against this time, you could come back some other time—better organized . . ."

"You don't understand," Jane said intensely, "if we're discovered
and if the decision is . . . negative . . . we couldn't come back. Your
people would be waiting for us."

"You won't be discovered," I said desperately. "Only Jane and
Morescu and I really know. Maybe Marie and René, but they don't
really know and I can guarantee all of us. We'll keep it a secret . . .
until you give us permission."

"We know that," Jane said solemnly. "Only there are other ways
in which our coming here will conceivably be known. So you see the
decision's got to be taken on what we will have uncovered by six
o'clock tonight, at the latest."

She started to move toward the ladies' can. I walked alongside of
her.

"Then for God's sake, don't ask me to meet my uncle," I begged.
"He's not typical. He'll give a totally wrong impression. It's not fair."

"Do you think it's fair to ask us not to meet him?" she pointed
out gently. "Especially when we have so little time and need every
possible means of finding out what it's really like here?"

She started to go down the stairs. It would have looked a little odd
if I had tried to follow.

I stood at the top of the stairs undecided. I was still trying to figure
out how I could avoid Debret.

A few steps down she stopped suddenly and came tripping back
up hurriedly as if she had remembered something of great importance,
kissed me very hastily and then twinkled off down the staircase and
disappeared.

I didn't even try to figure out what the hell *that* meant.

I walked out of the café and looked around.

Snookums was standing at a kiosk, elaborately choosing a midmorning newspaper. He turned to stare at me and it seemed to me he looked a little less sure of himself.

All I had to do was look where he looked—across the street.

My Jane was there standing between Marie-Ange and Wilfred.

The three were so deeply absorbed in each other that they didn't notice me or anything else. It wasn't hard to understand why. For the first time Jane was talking to people she knew to be from the other earth. Wilfred seemed to be doing all the talking, and even from that distance I could see Jane looking incredulously from Marie-Ange to Wilfred and back, and then back again, the way your head moves at a tennis match.

I rushed across the street, not remembering that it was no longer one-way at that point and neglecting to look in both directions, so that I narrowly escaped being run down by a taxi, the chauffeur of which came to a halt long enough to tell me I was a particularly offensive piece of old cheese, while Jane and Wilfred and Marie-Ange came hurrying over to me with such concern at my narrow escape that, among other things, I was deeply touched. Jane threw her arms around me and held me to her with a kind of fierce protectiveness and when we broke out of the embrace and I could look at her at arm's length, I saw that her face was aglow with excitement.

She was radiant—exhilaratingly happy. I was thinking that very few human beings had ever experienced as deep a feeling of love as I felt for this girl, and forgetting myself I leaned down and kissed her, and this time she neither pulled away nor showed the slightest signs of fear. A wave of joyous relief swelled over me, drenching me as I said to myself, We've got it made, she and I. She's mine now. She's mine.

Vaguely I realized that Marie-Ange was watching with a peculiar intensity, but I forgot about that almost completely when, as we slowly came out of the kiss, the way you would come out from under some delicious anesthesia, Jane looked up at me, then at Wilfred and Marie-Ange, and then laughed in pure delight and it was a heavenly moment as the four of us swung around the corner over toward my car.

Snookums, having crossed the street, was watching us and maybe puzzled why Jane was differently dressed. In any case I caught a fleeting glimpse of his reflection in a window and he did look perplexed.

There were others following us. I didn't see them although I was sure they were there behind us, but I didn't much care.

I think it ranks among the loveliest twenty seconds I have ever spent in my whole life. It didn't last longer than that, for I suddenly realized that Jane had been with *him;* that it was he who had brought on the radiance and the unreserved happiness, or at least been partially responsible for it, and I felt myself go hollow.

We stopped at a curb and waited for a traffic light. She was hanging on to my arm and looking up at me waiting for me to kiss her again. I didn't kiss her because even though we were in the heart of the existentialist belt, kissing a woman on the lips at high noon on the main boulevard isn't really done, and besides I shuddered a little as I realized that that first kiss of ours had been televised (I could imagine several hundred million teen-agers sounding off with wolf whistles) and besides, by then I was beginning to get worried again.

36.

THE TRAFFIC separated Jane and me from Wilfred and Marie-Ange, at least by enough distance so that we could speak to each other without being overheard.

"It is, isn't it?" Jane whispered in awe, leaning close to me as we dodged the traffic. "It's Wilfred! They're really here! Think of it, darling. Think of what it means . . ."

I gave her a sort of warning nudge because for a second there, I thought I felt a "Yippee!" coming on, but she managed to stifle it.

"They're here!" she repeated. "Really here! Will I have a chance to talk to him? Should I know his wife? She's very beautiful. They're both beautiful. Oh, darling, darling, darling . . ."

"I know," I said. "Now listen to me . . ."

But she was too far gone to listen.

"Will I be able to ask Wilfred questions?" she asked. "He said you'd just been with . . . Jane. What's she like? I mean as a person. Will I meet her? Four hours. I can't wait. Why don't you answer me?"

"You haven't given me a chance," I said.

By this time we'd crossed and were hurrying down the narrow street on which I'd left the car. We were far enough from Wilfred and Marie-Ange to be able to talk as we pleased, but not so far that they couldn't follow us.

"Now listen," I started to say.

"Has Wilfred told you anything?" she went on. "Or Jane? Do they still want us to keep the police away? What a morning! That strange policeman's still following us. He's just awful. Whenever he can, he even comes up very close and listens to you without hiding the fact that he's following or anything. Did I tell you this morning where Morescu and I went on Sunday? We went to Normandy. To René's brother's house. A little village called Nogent. Wonderful—feeling of life—"

"I've got to tell you something," I said insistently. "Before Wilfred and Marie-Ange come . . ."

"Marie-Ange?" she asked blankly. "Is that Wilfred's wife? Did you know her before? You're not saying anything. What's the matter with you?"

She looked at me with a slight frown. Something was worrying her.

"Give me a chance," I said.

"You were very—different this morning," she said and there was a note of reproof in her tones.

Of course it was my golden opportunity to tell her that it wasn't exactly me she'd been with in the morning, but something told me I'd better not tell her, so I didn't . . . despite the fact that I'm not at all sure one should listen when something tells you things. It's worked out at less than fifty-fifty in my favor in the past.

I turned quickly to cast an over-the-shoulder glance at Marie-Ange and Wilfred. He was goggling at everything and seemed to be murmuring to Marie-Ange, but I was sure he was using her as an excuse to get in a few educational words to his audience.

Jane was about to start off again.

"Now shut up a minute," I said sharply. "From the moment Wilfred and Marie-Ange join us, we'll be on the air. Televised. To their planet. We have already been televised." That held her. She looked up at me, openmouthed. Literally. You could see the two rows of lovely white teeth. "An estimated audience of something like two thousand million . . ."

"Two thousand mill—" Jane said weakly. "Why, that's two billion!"

She shivered a little.

"Give or take a few millions," I said grimly.

"Just now—" She gestured feebly. "The kiss—and all . . ."

"Yes," I said. I gave her a fast five seconds to land. "Now you've got to pull yourself together. You have to help me. We've just got to make a good impression."

Jane stared at me.

"You mean their decision—may be influenced by—" Again she made a vague frightened gesture.

"Sure as hell will," I said, "if you ask me. Now, we're about to meet my Uncle Debret—"

"You should've told me," Jane said. "I would have worn my other suit."

"I didn't know this would happen," I went on grimly.

"I would have worn my blue blouse," she said, "and . . ." she made a groaning sound as her hand flew up to her head, "my hair . . ."

"You look great," I said grimly. "Now listen. About my Uncle Debret. Whatever you do, avoid a fight with him. Am I coming through to you?"

"Vaguely." Jane swallowed. "Maybe I'd better turn the volume up a bit . . ."

"And for God's sake keep *them* talking," I said. "Don't let them draw us out. And promise you'll help me keep Wilfred and my Uncle Debret apart. And no matter what Debret says—"

"I'll be sickeningly sweet to him," Jane said. "Don't worry. Only what'll I say? What'll I do?"

"Just be natural," I heard myself say, and I tried not to feel too much of a hypocrite. After all I was a veteran interplanetary television hand by now—of over two hours' standing.

We didn't have a chance to say anything more, because Wilfred and Marie-Ange came up just then.

As Wilfred held the back door of my car open for Marie-Ange (who got in very gingerly; she really didn't have too much confidence in my car), he went on about how they had been looking at the windows of the antique shops, and how it was fascinating for him to consider how revealing of a nation an antique shop could really be.

The realization that we were being televised brought out an unsuspected big chunk of ham in Jane—she sat very primly and kept flashing smiles every which way (I suspect favoring her better profile), leaning over and pointing out to Wilfred that he hadn't really locked the door. (She meant with the safety catch. She always locks the door of any car with the safety catch.)

Wilfred thanked her and said they hadn't been in a motor-driven vehicle since they were children. As I started the car, this was a perfect lead in for Jane to ask sweetly how they traveled if they didn't travel with internal-combustion-driven vehicles.

I started the motor and both he and Marie-Ange sort of hung on, as if they half expected the car to explode.

"We travel on rays," Wilfred said, as we moved off. They seemed a little relieved when we actually got under way, the way some people feel in a plane when it's definitely airborne. Not completely reassured but not so bad either. "The ray is propelled down the streets and highways. We have specially built vehicles which have no motors of any sort. You simply get in and set the speed and direction, and the ray moves you to your destination." He managed to lean back a little. "But don't get the idea that transportation's free. Not at all. There's a yearly payment which you make for the privilege of using that energy to transport yourself and your family. Some of us feel that that payment's been much too high, and we've been carrying on a campaign—"

Marie-Ange took time off from worrying about driving in a motor-driven vehicle to stop Wilfred.

"I remember very clearly the instructions," she said sharply. "We were not to make any political propaganda of any kind while broadcasting. I think the instructions were meant mostly for you."

Wilfred hesitated a moment. "Sorry," he said finally.

Fortunately we hit Boulevard Saint-Michel at that point. It fascinated both Wilfred and Marie-Ange. It fascinated me too, as a matter of fact—it always does.

Thousands of students had just broken for lunch, spilling out of the sedate old Sorbonne buildings and cascading over the outdoor cafés and restaurants. They ran, they shouted at each other—there was such a crazy kind of animation that you figured that, aside from the traffic cops, a special corps of guardian angels must've been assigned special duty on the boulevard to keep hundreds of the students from being crushed in the mad noonday traffic.

"Well," Marie-Ange commented dryly, "there's not much difference between your Latin Quarter and ours—"

"Of course it's much cleaner," Wilfred interposed. "I mean ours is—" He then added hastily, "Not because of people's habits. It's because we've eliminated all smoke so that the façades of our buildings are quite clean. You see—we heat with the ray . . ."

I'm sure Marie-Ange nudged him. It was rude of him to keep insisting on their superiority. Anyway his voice trailed off apologetically.

"When did you discover the principle of this ray?" Jane asked.

Wilfred brightened.

"Matter of fact," he said eagerly, "I remember the date quite clearly. It was a world sensation—December, nineteen forty-one—a Japanese research team announced the discovery—"

I don't know whether you remember but it was December of 1941 that our Japanese launched their attack on Pearl Harbor.

"Can you tell us anything about the radiant substance Dr. Morescu and I found in our crystal containers?" Jane asked.

Wilfred thought a long time.

"I'm not a biophysicist," he said finally. "I can only give you a general idea—"

Either that, I thought, or he was under instructions not to do more than that.

He said something about energy representing a qualitative change in mass and that the basic life substance similarly represented a qualitative change in energy. The substance was energy developed to the point at which it became life.

Something about his voice or manner or what he was saying rubbed me the wrong way, just as he had done when we were kids, and the mild irritation set up a whole chain of sweet memories, like the smell of autumn leaves burning. I wondered vaguely why I had always felt him to be my best friend, why I had always felt so protected when I was with him and why his death had left this permanently gaping hole in my life.

He was going on about the radiant stuff—saying that it had enormous latent energy, but unlike radioactive material was not only benign, but had direct and extraordinary therapeutic and curative powers.

What was it about him? Then it hit me.

Wilfred was perfectly at home.

It didn't matter that it was another planet and that he had flown through space and that we were participating in a fabulous event. Wilfred felt at ease. He belonged. He was a part of it.

He had always been part of it. That had always been his quality whether it was a geisha house in Nagasaki or a London drawing room, or arguing with my Uncle Debret.

I think I figured out why.

It was because he accepted nothing as permanently fixed, people, institutions, values. There wasn't a darn thing you couldn't change— if you felt they needed changing.

When you feel that way you're no longer scared. You're at ease. You can do something about it, handle it.

Not like me. If you don't walk into a snug ready-made world with hot and cold running comfort you've had it, I hear myself say to myself. You can only cross your fingers and hope for the best.

That's why anything new scares you.

Wilfred finally bought it in a plane anyway but while he lived he was alive. He didn't let two-thirds of himself go down the drain in vague fears and apologizing for being alive.

Marie-Ange was leaning back a little watching it all with a distant interest.

Wilfred was telling Jane that there were no longer individual heating units. They heated the atmosphere of whole cities and countrysides.

I suddenly felt exhilarated. I had made a discovery as important, it seemed to me, as discovering a twin planet.

I'd found out why I'd been afraid.

37.

THERE WAS a whining overhead. A jet airliner was circling over the Orly area.

Both Wilfred and Marie-Ange watched it in fascination.

"You still fly in *those?*" Wilfred asked incredulously.

Of course that set him off on how *they* traveled. Apparently there was nothing to it. They flew at fantastic speeds and there were never any accidents. Wilfred and Marie-Ange only the other day had had some people from Rio de Janeiro in for dinner at their home in London. For their guests it had meant a pleasant fifteen-minute trip. Wilfred often fished in the Fraser River in British Columbia on a Sunday afternoon and was back in London the same evening.

While he was telling this, of course the traffic to Orly was impossible. There were bottlenecks. Drivers screamed at each other. Cops blew their whistles furiously.

Jane's father, Wilfred went on, not noticing immediately how the mention of Jane's father affected our Jane, and some of his cronies had a patch of garden in New Zealand. After work of an evening they'd potter about with their greens and tomato plants in New Zealand and would be home in London for supper.

Then Wilfred saw the tears in Jane's eyes and said gruffly, "Sorry —I'm terribly sorry—"

"That's all right," Jane said quietly. "I'd like to hear more—"

Wilfred hesitated, watching Jane.

"Nothing much more," Wilfred went on after a moment. "People in New York come to London for the theatre and vice versa. Touring has become the most popular weekend activity. There's no place on earth more than an hour away from any other point. If you're willing to take an hour's drive you can have your choice of the equator or the pole—and it's quite cheap—although we feel it could be cheaper—"

"Oh—you." Marie-Ange chided Wilfred with a pretense at playfulness and although there was still the slightest note of irritation, her manner was a lot friendlier toward him than it had been earlier. "Travel is so cheap now that I can afford to do most of my shopping in Paris—that is, whenever we want the real French thing. And didn't we go to Peking last week for a Chinese dinner? Of course we figured it cost us about double what a meal at a Chinese restaurant in London would have cost—but Wilfred loves Chinese food so—"

The cop at the Orly intersection was screaming so furiously at me to make the left turn which would lead to the airfield that he forgot to stop the opposite traffic and we narrowly escaped being smashed by a sleek Citroën, which caused the cop to whistle us to a stop, ask for my papers, bawl the hell out of me, and then wave me on with a polite salute.

Wilfred had time to say that they had finally abolished all passports and visas just as a small army of customs officers and airport police made their way to the main Orly building to await the new arrivals.

We parked and got out.

Not far off behind us Snookums had driven up in an unostentatious French car with ordinary French license plates and markings, and was leisurely backing into a parking space, and not far behind him, two men were just getting out of a black Citroën. Even before I could distinguish them I knew it was the sheepskin jacket and his colleague, because nearly all officials of any importance at all in France use black Citroëns.

Our little decoying tactic was working.

The cops were following *us*.

The plane from Montreal was announced as about to land just as we entered. Wilfred and Marie-Ange wanted to watch it as it actually touched earth, so we marched upstairs to the terrace, where there was a completely unobstructed view of the landing areas.

As the huge silver airliner began its descent both Wilfred and Marie-Ange stood there tense, she almost afraid to watch; their whole attitude was that they really didn't believe those contraptions could actually fly (while I was thinking that they seemed to me the latest word in modern design and engineering) and they insisted on remaining on the terrace until it had actually landed and the passengers had disembarked. Then as though the first time had been an accident, they waited for a second airliner to land, and it was only when I pulled them away, telling them I would miss my uncle, that they agreed to leave.

Snookums and the other two police followed us down the stairs, in no way acknowledging us, pretending not to know us or each other.

"By the way," I said casually to the others on the way down the staircase, "you mustn't pay too much attention to my Uncle Debret." It was a speech I had carefully worked out on the way over. I enunciated as clearly as I could and spoke sufficiently slowly to give all their simultaneous translators lolling on the manned satellites a chance to translate accurately. "You mustn't attach too much significance to his opinions."

"How do you mean *that?*" Wilfred asked.

"The way we say in our movies," I said. "The opinions expressed by my Uncle Debret represent only the opinions expressed by him and practically no one else."

Wilfred looked puzzled.

"Do you mean by that," he asked, "that we are not to take his views as representing any important body of opinion?"

I wasn't sure that that was a better way or a clearer way of saying it, but I let it go.

"That's right," I said. "The only body he represents is his own."

"Well, *that* should be fascinating," Wilfred said grimly. By the time we got downstairs, the passengers from the Montreal flight were being cleared by the air police and we could see them through the glass paneling.

It was Marie-Ange who saw him first.

"*Mon dieu!*" she exclaimed, and pointed.

We all looked and of course there was Uncle Debret who hadn't as yet seen us.

"But you and he look so much alike!" Marie-Ange explained to me, but not without a slightly reproving nuance in her voice, a nuance which had unconsciously slipped out. "He's a very handsome man," she went on quickly, trying to make up for the nuance, "but I was not at all prepared that there should be this family resemblance . . ."

She made me feel as though I had cheated her somehow.

I examined Debret carefully. There was no question of it. We do look alike and the idea seemed very unattractive to me, even though, I think objectively, if I hadn't known him, I would have thought of him as a decent enough looking type.

Uncle Debret suddenly saw me, or I should say saw Jane and me, and not realizing yet that Wilfred and Marie-Ange were with us, flashed her and me a great smile, and made a very gay dumb show asking about Jane, indicating with his head that he was asking, "Is that she? The very special she?"

I nodded back with very big nods since they had to travel quite a distance through the glass paneling and all, indicating it was she, and he smiled again and made a jocular face intended to convey the idea that he thought she was quite a dish and much too good for me.

I began to let myself relax a little. I began to think maybe this was not going to turn out as badly as I thought. Debret seemed so gay and debonair, and I tried to suppress an unpleasant feeling that I was kidding myself, it was all going to turn out to be bloody awful, and that Debret's smile was one of his great assets and he knew it, and used it, and his not inconsiderable charm, to great effect deliberately.

He swept out of the customs room making a show of his youthful stride. He greeted me warmly, shaking hands profusely. I presented him to Jane and he shook hands with her in a way which was one step removed from making love to her, and dumped his charm on her the way a gravel truck dumps its load. Only he spoiled the effect a little by saying:

"So this is the young lady who's causing all the trouble," and when we didn't laugh very heartily, tried to smile it away.

He had turned much grayer than when I had seen him last, but he carried that off too with great effect, looking the perfect image of a slim, well-dressed, youthful senior executive.

He tried to sweep us out of the room by putting his arm around me and going forward, thus establishing, from the very beginning, that the rhythm of events was being set by him, except that even if I hadn't really wanted to oppose him at that point, it was still necessary to introduce Wilfred and Marie-Ange.

"Some friends of mine from London," I explained a little haltingly, as his face froze, especially when he heard the name MacIntosh. "They have only a few hours, and your cable came so unexpectedly, I thought you wouldn't mind their coming along . . ."

"Not at all." Debret needed a second or two to get himself back into character. He turned to Wilfred. "Not related to Wilfred MacIntosh?"

"Most MacIntoshes are more or less related," Wilfred said. "I think you're probably referring to a sort—of cousin of mine."

38.

IN THE background I caught a glimpse of the sheepskin jacket and his pal looking over the passenger list which the stewardess had just brought them, then glance up at us.

I don't know what had happened to Snookums.

Although Debret had certainly noticed Marie-Ange before, it was only as we were on our way out that he seemed really for the first time to feel her full effect.

Now despite the fact that it was obvious that he had come on special and important business, he was able to put it aside for the moment and suppress his first impulse, which had been to ask me to get rid of the MacIntoshes as quickly as possible. He began to make a big play for Marie-Ange.

I could almost see the wheels of his psyche at work. I've escorted too many visiting firemen not to know the symptoms by heart: the sudden realization that it was Gay Paree and not Montreal, and that you were in your late fifties and free and that you'd bloody well hurry and make time while you could and that here was a beautiful sexy French lady.

All in the youthful vagabond vein, Debret had brought very little luggage (the implication there also was that he'd be able to take care of whatever he'd come for in very short order) so that we were out of customs and the rest and in the car in a few minutes.

He insisted that Jane and Marie-Ange sit in the back with him, and arranged it so that it was necessary for him to put his arm around Marie-Ange. She watched him with that assured and objective detachment with which I'd seen many young French matrons watching the gay old Western hemisphere dogs in action, knowing that at any time they wanted, they could coolly call a halt, but mildly interested in the way it would unroll, while Wilfred pretended not to be aware of any of it, and sprawled casually in the front seat next to me.

Somewhere off to one side on the parking lot the two French cops consulted with each other and decided to follow us after all, even though by then, I had a feeling that their cops' instinct must have told them they were barking up a forest of wrong trees.

We drove out to the highway. For me, the general atmosphere was that of knowing you were sitting not on one, but on three or four bombs, fuses lighted and ready to go.

At any moment Uncle Debret might get his mind off Marie-Ange long enough to sound off on something that would be disastrous; or if he didn't get his mind off Marie-Ange, Wilfred, who was smoldering at my side, might conceivably sound off at Uncle Debret; or Debret might put *me* on the spot and this time, if I didn't want to lose Jane forever, I knew I'd have to tell him off once and for all. Besides which, I had a feeling a little fuse was burning inside of Marie-Ange too.

Well.

Everything went along fine until we came into Paris. I think Wilfred tried very hard to be sweet up to that point, and help us present ourselves in the best possible way. Even though anyone with half an eye could see that Debret's hand was on Marie-Ange's shoulder in a way it shouldn't have been, and that he was leaning toward her every chance he got, while she kept watching with that objective interested eye, making no move to stop him.

I could feel myself getting more and more irritated. I had been prepared to be provoked by Debret in every conceivable way except this one. I tried telling myself that it was really none of my damn business anyway, what was I getting so excited about, I was in love with Jane, and besides which it couldn't possibly amount to anything—there was no place for Uncle Debret to take it from the hand-on-the-shoulder and accidental-brushing-of-the-knee phase.

Just about the time I was ready to explode, Debret stopped telling us what an up-and-coming country Canada was long enough to ask me to stop at the first florist's shop, which I did. Then he got out of the car with that youthful, energetic, no-nonsense manner of his and dashed into the shop.

While we all watched in speechless fascination, he bought up what seemed to us all the most expensive flowers in the joint (including some beautiful chrysanthemums which the French consider are only for decorating graves, and which must have astonished the hell out of the florist lady) and came back into the car loaded, presenting the flowers to Jane and to Marie-Ange, and there was a special significant sidelong glance as he gave Marie-Ange her flowers.

For a few minutes Debret's gesture worked. First of all it was so lavish, and secondly the flowers were beautiful, and thirdly the wonderful scent filled the tiny area which is the interior of a car so that the air was intoxicating and heady. Even I was beginning to think maybe I had been wrong—he was just a lonely, aging man trying to be nice.

Debret then asked Marie-Ange where they were staying. Wilfred replied that they weren't sure yet, their plans were indefinite; to which Debret replied that he wouldn't hear of their leaving before having dinner with him. He was talking directly to Marie-Ange. When she didn't answer, and Wilfred replied for her, that they wouldn't know for a few hours, Debret kept on at it, saying that he hadn't been surrounded by so much youth (we weren't really *that* young) and by so much feminine loveliness for a long time.

Nobody said anything at all to that. I opened the wing of my front window because what with the flowers and all, it was getting a little *too* heady and the glass was misting. I leaned over and wiped the mist off, saying that I wouldn't want Debret to miss anything of Paris. It was his first visit in many a year.

Debret made no reply to me, instead asking Wilfred if both of them were going to be busy the rest of the day. Wilfred scrunched around in the seat to get a better look at Debret, and to make sure he had heard aright, it was all so blunt. Then Wilfred said he thought both were going to be busy the rest of the day. To make it completely official, Marie-Ange added that she for one was going to be very busy indeed.

Apparently the way she said it irritated Debret, so that he leaned back a little. It was only then that he took up my crack about his first visit.

"Paris is great I'm sure," he said, "but you know Montreal is good enough for me. A man has everything he needs in the place he calls home or there's something wrong. Wouldn't you say, Mr. MacIntosh?"

Wilfred thought that one over.

"Well no," Wilfred said quietly, after having thought it over for a long time. "I think I would say pretty much the opposite."

"Oh, I see," Debret said sententiously. He was going to enjoy this one with both feet kicking and both fists slugging. "You wouldn't say so?"

"No," Wilfred said seriously. "A position of that sort would seem to imply that only one place or one country had all the good things of life when obviously . . ."

Well—

That did it.

"Maybe that's what the trouble is," Debret said with a kind of heavy conviction. He was still only warming up. I tried to switch him off onto something else, but he paid as much attention to me as an elephant would to an ant.

"Maybe if you young'uns really knew where your home was, there wouldn't be all this mess. I say that the man who knows where his home is and is willing to give his all for it, is two-thirds there. Wouldn't you agree to that, Mr. MacIntosh?"

"No," said Wilfred, "not at all. And besides—which mess are you referring to, Mr. Debret?"

"Which mess do I mean?" Slightly purple with rage, Debret looked us all over and decided to take it out on me. "Now listen, you!" he shouted at me.

I hadn't said anything. In addition to everything else the injustice of it all was infuriating.

"Wait a minute!" I said. I made a big effort and succeeded in partially controlling myself. "I'm sure we can talk about this later—"

"Why later?" Marie-Ange surprised the hell out of me by asking.

We all stared at her for about a fiftieth of a second, but she looked right back at us, wide-eyed, beautiful and innocent.

Debret gave Marie-Ange another look, opened his mouth, closed it, then turned to me.

"Stop this car," he said sharply.

I swung over to the curb with an alacrity that surprised even him.

"I'll get you a cab," Debret said huskily to Marie-Ange, although he obviously included Wilfred in his offer.

"We're not going on with you?" Marie-Ange asked.

"No," Debret said paternally, "no point in subjecting you to what's about to happen."

"We don't mind," Marie-Ange said.

"In fact I think we'd rather enjoy it," Wilfred said evenly. "Nothing like an exchange of opposing ideas . . ."

Debret turned to Wilfred.

"Some other time," he snapped.

He opened the door for Marie-Ange and Wilfred, and helped her out the way you would help a pregnant empress get out of a car, then swung youthfully off and energetically flagged a cab for them.

Jane and I got out too. The four of us watched Debret blankly.

The second Debret was more or less out of sight when Wilfred handed me the vial.

"I'm sure none of this can be of real interest to your television audience," I said.

I handed it back to Wilfred.

"You're wrong." Wilfred said quietly. "It's of tremendous interest."

I took back the vial. What else could I do?

Debret had found a cab and was heading for us.

"We must see you," Marie-Ange said. "We still have something to say to each other."

I nodded.

The cab came up.

We shook hands all around.

Debret held Marie-Ange's hand so long it got embarrassing.

"It's been very fine meeting you, Mrs. MacIntosh," Debret said.

"It's meant a great deal to me too," Marie-Ange told him.

"And to me," Wilfred interjected.

Finally Debret let go of her hand.

"I'm at the Hotel Prince de Galles," he said to her. "If there's any-thing you need—"

"We'll be sure to call on you," Wilfred said dryly.

The cab went off.

Jane, Debret and I stood on the curb for a few seconds staring after them.

"Beautiful woman, Mrs. MacIntosh," Debret said.

"Lovely," Jane said.

It irritated the hell out of me that he kept calling her Mrs. Mac-Intosh.

We got into the car and drove off.

"That dark Mediterranean beauty appeals to me," Debret vol-unteered.

"It appeals to a lot of people," I said sharply.

He didn't like that last crack.

We drove along in silence for about thirty seconds. I had the feel-ing Debret was waiting for Jane or me to say something. But neither of us did.

"Well," Debret said finally, "if neither one of you will ask me why I came, I'll have to tell you on my own."

"I was hoping you came to have a nice friendly visit," I said.

"I didn't come to have a nice friendly visit," he said tartly. He turned to stare at Jane. "They warned me you'd look young, but you look like a little girl." His tone implied that she wasn't such a nice little girl. "I've been led to understand that you've discovered something of great military importance and that you're not being very co-operative. You haven't yet informed any of our authorities." He looked at me. Without turning, I could feel his look. "Either one of you."

"The military aspect of the discovery," Jane said carefully, "is really minimal."

"No military aspect is minimal these days," Debret said loudly.

"I hate talk about military aspects," I said. "I've had enough military aspects for a whole lifetime."

"Well that's just too bad for you," Debret said, "because that's what we're going to talk about whether you like it or not."

I was saying to myself in a panic, How did we get ourselves into this? I had to stop him. Had to—

Before I could think of anything, he turned and pointed a finger at Jane. "Young lady," he said accusingly, "have you or haven't you invented a device that can kill at a distance?"

"Kill?" Jane asked, shocked. "It wasn't conceived that way, it—"

"Maybe it wasn't," Debret clipped off at her, "but I understand that's what it does. Or could do."

"I don't know," Jane said, moving away from him. "I don't think so—we don't know yet."

"What do you mean, we don't know?" Debret asked pugnaciously.

"Uncle Debret . . ." I began.

By now they were both disregarding me.

"If you don't know," Debret said, "that means there's a possibility that it's true. That's all I need to know. A possibility that something you've invented could be the greatest weapon of all time—"

"Uncle Debret," I said, and this time my tone was grim.

He turned and looked at me for a long time without saying anything, just fixed me with his dead-fish look. Finally he barked, "This is important."

"Who gave you the idea it could kill at great distances?" Jane was asking him quietly.

"Never you mind who told me," Debret snapped. "It was intimated to me that your invention had fantastic possibilities. They know, for example, that in the villa in which you were working there was not any unusual consumption of electricity and yet you were able to generate a beam that stopped a four-motor airliner dead in its tracks. Imagine what could be done with a *real* push of power behind that!"

"I'm afraid I can't begin to imagine," Jane said. She was very white.

He cut her off.

"You can't imagine?" he asked outraged. It was as though the idea was so outrageous it choked him. "Have you any idea what it means? It means we'd have them! We'd have them!" His face came alive with real passion. "We could wipe them off the face of the earth once and for all!" If you hadn't heard his words, from the look on his face you would have sworn he was talking about some beautiful dream. He was aglow with happiness. "Blot them out!"

Two billion people heard that, I thought. It was done. Over.

39.

"UNCLE DEBRET," I said quietly. "There's a great deal more to this than meets the naked eye. Now—"

He wouldn't even let me finish.

"There's nothing more to this than any man can see with half an eye!" Debret shouted. "Anything beyond that is treason!"

I almost let go of the wheel.

"What do you mean, 'treason'?" Jane asked, stunned.

"What anybody means by it!" Debret barked at her. "The foulest most unnatural crime a man—or woman—can commit."

Maybe it was because he had shouted at her. Or maybe it was because it had all gone too far, but suddenly I didn't care any more.

"How did that word come sneaking up so soon?" I yelled at him. "I wasn't expecting that kind of brutality from you for another good three minutes."

It was out. There we were—he and I—ugly—circling each other like two gladiators, sword and trident poised for the kill.

Jane had curled herself as far away from Debret as she could get.

"Listen, you!" Debret became calm the way a white-hot poker is calm. That was part of his strength. He could get into a fury without losing control. "In these last couple of days I've had to stand by and subject myself to the most horrible experience of my life—stand by, while wonderful, important people" (in his vocabulary those two words "important" and "wonderful" went tearing around, inseparable pals) "tried hard—tried hard I tell you, to avoid implying that my own flesh and blood, my own nephew, was a traitor. A man in my position. Oh, I knew that some day it would come to this. Now Miss Bridon-Jack is someone over whom I have no right or claim whatsoever—"

"What the hell," I said generously, "lump us both together."

"Spare me the wise-guy stuff," he said. He was venomously quiet now. "Asked by these people would I fly to Paris and help persuade my very own nephew, who is close to this certain young female scientist, to turn over her secrets—secrets we're desperately in need of, what with every man, woman and child of us in danger of being blown off the face of the living earth—what with those bloody moons hovering over our heads right now and missiles that can travel across continents . . ."

There was no point fighting it after that, no point in trying to hide anything from the other world.

"Hydrogen warheads on intercontinental missiles," Debret went on. "Guided missiles . . ."

He was like a monstrous boy with monstrous new toys. The new words fascinated him. Intercontinental missiles. Warheads. It was the latest way of making small puddles of sensation on people's living-room rugs. "Half-life. Countdown. Launching pads. Non-ballistic . . .

"And you," Debret spat the words at her, "say you don't know—you don't know—"

I figured to hell with the television audience. To hell with everything. I don't think I even decided these things consciously. My calm blew up like a land mine in my face.

"Who are you to ask questions?" I shouted at Jane. "You're nothing but a silly little egghead who happens to have stumbled on something! You just go along inventing with that little egghead of yours and leave the important problems for this wise, thoughtful, reasoning man—"

"You no longer work for me," Debret said.

I swear he said that.

"Even though you're an old man and my mother's brother," I said, "I want to tell you the truth. The truth is you've plagued our lives from the time I can first remember. Father's—Mother's—mine—I don't want any more of you. I'm through. Keep your job."

I stopped the car. Debret was staring at me strangely.

I could hear him breathing hard. I remembered that he had cardiac asthma.

I could feel Jane alongside of me, rigid.

I couldn't bear to look at him.

"You'll want to apologize to me," Debret said. "Won't you?"

"Yes," I said. I remember Jane turning to look at me. "I don't see what good it does to hurt you at this stage of the game."

"I don't understand," Debret said uncertainly. "Are you apologizing or not?"

"Take it any way you like," I said wearily.

Debret decided to accept it as some sort of an apology.

"I've come a long way to try to talk reason to you two," Debret said. "Now maybe we've all been a little overwrought. *Un peu nerveux,* as the French say." His accent was horrible and the French never say that. Suddenly I looked at him and he seemed to me an old woman, a querulous old woman who by accident had strayed away from her tea cozies. "Let's all calm down." He waited a second. "You can have your job back. But only on condition that you help persuade Miss Bridon-Jack to see the light."

I started the car.

We moved off.

"I don't want to work for you," I said. "I don't want to work for anyone who makes a condition of work anything other than that the work be done well. For years now I've been nothing because I could work for you only if I thought the way you did. No more—"

"You haven't any money," Debret said. "You're in no position to talk to me that way. You've been doing a very special kind of journalism. There isn't much of a market for what you do . . ."

He understood clearly. He'd understood it always—and used it.

"Where can I take you?" I asked.

"The Prince de Galles," he said. Now he turned to Jane. "You mustn't let this difference between my nephew and myself influence you. It's come as a great shock to me to discover that there's this animosity for me after I've done so much for him and his family." I guess he couldn't tell from Jane's face how it was going over. He changed tactics. "Miss Bridon-Jack, believe me. You have no right to decide what should be done with your discovery—"

"I think she has a right to think about it," I said. "Her whole family was killed by an unguided missile with a warhead. She's got as good a right as anyone—"

"Right?" Debret shrilled at me.

He's gone to pieces, I thought. He's lost control. I could see his face in the rearview mirror. It was contorted with hatred.

"A right to think about it!" he went on almost hysterically. "The fact that you two could have any doubts at a time like this makes me sick with shame! You ought to be publicly flogged! Both of you! Dragged out in the streets and whipped!"

Debret had been carrying on a campaign for years to reintroduce the whipping post as a form of punishment. It was one of his favorite subjects.

Jane made a little sound of horror and Debret realized he had gone too far. He leaned back against the seat wheezing asthmatically and from there on we drove along in silence.

After you've introduced the whipping post into the conversation, there's not a great deal left to talk about.

Debret got out of the car as a hotel porter came up to take his bags. I got out to help the porter, but I let my motor run so that there would be no mistaking the fact we'd stopped only long enough to get rid of him and his bags.

The old man started toward the hotel entrance with that youthful stride, got a few feet and realized I hadn't followed him, stopped a little puzzled as if trying to understand why, then remembered, and looked at both Jane and me.

I had just finished giving the porter Debret's handbag and had swung over to the front seat. Jane hadn't moved and was watching us both.

"If you kids are free for supper tonight," Debret said heartily, "I've heard a lot about the Tour d'Argent. Would you like to join me?"

As you probably know, the Tour d'Argent is one of the most expensive restaurants in the world.

He was standing there as though nothing had happened. The gladiators had run into each other after the little incident in the arena and had slapped each other on the back to indicate there were no particular hard feelings. It's true they'd tried to kill each other, but that was in the arena.

"Think it over," Debret said gently. Then he flashed that smile of his on Jane. "I am very pleased to have made your acquaintance."

Jane was so astonished she could barely nod.

"I'll see you later," he said to me.

When I got back in the car, Jane was curled up again. She didn't look at me as we drove off.

For several minutes we drove in silence. She took hold of my arm and held it close to her.

"Well, St. George," she said in a shaky voice as she nestled her head against my arm.

"St. George?" I asked.

"Wasn't it St. George who killed the dragon?" she asked. Her voice was soft and strange. "Oh, darling—I thought you'd never tell him. I know how frightened you were of him. But you told him and I'm so glad. You told him and whatever else happens I won't mind. You're free. You're my own St. George . . ."

She started to cry, her face buried in my jacket while we drove across the Seine and up the big boulevard. She was still crying when we drove up in front of her hotel. Gradually the sobs subsided. She lay like that next to me for a long time, with me stroking her hair. Then without looking at me she asked me if I would like to come up with her.

I took her in my arms and her lips came up to mine tenderly and I kissed her. There was a fraction of a second when again I felt the tremor of fear shoot through her body but I had pulled my lips away so quickly that it seemed as though it had been all right. She had kissed me on the lips and hadn't pulled back or grown rigid. So it seemed it would be all right.

As we got out of the car I looked around. We had lost the cops. Either that or they'd decided on their own there was no point in following us.

The concierge at her hotel looked at us with real surprise.

"But I thought you were upstairs," he said. He made a startled gesture behind him.

Jane looked quickly over at the keyboard and saw that her key was not there.

"I slipped out for a second," she said quietly.

We got into the lift not saying anything. I held her hand and could feel the excitement surging through her.

We stopped at her door and she looked down the corridor, then when we'd made sure it was empty, she tapped lightly on the door. "It's me, Jane," she said.

There was a second of silence, then the door opened noiselessly and the two Janes were face to face.

Jane went in and I followed and shut the door slowly behind us.

The two girls stared at each other, just looking at each other; then at exactly the same split second held out both hands to each other, then exactly at the same second touched cheeks with each other; then held each other off in awe, realizing, I suppose, that they were reacting exactly alike.

For me, watching them, it was like looking at a strange mirror which doesn't reflect exactly alike even though the images are the same.

They kept on looking at each other and never in my whole life have I seen two more radiant creatures. Confronting each other this way, they both felt that the glorious thing that had happened was deeply true and real and it reminded them of a great and incredible future to come.

Then they burst into a wonderful exciting kind of laughter, still exactly at the same moment, only suddenly our Jane was crying and their Jane stopped laughing.

Our Jane turned away and wiped her eyes and wrote on a pad, writing with very large letters MICROPHONE, and pointed to a corner where there was a cluster of so-called modern wall lamps.

Their Jane laughed and whispered that whoever was listening would think she had gone crazy because they would hear one voice. Just the same, I went over to the wall lamps and knocked on the wall with my pipe so that the sound would drown their voices.

At that point, our Jane laughed, and they both sat down with that astonishing simultaneity.

They talked rapidly and spontaneously to each other. There was absolutely no strain and I was amazed at how rapidly they accepted each other. It seemed to me it was as though they had somehow been together all the last years.

Their Jane talked about Phnee and Mundy and her mother and father. I think she said Phnee was studying architecture because there was still a great need to adapt all the buildings to the modern way of life. And Mundy wasn't sure yet what she wanted to do. She was a wonderful ice skater, of all things, and had talked several times of becoming a physical instructor. The idea seemed to disturb Mother and Father.

Our Jane stopped her and asked her how much time there was left for them to talk and their Jane said regretfully that there wasn't much time left.

Our Jane got up and asked if one of the reasons their Jane had talked about the family was because she had not wanted our Jane to ask questions she wouldn't have had the right to answer.

"Yes," their Jane said. "That was partly the reason." She took our Jane's hands impulsively. "Just a little while longer. We'll talk freely —about anything. We'll be able to say exactly what we think and feel —out loud and it won't matter who'll hear it." She turned to me quickly. "Would you mind taking me back to your place? Because if anyone did try to stop me—you could help—"

I minded. Very much. The last thing I wanted to do just then was to leave our Jane.

But there was too much else involved and besides we'd see each other shortly.

Then the two girls came close to each other and touched cheeks again as though they'd seen each other often and knew they would see each other as often again.

So I kissed our Jane and whispered I would be back very soon. From the way she whispered that she'd be waiting for me—there—she wouldn't move—there was no mistaking her meaning.

Then their Jane and I left.

No one tried to stop us in the hotel lobby and we made it to my car without being seen by anybody special.

We drove to my place in utter silence and it wasn't an uncomfortable silence either. We were too absorbed with our own thoughts.

I parked the car a safe distance from my place and their Jane and I walked as quickly as we dared without attracting attention.

A couple of hundred yards from my door Snookums materialized out of nowhere—actually out of one of the parked cars.

We didn't slow our pace and broke into a half run without missing a step. Snookums had done it beautifully, so gracefully that we hadn't even been startled; except that I had a terrifying feeling that it had taken enormously careful organization and planning for him to have been able to present himself that unostentatiously at our side at that very second.

"If you don't mind," he said in French, "I'd like a few words with you—just between now and the time we reach your corner and before we turn it."

"We are in a hurry," I said. We increased the pace.

"I want to tell you something." Snookums said very quickly. "You and Morescu—"

"We're not interested," I flung back at him.

I could see their Jane was listening intently.

"There's a right and wrong side in every conflict," Snookums said.

"You represent the right side," I said.

"Yes," Snookums said. "I want to tell you what side that is."

We were nearing the corner. Snookums had become agitated. He had lost that cold aloof calm. He was involved now.

"I'm not sure you know what's at stake here," he said, a little out of breath.

"I think we know better than anyone else on this earth," I said. I was beginning to puff too.

We turned the corner. He didn't dare follow.

"We'll never know what side he was on," their Jane said quickly.

"Never," I said.

Mme. Fénelon tried to stop me. She's a lousy actress and it was easy to see that there was someone behind her, out of sight, watching and listening in the shadows of her cubbyhole.

She made a great pretense of good cheer and of being glad to see us. When I responded curtly and kept right on, she hurried to keep up with us, smiling comprehension as if she understood people of affairs such as ourselves couldn't be bothered with passing chitchat with the likes of her. Nonetheless, she intervened physically to stop us from taking the elevator.

"A large man," she said, "with very loose clothes; a tall woman and an Indian lady, and many others. They were all carrying loads of papers. You know these people?"

"No," I said impatiently. "They must be visiting someone else. After all, there are many other tenants in this house."

I rang for the elevator. It began its oozing descent from very high up. (It took so long in coming, I assumed it had been at the seventh floor.)

Mme. Fénelon hesitated. She glanced behind her as though she'd like nothing better in the whole world than to hurry back to her cubbyhole and to whoever was waiting for her there and get further instructions.

"A young man and a young woman. French. Do you know them?"

"I know many people who could answer that description," I said. "Did you ask them what their business was here?"

"Indeed," said Mme. Fénelon tartly. "They all replied in English."

"Even the French lady?" I asked.

"Even she," Mme. Fénelon said. "So I do not know what they want or whom they came to see. And the young people were loaded to the eyebrows with documents."

"I was expecting no one," I said. "Especially not people who would read that many newspapers."

The elevator arrived. I excused myself hastily, and we made our way around her and into the cage. As we were slowly pulled up, I caught a receding glimpse of Mme. Fénelon as she bustled off. Her manner was that of a noncommissioned officer hurrying to make a report to headquarters.

40.

THERE WAS no one on the landing when their Jane and I got out at the seventh floor. I was surprised at how relieved I was. I guess I'd really expected the police, the army, the navy and the marine corps.

Their Jane knocked lightly on my door. Almost immediately it was opened.

Marie-Ange came out quickly. She had obviously been waiting at the door.

Marie-Ange held the door open and beckoned their Jane to come in quickly. Their Jane hesitated a second, then flashed me a tight worried smile and went on in, while Marie-Ange came out and, holding the door slightly open (almost closed) behind her, kept me with her.

"There's something I want to say to you," she said urgently.

My impulse to go on into the apartment was so strong that I really didn't hear her for a few seconds.

"You must not worry about your Jane," she said quickly. "*He's* with her now—"

I was supposed to find that reassuring, but I caught my breath—sharply.

"He? Why?" I demanded.

She seemed startled by the vehemence of my response.

"We thought it best someone be with her now," she said gently, "and if need be—they could draw off any unwelcome visitors. Don't you trust him?"

I avoided her eyes.

"Sure," I said, "I trust him . . ."

She continued to watch me that way until some small sound from down below brought her back to the moment we were then living. Then she took my hand and held it gently and said softly:

"*Chéri, chéri*—this is what I wanted to tell you—I understand now about the bombings. It took me a little while—but I understand." She leaned very close to me so that I could feel the fragrance of her body. "It was good that I came and that we met. Because now you know that your Marie-Ange and your Tou-tou would have understood too and forgiven you—just as I have—with all my heart."

As she spoke, it seemed to me that Marie-Ange and Tou-tou were suddenly standing before the great wall, holding hands and watching Wilfred and me, and they both had that serious look that people get on their faces when they watch someone who is about to go and try not to cry. They were waving at Wilfred and me and the bus pulled out and I thought I heard them whisper, "We forgive you—"

"I am glad that you came," I was able to say at last.

A weight was sliding off me, a terrible weight that I hadn't known was there. Something began to sing out loud inside of me.

"Tell me something now." She spoke in rapid whispers. "The idea of seeing me—alone—from time to time—in odd places—for a few stolen hours—"

I looked at her oddly, perplexed.

"Would be exciting—wouldn't it?" she finished.

"Yes," I whispered back out loud. "Yes—yes—immensely exciting—"

I stopped myself, shocked at the readiness with which the words had popped out of my mouth.

"And yet Wilfred is your best friend," she said wistfully, "and yet you are deeply in love with Jane—"

"Strange," I said, dazed.

There was no question but that what I had meant was, that if she had asked me, I would have come running—even now. The idea shook me, baffled me.

"Not really strange," she said very gently, "only strange to you of the Anglo-Saxon puritanical world who think all human beings must be exactly thus and so and no other way. But we are not like that." She shrugged gracefully. "Still—you are right—in one way. There must be a certain discipline if we are to live together—and we must be very clear—" She pulled herself together with an effort, then smiled wanly.

"Don't be angry with me," she went on, "but it was when I saw your uncle and saw how alike you were, and watched him carefully —that it became clear to me. I understood about you and about the man who is you in our world, and what it really was between him and me." It took her another beat to get up enough courage to say, making it half a question, "It's not a thing on which a man—and a woman—can base a life—"

She was waiting for me to give the final *coup de grâce*—the shot in the head to a dying idyl—

"No," I said. "It's not anything upon which a man and woman should base a life together."

She nodded heavily and for a second I had a feeling my Wilfred was standing at my side and smiling at me and making a gesture indicating he too forgave me and I felt a momentary flash of hot resentment— What had I ever done to *him?*—but at that very same second I suddenly knew that all these years I thought that I had betrayed him, and now I knew I would no longer feel that way.

The singing inside of me became a full golden voice pouring out in shimmering song. I felt I had a right to live the moment I was living, to live it the way I wanted to and to look at the future with anticipation and pleasure.

Marie-Ange was standing motionless now, looking at me.

"You know I do love Jane," I said.

"I know that now," she said.

She turned to go back in.

I stopped her.

"That summer night," I said, "at Saint-Malo—"

She looked at me in amazement.

"What about it?" she asked.

"I don't know," I said painfully, "she was only fifteen—"

Marie-Ange burst into soundless laughter that trailed off quickly.

"Guilty about that too?" she said with a kind of maternal weariness. "An unknowing trusting girl-child," she said with a gentle mocking, "seduced by the wicked man of the world who was then a whole sixteen years old. But don't you know, my poor Anglo-Saxon, that you had almost nothing to do with it?"

I looked at her in bewilderment.

"You just happened to come along at the right moment," she explained. "She'd decided long before you came that it would be that summer. It could have been anyone. It almost was the *notaire's* son, but he was such a fool—and when she did finally meet you, your Canadian-French was so winning—she made up her mind it would be you when she'd first seen you on the beach the first day you came— or does that hurt your pride?"

It was definitely liberation day for me.

Marie-Ange sighed.

"If this all works out," Marie-Ange said quickly, "you'll come to visit us—with your Jane. We'll have Tou-tou who'll be so thrilled to have you. You'll be a celebrity by then, you know—and you'll love our little girls."

Before I could say I'd be delighted to come, Marie-Ange got on her tiptoes and kissed me.

I don't want to think about what had been going on between the other me and Marie-Ange up in their world, and don't anybody try to tell me.

But I know this.

That, my friend, was a good-by kiss. Long, tender, regretful, but meant to last forever.

Marie-Ange opened the door and we both stepped into my apartment.

41.

It LOOKED like an American press room on election eve—

Dr. and Mrs. Whitman, Mme. Sen and Dr. Soukhanova were over near the dining table, elbow-deep in documents, furiously consulting, leaning over toward each other every few seconds, conferring with each other. Before the great window, Walter Carr was pacing back and forth, writing rapidly on a pad as he paced. (I've never seen that done before. He never once looked where he was going. When he'd come to the wall, he'd make a very good about-face and start in the other direction.) Through the open bedroom door I could see Wilfred turning pages of magazines and newspapers as fast as he could. He looked up as Marie-Ange came running toward him. Even at that distance I could see him brace himself as though he knew she had come to some sort of a decision.

Then I think she whispered something to him—and doughnuts will get you dollars that it was "I love you" because he swept her in his arms and crushed her to him.

A noise behind me from outside made me and all the others except Wilfred and Marie-Ange who were too far away in more ways than one—turn.

It was the elevator. It came all the way up and stopped at my floor. There was a knock on the door.

I never did find out who it was that knocked, but whoever he was, he was persistent. He just kept right on knocking, while we all waited without moving or breathing or making any sound.

Finally we heard footsteps and the sound of someone going down the stairs, from which I gathered that our caller was probably a Frenchman or European. They have no faith in elevators for the descent and invariably prefer to go down via the stairs.

Everyone watched as their Jane went to the door and opened it cautiously. There was no one on the landing. She shut the door behind her.

By the time I turned, the others were looking toward Wilfred who had come hurrying up in great excitement.

"We're to stand by," Wilfred said excitedly. "The World Council has come to a decision."

My heart stopped beating as their Jane came over close to me.

Wilfred carried in a huge vial about the size of the face of a clock. It was full of the luminous substance. Wilfred put it down carefully on the table.

One by one we all gathered around it. I noticed Wilfred and Marie-Ange were holding hands, the way people who are waiting to hear news of a disaster might hold on to each other. Everyone was watching that vial.

Then a soft effortless English voice emerged from that vial, clearly, distinctly and with exactly the conversational timbre of a voice in that very room:

"*This is LXI London,*" the voice said. "*The following is the authorized statement issued by the World Council which we broadcast simultaneously to the peoples of our planet and to our delegates who are now on our sister planet: 'It is with profound regret that the World Council has come to the unanimous conclusion that the peoples of our sister planet have not yet achieved that degree of development which would permit us to place at their disposal all the scientific and technological data which they do not possess.'*"

There was a sighing sound from Jane.

Madame Sen turned away from the rest of us.

Dr. Whitman moved heavily.

I felt as though a hobnailed boot had kicked me in the face.

"*Our eight delegates now on sister earth are hereby ordered to return at once and without any further delay of any kind whatsoever.*"

I tore my eyes off the trembling radiance within the vial.

They were going. It was off. We had failed.

They couldn't leave us. They hadn't understood. Something hadn't been explained.

Dr. Soukhanova and Madame Sen were hastily gathering their notes. Wilfred was frantically turning a few more pages of an article I'm sure he felt was of crucial importance, while Marie-Ange was tugging at his sleeve urging him to leave. Once they looked up and their eyes met mine and they both had stricken looks.

"Take only essential documents!" Dr. Morescu was calling out.

He and Walter Carr were working furiously.

Only their Jane hadn't moved. She stood looking at me the way you would watch a dream fade away—bewildered, incredulous.

"Documents! Documents!" Dr. Morescu called sharply.

Jane moved just as I was about to reach for her.

"Great differences prevail between the two systems on the sister planet," LXI went on. *"Relations with them at this time could not but create animosity among our own peoples. Thus, in the interests of maintaining our world harmony, which has been so difficult to achieve and so difficult to maintain, and for our security, it is with the greatest sorrow that we are forced to dissociate ourselves from the unresolved conflicts of our sister planet."*

They had quickly arranged piles of documents which they were to take with them. They worked with such an intensity as to make me feel I was not there. I went from one to another trying to say something, but they didn't even look up at me.

I pulled at Wilfred.

"No," I kept saying to Wilfred. "You can't leave us. You don't understand. It's wrong . . ."

He kept on looking for the essential documents.

Behind, the voice of LXI continued:

"To the millions of volunteers who have offered to undertake the flight to the sister planet we have this to say: Our delegates now on the sister earth have already disposed devices which will be left on the sister planet and by which we will be kept in permanent contact with that planet. Thus when we receive word that the differences on the sister planet have been resolved, normal flights will be undertaken between the two planets. Until that time however our international police have been instructed to patrol the skies and prevent any unauthorized attempt to contact the sister planet."

Whitman and Wilfred began to carry some of the bundles of documents upstairs. I hurried after them. Below, the Chairman of their World Council was making a statement, but I couldn't hear it.

"You didn't have time to make a fair judgment!" I said to them. "You've got to ask them to reconsider!"

That did stop them for a second.

"How could you make a judgment?" I demanded. "Surely not on the basis of what you saw here—in a few hours—in one spot of the world?"

Dr. Whitman shook his head sorrowfully. "We could make a judgment," he said sadly. "The evidence against you is so obviously conclusive. It was only a question of finding that evidence—and we have. Do you realize what you've already done? Do you realize how you've already filled your atmosphere with poisonous radioactivity? And that you are actually threatening each other with annihilation?— What do you expect us to say?"

"You're wrong," I said. "It's not that way, not really—"

Dr. Whitman turned away from me.

"That's our World Council," he said gravely. "*We* carry out their decisions."

I rushed down the stairs.

"*In this latter half of the twentieth century,*" the Chairman's voice was emerging from the vial, clear, in English, "*there is no place for fear or pessimism. Let us all continue to work together, as we have over this last most fruitful quarter of a century, for the ever continuing betterment of our way of life.*"

Dr. Morescu was looking over documents with Madame Sen and Jane. They were so deeply absorbed there was no way to reach them.

Marie-Ange was making bundles of several magazines. I touched her arm. She looked up at me, then very gently pushed me away.

I rushed back to Walter.

"Walter!" I pleaded. "Why didn't you make your presence known to our people here? If people knew what you could bring them, there wouldn't be any differences—"

He shook his head. "That has all been taken into consideration," he said gently and turned away. "All of it."

"*We are now on the way toward the solution of the problems which are the real and great problems of mankind,*" the Chairman's voice continued. "*We can now ask ourselves: 'Who are we? Why do we live? What is the phenomenon which makes of us thinking and feeling creatures?' The last few dark chambers in the house of man are about to be lighted. Can it be asked that we risk that in order to help our sister planet? No. It cannot be asked. They must work out their own destiny. To our delegates on sister earth, may God grant them a safe return to us, and to the peoples of that planet, may God grant them the wisdom and strength to work out their differences.*"

There was a second's pause, then the voice of LXI:

"This ends the statement from the World Council," and even in his professional tones there was a note of deep regret.

"Are there any questions from the delegates? An appropriate period will be allocated to them."

Dr. Morescu called out to those who were upstairs.

No one had any questions. It was all clear.

Those remaining below hurried toward the steps.

Wilfred came dashing down to help them.

"Wait!" I shouted. "Wait!"

They all turned and stared.

"It can't end this way!" I pleaded. "It can't!"

Wilfred and Marie-Ange and Jane came over alongside of me. "Don't give us any military secrets," I said quickly. "Give us only what will help us beat back disease and poverty—peaceful things—"

Wilfred turned to Morescu.

"I'd risk it," he said. "I'd stay . . ."

Dr. Morescu shook his head.

"You'd risk it," he said, "but we wouldn't permit you. It's not just your life. It's our security. No. We've been ordered to return. No one can stay." He turned to me. "But there is one thing we can do. We can talk to you while we are preparing for the flight back. We will answer all questions which will not endanger our security. Only—we must hurry. I cannot permit any unnecessary risk . . ."

They moved off quickly up the stairs, with me, in my anxiety not to lose a second, stumbling after them.

Wilfred, Marie-Ange and their Jane had dumped the books and magazines and papers on my bed and were tying them in bundles, while the others were applying layers of the luminous stuff to each package.

It had got dark and the only light in the room was from the window which faced the quai. Outside it was cold and blustery and far off in the black skies you could discern ashen clouds shuttling back and forth.

"Hurry," Wilfred shouted at me. "Ask your questions."

I couldn't think.

"Tell me anything you think will be useful to us," I said frantically.

They stopped whatever they were doing for a second, but it was no good. They couldn't organize their thoughts under the stress of having to leave. They had no real idea of what, among the things that they could tell us, could be told simply, to a layman like me, and would be most useful, and what we didn't know.

"Come on!" Wilfred shouted at me. "Ask what you *think* you need most! We'll answer as best we can."

"Cancer," I said. "Have you learned to cure cancer?"

"The beam," Walter said. "The ray. We use the ray—"

"But they won't have the ray!" their Jane said tensely.

"I remember the work of an American researcher named Griffith." Dr. Morescu spoke rapidly. "From what I remember, it seems to me that he was on a path which might be useful to you here. Find the American Griffith . . ."

"Griffith what?" I asked frantically. "Griffith is a common name. What's his first name? Where will I find him?"

"I've already inquired about him," Walter said. "It's no use. He was killed in Italy in their last war."

"Then there's another," Dr. Whitman said. "The Pole Wyncygstern of Warsaw . . ."

"I inquired about him too," Walter said gently. "He was a Jew. He died in the Warsaw ghetto. There was a massacre there."

Maybe I imagined it, but it seemed to me they all stopped and looked at me accusingly, as if somehow I was responsible that so many of our great people had been killed in the war.

Maybe I was—in a way—

"Surely there must be someone living," I said.

"Someone young," Dr. Morescu said urgently, "very young. Who could have escaped the war."

"There is Rufus Boehm," their Jane said finally. She had been thinking hard. "I think you know him . . ."

"I do," I said. "Only the last time I saw him he was very pessimistic about his work."

"The Boehm-Vas Test!" Dr. Morescu said in triumph. "Of course! Tell your Rufus Boehm to contact a young man named Vas! Stanislaus Vas! Do you understand?" He was very excited. "Write his name down."

Their Jane spelled the name for me. V—A—S— She made me spell it after her. I repeated it after her in the darkness. V—A—S—

They began to help each other put the stuff on. Their Jane came over to me and without her saying anything, I knew she wanted me to help her. I touched her body and looked out of the black window at the sky, and realized with horror that in a very few minutes, covered only by that luminous stuff, she would be hurtling through those ashen clouds. I remembered the old terror, the moment when the engines were being warmed up, the second before we were to take off, when you felt you couldn't do it, you couldn't move, and then it would be as though someone else took over for you, as you watched your hands make the skilled motions they had been trained to make.

"Vas is a Czech," Dr. Morescu was saying. "If Boehm combines his work with Vas's they will produce great results. You remember the name?"

"Yes," I said, "Vas—"

"Your fiancée," Dr. Morescu said, he was speaking staccato, "and your Dr. Morescu, they should continue with their work. It can only be for the good. The weapons which have already been developed are ultimate. You have reached the sad state where the means of destruction are so powerful that it is now no longer a basic issue as to whether a discovery can serve as an additional weapon."

There was a sound which at first seemed like something I was hearing only inside my head, it was so strange and far off. It was my telephone. The one in my bedroom. Jane answered it. She spoke for a couple of seconds, then handed me the instrument. It felt cool and strange in the darkness.

"You've got to help me," my voice came over the telephone to me.

It took me a second to get over the shock.

"Help you how?" I asked.

"Your place is surrounded," he said, "or at least I have that impression. If I came up now, they might think it was strange since they've just seen you. Now look. Can you come down in an overcoat?"

"Where will you be?" I asked.

"I'll be waiting for you in your car," he said.

"You know my car?" I asked, startled.

"Yes," he said dryly. "I had one like it fifteen years ago."

He hung up. I replaced the receiver on the cradle and turned toward the others.

They were ready to leave now. They were watching me in a way which made me realize that when I got back, they would be gone and I would never see them again.

Dr. Soukhanova came to me. I could barely distinguish her in the darkness.

"I wish to return some day soon," she said softly in French. "Or better still you must come and visit us. It is up to you now to make it possible . . ."

Dr. Soukhanova touched my hand and turned away, fading into the deeper shadows.

It seemed to me in the darkness that Madame Sen had taken the gold ornaments out of her hair, and her long jet-black hair had fallen over her shoulders.

"Once you make it possible for us to return," she said quietly, "it will also mean that you have lifted all those people whose skin is pigmented as mine out of the abyss of famine and disease and into the world of the future. You have no idea what human riches lie buried in those starved and diseased beings and what contributions to knowledge and to beauty they will make once you have given them the opportunity."

She gave me her hand, bowed, and moved away. I felt as though I had just had an audience with a queen, and that she had been fully clothed, and it was I who had been standing there naked.

Then Jane walked sadly with me over to the closet where I got my overcoat. Dr. Whitman came over to me and we shook hands.

"If this thing had worked—" he said wistfully, then stopped and said no more, turning away.

I shook hands with Wilfred and stood there looking at him and Marie-Ange a long time.

"This is all going to work out," Wilfred said cheerfully. "It's just a question of time. We'll soon be going back and forth. When you and Jane come to London, you're staying with us. And don't worry —it's going to be great."

"Sure, Wilfred," I said. "It's going to be great. Remember me to Tou-tou."

"We will," Marie-Ange said.

"Does she still laugh as easily as she did?" I asked.

"She laughs very easily," Marie-Ange said and went away, for she and I had already said our good-bys.

Jane accompanied me to the door. Dr. Morescu was waiting for us there.

"Hidden among the pages of your journal," he said to me, "is a photograph of my wife and daughter. I . . . I thought perhaps it . . .

44

it would mean something to your Morescu. But that will be for you to judge."

"That was considerate of you," I said.

"Vas," he said. "You won't forget Stanislaus Vas."

I shook hands with him, then with Wonderful Walter.

Now Jane and I were left facing each other.

"When he spoke to me on the telephone just now he sounded glad to hear my voice. Very glad," she said, her voice throbbing with excitement.

"You see?" I said. "It wasn't a total loss after all, your coming here."

"No," she said.

"Your World Council might not trust us," I said, "but for affairs of the heart, we're the best."

"Tops," she said.

We kissed. Long. Sweetly.

I looked out against the black sky, then I looked at her. I think I shivered.

"You'll let me know?" I asked.

"Yes," she said, and she too went away.

"The roses!" a voice called to me—it was Mrs. Whitman's. "Take good care of the roses!"

It was the last thing they said to me. I thought it was odd at the time.

I looked at them all but it was too dark now to see their faces.

Then I waved to the darkness and left.

42.

MY CAR was on the quai a distance back. As I stepped out of the apartment house, I knew that many eyes noted my appearance and I think I was followed.

When I got to my car there was no one near enough to notice anything.

I opened the door.

He was sitting in the front, in the passenger's seat. I slid in behind the wheel.

It was dark and I saw him in profile. I'd never been sure what I looked like in profile, but I knew then it was like that.

We sat for a second, I guess it was to give each other a chance to get over the shock.

Finally I said, "They're all going back."

"I know," he said. "I've been listening in too." His voice was exactly like mine. "Drive up a little distance away. I want to look at you."

I started the motor and he ducked down so his head wasn't visible.

I drove a few blocks and pulled up in front of a café where there was enough light. I was parked in such a way that no car could get in behind us.

Then I stopped and for the first time we looked at each other.

Medium height, I was saying to myself. Pleasant face with slightly irregular features. He has a mole on the right cheek, in exactly the same place I have.

"I just left your Jane," he said, and it was only then I realized he was talking the way a man who has just been through a hell of an experience talks.

I didn't say anything.

"That's quite a woman," he said.

"What does that mean?" I asked. I felt like a clock which had stopped.

"Exactly what you think it does," he said. "There's no reason for you and me to kid each other, is there?"

"No," I said.

"Your problems are over," he said.

"Thanks," I said. I would have said you son-of-a-bitch in the same tone of voice.

"Listen," he said, "there was a moment there where I had to make a choice. For you. Understand? If I'd hesitated, I think you would have been cooked for good."

"How will I ever be able to thank you?" I asked bitterly.

"All right," he said harshly. "I didn't go there with the intention of letting anything like that happen. But it did happen. I . . . I didn't realize how much I was attracted to her . . ."

"I know," I said. "It was bigger than either of you."

He didn't follow through on that one. "I think I ought to tell you how it happened," he said.

"Never mind," I said, but I braced myself the way you do at the dentist because I knew he was going to tell me, no matter what.

"You ought to know," he said. "The minute I got into that room she walked right into my arms. I don't know exactly what had gone on between you two before—but there she was. I kissed her and she reacted very strangely. She began to pull away and at first I thought I ought to let her go, and then I reacted without really thinking." My throat was harsh and dry. "I lifted her off the floor and held her to me as tightly as I could and I kept telling her it was going to be all right. Everything was going to be all right. It was as simple as that."

He stopped.

He was a little astonished because I had laughed.

You might call it a poor man's Homeric laughter.

"You didn't mention a milk bottle while you were at it?" I asked hoarsely. "A broken milk bottle?"

He frowned. "Milk bottle?"

"Never mind," I said.

We fell silent.

I was thinking what if, that first night at my place, after the party when they had all gone, what if I had done something as simple as that?

"I think I understand what the matter is," he was saying. "She's afraid to love. *Was* afraid, that is. Because the last time she really loved anyone she felt they betrayed her. Her family. She really loved them. Then they got killed. To a kid that meant they left her. Betrayed her. Therefore anyone she really loved might leave her. It was too terrible to live through again. So what you have to do is reassure her. Hold her to you. Don't let her go. Make her realize you're here to stay . . ."

"Okay, Doctor," I said harshly.

"That's quite a woman," he said again. "You're a lucky fellow."

I wished he'd stop saying that.

"So are you a lucky fellow," I said.

He stared at me for a couple of seconds.

"How do you mean that?"

"There's no reason for you and me to kid each other, is there?" I asked.

"No," he said after a moment.

"That's quite a woman," I said, "and you've been a prize horse's ass all these years."

"I guess I have," he said quietly.

He thought for a couple of minutes.

"Listen," he said. "You've had a rough time. And you're in for a rough time from here on. I could take it better than you. I'd be willing to change places with you. You go in my place. I'll stay." I guess I blinked in noncomprehension. He smiled wanly. "There's quite a difference in the way we live. You can't imagine what it's like."

He was pale. I think he was scared to death I'd take him up on it. I shook my head.

"Never mind," I said. "I'll stay. It's not much of a world but I'll take her the way she is, mixed up, confused, difficult, and full of problems, but I'll take her—and that goes for my girl too."

"That's not why I offered," he said.

I looked at him and realized it hadn't been why he'd offered.

"I thought maybe I could be useful here," he said.

"They want you to go back," I said. "And I'll try to make myself useful instead. But thanks anyway."

"Don't mention it," he said with a tight smile. "I'll need twenty minutes." When I hesitated, he went on. "I know how you feel only you've got to help me. If you go back sooner, it might foul things up."

"Okay," I said finally. "Twenty minutes."

I got out of the car, took off the overcoat and gave it to him. He put it on. That way if anyone had noticed what clothes I'd been wearing when I'd come down, they wouldn't notice that he was wearing different clothes.

We stood there looking at each other for about ten seconds.

"That's it," he said.

A car came by and in its light we saw each other.

That's me standing there, I was thinking. Good or bad, that's the way I look to other people. And good or bad, that's pretty much the way I am.

"Goddamn it," he said suddenly, his voice thick with emotion, and I threw my arms around him at the same split second he threw his arms around me, and we clasped each other close.

I've accepted myself, I thought. At last I accept and respect whatever I am. And I will try to live with what I am and make the most of myself and the world I live in.

I watched him walk away in the darkness and remarked the cut of his shoulders and the slightly loping quality of his gait—and that he didn't limp. I felt confident and reassured.

Near the café up ahead, he turned and waved. I thought he looked gallant the way he saluted. I waved back to him but he couldn't have seen it because of the darkness.

The moment he disappeared I realized there were a thousand things we should have talked about. Maybe he wouldn't have known, but I should have asked him anyway.

But he was gone by then and I had promised to wait.

Those next twenty minutes were among the hardest I've ever done in my life. Suddenly I needed to get back, to talk to them, to beg them to change their minds. Yet I knew if I did, it was conceivable that some of the people who were unquestionably watching the apartment house might decide it was all too strange, there were too many of us who looked alike, coming and going, and might decide to break in. It would have been betrayal. Maybe I'm wrong—but I've always been against betrayal no matter how justifiable it may seem.

When the twenty minutes were up I broke into as close to a run as was possible without attracting too much attention.

Snookums was waiting for me again, lurking near the same corner.

"I've got an answer for you," I threw at him on the run, "and the answer is as follows. They don't give a good goddam what government you represent," and hurried on.

Henneman was in the doorway of the apartment.

"Where did you come from?" he asked. "I just saw you go up."

"It's possible," I said, swinging right on. He hurried to keep up with me.

"There's no other exit in this house," he said. "How did you get down?"

"I slid down the beam," I said, "all pink and bare and looking like an angel."

He looked at me in disgust.

"I've got to talk to you," he said.

"I bet you do," I said bitterly.

Madame Fénelon was frantic when she saw me. "I know," she said shrilly, "I know now. There is another way out. I was sure that Monsieur Turoffsky built a tunnel or something."

"If he had," I said, "he might have been alive today."

43.

I WENT up in the elevator. It seemed to me the slowest means of movement I'd ever encountered.

Of course they had all gone by the time I got to my apartment, and of course I had known they wouldn't be there, but still I rushed frantically from one room to another looking for them.

After a while, when I had convinced that part of me which is outside of logic that they had really gone, and what was more that they had left no trace whatsoever of their ever having been there, I sat down in a heap—beaten.

Then I heard the sound of the elevator and I held my breath and waited. The elevator kept grinding on and on and not stopping and my heart started to pound.

I got to the door and opened it as the elevator stopped at my floor.

Jane was in the elevator. She waved to me and promptly got all tangled in the swinging impossible doors because she was carrying something in one hand.

She was carrying a valise.

We just looked at each other for about one heartbeat. I think she knew even before she asked me.

"They've gone," she said gently.

"Yes," I said.

She came over to me and I held her close for a very long time.

Then we pulled apart and she said, "They'll be back," the way you would say something you were absolutely sure of.

I took the valise from her and stepped back a foot or two to catch the image of the way she looked and fix it in my mind for the rest of my life, golden hair and soft golden eyes and a bridal radiance.

Then she asked me, exactly as their Jane had asked, if I would "belatedly carry her over the threshold."

I picked her up tenderly, and holding the valise in one hand, carried her into my place. We kissed, lingering over the sweetness of it, and then I set her down.

There was a second there when I thought that I ought to tell her that it had been he and not me, but I don't think I have to explain why I didn't—not with her looking at me the way she was.

Then she caught sight of Elmer and the two of us walked over to him.

Elmer was glowing as he had never glowed before. If he had been a dog he would have wagged his tail for all he had, but being only stuff, he sent us his soft radiance, enveloping us and bathing us in a glow of swelling promise.

I thought again of the clean streets with airlike crystal, about the people in London who pottered about in patches of gardens at the other end of the earth, about a planet which was free from the terror of our terrible diseases, where people could conceive of controlling their climate and could turn to such questions as who we are and why we are.

Suddenly Elmer dimpled and as we both watched I spelled the message out loud for Jane:

"*All arrived safely. Good luck.*"

"Good luck," Jane whispered softly.

Slowly the substance in that container began to die and we knew they had withdrawn their ray. It was as though a feeling were dying, a feeling of joy and gaiety and youth and promise were gradually disappearing. It seemed to me the stuff hated dying, passionately. It wanted to stay warm and glowing and alive and to continue to be. I looked again and I knew I was looking at ordinary sterile water. The stuff was dead.

Mourn the dead promise.

Mourn the dead hope.

We stood a moment of silence, in memoriam. Jane sighed, and the sigh was like a punctuation mark, then she smiled and the smile was the beginning of another paragraph, another chapter, another volume.

She took off her hat and remarked that it was her going-away hat, and that she had not realized before how fond of symbolism she was, as for example, wearing the hat the short distance from the hotel to my place had given her a sense of having come to me. She said that there were several other bags, but that they would be brought over in the morning.

She talked on about how surprised she had been on how many things she had accumulated. She had decided not to take time off now to throw things away even though she disliked "savers," people who kept useless things. She said that the concierge at the hotel had realized what was happening and that he had sent me his felicitations and had been very warm and sad at her leaving. I was wrong to call him names.

Pops and Bunny Whitman had arrived. She said that she had already met them. It had been a warm and wonderful reunion, although they had not really said anything to each other.

They were on their way up here. Did I mind that she had asked them here? It was a gentle way of telling them about her and me without saying it out loud.

I said I didn't mind.

Then she said that Pops had implied that there would be others who would come up.

The elevator started to whine away. I took Jane's bag upstairs with me into my bedroom.

There was a knock.

I asked her to answer it because I got a good look at my bedroom and it was a shambles. I wanted to straighten it just a little bit. I had a hunch I wouldn't have a chance to later.

When I came down about five or ten minutes later, Jane and Morescu were sitting in the living room staring at each other. I could tell from the dazed look on his face that she had told him.

It was a shock for me to look at Morescu, almost unbearable. I wanted to reach out and say, "Wipe off the make-up, you're still a young man."

He was nodding his head sadly to me now—rocking a little.

I nodded back as though agreeing with him that it was too bad. Jane said gently that we ought to decide what we were going to tell the people who were coming.

"I'll tell you what I thought," I said. "I'd like to call in Izzy and Henneman and all the radio and newspapermen here and break it tonight—"

Morescu looked at me quizzically.

"Break what?" he asked with kindly interest.

"The news," I said, "the story of the century. The visitors from a twin planet. We'll get all the major radio chains all over the world, but I would like to have Izzy and Henneman first—"

Morescu stopped me.

"The visitors left something behind?" he asked gently. "Something we could offer as proof?"

"Of course they did," I said quickly. "They—"

I stopped.

They waited anxiously for me to go on.

"We were just discussing that aspect of it," Jane said to me, "before you came down, and it seemed to us there is no real proof."

"There must be proof," I said incredulously. "There's got to be—"

They waited again, very hopefully. Frantically I fumbled in my pockets and pulled out the vial.

"This!" I said almost hysterically. "They televise on this! We televised a whole day here! One planet to another—"

They were both studying the vial carefully, Jane less hopefully than Morescu.

"I think you'll find that the metal is platinum," Jane said.

"Platinum?" I repeated stupidly.

"And still wet," Morescu said.

"With water," Jane said, "sterile water—"

Morescu handed it back to me.

"It will make an interesting souvenir," he said.

"There's nothing unusual about it?" I demanded.

"Nothing," Jane said. "I had a few seconds alone with Wilfred. I asked him. He told me it was ordinary platinum."

I looked at them uncomprehendingly.

"But you saw Wilfred," I said, "and Marie-Ange with your own eyes."

"I'd never seen them before," Jane said, "and even if I had—nobody will take our word. Not if people want to start out with the assumption that we're perpetrating a hoax—"

"The angel the pilot saw—" I protested.

"The pilot," Morescu went on, and I wished he would stop sounding so patient, "has just agreed that it probably was a hallucination."

"That girl in the tree was no hallucination," I said. "I saw her—I—well. Never mind, but I *know* she was real—"

"No one else saw her," Jane said. "Except me—later—in the hotel. But it's still just our word, isn't it?"

"We can't let it die this way." I was in a sweat now. "All sorts of people saw strange things. The concierge at your hotel was startled—"

I stopped again.

"If another newspaperman," Morescu said, "tried to relate a story such as this—and base it on a concierge's bewilderment—"

"I wouldn't believe him," I said. "But then there was the plane. Caught in mid-air—almost crashing—"

"We could never duplicate that ray," Jane said. "It came from them, from our twin planet. We can't produce that ray ourselves. We don't know how. If we make any claims of that kind it would be only natural that a demonstration would be asked for."

"All right," I said. "But the messages—"

"What have we to show there," Morescu asked, "but some paper you scribbled on—"

"Maybe somebody else picked up those messages," I said.

They both shook their heads simultaneously.

"Not unless they were at exactly the same point in the same research we were doing," Jane said.

I sat down and thought.

The dream of exploding this story like a bombshell on the world had become so much a part of me that I couldn't let it go.

"The roses," I said at last. "They left those roses for me."

They both walked over and looked at the roses carefully.

"They are very beautiful roses," Morescu said. "Freshly picked. But they are extraordinary only for their beauty—nothing else—"

He was wrong there, but we didn't find *that* out until later.

I must have looked very forlorn, because Morescu made an equally forlorn attempt at humor, I suppose to cheer me up.

"You could probably win a prize at a flower show with them," he said.

"Let's just break the story anyhow," I said. "Maybe they'll take our word for it."

They were both silent for a long time.

"It doesn't matter for me," Morescu said, "because I've lived through so much. But for Jane—a scientist—to make such sensational claims—without absolute proof—"

He didn't have to spell that one out for me. I could see it.

"All right," I said. "But maybe they were seen on radar screens. Maybe people in other countries saw things—"

"People in all countries have been seeing things for years," Jane said. "If there has been other evidence we could consider it."

We went on like that for a few more minutes, always making a full circle back to nowhere.

Then people started to come.

44.

THE FIRST under the wire were the corduroy kid and the sheepskin jacket, but Pops Whitman and Bunny were a respectable second, with Jason Foster and Henneman almost a dead heat.

I think you remember my mentioning Jason. He was still working for some American agency.

I kept waiting for my Uncle Debret to show up but he didn't, so the proceedings started (and finished) without him.

First of all, all of our visitors pretended not to notice Elmer, although they kept looking at him every chance they got.

Henneman tried to draw a sketch of it, but the two Frenchmen came circling around him so he ostentatiously crumpled the piece of paper up and threw it in a wastepaper basket. From then on the two French cops never took their eyes off the wastepaper basket for a moment for the rest of the time they were there.

It was Jason who, in a subtle way, was in command. I can't remember exactly how it was he took over, but he did. I watched him operate. He was awfully good. He knew exactly how long to wait while Jane took me by the hand and brought me over to Pops and Bunny, and Pops kept saying over and over, as he looked at me, "Well, well, well," and Bunny just kept, not staring, I guess gazing, at me and Jane.

At precisely the split second which was indicated, when I was wondering how Jason would handle the situation, he moved in, just when people's nervous expectations had reached the boiling point.

"Well," he said in French, "there's no reason why we can't be open and aboveboard about the reason we're all here. We're among friends—"

Henneman started to translate for Pops and Bunny, but Pops replied in perfect French that they both spoke and understood the language.

The sheepskin kid then said, with a little less certainty, that it was correct—we were among friends. Although research was completely without restriction in France, they had reason to believe that certain research had been carried on near Paris by Monsieur Morescu and Mademoiselle Bridon-Jack and that there was reason to believe that this research could conceivably have implications for his country's security—even though the two savants were not French nationals, nonetheless asylum had been granted to Monsieur Morescu and perhaps Mademoiselle Bridon-Jack.

He was stopped by Pops who said that he would like to point out that the research had been begun in the United States, where Dr. Morescu had first been given asylum.

Jason developed that point a bit further.

They finally realized that Morescu had been trying to say something.

"I believe," Morescu said, "that you are interested especially in knowing exactly what was the nature of a particular phenomenon which occurred the other day near my villa—when a powerful airplane was ostensibly immobilized in flight?" Although nobody answered, the fact that they all held their breaths was answer enough. "I regret, gentlemen, that the data which Miss Bridon-Jack and I have in our possession does not offer a satisfactory explanation of why that phenomenon occurred."

They all breathed again—in disappointment.

"We are so sure of this," Jane said, "that we have no hesitation whatsoever in suggesting that a committee of scientists study our data. We will give them every co-operation—in fact we will welcome collaboration because we are as anxious as anybody that a real explanation be found."

They knew they'd had it then and everything after that was a lot of polite palaver.

Everybody was anxious to get rid of the skeepskin kid and the corduroy kid, but they understandably refused to get out until both Jason and Morescu had given their words that nothing would be moved and that Jane and Morescu would co-operate with the French as enthusiastically as they would with anybody else.

The corduroy kid turned to me and said there was one feature of the situation that he still found somewhat disconcerting. He apologized for his insistence but, in view of what had seemed to them a singular lack of co-operation on the parts of Morescu, Jane and myself on the occasion of their first meeting with us, we would understand.

"You had a number of people up here during the last few hours. They could conceivably have had access to the data which you were guarding. Would you mind telling us who those people were?"

Why, they were people from our sister planet, I could have said.

Sister planet? he would have repeated politely. Have you got anything to prove that?

Why yes, I would have said. I have a dozen roses to prove it.

They were beginning to look at me suspiciously. I was taking too long answering.

"Your radar didn't pick up any unidentified objects last night?" I asked. "Several unidentified objects?"

Jason and the others exchanged glances.

"No," Jason said. "We've been keeping a twenty-four-hour vigil. And I've been checking. Why do you ask?"

"Just generally," I said. "I'll tell you who those people were," I said to the two French cops. "They were helping me on an article I am writing. It's a long article. It's a little bit like the thing the President of the United States does every year. You know, 'State of the Nation.' Only this one's going to be on the 'State of the World.' How things are on this planet."

They all looked at me with interest, each coloring the look with whatever individual attitude they had toward me. It was a nicely varied look, with many facets. Henneman's could have curdled milk at ten paces.

"I see," the corduroy jacket said finally. There was a slight tinge of suspicion in his tone. Still, the others accepted that as an official exoneration of me.

"I guess you would need lots of help with an article as ambitious as that," Jason said doubtfully. "That *would* account for all those people."

"And I'm going to need more help," I said. "I was thinking of even coming to you."

"By all means," Jason said graciously. "Anything I can do, please don't hesitate."

"You are very sure those people had no access to any of the data?" the corduroy kid repeated.

"Absolutely," I said without hesitation.

And then the two French cops left.

Jason had been sort of eying me.

"There's no particular reason you asked about several objects?" Jason asked. "The several unidentified objects you mentioned?"

"Oh, no," I said. "Just asking."

"You did have something on your mind," Jason encouraged me. "Why don't you tell us what you were thinking?"

Jane and Morescu were watching me intently.

"Just a crazy idea I had," I said. "Too crazy—"

"No, go ahead," Jason said, the way you would talk to a bashful kid.

"Go on," Henneman said.

"For a while there I was playing with the idea that it could have been someone from another planet," I said with a boyish smile. "For example from another earth—the twin of ours. . . ."

Pops smiled very good-naturedly.

"That happens to be a mathematical impossibility," he said. "It is physically impossible for such a planet to exist in our solar system."

"I see," I said.

Henneman looked at me as if I were a disgrace to the newspaper business, but I felt better.

I couldn't have let the evening go by without having said it any more than most people can resist putting their fingers on the paint underneath a WET PAINT sign.

I had to say it, and I *had* said it.

Well—that broke the back of the agenda for that meeting.

There was some desultory talk about how Jason would arrange with the French to have Elmer moved to some place which would be mutually agreeable and arrangements were made about the notes.

Just about then my Uncle Debret called and Bunny insisted he join us and we all went out to a very decorous dinner. Debret was very pleased and I'm sure he felt he was responsible but everyone avoided talking about anything meaningful.

The rest of the dinner was full of Bunny looking at Jane with love, with Pops making professorial jokes, and Jane and me looking at each other with excitement every time no one looked at us.

A little after midnight it all broke up and people went off to their various domiciles, leaving Jane and me to go to our domicile.

Jane began to unpack, but then decided the hell with it, she would finish in the morning. She disappeared into the bathroom and when she came out she had on a very flimsy nightgown and had once more wiped the lipstick off her face.

"You know," she said thoughtfully, "there are one or two things I meant to ask you about. For example this afternoon—"

"Can't we talk about it another time?" I asked.

"Yes, but," she said, "I had a strange feeling—"

I never did let her tell me about the strange feeling. Instead I kissed her very tenderly and she responded very tenderly. For a second there I thought I ought to tell her that it hadn't been me who had written those letters, that it had been Wilfred.

But instead I told her how much I loved her and when I held her close I could feel the surge of her response, open and free.

45.

WHAT SHALL I tell you?

If you've ever experienced loving and being loved, I don't have to tell you anything. Just go back to that time yourself and relive it, because that's the way it was.

If you haven't ever experienced it, it can only be told to you distantly, the way colors are described to the blind.

We spent half the night talking about the honeymoon in Vancouver in the spring and about where we would eventually live and how many children we would have and how I'd no longer work for Debret. We decided that I'd look around first for a little while, and give myself a chance to find something.

I was happier than I've ever been before at breakfast, with her next morning, especially because in the cold clear raw light of that Paris

Tuesday morning, the idea of quitting my job with Debret didn't scare me.

Nothing really scares me now, because each time I begin to feel doubts all I have to do is look up and I can feel and see that mathematically impossible sister earth of ours somewhere in the heavens and in our future. I can see and feel it as clearly as Turoffsky must have been able to see that beautiful hand he carved, somewhere implicit in that piece of white marble from which he eventually fashioned it.

Debret left a couple of days later. His whole manner was exactly as it had been after the fight. Nothing at all had happened.

Pops and Bunny hung around Paris, Pops working with Morescu and Jason and a lot of other experts, French and otherwise. Jane and I had our banns posted at the local *mairie* and Bunny helped her buy a trousseau.

Pops and Morescu kept working very hard and there would be frequent huddles with a lot of other people.

Finally Pops, Bunny and Jason took off for the States.

During all the time they were in Paris, something bothered me. I didn't know what it was until after they'd gone.

The roses, those wonderful red roses, hadn't faded.

Morescu and Jane were just as excited about it as I was. Each morning the moment we got up, Jane and I would go rushing down to see if our roses were still alive—and they were.

It was too late then for a press conference. Weeks had passed and besides we couldn't be sure the roses wouldn't go just the day we'd call the boys together.

Finally we decided that I ought to write this up. What happened had to be recorded. So I sat me down to write this book as quickly as I could.

46.

THE ROSES haven't faded yet. They're just as alive and as bright as the day their Bunny Whitman gave them to me.

I've finished the book now and tonight I'm giving it to Jane to read. And I know now what we'll do with the roses.

When she's finished reading the book and knows that it was Wilfred who wrote those letters and all about the other me and if she still wants me, we'll get married tomorrow. Late tomorrow night, when no one is watching, we'll go together to the Étoile and there, under the Arch of Triumph beside the eternal flame, we'll leave one rose on the tomb of the Unknown Soldier.

The day after we'll go to Saint-Malo and we'll leave another rose in the cemetery there for Marie-Ange and Tou-tou. Then we'll leave one rose for the American boys who stayed behind forever on Omaha beach. We'll fly to London and leave one rose outside the Kensington flat where Jane's family lived. We'll send one rose to Stalingrad, one to Berlin and one to Hiroshima and one to Nagasaki. And we'll send one rose to Lidice and one to Coventry, and the eleventh rose is for Wilfred and the twelfth rose is for Jane to keep for us.

Maybe people will notice that the roses don't fade.

Maybe they'll ask why.

We'll tell them and then maybe people will begin to think.